GUNBOY

GUNBOY

SHREYAS RAJAGOPAL

HARPER
FICTION

An Imprint of HarperCollins *Publishers*

First published in India by Harper Fiction 2025
An imprint of HarperCollins *Publishers*
HarperCollins *Publishers* India, Cyber City, Building 10-A, Gurugram,
Haryana – 122002, India
www.harpercollins.co.in

2 4 6 8 10 9 7 5 3 1

P-ISBN: 978-93-6569-422-2
E-ISBN: 978-93-6569-618-9

Typeset in 11.5/15.2 Adobe Garamond Pro at
HarperCollins *Publishers* India

Printed and bound at
Replika Press Pvt. Ltd.

MIX
Paper | Supporting responsible forestry
FSC™ C016779

This book is produced from independently certified FSC® paper to ensure responsible forest management.

HarperCollins *Publishers*, Macken House, 39/40 Mayor Street Upper, Dublin 1, D01 C9W8, Ireland

To Laali. You believed when I didn't.

To Michelle, for everything.

God made men,
Samuel Colt made them equal.

I

WEAKNESS

ARVIND

It is after school when the senior boys grab them and it all goes to shit.

The boy stands alone, a forlorn statue in the centre of the loose circle of schoolchildren, his peers and never-friends, his eyes fixed on a small stone a few inches from his feet. He does not dare look up. Little puffs of dust blow off the stone as the breeze, hot, liquid, singes his thin bare forearms, legs and the nape of his neck, all the parts of him left uncovered by his uniform.

It is high afternoon in the brutal summer of Rannwara and here in the football ground of the Rannwara Sainik School the sun beats down on everything like the hammer of hell. It beats down on the threads of dead grass, the wooden husks of trees, and the birds that don't fly and the dogs that have vanished altogether. It beats down on everything and everyone, but most of all it beats down on Arvind; where he stands there is no shade, no succour, no protection.

The boy's full name is Srinivasan Arvind. He is south Indian. He is twelve and twelve is a strange age for the boy who feels he is younger and older in parts. His body is small, short, only the twenty-seventh tallest in a class of thirty-two children, more fitting someone in the fourth or fifth standard rather than the seventh the boy is in. He feels older too—older in his eyes, older in all the ways he knows how the world works, and older in his awareness of his inability to change it.

The only power he can claim is that of denial and it is something he puts all his energy into—blocking the heat and the dust and the engines of the school buses and the buzzing whispers of the kids around him. The thick anticipation of violence that hangs on everything. He just focuses on the pebble.

It is brown and tilts to the left.

This is something he does. Something that helps him in times like this. He sees an object, inoffensive, regular, and he focusses his attention on it, every sense and sensation flowing into the object, sinking into it—and whatever bad is happening to him does not hurt him too deep, and he can come out when it goes away.

'Look up, you black fucking loser.'

There it is.

The voice is high-pitched, stretched out, nasal—knife-sharp in its aggression, and it pierces through all the layers that hid his self. The sanctuary of the pebble shattered, he looks up to take in the scene around him.

Before him stands Jaggi, his chief tormentor, tall and dark, almost as dark as him, imposing, smiling with perfect white teeth. With him are the other seniors: Mahesh and Swapnil. They are holding up Sudipto, his soft fair arms squeezed into their oversized fists.

Sudipto, the boy's best and only friend, is short, round, fair—the skin of his face is already bright pink from the sun and the stress. He too stands in place, resigned to the grasp of the much larger senior boys, and does not try to break away or struggle against them in any way.

This is not a fight.

The boy cannot bear to look at his friend in this situation, so he decides to look at Jaggi instead. Jaggi who is pacing with large strides between the two friends, looking like something predatory, a panther maybe. Jaggi who is screaming obscenities in Sudipto's face, eliciting nervous sporadic laughter from the gathered audience—the circle of faceless brown and white uniforms enveloping them. Jaggi who has big arms with bicep muscles bulging under folded shirt sleeves. Jaggi who is in the tenth standard and who they say failed a couple of times, which makes him older and larger and nastier. Jaggi who glares at the boy even as he fakes sporadic punches at the trapped Sudipto, making him flinch and whimper at every turn, fat silent tears rolling down his pink face.

The moment builds and the boy keeps his eyes up, fixed solely on Jaggi, determined to not look at his friend at all, not wanting to drown in whatever he finds there.

It is a gut punch.

There is no wind up. In a flash Jaggi's fist sinks deep into Sudipto's soft stomach.

Sudipto's face turns red and lips blow out—no sound—just opening and closing as the impact scrambles his nerves.

Mahesh and Swapnil release his arms on cue. Sudipto collapses on the ground. And there it is, right on schedule, the rapidly growing wet patch on the front of his brown shorts and the sickly sweet scent of piss.

Jaggi laughs like a rabid wolf. 'Today, boys and girls,' he crows, 'it took just one hit!'

Swapnil laughs. Mahesh laughs. The uniforms laugh. The world under a boiling sun laughs.

And Sudipto lies there, curled up in his own piss, crying.

Arvind has still not moved a muscle.

Jaggi leaves with his minions, stopping to ruffle Arvind's hair on the way. The crowd fades. Arvind walks to his friend and helps him up, careful to not step in the puddle under him.

•••

The friends walk home, side by side, each alone in his world.

They take this route often. Every time they miss the bus, every time they leave early, every time they hide in empty classrooms and leave late. Every time their plans don't work, and Jaggi gets his hands on them. It is an unpaved path that leads out from behind the school and then runs parallel to the railway line entering the town of Rannwara. The train tracks, two sets of them, sit high on an embankment with wide tracts of open ground sloping down on both sides, the dry brown landscape broken into pieces by the shining grey of abandoned quarries.

There are no trees and no shade, and the path's featureless length seems to stretch out forever but it takes only about twenty minutes to get to the back gate of the Rannwara Steel Company Colony where the boys live.

On their walk back, as usual, Arvind does not say a word to Sudipto, knowing that his friend will break the silence when it is time. Overt sympathy now is not the answer. Pity does not help. His friend needs this time to collect pieces of his shattered pride. Sudipto is still wearing the piss-stained shorts, no longer conscious about it, taking a long sip of water from a bright blue Power Rangers water bottle, foreign-imported—just like his foreign-imported Ninja Turtles bag and his foreign-imported bright yellow pencils.

Sudipto is foreign-imported too, having arrived in Rannwara less than six months ago. A short time, but enough for Arvind and him to have become best friends. Declared and witnessed, with all the weight of such things at the age of twelve.

They have many things in common: both are outsiders—Sudipto is Bengali and Arvind is Tamilian—and new to the school, both speak broken Hindi with funny accents, fitting in at school, or even the steel colony that is filled with boys who seem too athletic, too rough, too north Indian …

They have other things in common too, and spending time with Sudipto is fun, but Arvind is able to look at the truth of things.

It was their outsiderness that had brought them together, and Jaggi, of course, had proved the welding flame to fuse them.

'I am sorry about this. You get delayed all the time because of me.'

There it is. The crack in the silence.

'It's okay. I don't mind,' he replies, and then, 'I told you we needed to leave immediately at the bell.'

'I know. You are right. I just did not think ...'

'That's your problem. You don't think. Next time just listen to me.' It is sharper than he had intended but it needed to be said.

Sudipto slows down. Almost stopping.

'But there was no reason today.'

'They do not need a reason.'

Arvind does not stop. His anger is making him walk faster.

Sudipto half jogs to catch up, his voice going up in pitch with each laboured stride. 'Back home we had classes about bullies. They would teach us that bullies are not bad people, just confused and need some talking to from a guidance counsellor ...'

Sudipto's accent is slipping in again and Arvind has to concentrate on following the potent American twang that emerges, stretching syllables.

'Not bad people?' Arvind can feel the blood push against the skin of his face. 'He and his friends beat you up every second day. Jaggi is a mad dog ...'

'His parents, the teachers ...'

'It won't help, Sudipto. We have been over this. His father owns all of Rannwara, he owns half the state. No one is going to touch him ... We have to save ourselves.'

Arvind thinks that this—like many other things—should be obvious to his friend. But he just does not seem to learn.

'What can we do then?'

'You listen to me more, that is something we can do.' And then, because it is important, he says again, 'And we tell no one. Any complaints, and well, it'll get a whole lot worse.'

'It's not right. Why does he do this?'

'Because he can.'

With this Sudipto gives up the debate and visibly deflates. This makes Arvind feel better. Not good exactly, but validated.

'Forget it now. How are you? Are you okay?'

'Yeah. Today, it was just one punch.'

Silence falls again but it is an easier silence, lighter than what had come before. He should not be shouting at his only friend. But he had been right, he had asked Sudipto to leave the instant school got over, to not wait for the buses or other class-boys or the bathroom or the refilling of water bottles. Every instinct had screamed at him to get out, though he was not consciously aware of the reasons. He had learnt to trust his instincts. Learnt it the hard way over the two years he himself had survived at the school, alone.

They reach the handpump. It stands on a raised platform. It is an ancient thing, made of cast iron, grey, with patches of dull rust along its body. It stands taller than the boys.

With no words spoken, with the motions of ritual, Arvind reaches out to grab the long iron handle. It is high and very heavy to move. He has to hang on it, hop off the ground and pull with his entire body until, with a creak, it starts moving. All the way down and then with his shoulders pressed against it he pushes up.

As the water begins to weakly sputter from the nozzle, Sudipto washes his hands and face. He then takes out a change of uniform and underwear from inside his bright green Ninja Turtles bag.

Arvind closes his eyes and turns his head as Sudipto washes himself. He keeps working the handpump, feeling the strain alternate between his shoulders and his legs, and thinks many things.

How the handle is heavy and the mechanism feels rusted, each point of friction vibrating against his body. How Sudipto is able to change into a separate uniform without his mother finding out. 'The clothes just go to the didi who washes them again,' he had said matter-of-factly and Arvind had wondered then as he wonders now about mothers who do not know exactly what is happening in their homes ...

And mostly he thinks, even as his shoulders and arms start burning from the effort, of how the direct suffering of Sudipto correlates with his own life being so much better: Arvind is no longer the easiest and most convenient target for the senior boys. Earlier, he had to outrun all the boys; now it is sufficient to outrun his friend. To just be a slightly faster target.

It is a hard lesson to learn and a harder thing to face—but what can you do?

In time, Sudipto is done. He is wearing a bright and fresh uniform and the soiled clothes, wrapped in a polythene bag, are hidden between schoolbooks ...

It looks suspicious, Arvind thinks, the cleanness of him. He does not look like a boy who has spent a day at school. He would have thrown some dust on it, rolled a couple of times on the ground, but that is neither here nor there.

They change spots. Sudipto works the handpump handle. He is awkward, even though the two of them are the same height. The flow is weaker, more uneven now. Arvind washes his face and wets his hair. It makes him feel better. Parts of the day slip away.

As he picks up his bag from the ground, Sudipto turns to him. 'I am going to tell you something, but you cannot tell anyone.'

'You are my best friend.'

Sudipto takes a deep breath and looks at his own feet as he speaks. 'Today I did it on purpose. I was waiting for it. I was waiting for the first hit so I could piss myself. He always stops hitting me when I piss myself.'

At these words Arvind is once again elsewhere, any place but here, soaring through another universe and dreaming of space ships and laser guns as the rest of Sudipto's confession is swallowed by the wailing horn of a train that rushes past behind them.

AMAR

Amar is in a train, looking out at the town and he decides that it is a shit town, and he pities every backward inch of it.

It expands outwards forever, this micro example of hinterland India, small and crowded and dirty, the exact flavour of the once-home he had run away from. It was a long time ago, but still, looking at this doppelganger, he feels threads of an old desperation twitching around his muscles.

It has been almost ten years since he arrived in Bombay, reaching the big city stowaway-ed in a train much like the one he rides now. It was the day after India won the '83 World Cup and it was a good omen: the city was good to him—it had taken him in and reared him and in these ten years he had never found a reason to leave. And so it is with much younger eyes that he looks at this town that is not the town of his birth, and this state that is not his home state, but enough is the same in the non-Bombay-ness of it that it all rushes back. The brown streets under brown skies that flow outside seem to exercise a claim on him, as if to say this is who you are and you will never not be it …

And so it is that the shooter, Amar Singh, twenty-five but an old twenty-five, is not entirely happy as he stands at the open door of the train compartment, smoking his second to last cigarette. He has been told that the stop here in Rannwara is quick, less than a minute, so he is ready with his bag sitting solid between his feet. He perhaps does not need to do this, there is no one else waiting to get off, but it is not like him to take chances.

The world outside slows and gains texture and shadows gain faces, fleeting glimpses of farmers and goatherds and half-naked boys with sticks, shining dark in the bone-white afternoon. The fields are behind him, now it is ancient warehouses and shells of factories, abandoned and in disrepair, broken windows staring like so many silent howling mouths.

The train is seven hours late, but he is not bothered. Time, for a change, is something he has.

The station appears almost as an apology. He tosses the cigarette, reaches inside his dark brown shirt and takes out a taveez with an image of the God Hanuman on it. He kisses it before tucking it back in.

With a deep breath, he steps out on to the platform. Bhenchodh Rannwara. He hates it already.

•••

His bag is heavy. It is green, made of thick military canvas. He holds it at his side, his left arm stretched tight by its weight. He is a strong man and it takes visible effort. A coolie steps forward from the gloom behind a tea stall but is waved away. This weight is his own.

Walking out of the station, he makes his way past sleepy traffic. A white jeep, its skin bleached in the sun, stands parked under a tree—holding women in its dark depths, seen only in hints of bright colour and mirrorwork. A bullock cart crawls through, with the animal thinner than the man whipping it, both a collection of ribs and flies. A man in a brown kurta, riding a brown scooter. He takes it all in, discards it and makes his way into the web of shaded lanes, careful to not step in puddles and cow shit.

It takes him a half hour before he finds the hotel. It looks suitable. A large painted board over a dark hole of an entrance—Hotel Jaipur, written in faded red over a once-white background. It looks forgettable in the best way. At three storeys, it is taller than the flat buildings that surround it. The corner rooms on the high floors should have views of oncoming traffic in both lanes.

He continues to walk, bag still in hand, tracing the perimeter around the property, filling in the grid in his mind with the paan stalls and the tiny shops—holding within printers and metal scrap dealers. The circuit complete, satisfied, he stops and buys a packet of Capstan cigarettes at the paanwala, tipping him five rupees.

•••

The insides match the outside.

There is no pretence left. Hotel Jaipur stands naked before him—a hole for drinking and whoring and for faceless travellers who come from a deeper nowhere, stopping a night before heading upriver to civilization. The lobby, such as it is, is inviting, cool and dim, closed off to natural light ... The floor is clean and the walls mostly free of spit stains. An ancient wood and iron staircase on his left, leads up into shadows. Next to the stairs is an ornate wooden desk that serves as a reception. A man, thin and balding, sits reading a tattered book in the weak light from a small bulb hanging over his head.

Amar walks straight to him. The man does not notice. On the desk is a cup of tea, now cold, with a thin crust of malai coagulated on top. A fly walks on it, confident, slow, in no hurry. Amar knocks on the table, sharp. The thin man is startled. The fly stays. The man looks at him with creamy eyes that take a moment to adjust to imposing reality. The book stays alert in his hands, on the cover a plump-faced girl running with blood pouring from her forehead. The title, in big yellow letters, is hidden by bony fingers.

The formalities take moments.

Amar asks for a particular room—'Top floor, looking west'—and the man nods, extending an unnaturally long arm. It stretches out like a magic trick. The whole time, he does not get up from the chair. He grabs a key from a board on the wall. There are others like it, hanging; almost all the keys are still there.

'There is no food, there is a problem with the kitchen,' the man says. 'Come and go as you like. Do not get girls, we are not that kind of place.'

It is exactly that kind of place. Amar knows that the man knows that Amar knows it.

As he hands the key, he pulls out a tattered register from deep inside the desk.

Still holding the green bag off the floor, Amar writes an obviously fake name and adds a made-up signature with a flourish. The man does not look at the name. He simply closes the register with a flat crack.

With that—and for hundred rupees a day, paid in advance—the room is Amar's.

•••

It is a heavy climb up with the bag and Amar is sweating by the time he reaches the room. It is one of five along the corridor, and the one closest to the stairs. The others, he knows from the unclaimed keys on the board, are unoccupied.

The room is run down, but has the vantage Amar wanted—the large open window looks out onto the main street and another smaller window opens onto the bylane. There is a small TV, a bed and a large out-of-place dining table with two mismatched chairs.

Amar keeps his bag on the table. It creaks with the weight and bits of dust fall off the underside.

Now alone, Amar moves with some urgency, shutting the door and window and fastening all the latches. He unzips his bag and removes a length of chain and a fat padlock. Not trusting the simple latch on the double doors, Amar loops the chain around the door handles before pulling it tight, fixes the padlock in place and locks it.

With the room secure and in the almost complete darkness, he takes his shirt off. Underneath, his white banian is soaked through with blood streaming from his heavily bandaged shoulder.

He collapses on the floor.

ARVIND

It is evening in the Srinivasan household and Arvind is feeling the smallness of his small desk in the small room, smaller still for it must be shared.

It is larger than his old small room in Trichy, but that was his very own space. Unshared, private. These things make a difference. Here, the square footage of the second bedroom of the Srinivasan apartment on the top floor of Building C-19 of the junior officers' quarters of Rannwara Steel Colony is shared by Srinivasan Arvind and his elder sister, Srilekha.

There is not much by way of furniture, just two skinny iron cots set against adjacent walls forming an L and two desks alongside the other two walls. An image, a calendar cut-out of Sri Balaji, stuck on the wall with tape right above Srilekha's desk, stares with omniscient benediction at her stout form as it bends almost double over her impossibly thick H.C. Verma's *Concepts of Physics* 3rd edition.

Srilekha, tall and solid, has not so much outgrown her desk as enveloped it entirely. On a footstool at her side sit the cousins of the Verma—the M.L. Khanna and the O.P. Tandon, each volume thicker than all of Arvind's school books put together. These are books that Arvind has stared at since they entered the room a year ago, and such is their terrible density that they now seem to occupy it all by themselves: Srilekha and he and the beds and their dreams mere planetoids to their combined Jovian mass. They are big, their spines wider than his palm, hundreds of pages, each crawling with equations and definitions in small type, challenging like mountains—not to be conquered in the brilliant work of a weekend. Come take us on, they say, we take will power and time and effort—all the things that Arvind, now in Class 7, can already see being demanded of him with paralysing dread. The books scare him shitless. And powerlessly he hates them. And their presence in this room, their dominance in his sister's life has made her a stranger to him.

His scrutiny goes unnoticed by Srilekha, and he turns his eyes back to his own notebook pages that lie empty, accusing, and then draws circles along the margins, carefully small, one running into another, and then his pencil moves faster and faster as the circles devolve into a scrawl and he does not understand it but he likes the shine of the graphite as it falls in interlocking patterns and ...

'Stop it, Arvind.' Sri has not even lifted her head from her own books, her pen is still moving as she talks. 'You are distracting me.'

Stop what, he asks in Tamil, innocence itself, I didn't do anything, using the whining tones that should bait a reaction out of her, but there is nothing. No response from her as she once again fades into her work.

He resents the Verma more now for stealing his sister so completely that she won't look up even while admonishing him. He scratches harder, the red and black Nataraj pencil stabbing into the thin paper of his notebook, digging in, tearing it in parts as his circles become larger, more violent, as they cut into each other with a manic ...

'Stop it, Arvind, this is a timed test ...' It is not a plea and thus not the beginning of a negotiation, but an order, stern and irritated, all too symptomatic of where their relationship has been lately.

The scratching is not enough and so of course he throws his eraser at her. It is not well aimed and not thrown particularly hard but it bounces off of her shoulder. This should give him something.

She turns to him, and in her eyes is a blankness he does not like.

'Amma!'

Calling the parent is a final, uncalled for, escalation. A declaration of defeat, a nuclear option, pre-emptory, skipping all the fun parts in between. It is disappointing to Arvind who is stewing when all thought drains.

'What is going on in there?' It is the father and not the mother. The Srinivasan—and the voice booms through the walls like a concussion. ARVIND, it says in capital letters, ARVIND, leave your sister alone, and then, 'Do I need to come in?'

'It is nothing, Appa.' His voice, squeaky again, rising in pitch. An imploring look to Sri who pipes in, 'No, you do not, it is okay ...'

Then to him, in Tamil, sweeter tones, softer eyes … once again it is the face of his sister. 'Please, Appu, I need to get this done. It is important ... and it is hard enough without you ...'

Arvind nods in silence and thinks his options through. 'Okay, I am going up, call me if they ask for anything,' and then silently he moves off the chair and onto the cot and with practised smoothness Srinivasan Arvind is out the window.

•••

The route to the terrace is precarious but Arvind has some experience now. One hand to the thick paint-covered pipe, a bare foot on the outside shutter—a push and a pull and you are scrambling over the ledge, and now, digging both feet in with no thought of the giant fall behind you, you spring up, fingers grasping the top of the parapet wall, a quick climb over and into the sky …

The terrace is warmer than the evening around him—the concrete underneath his feet is shedding the heat of the day, of which there is a lot. It will barely have time to cool before the sun rises again to beat it into submission. Arvind does not care much for the heat or the sun, for him the sky and solitude are enough. Here he believes he can breathe, and he smiles his very first smile of the entire day.

It has been like this for two years, a tough twenty-two months for Arvind who, until his father's transfer to Rannwara, did not understand the idea of persistent unhappiness. They had lived in Trichy for a long time before this—and it is those days, filled with underarm cricket and bikes and overall optimism, that dominate his memories. It was not perfect, nothing was, and details are already losing their sharpness, but having been here a while he now realizes the past was pretty good.

They play cricket here too, in the evenings. He can hear their shouts in the distance—the kids from the colony whom he does not play with. They are too old, too big, too loud, too different. Here they play overarm with a season ball.

He acts like he cares little and heads to the water tank behind which are hidden away all of his treasures. They are in an old schoolbag from when he was younger, a true child. The bag is small and blue in colour—on its front is a very eroded Spiderman, now just a red shadow of human shape but still leaping clear and vivid in his memory. There is no contraband here, nothing that is stolen or not okay for him to have—but he still feels better with his bag on his terrace, a simple space which is marked as his, unshared.

In the bag are a couple of action figures—GI Joes—with limbs missing, a tennis ball, pieces of string, a toy gun, a yellow plastic helicopter. He takes them out and arranges them at his feet.

AMAR

In the bag are five immaculately packed weapons.

Each is wrapped in paper and then plastic and then paper and then duct-taped all around—they look like oblong stones, stolen from an ancient temple or a tomb. They do not look like guns at all.

Four of these packs are medium sized, with one that is slightly larger at the very bottom of the bag. Alongside them are other parcels—more rectangular in shape. Each placed snug against the other, all hidden under a layer of hastily thrown in clothes.

In the light of a naked bulb, Amar, sedated by painkillers, activated by nicotine, goes to work. At his side: the empty packet of Capstan, flap open, seven cigarettes lying flat like so many bullets; a quarter of Royal Crown and a steel glass; a knife, unsheathed, small, sharp.

He removes each plastic egg from the bag and arranges them symmetrically on the table—the largest of the five sitting on top of the rest. A surgical cut along the length, just so deep, slicing through paper and plastic and no scrape against the contents, yields black metal.

The first gun.

It is a CZ75.

A pistol, impossibly beautiful, perfectly proportioned; it sits heavy in his hand. Gleaming under a bulb, he feels he can see his smiling teeth reflected on its skin. It is a cold thing, a thing of death and astounding accuracy. It is truly a master's instrument, a gun built for the Olympics, to shoot down the eye of a flying bird at a hundred metres. A gun wasted in the hands of amateur shooters squeezing triggers with their eyes closed. He believes in it. Absolutely. And he believes he knows much about guns. He feels that this gun is the greatest thing the Russians have ever made.

He feels the pattern of the textured grip, the coldness of the steel, the final potential of the un-cocked hammer. He pulls back the sleeve of the barrel, a single smooth motion leading to the double click. He checks for a chambered round. He does not need to—he packed these guns himself forty hours ago—but when it comes to guns, good habits are mandatory.

It is time to begin. He pours his first drink, drains half in a single swig.

Picking up the gun again, he retracts the sleeve just enough to de-couple the mechanism, splitting the gun into two. Then the recoil spring and the guide—along which the top half barrel moves in the moment of shooting—that absorbs the force of the recoil as it slides back, throwing out the spent cartridge and allowing its fuller brother to take its place. They come off without a hitch. And, finally, he pops open the barrel.

The weapon sits in front of him in eight pieces. It should seem harmless now, a mechanical curiosity, like an old watch taken apart. But like the old watch—within whose parts the ghost of the whole remains, ever present—the gun in parts applies gentle pressure against the fabric of the real world, vibrating with a spectral heartbeat.

It is now long slow minutes of cleaning and rechecking the oil—he always rechecks the oil. Check the barrel for powder deposits. Check the sleeve for rust and scratches. His world shrinks to a paintbrush and a small plastic bottle of gun oil and in this task there is pride and focus and much nobility.

In time it is done and the gun takes its shape again under his practised fingers, the body reformed from its constituent parts. The final click, satisfying, perfect in pitch. The CZ75 lies complete now, looking like it did fresh from its egg of paper and duct tape. A simple end. He lights a cigarette and finishes the drink.

And so it continues for Amar Singh in a corner room of Hotel Jaipur in a town he did not know existed a week ago under the heat of a bulb—gun after gun, black steel, the lot of them. Next, a Taurus revolver, custom barrel—if the CZ75 is an Olympic archer, the Taurus is a bulldog, a bar fighter; not a sword but a hammer, sitting hot and angry in his palm. A close-range weapon, the Taurus is made to be hidden—in ankle holsters and handbags, to darkly ambush and shoot into the backs of heads. It can blow a man's skull into eleven pieces—he knows, he has counted.

The same pattern in the sweating heat—strip, check, clean, re-assemble, all in the dance of the fingers, even as his eyes heat the fever of absolute concentration. The sheathing sigh of the mechanism coming apart and the click-clack of the mechanism falling together, and with it like added percussion, a drink, a cigarette and then another drink. The repetition, the sounds, the touch of the steel connecting him to the Amars of the past and the Amars of the future and in this moment all his selves are within him

Next is the Walther PPK, small, deadly, super concealable—a weapon of spy films and movie stars. Shiny and well-made but with a nasty recoil that won't let you shoot the same man twice. A thing for amateurs, he feels, but it sells well enough.

Another Taurus—a revolver, longer barrel, a cannon to make men shit themselves—assembled again and with a final spin of the cylinder he rests it in place.

He opens a second quarter of whisky. The large egg. Black menace seems to leak out of the packaging. Inside is an Ingram Mac-10. A submachine pistol, this one with an extendable stock. It sits there in front of him, an ugly fucking thing, heavy and square, industrial, a thing of no grace, a brick of death. It punches through destinies a dozen at a time. One pull of the fat trigger and an entire room stops breathing, torn to shreds by the thick rain of soft-bellied .45 ACP rounds. This is not his weapon of choice. It merely serves a purpose, an ugly instrument for an ugly task—the form following the function, as it does with them all.

They sing to him, these guns, with their own individual voices. They are all his, these five in the bag, to the extent that all guns belong to all men. Further than that, they serenade to his training, experience and his hours of incessant drilling of their protection and aftercare; yes, they are his as they lie before him and they belong to him but they are not his to the point that he belongs to them.

That one only comes now. The best he has saved for last.

•••

The Gun is strapped to him, sizzling against his chest, heating up slow and patient in the hour he has spent with the others.

With hands that shiver with devotion, he removes it from a shoulder holster with his eyes closed, and with eyes closed he begins the work—the Gun erupting to life in his mind's eye. The Gun, his Gun, his God, a Berretta 9mm, the custom sleeve with engravings of cool chrome, the custom grip finished in enamel and gold, the body blinding white …

It is blessed by Lord Hanuman himself—the monkey god's image, worked into gold leaf and perfect bright enamel, shining along the grip as He stands hoisting a mountain, victorious. The tip of Amar's thumb traces the lines of His smile—wide with benevolence, blessing all the killing that is to come, all that is true, all that is dharmic.

Now his breathing slows as the love grows and the worship begins. The patterns of movement are similar but unhurried and ever more deliberate: the unloading of the magazine, the unchambering of the single bullet in the barrel, and this jewel is disassembled. The insides are carved and mirror-bright and Amar, even with his eyes closed, can see his life gleaming at him from every plane of shining perfection.

When he is done, when the Gun is re-assembled, he is spent, the perfect sphere of his concentration shears along its surface. He sits with eyes open, staring at his weapon in his hands and this is how it is for many hours, words of true prayer buzzing through thinly parted lips.

ARVIND

All the stories he imagines are about death and revenge, and they run on fast-forward in his head, all motives lost and options discarded till it is the climax, the good guy beaten but not broken and the bad guys about to be dead.

He plays these scenarios out with his toys and on paper—entire pages of his sketchbook are now smeared with red crayon scratches, spouting from brown figures torn apart by so many lasers, limbs flying everywhere. Scenes never shown in the cartoons on cable TV are played out here in all their gory detail. It seems logical to him—the lasers that pierce metal and take down aircraft, surely, they should burn through mere flesh.

The sounds of cricket are still audible—the shouts louder, the language worse. It is dark now and the younger kids have gone home but the older ones continue playing in the streetlights.

He is done with his toys and sketchbook, with his imaginary worlds of reciprocal violence, and now he sits. He is not ready to go back yet, not ready to face his family, or anyone at all really. He is contemplating the pressure inside his chest which sometimes grows, he does not understand the nature of it nor can he surmise the actions to release it. As it grows, this pressure sometimes brings him to tears, but he swallows them. For tears are what the world wants from him and he does not give them up easily anymore.

He is tired of running, of keeping his eyes open at all times. He is tired of spotting ambushes, of listening for their laughter, of always looking for the slightest change in the body language of the senior boys, of watching for anything that signals a beating is on its way.

He is too weak to fight back. He had tried then, when he was fresh into this—his punches ineffective, his kicks bouncing off their legs. It was a mistake, all his attempts had only exacerbated his own agony. Oh, they liked to hunt him down then, didn't they? The strange small kid who does not cower and beg … not immediately anyway. All the more fun to break him after…

The things that he could do …

Throw stones at them. That would teach them. Store the stones in his schoolbag and wait for the right moment. Run when they give chase, lead them into an ambush, then turn and unleash. He would not miss, no, not then, not as he pictures it, his hands a blur as he flings the stones at high speed, catching faces … That would teach them, would it not?

If not, if not, he could always push them down the stairs. Vatsal, who was then in VI-B, had fallen last year and had broken his arm. A boy from pre-primary had run into him, tipping him over. Vatsal was out of school for weeks. Arvind had seen it happen and realized how little it took, it was just a question of timing. Even the bigger ones could be tripped easily, and crash down and he could get away … But they would come back. They always did and each time they caught him was worse than the last and this is when he hears a clear clicking sound, a wooden ruler tapping against the metal pipes. It is the signal from Sri …

He packs his thoughts inside his chest, stuffing them deep and the pressure seems to increase but what else can he do … The process is then repeated, but in reverse, as Arvind packs his treasures into the

Spiderman bag and parks it inside the waiting crevice under the water tank. Once secure, he leaps the walls and swings down the ledge and in through the window, back home in time for dinner.

•••

Family dinner is a constant thing, every night, without fail. They sit—Sri and Arvind—on one side of the wooden table, Arvind's feet dangling some inches off the floor and Appa sits at the head in his white banian and matching veshti, showered and powdered, smelling of sandalwood, deep-set eyes dark with intelligence, on his face the gracious smile of an emperor reigning over his little empire. The effect is spoiled somewhat by the lights reflecting off of his shiny bald head, pulsing in interchanging primary colours bursting from the altar of Lord Balaji—the God Himself installed, resplendent, beside the dining table, drowned in flowers, exalted by oil lamps and, to really drive the point home, garlanded in bright electric light. Later in the night when the house is asleep and all else is shut and the tube lights have winked out, these bulbs stay on, grading the entire living room in nightmare hues of red and green.

Now, however, they are not as offensive and Arvind finds them easy to ignore, his eyes on Amma as she makes several trips between the kitchen and the dining table, carrying plates of steaming food, always too many at once, balanced on her thin arms, served in courses for the rest of the family.

Next to him, on the seat to the right of Appa, Srilekha looks pleased with herself—her test must have gone well, he thinks.

Arvind is not hungry. The storm inside him has not yet blown over, and he has little appetite but he serves himself almost the usual amount of food so as to not excite comment.

'I was talking to Ramani periyappa yesterday,' Appa says, 'and his son, Shankar—you've met him—has just cleared IIT.'

The words are directed at Srilekha but Arvind senses that he is meant to hear them too.

'Oh wow, okay …' his sister's voice from his left. He cannot tell if she is sincere though she has stopped chewing and is looking at their father.

'So I asked him what Shankar had done for physics and periyappa said he had some textbooks that he had bought in Germany for Shankar when he was there ten years ago—great textbooks. Smart man, he knew they would be useful.'

His smile is endearing. 'He said he will lend them to us … They could be good for you, Sri. These Germans … very smart people. Dedicated.'

She thanks him for thinking of her and helping her in this, and the whole time a voice inside Arvind is screaming that these are his dreams for you and not your dreams for you and then Appa praises her again, and it is all about her commitment and focus and hard work and these words Arvind knows are not simple appreciation and encouragement for her but searing red lasers aimed at him and he can do nothing but take them on the chest and nod along and not sulk as he plays with his food.

Appa and Sri continue talking and she is animated and going on about prep tests and Olympiads, while Arvind has tuned out. He is thinking about Jaggi once again. How maybe he could throw some boiling water on him, carried in a thermos from home, the one Appa uses for his coffee … but it is hard to focus on these thoughts of revenge, they seem thin like air, tiny impossible dreams, scratching against his throat. Amma has now joined them on the table, wiping sweat with a white hanky, and on the TV in the background, the news anchor in the sari is talking about the attempted assassination of a builder in Bombay and the mafia wars raging in the city and …

'Arvind, learn something from your sister.'

And with that he is back at the table and it is Okay Appa and Yes Appa and Next Time Appa as they go over his test results from school and his lack of a work ethic and then there is silence again but for the scraping of spoons on utensils.

'Amma tells me you have a new friend—Mr Chatterjee's son?'

'Yes, he is in my class, his name is—'

But Appa has moved on, barrelling through the conversation the way he has done all his life. 'Good good. Brilliant man, Mr Chatterjee. Brilliant. Really changing things at the plant. He was in the US, you know, before this? Working in Dallas. Stay close to him, this kid—what's the name?'

'Sudipto—'

'Yes, Sudipto, stay close to him. You will learn something. He is Bengali. Intelligent, yes, like us. Man of principle, his father, hard-working. At his desk at 9 a.m. Stay close to him. I tell you there is something about Mr Chatterjee ... So different from Sharma ... Something in the genes, Bengali Brahmins are very intelligent. Yeah, he too is from IIT, I think, I do not recall which ...'

And that is about all that Arvind can take about IITs and exams and work and casual afternoon violence and the pressure building inside him explodes and the words come tumbling out.

'If he is so smart why does his son get beaten like a dog every day in school?'

•••

Later in the bedroom Arvind is awake and completely still. There is some pain on his cheek where his father's slaps still resound in the nerves, and there is no sleep, but the pressure, the unbearable pressure that had been building all day has dissipated now, replaced by confused thoughts percolating in lazy circles.

'I know you are awake.'

It is Sri. He does not respond nor change the pattern of his breathing.

'What happened was not okay, but you should not bait him with such things.' And then, 'The kids in school trouble you. They beat you. I see it.'

He stays silent.

'It has happened to me. We are targets. 'Cause we are new. 'Cause we are not from here. We are different and make for easy game. I hate it here. I really do. Why do you think I study so hard? I want to get out of here. I am going to give that exam, leave and never come back. You can do the same thing, Appu. It is just a few years. Then we leave and never come back. Ever. Be strong. Just a little longer.'

ARVIND

The very first time Arvind played a video game was at Sudipto's house.

It was early in their friendship, and Arvind went to meet his then new friend, dressed in his best birthday clothes that Amma had taken out—after all he was visiting the Chatterjees, who lived in a Grade A – Director Level Bungalow in the Rannwara Steel Company, Officers Colony.

He had known that Grade A existed and had ridden his bike through these lanes before, feeling like an interloper, smaller than his small stature, awed by the poles of the street lights that were painted dark green, and by the wide flat banks of manicured lawn that extended between the shining road and the boundary walls of the bungalows, the walls themselves made of textured Kota stone with thick hedges of pink bougainvillea growing over the tops so that nothing of the houses inside was visible.

He had still felt like a stranger when he had visited Sudipto the first time, found the right bungalow, it was not hard even though they all looked the same for there were only six of them, and he swallowed with much nervousness as he opened the large sliding gate before walking into the mystery and promise lying inside …

The lawns were large, and Sudipto's mother was exceptionally pretty, making Arvind blush with her attention, but these were not the scenes that embedded themselves in his mind. What was significant was Sudipto sitting on the living room carpet, smack in front of the television, with a plastic controller in his hand—and on the big foreign-imported TV were the brightest colours Arvind had ever seen.

He was instantly lost in the 16-bit perfection of the Super Nintendo, his eyes popping at the exploding pixels of Super Metroid and Mario World.

The TV was suddenly no longer a TV, but a window into a better world, of weekend morning cartoons come to life, where play did not need other people. A world of magic and sprite explosions and enemies that flicker into cartoon smoke. It was his first time playing anything like this and they played the whole afternoon and ate sandwiches and drank Frooti, and Sudipto let Arvind take turn after turn, laughing along the whole time, and it was easily the best day since Arvind's family had moved to Rannwara, probably his best day ever …

Later Arvind would conclude that the extended playtime and even the whole afternoon was perhaps a bit of a bribe, a price paid for friendship, and Arvind, while isolated here in Rannwara, was not nearly as isolated as Sudipto. The bribe, if that was what it was, worked and much later in the evening—a full hour past the time he should have been home—fingers clawed over light grey plastic, Arvind thought, this is my new best friend.

•••

He could never quite get his fill, for Amma would allow him to visit Sudipto only once or maximum twice a week, sensitive as she was to appearances, especially in the subtle hierarchies of the Steel Plant, and how it must never seem that the Grade C Srinivasans were taking advantage of the hospitality and largesse of the very Grade A Chatterjees.

And so on Friday morning at school, in the half hour before the assembly, when Sudipto shows Arvind his brand-new Nintendo Game Boy—a light grey box the size of a large calculator, with a green screen and tiny purple buttons, and containing thirty-two different games—fitting inside a pocket and a schoolbag, and running on batteries … Arvind's mind explodes with the possibilities. This machine is the answer to dreams that he, Arvind, had never even known to dream. A portable video game, who would have even thought it?

'I brought it here to show you,' Sudipto says by way of explanation. 'Papa got it from Israel.'

The classes begin and the Game Boy vanishes into Sudipto's schoolbag—but it is all Arvind can think about through the morning classes and through the lunch break. After lunch they have PT and Arvind insists that Sudipto smuggle the machine in his pockets as they head out. Come on, he says, you know I want to see it.

Arvind and Sudipto are not athletes by any measure, and are outcasts besides, so football with the rest of the class is never really an option. They usually spend their PT classes playing a slow and listless game of underarm cricket with the other fatties and asthma kids and the PT Sir, Chanchal Singh—tall, moustachioed, Nepali, a monster with an eager cane and a litany of unbroken verbal abuse—sees them as sub-human and leaves them to their own devices.

As such it is not a big thing to break away from and find a rare, shadowed spot under a wall next to the equipment shed and the pump room and it is here that Arvind plays his very first game of Super Mario in black and white 8-bit glory, the boys hunched together, thick as thieves.

And this is how Jaggi and his gang of friends find them as they jump the school wall, returning from a sneaky post-lunch cigarette.

•••

'What is that?' Jaggi asks. 'Show it to me ...'

He is calm and not rushed even as Sudipto and Arvind scramble to their feet, Sudipto hiding the console behind his back and repeating, 'It's nothing, it's nothing, it's nothing,' as if that will somehow help but of course it does not and Arvind has his eyes on the other boys who are spreading out naturally to block attempts at a getaway while Jaggi lunges for Sudipto's arm ...

Sudipto wrestles his arm out with genuine ferocity, surprising everyone, Arvind included, but the effort is of little use as Jaggi grabs him again and twists with the muscle memory of a lifetime of bullying and nearly succeeds in snatching the device, when Sudipto, berserk, stricken by madness, bites his hand.

Bites it deep.

Blood.

Blood everywhere.

Blood streaming over Jaggi's wrist and across the bottom of Sudipto's face. Arvind takes a hold of his friend and they run, pushing through the seniors, towards the football ground and the other kids and the relative safety of tall, tough Chanchal Singh. Looking back Arvind sees Jaggi standing where they left him, bloody arm raised in the air, giving a bloody thumbs up, and he is laughing like a mad dog and the boys just keep on running.

AMAR

Amar stands at a payphone, chewing on the end of an unlit cigarette, flicking it from one side of his mouth to the other, all the while glaring knives at the owner of the tiny restaurant who seems all too curious …

There is no dedicated booth to make calls, no real privacy, just a phone screwed into a wall right by the entrance and the phone rings against his ear even as the owner shies from his gaze and, looking down, begins to count through a thin wad of tattered currency with exaggerated care.

Amar knows the old fucker is listening in.

The phone has rung out about four times. Amar dials again. He knows that Boss is a busy man with many phones.

This time, it connects with a click.

'He is alive,' Boss says, voice full of gravel and static.

Of course Boss knows it is Amar on the line. Amar does not question the things that Boss knows. He knows many things. Amar lets those words settle in his chest and thinks long and hard about possible responses. 'I can come back,' is what he says finally.

Boss says no, and to stay there and finish the delivery and take his time.

'Too much heat over here,' and then, 'Okay, so this is the part I did not have time to tell you. Over there, you have to meet Bilal. Do you remember him?' Yes, Amar remembers him and remembers not liking him, but then that is Amar's own business and not that of Boss so he just says yes.

'Go meet him in two days. The packages are for him.'

'Then I come back?'

'No. Not now. Stay there. A few weeks, a month. Rest. Eat. Sleep. Go shopping.'

'I am absolutely fine,' Amar protests and Boss replies with an 'I am not asking', and that is the end of the discussion and then Boss is giving him an address that is too long and convoluted for Amar to instantly absorb.

He asks Boss to hold on and borrows a notepad and a pen from the owner who is now writhing in curiosity.

Back on the line, Amar takes down the address. He asks Boss to repeat it and ensures that he got it right the first time. It is not a place he knows, but he is confident he will find it.

'Meet him. We will talk next week.' Boss has other things on his mind.

Amar tears off the sheet, and the two sheets beneath the page he wrote on, and puts the lot in his pocket. He returns the notepad and pen, paying the man for the call and a small tip for the borrowed paper, and walks out into a street choked with cows and dogs and beggars and scooters and all the dust in India. He squints against the glare of the day, piercing through a sky crowded with electrical wire. He spits out the mangled cigarette from his mouth before walking on.

At a paan shop he buys fresh cigarettes and a Gold Spot. He takes out his painkillers—little white pills sitting loose in a plastic pouch—and pops two, slurping them down with the tart orange cold drink. His fever did not return this morning, but he is taking no chances.

There is nothing pressing to do now. He thinks about a paan.

A police jeep turns into the narrow lane and stops on the opposite side, engine running. A hawaldar in uniform gets out of the back—heavy and uncoordinated—and waddles his way to the same stall.

There is no change in Amar's demeanour. Nonchalant, easy, he keeps sipping on his drink.

The hawaldar picks up a bunch of paans kept ready, wrapped in paper, waiting for collection. It has all the signs of a daily ritual. The paanwala hands the man a cigarette along with the packet of paan, his Adam's apple bobbing with feigned joviality.

The hawaldar has thick solid arms, strong, good for slapping civilians and beating detainees with thick regulation belts, but not much more. His belly presses against the wooden stall as he bends to light the cigarette. Short fingers like railway spikes. On his shoulder is a vintage .303, single-shot, bolt-action rifle, aged and scratched—a good weapon for its time, robust, in good hands it could place a bullet accurately at truly enormous distances. It is slow to shoot, slower to aim. Anything less than fifty metres and it is better used as a stick. Amar reckons that this policeman has never shot his in a combat situation.

A honk from the jeep, a glaring fat man in gold-rimmed aviators staring out from the front passenger seat, his white skin pink and damp in the heat. The senior officer in civilian clothes. Scowling at the world for existing without his express permit.

Amar enjoys the hobbled jog of the hawaldar rushing back to the jeep, which begins to move even as he scrambles in. They drive off in a belch of smoke.

When his own paan is ready, Amar drinks the entire Gold Spot with a slurpy straw suck. He reads the piece of paper with the address. Details memorized, he crumples it, pops it in with his paan and keeps on chewing.

SUDIPTO

Civics class and Sudipto can barely hold the pen in his fingers as he takes notes while Bakshi Ma'am goes on about Directive Principles of State Policy. Her voice, with its heavily accented English, is something he barely understands even on the best of days, but today it is coming to him from the other side of an ocean—vague and disjointed. It does not matter what she has to say about the topic, he knows she is merely reading the relevant parts of the textbook aloud in class and it will take him minutes to find the passages but he still tries out of habit. And it is something to think about, rather than how he is going die.

He wants to stand and tell her—this teacher—that he is scared and he wants to go to the principal's office and call his family from there to come and pick him up, and then put him on a train or a plane out of here ... But there are stories that Arvind has told him, that other boys have told him, about what happens when you complain ...

They told him that Jaggi had cut off a boy's arm.

•••

They have a plan, Arvind and he, more Arvind than he, on how to escape from school today. He is worried about tomorrow though, and the tomorrow after that and the endless sequence of tomorrows to follow in the weeks and the months … but Arvind tells him to survive today—and they should escape the worst of it.

It is the last class of the day. They have switched seats with Ankit Pujari and Rohit Nagar in exchange for a box of imported tennis balls that Arvind knows Sudipto owns but doesn't use, for their desks are closest to the only exit.

'We have to leave before school ends,' is what Arvind has told him, 'they will be waiting for us at the bell.' His throat is dry, he thinks he can taste the blood in his mouth, Jaggi's blood, blood that he has washed and rinsed and rinsed for all of the lunch break but which still seems to seep from the gaps between his teeth.

I will run today, he thinks, and then tomorrow is Saturday and then it is Sunday, and then in the new week Jaggi will find me and kill me, destroy me, beat me into a pulp, strip me naked in the school halls, rip my skin off with his teeth …

Nothing he has been through, nothing in the last six months of hell, is going to match up to the shape of Jaggi's vengeance now.

He feels panic rise inside him again, much like during the break in the bathroom where he was shaking too much to even come to class while Arvind spoke about initiative and movement and how today they must run—in this Arvind is clear, but the timing of it must be perfect. The idea of staying in class till the end of the day, and hiding in the vacant classes even as the school empties bit by bit, waiting for the slimmest opportunity and sneaking out—all the while being on the lookout for predators is not appealing in the least. They must leave before school gets over, before the senior boys can begin searching for them.

In this moment, as Bakshi Ma'am goes on, it is like Arvind knows what he is going through because his friend has turned now to look at him, and there is a determination in his gaze. No fear, just an intense concentration and it makes Sudipto feel a little more assured that the plan such as it is will work and today will be taken care of, and while that leaves the crisis for later that is all that they can do now … With the slightest nod Arvind begins to pack his books and pencil box into his bag, really quietly, not drawing any attention and Sudipto copies him, swallowing his own distaste at closing the book while the teacher is still teaching. The instant Bakshi Ma'am turns to the blackboard to write, Arvind pinches his arm, sharp, and begins to move, and he moves as well, somehow slower. He can feel the eyes of the entire class on him and it is difficult to slide past the desk but he keeps his eyes trained on the back of Arvind's neck even as some of the other boys start shouting but Bakshi Ma'am has not yet turned around and then they are out of the door and behind them the whole class explodes in sound …

They run through the corridor of the secondary section, crossing the other eighth standard classrooms and down the stairs, and it is at the next landing that Arvind slows down, 'Easy now, we should look as normal as possible,' and Sudipto nods, and says, 'She is going to complain to our parents,' and Arvind says, 'Jaggi now, parents later.' It is always the first things first for him, a credo or a guiding philosophy, and Sudipto realizes that in all his years alive he has not genuinely imbibed this natural, and very obvious, truth of survival …

They cross teachers and peons at an even walk as they head to the PT rooms in the back of the school, and no one looks at them twice. He turns to Arvind and asks him if he has ever done this before and Arvind turns and smiles and says, 'You forget, I have already been here two years.'

AMAR

Amar walks out of a shop wearing his very own pair of imitation Ray-Ban aviators, and the world seems kinder. He has been shopping.

In his right hand is a bag with two trousers, four boxes of underwear, four boxes of vests and three shirts in dark colours. Dark in the summer heat, dark because his shoulder still bleeds—the wound reopening at the slightest excuse, seeping thin yellow plasma from the cracks in the clot. He had dressed it again himself this morning—it is not healing as well as he had hoped.

He needs a doctor. He should have seen one in Bombay, but there had been no time. Things had been frantic. He could look for one now, but he does not know whom to trust. It cannot be just any doctor; it must be one who is willing to look past the origins of bullet wounds. In these matters a cash bribe is not always sufficient.

He would have asked Boss if the bhenchod owner hadn't been listening in with so much interest. No matter. Maybe Bilal will know someone.

Amar takes a circuitous route back to the hotel. He is in no rush—there is nowhere he has to be—and as the afternoon progresses the traffic in the town dies down … even the cows have found patches of shade to collapse in.

The painkillers do their work inside him, his fever now a thin layer of cold sweat on his body, and with his shoulder settling into a dull throb, Amar finds something akin to well-being.

This, Rannwara, this smells like his old home to him, a home discarded, that lies in another crowded dusty lane, much the same as the one he walks on now, a reflection that lives a thousand kilometres to the east, where they dream in a different language. He cannot shake it, for enough is mirrored in the corrugated shutters and the wooden shop doors patched in fading blue paint …

The path of his life, which he can now trace clearly, has been a mad dash to get as far as possible from that one terrible point of origin, now well beyond the horizon, to where its venomous breath can no longer reach him. He thinks, as he walks in streets that threaten to melt into his past with every step, that the hate that drove him once might just be fading … Age levels these things, the mountains of youth erode away with time. It is the kind of thing Wendell was likely to say. Fat bastard with his extra fat brain. Was it possible to go back? Would he even want to?

It is amidst this reverie that the first hints of temple bells reach his ears, the sounds hammering a spike through his heart. All thoughts are dust instantly, and his feet begin to move, the pain in his shoulder forgotten … He walks towards the sound unerringly, the ringing deep and regular, a brass heart in complete resonance with his own.

He turns left, then right, and left again, floating over the ground, ever closer. The narrow streets are now behind him and the roads are wider and the shops have given way to old houses with grand gates, and another right and then a left and he is face to face with Lord Hanuman.

The Lord smiles at him with big yellow teeth.

It is a man with a mask on and it is not just the mask, Amar notes, but an elaborate costume with a colourful dhoti tied at his waist and his bare chest covered in saffron and ash, and a fake tail and a plastic mace in his hand. Amar is still in shock when the not-Hanuman closes in on him and lets out a loud undulating hoot which sounds nothing like an actual monkey …

He passes Amar by and there are others behind him, lots of others, a riot of Hanumans, an entire procession of young men dressed as the monkey god flows around him, jumping and yelling and hooting in chorus.

Moments later they are gone, vanished around the corner, and Amar Singh, bhakt of Hanuman, an ardent faithful to the monkey god, a faith resworn a thousand times for a thousand reasons, has no choice but to follow the throng, dazed absolute, his right hand reaching inside his shirt and touching the small gold image of the God he holds next to his heart.

MAHESH

The little fuckers are in sight, and Mahesh's hands squeeze tighter around the scooter's handles. He is excited, he is going to grab them and he, himself, will get to be the first one to fuck them up.

Mahesh's kismat has truly been shining on him today. First, he had not been in class, having bunked the last lecture to smoke cigarettes and listen to the cricket commentary on Jaggi's car radio, and was thus perfectly placed to make the pursuit. Then, he had been correct in assuming the boys would escape along the tracks, taking the short cut—a road deserted enough that any beat down would not be interrupted—to the steel colony. And the luckiest break of all, today was also the day he had his fucking scooter with him.

The scooter, a Bajaj Chetak '89 model in pearl blue, belongs to his father and as such is not something that Mahesh gets to use very often. Forever subjected to the shame of riding pillion to Swapnil on all their joyrides, Mahesh treasures any circumstance—his father's current battle with jaundice not excluded—that allows him to have the scooter to himself.

To have his own ride, and to have these little bastards to chase down … it is truly a blessed day.

Mahesh had been very surprised that the boys had been allowed to walk away. Surprised that they, the seniors, had not thrashed the fuck out of the boys then and there, at the time of the bite and the blood—it would have been quick and effective with no teachers nearby and no witnesses. But no, Jaggi must have his fucking games, and he said he likes his rage to build. Mahesh does not always understand Jaggi, but allows him his ways. He holds no illusions about any equality in this relationship.

It was supposed to happen after school though. The senior boys had parked themselves outside the secondary class corridor to make it easy to catch them. It would have been something really special. Of course, they got there only to learn that the bastards had jumped class and run off early. Thus the chase, and now Mahesh is here on his flying scooter and here they are in his sights.

Though both the boys are together, Mahesh's dreams of violence are focused on the Madrasi boy, the one with the ashy lips and the shifty eyes. He looks like a rat, he thinks, and I would like to pull his tail out.

All these fucking colony rats. Everywhere, in every class and every corner of the fucking school. Mahesh hates them. Acting like they are better than the rest of us, with their high marks and English words and strange long surnames—hard to fucking pronounce.

Well, they will learn better soon enough, learn who actually runs this place, and it is Mahesh who is going to teach them.

He can see them rushing now, the fair one faltering already. This will be fucking easy. He considers running them over—the fat one should be okay, he feels, turning his wrists to push the motor forward, he will fucking bounce.

They have seen him now—the Madrasi turned around and looked—and they go a bit faster but it is not really a lot of use. The slope along the sides of the road is quite steep, so they can't simply move off it and they can only keep going in a straight line away from him. Idiots. He would have tried to descend towards the tracks had it been him, not an easy path, what with the evil-looking shrubs and the rock, but it is what he would have done.

The fat one cannot run anymore, and Mahesh is gaining on them now, fast. He has to slow down a bit as well, the broken road doing the tyres no favours, and bite down his jaw to prevent his teeth from chattering, the scooter shuddering under him.

The south Indian takes his friend's schoolbag on his own shoulders, he is pushing him on. Skinny bastard could have run and saved himself, but didn't. Well, he will pay for it. Mahesh thinks he can sort both of them out himself, one slap and one punch should do it. The small one might run away once he comes off the scooter, but the fat one is fucked. And there is always time later … What a story he is going to have to share with the others!

Jaggi is going to be annoyed, though, that Mahesh got to them first.

The fat one cannot run anymore, he has slumped to his knees. It looks like he is puking. Pathetic. Always leaking from somewhere, that one. Got to be careful when I grab him.

The thin one is standing now in the middle of the embankment. Less than thirty metres away. He has his friend's bag in his hand, holding it by a strap … twenty metres. He extends one skinny arm and lifts the bag over his head, and swings it around so it forms a wide arc, and pivots on his feet, taking one big circle—Mahesh doesn't like the look of this and he should maybe slow down and brake but his brain is not responding—and another big circle and lets it go. And now it flies, and Mahesh can see it coming towards him, almost in slow motion … Its path leading directly to his face, getting larger and larger, and he is scared and he ducks to the handlebars of the scooter and the bag sails over his head just about and the fucker missed, the sisterfucker actually missed and now he is going to ram this—

There is a sudden pulling sensation as the rear wheel of Mahesh's father's scooter locks up around one of the extra-strong extended straps of Sudipto's American-made Teenage Mutant Ninja Turtles bag and the momentum causes the entire scooter to flip over the front wheel—Mahesh shooting over the bars and the scooter flying over him …

ARVIND

Mahesh has slid down the slope at the side of the road, an unholy mess of man and machine, fat legs still trapped under the scooter, and is crying fat tears from little eyes, face messy and bleeding from a hundred tiny cuts. Throaty words mingle with the wails—he wants help, he wants a doctor, he wants to kill Arvind but mostly he wants his mother. The words and the wails keep spilling out of his mouth and the tears keep spilling out of his eyes and the whole time Arvind is simply looking at him, taking it all in, shining with adrenaline and righteous vengeance.

The hero stands over the broken and bleeding body of the villain. It has happened, finally. In this moment the world has changed.

Arvind turns to Sudipto, who is still where he had fallen, mouth agape. Arvind rushes to him and pulls him to his feet.

'How did—'

'It does not matter—we need to leave. Let's go,' he says, 'before people come.'

'I need my bag—'

'Forget it—you can get new books. We need to get out of here—'

'The Game Boy is in there.'

And so, Arvind climbs down to the scooter, foot after careful foot, minding the loose pebbles under his feet till he is within an arm's reach of a shattered Mahesh, who swipes at the air in vain, cursing the gods in between gulps of air—all to disentangle the bag from the back wheel of the scooter. The whole time he makes it a point to not look too closely at where Mahesh's leg is bent in a way a leg is not supposed to bend.

AMAR

Amar follows the boy Hanumans across what feels like all of Rannwara as they pass through crowded markets where customers stand to the side holding their palms together in supplication, muttering prayers under their breath, and through choked by-lanes lined with crooked houses in lurid pinks where more children join them, some masked, cheering as the monkey-men jump and dance, and women stick their heads out of small windows to shout Jai Bajrang Bali …

A walking meditative state, an ocean of sensation with no conscious thought, the act of movement itself building into something religious, and abruptly he is there, the destination, a large market square—decorated in red and gold cloth, packed with hawkers—at the end of which stands a large temple complex that dominates all of it. He is struck still at the sight of the temple even as his gang of monkeys mixes into the crowd, joining the multitudes of others like them, painted and laughing …

The temple is old, royal, carved into the face of a hill, sitting high above him. Its ancient walls covered in figures that are too far to discern, but he can feel their eyes, all their eyes, staring as one, reaching past the entire mass of humanity to stab into him, following him unerringly as he moves, their gaze saying yes, yes, it is he and he alone among them all—and the call is real and true and it will not be denied.

Around him the fair burgeons—people and more people grind against the brightly decorated carts filled with garlands and figures of gods, children run with wooden swords wrapped in golden paper, while the rest walk with ice lollies and technicolour drinks in thin plastic glasses, soap bubbles and clusters of balloons bouncing just above the tops of brown heads and everywhere a million pinwheels sitting still in the thick air like dead fluorescent butterflies.

Access to the main entrance of the temple—a wide avenue of stairs cut into the hill that rises from the edge of the square to his left—is through a makeshift bamboo corridor to give some order to this chaos. Next to it lounge policemen, eyes blank with professional boredom. To his right are stores overlooking the square, some shuttered, some festive. Parked cars and two-wheelers, a jeep with political stickers and a cop, this time in plainclothes, standing to its side, fanning his face with a folded newspaper. Boys in school uniforms sitting on the bonnet and eating ice cream.

Back in the square anticipation builds as the bells rise to a crescendo, the clanging going through his bones like holy water. He needs to be there for the big aarti, to make it for this darshan. The timing has been immaculate—the events of the last week and month seem to stretch behind him like a rocket trail, impelling him forward, bursting through all reality to bring him here.

He heads to the stairs, aware of the bag in his hand and the Gun at his shoulder. It sizzles with absorbed vibrations, a deep resonance. Closer to the barricades rise giant tents within which the hopeful swarm—and men scream over each other, selling wicker baskets filled with fat brown coconuts, garlands of marigolds and a local pink flower he does not recognize. Families crowd around stalls with open shelves, dumping their shoes and bags, exchanging coins for coupons, as they grab their baskets and head into the press, all barefoot, children holding ends of saris and kurtas in tight fists.

This is when he sees the metal detector.

It is a harmless looking rectangle of metal standing at the top of the stairs, just outside the temple itself. A sleepy-looking cop sits on a plastic chair next to it, waving people through even though it beeps, barely noticing anyone who goes through.

He pauses with his hands raised to the sky—palms together. Saluting the house of God from the outside, he thinks.

There is little risk here, but Amar Singh likes to deal with certainties. Every bit of unnecessary risk counts and accumulates. He is still making calculations when the temple bells sound again, ripping through his thought structures and determining his answer for him.

•••

A little while later, Amar joins the line of devotees on their way into the temple, a big hundred-rupee basket of coconut, fruits and other offerings in his hands. It is the largest they are selling. He does not see the burst of commotion at the jeep parked behind him or notice the schoolboys abruptly disperse, moving with sudden purpose through the market. His attention is entirely on balancing the basket in his hands even as the crowd pushes him around.

He walks into the temple and the detector doesn't beep.

ARVIND

He might have to leave the city after this.

He cannot stay here. Jaggi and his boys will hunt him down. He could go and live with his chinnamma in Chennai or some boarding school or hostel somewhere. Maybe back to Trichy even—but what will he tell his parents? What words can he use to explain his predicament? He has never spoken to them about something important to him before. Those channels of communication do not exist. There are no precedents and no procedures. He toys with words, forming them in his mouth but they feel alien, sounds without meaning.

Any explanations will breed violence—foremost among them, the violence in his father's hands and then the sharper weapon that is his father's disappointment standing like a sword at his throat.

This is a problem for later, all for the tomorrows. He must focus now because today is not over yet.

He walks behind Sudipto, pushing his friend forward, urgent, unyielding. Sudipto's steps falter, his new shirt is already covered in dust, translucent in his sweat, stained in his puke—his white vest is showing through under the light green straps of his schoolbag. Foreign-imported straps that did not break even when entangled in the wheel of a scooter.

'Why are we heading this way?'

'They know we were on the back road … They could catch up with us.'

The road along the tracks is empty and long. They could not possibly have continued along it. It would take another fifteen or twenty minutes to reach the back gate of the colony, to safety. Anything could happen within that time, any number of pursuers could overtake them. Mahesh may not have been alone, his friends might have been following him on cycles and on foot, or in cars even …

By now, Arvind is sure Mahesh is screaming, and has drawn passersby to him, maybe even other kids from school, other seniors. The police? He is not sure—and so they push on, across the tracks, through the smaller colonies where the houses are made of exposed brick and the narrow roads are just shallow drains, and from there they cross into the town proper.

He will need to change towns. Maybe just changing schools will do, that way he can still stay with his family. And still have Sudipto. He knows there are other schools in Rannwara, though he is unsure if they are English-medium. But he does not think that changing schools will stop Jaggi now.

'How are we going to get home? I have never been here ...'

Sudipto's accented voice brings him back. His friend is, once again, difficult to understand, the words are fast and shrill, American, shedding nervous energy in bundles.

'We take a tempo. It costs four rupees. From here straight to the colony main gate.'

Sudipto nods. 'Are you sure it is safe? I have never been in one before …'

'It is fine, don't worry.'

The tempo stop, such as it is, exists informally under a large tree at the corner of the main street, opposite the bank. Here they wait, surrounded by blaring horns and angry shouts. Sudipto, beside him, is a bundle of nerves, flinching every time a stranger brushes past.

But he does not complain and no longer asks questions. Arvind senses within his friend an acceptance or merely an exhaustion so deep that no outrage can be summoned anymore.

The wait is longer than usual. To his right, a tight group of blacksmiths sits under a tree. Nomadic tribesmen, the lohars hammering out small tools on burning coals, the iron a soft red glow, sparking in the shadows as the hammer comes down. Arvind counts his breaths, inhaling and exhaling with each strike of the metal, ringing clear like a temple bell. Pouring all his apprehensions into the incandescent metal till he can feel his frayed nerves settle.

Eventually, a tempo arrives. It is an ancient hulk of rusting metal, a triangular driver compartment carrying a hollow square upon its back. It stops when Arvind waves it down, and is packed full, boys older than them stand on the edge, hanging off the frames. Inside, the passenger box is crowded and dark, holding within its confines a thick awareness of humanity and sweat. Thin men in pale dhotis slide and shuffle, creating a few inches of space where there should be none.

Arvind pushes Sudipto in before getting on the frame himself, balancing his feet on the floor, most of his body sticking out, wrapping a hand around a holding bar that is wet to the touch. He hopes it is just sweat.

They move by inches through choking streets, deeper into the city. The crowds around them swell as they get closer to the temple square. Arvind is happy to have his head outside in the air, taking in the colour and the sound—the clamour outside blissfully washing over the one within him.

It is how he sees the senior boys seconds before they spot him from where they are sitting on the hood of a jeep. Arvind's eyes meet Jaggi's and there is a shock of recognition and it is the worst luck in the world but there is no getting away on this tempo, moving like a snail, so he screams at Sudipto to keep going till the Colony and hops off.

And then stabbing deeper into the press of towering bodies around him, Arvind runs.

AMAR

Amar, on his exit from the temple, fresh teeka still wet and glistening on his forehead, shoulder sore from holding the heavy basket of now-blessed offerings, finds everything in uproar. A fight has broken out among the stalls within the tent—the epicentre of the disturbance is in the largest stall where, amidst the shelves, sit his things … In an instant he moves, the basket dropped and forgotten behind him, ignoring the shouts as people trip on coconuts rolling under their feet … He must get to his things … he must.

He pushes through the agitated throngs—his shoulder burning up, things tearing inside, the bandage feels wet to him as he nears the chaos only to find a bunch of school kids, the same ones from the jeep earlier, scuffling with each other. A couple of cops enter the fray, their wooden laathis swinging before them, even as a portion of the tent collapses, the thin bamboo holding up its cloth roof coming apart, and Amar, not minding his own shoulder, pushes pushes pushes ...

And then another crack as a second bamboo structure gives way and the colourful pandals collapse onto themselves and all the men are stuck underneath. It is all blindness and chaos but he is relentless and he is close, and the shelf that holds his bags and his shoes is just ahead, within arms' reach, when a boy, a fucking little bastard monkey of a boy, small and dark, runs under his feet and then a larger one dives at him, landing on his leg. It takes Amar no effort and no thought to just lift him and heave him to a side and there it is, in the middle of everything that has fallen, his bag, and just as he gets to it, another push—it is the same school kid again—and he collapses onto the shelves.

His shoulder is screaming in agony and he can feel the blood beginning to trickle down the side of his body. The shirt while dark is not black and with the police here, right on top of him, it is getting very dangerous, and the same bells that rang in his head on the way here are still blaring now. Amar needs his bag and then he can get the fuck out, and there it is and he picks up the shopping bag and shoes and new sunglasses and walks, not wanting to get caught up with the police. There is no explanation he could possibly give and even the most distracted cop will certainly notice his bleeding shoulder. So it is a good thing that no one pays him any attention at all.

•••

Head full of blaring bells, heart racing at two hundred, shoulder tearing itself apart, Amar limps away and after what feels like hours finds some seclusion. Looking around him with eyes that do not have the confidence they did an hour ago, he reaches into the shopping bag and of course the Gun is not there.

GUNBOY

Twilight falls on the steel colony, and on the terrace of building 34, Arvind can hear the ringing of the metal pipe, Srilekha's signal to come back down, for there is dinner and waiting parents and much chagrin and pain. This is her second or third time calling him, and he will surely get into some kind of special trouble for not being home.

However, the sound leaves no ripples on his young mind.

His attention, his heart, his very being is focused, with eyes so wide that they seem demonic, on his hands for they hold the most beautiful thing he has seen in his entire life, glowing with an internal light, like the will of gods made material—every prayer answered. An angel, yes an angel, has come and revealed the instrument of his deliverance.

In his hands, glowing alight in white splendour, crackling with all the lightning of possibility, pregnant with thunder, sitting dense and heavy as destiny itself, is the Gun.

Interlude

SECRET ORIGINS

THE MAN IN WHITE

Bombay, some years ago

Trilok Kamani always wore white because his father always wore white. It was something he never even thought of, the colour being as much a part of him as his skin. He wore a white shirt with white jeans stuffed inside white ankle boots bought from Italy, from the same place where he ordered his belts, also white—this one with a roaring tiger motif stamped on the white metal belt clasp.

To Trilok the colour white was not just an aesthetic choice, once inherited and now obsessed over, but a deep philosophical concept tying within itself the ideas of truth, purity and unmitigated focus.

White allowed no mistakes, no slip-ups. All scars and shortcuts became visible, there was no hiding and there were no lies in his white world, and with the grace of the Waheguru his white world would stretch all over and around this little planet …

On that Tuesday, Trilok sat at a large white desk, flipping through a fat white binder, white light glinting off his white-gold Rolex with its white dial and diamond hour markers. It had been an easy day for him so far, and it would continue to be an easy one even as Bombay boiled in its own heat outside. The three General air conditioners in his room had turned it into a refrigerator, ensuring he did not sweat through his white clothes.

He looked through the neatly written columns of numbers that weighed timber and gold and land prices in four countries, columns that measured the lives of men, the worth of their dreams and the price of their deaths ... So lost was he within this map of his empire that he did not notice the tiny broken pixels of movement in the top right CCTV, one of nine CCTVs, organized in a 3x3 grid on the display mounted next to his desk, as three shapes jumped over a wall and there was a scuffle and a bright burst of white static.

A second later, the sound of gunshot reached him, and although subdued and suffocated by the layers of concrete it transitioned through, it pierced his mind as he read about polyester factories in Indonesia. Trilok knew many things and the thing he knew most about was the sound of a handgun. He closed his binder, making a note of the page at which he would have to restart, and focused on the grainy footage of the security screens, trying to zero in on the exact location where his bastion had been breached.

The giant double doors to his cabin opened and Sahil and Dubash entered—his boys, adopted as street cats, now grown to be tigers, fearless, with fast hands and keen eyes. They closed the doors behind them and took up positions on either side, calm, resolute, made of stone.

'There are three of them,' Dubash said, his eyes drilling holes into the doors as if to look past and spot the attackers. 'They won't make it past the back office.'

The back office, a deliberate maze of zigzagging corridors with no clear line of sight, contained infinite ambushes. It would take an army and a half to get through.

'Should I call the police?' Sahil asked.

Trilok replayed the question in his head as it deserved some thought, and a quick analysis of the risk, for once the khaki boys came they would ask a million questions and would need to be paid off and there were those eight open cases against Sahil here, and look at him, the fucker knew it but asked the question himself. His boys were the best, he had no doubt.

'No, fuck it. We will bury these bastards in the garden in Alibaug.'

With that Trilok opened the right-hand-side drawer of his desk in which a white wood and ivory box, inlaid with gold was kept. Inside was the Gun, the white death, the perfection in everything. He took it out. Maybe he would get lucky and shoot one of the gutter insects that had arrived so unceremoniously, hopefully Sahil's minions would leave one of them alive at least. Chances were low—they were good boys, but excitable.

He settled in his chair again, right hand cradling the Gun in a loose grip, the thumb idly tracing the carving of Lord Hanuman on the enamel handle. Now there was nothing to do but wait.

It took another five minutes of gunshots and activity in screens four and five before Trilok got worried and glanced at Dubash who was looking at him, and then there seemed to be gunshots from the lunch hall, which was past the back office and past the maze and a lot closer to his own room than he would have liked. He could see them now on the screen, two shadows—a companion lost somewhere along the way—firing and moving and moving and firing like demons, inching nearer. Sahil nodded and his nod said he would go and deal with them and in his hand was an Uzi, his wedding gift from Trilok, a gun he had wanted since he had first seen it in one of those imported Hong Kong tapes he liked so much.

There was nothing to worry about, Trilok knew this even as Dubash switched off the lights in the cabin and moved to one side of the door and Sahil stepped out into the corridor, the door closing behind him.

Sahil appeared in front of the door in screen nine and moved quickly down the corridor, light on his feet, Uzi cradled in two hands at waist height and he slid into view on screen eight, taking cover behind a turn, waiting for the shooting at the end of the hallway to cease.

The attackers were somewhere between screens six and seven and then one of them, a young boy, noticed camera seven and shot it and now there were no eyes on anything ahead of Sahil who was just waiting on eight and then he fired and fired and it was the whole damn clip in one go. At 1200 rounds per minute it took merely two seconds for the flood of hot metal to burst through the narrow corridors, and nothing should have been left standing anymore but then more shots echoed through the halls and Sahil was on the ground, clutching his body. A young man, alone, his friends dead, thin and dark in a loose t-shirt, the same boy who had shot the cameras, limped past Sahil and shot him in the head before continuing—a thin trail of tessellated blood behind him.

'There is just one of them now,' was all Trilok, who was standing behind the desk, the Gun raised in two hands, needed to tell Dubash. If there was pain in Sahil's passing, Dubash did not show it. A silent nod and some repositioning. He moved to where Dubash pointed.

Minutes. Hours. The dark room was striped with sun, bands of light leaking from between closed venetians. Time felt thick like sweat. Mouth tasting of blood from a chewed up cheek, Trilok shook in his own den, the smell of his own fear making it hard to breathe. But there was comfort here, comfort in the form of Dubash, the best boy, only Dubash, ever dependable, stood unmoving, a perfect predator, waiting, waiting, and every breath was hard in Trilok's throat. Then there was movement on the outside and a flicker of a shadow under the door. *Boom. Boom. Boom. Boom.* Four shots from Dubash at chest height, each perfectly four inches away from the other and then a thud outside the door and Trilok let out a long exhale.

As they repositioned soundlessly, three shots rang out, blind, through the door at impossible angles, and one caught Dubash in the throat and he fell to his knees, blood pouring like a fountain from the side of his neck.

Trilok rushed without thought, the Gun white hot in his hand. He swung the door open to find the boy crumpled along the wall opposite him, more than half dead, dark red blood on light red t-shirt, eyes made of fire. His gun must have been empty for it lay smoking at his side, sleeve retracted, his right hand clutching a taveez at his neck.

Trilok raised the Gun, it weighs as much as the whole damn moon, and pointed it at the boy who did not blink, chest rising quick and shallow, squeezing as many breaths as he could into the last bits of his miserable little life.

Sahil dead, Dubash dead, half his boys dead. His empire of white painted red. How he hated all of this, what a waste of a fucking day, and all this despair escaped him with a 'you lucky madharchodh' and he pulled the trigger and the Gun went *click*.

II

GREAT POWER

AMAR

Amar Singh holds his breath as the old barber uses his blade to scrape the stubble off of his throat. It is an uncomfortable feeling, this fear that he feels, corroding his insides.

It is also a new thing. Fear. Or rather an ancient thing that had gone away for a really long time. He had thought he was free of it. Now it is back and he does not like it.

As to the root of the fear … Amar thinks about God.

He did not start off in this life a believer in destiny, or of gods or powers outside of man's understanding. As a child, he had seen what his bastard father had shown him, and concluded that a God who does not see injustice and pain—such a God is blind. And even worse than a blind God, is a God who sees but chooses not to act. Well he had no room in his life for such a God.

And with no God and no destiny and only the hell of the present burning his feet, a young Amar had run into the wide expanse of man's world and demanded a very human accounting.

But that was then and this is now and it has been years since that day of blood when he picked the Gun, and his own personal God apparated and walked in step with him. Lifting him, encouraging him, making his aim true and striking deep into the very hearts and livers of his enemies. Ever since, he had thrown himself into the worship of Lord Hanuman, the great warrior monkey, the avatar of Shiva, the instrument of holy redressal, and it was the lord's blessings, his avatar as a weapon, that made Amar strong, invincible.

He could do anything with his Gun-God at his side. Walk into the worst fights with bullets spraying like rain—where men turned to pieces of bloody meat—and survive. Dive into ambushes while laughing on the inside at the stupidity and terrible karma of his enemies, that they would serve themselves to their deaths in this manner—he the mere packager, gift-wrapping their souls enroute to the afterlife.

He knew shooters became superstitious. It was a problem in the profession, and it was not hard to find veterans festooned with a dozen holy threads tied on their hands and feet and around their cocks, and rings and necklaces to win favours of deities and fakirs. Always, there were temples to be visited, and bar girls to be held one last time, lovers whose lips and voices drove away the spectre of death that haunts a man who had chosen to live his final hours on repeat.

As more and more comrades around them died, it became natural to build rituals that protected them, to give meaning to continued survival, to another few mornings of life won back in a world of terrible randomness. A world where a lucky roll of the dice determined if the bullet clipped an ear instead of entering the eye. And then like any gambler, there was nothing to do the next day but to go and gamble again, knowing that if it indeed was truly random, then the bad number was up, for luck had stayed around for far too long.

So they all, all his fellow travellers, stayed up nights, smoking cigarettes, building castles in their minds, clawing through waking hours to spot patterns within smoke and dream. Invented reasons for still being alive. Wrote stories. You will never die on Tuesdays.

A silver coin with a black thread through it will avert the eyes of the God of Death.

He knew these things as superstitions in others, and knew his own circumstance was different. His was no longer a God who looked away. His was a God he had held in his hand.

His story had begun with the assassination of Trilok Kamani.

He did not know it then, young and stupid as he was, but it had been a bad plan with no chance of working. In darker moments he believes that it was never intended to. Three boys, barely trained, expendable, hopped up on pills and booze, holding tight their very first pistols—shot like an arrow into the dark. It was merely a piece of a message, sent via those who were meant to die as they failed. A mere pacing comma in a larger conversation.

But it had worked. Fortune had decided. Amar had crawled out of the belly of the beast, covered in the blood of a dozen men. He had made his way limping and falling, in pain and confusion, leaving a bloody trail on glinting white marble floors and walls, and in that blood were left all traces of the boys who walked in with him, his first soldiers-in-arms, their names and faces melting away as he made his way out, impossibly so, climbing over a wall mere feet away from the gate through which the police were rushing in.

Each excruciating inch of the escape is clear in his mind, while the attack is all fog and nerves and rum and the magic pills Wendell had handed to him. He is not sure he came back either. Sometimes he feels that he died there in that house, with those nameless, faceless boys, and a new Amar crawled out, the Gun clasped to his heart.

God had confronted him in the form of the Gun, and impending death and a young bleeding Amar had smiled, and the Gun-God had liked the idea of him and chosen him.

That was it really. This was not superstition but true faith.

Believing in God was being okay with the idea of being chosen, it was there in the stories if one read them carefully enough.

With two bullets through his torso and one in his leg, Amar Singh was the sole survivor of the assassination of Trilok Kamani. It was a miracle he survived the afternoon, or the month that followed, wracked with pain, coughing pieces of his lungs out—black and wet—and the fevers, all the fevers and the dreams pushing against open eyelids that spoke terrible things true and otherwise.

In those fractious weeks, as Boss rushed him from one backroom hospital to the other, stitched up by fucking horse doctors in the back of trucks, his bones rattling in the back seat of a Maruti Omni as they crisscrossed the city, always puking blood, always leaking from somewhere—through it all he kept the Gun in his hand and never let go even for a fucking minute.

He was sixteen then.

He is twenty-four now, and today, for the first dawn in eight years, he woke up with fear taking hold deep in his heart. He can feel thick fingers of it under the soft part of his throat where the blade goes brrrrrrrrt against the grain of his hard stubble. Today he woke up with the confirmation that God has forsaken him, and he is chosen no more.

He swallows it down.

Amar Singh sits at a barber shop on the edge of the temple square, quiet in the early hours, two round-bellied priests sitting on the stairs, drinking tea from steaming cups, behind them the entrance unguarded like an open mouth—no cop and no chair, and the metal detector pushed aside like old furniture.

All his other missions are forgotten. He must prove himself once again. Win over the Gun. Not falter in his faith. Not drown in the despair collecting at his knees. There are a million and one myths out there, about men being tested in their devotion, to only find themselves, to be never not-chosen. Thus, it shall be with him. He is determined in this.

Shave done, he asks the old man to oil his hair.

'I was here yesterday,' he says with closed eyes, as the old man kneads his granulated knuckles firmly into his scalp, 'and there was some chaos here.'

'Heh, just the usual. Some local boys … a fight that got out of hand a bit …' Then, 'Raghu got fucked, the shopkeeper? His tent collapsed and he lost all his goods in the chaos, and then had to fucking feed the cops also.'

'Why the cops?'

'Well, if you start a fight next to a mandir, the cops are bound to show up. And when those fuckers arrive, they will not leave with an empty stomach … Now they couldn't really touch those schoolboys, but someone had to pay the bill …'

'The schoolboys ran away?'

'Well, sahib, that is the thing. The boys involved are famous around here, you know … they have a proper reputation. One of them is the son of the local leader, his father rules this district. The cops recognized him and shat their pants … They were pissed, so of course poor Raghu got fucked …'

ARVIND

Arvind opens his eyes in a new world.

It is early and still dark and the lingering coolness of the air inside his room rests against his skin. He feels good.

His face stings but it is a sensation from far away. It is just pain, completely superficial. Easily ignored. There is no emotional component to it—more akin to stubbing your cheek against your father's hand as you run across the house than an actual beating.

Appa was in a hell of a mood last night.

Arvind, through his adventures, had never missed dinner before. Never returned home with his uniform being in quite this state of disrepair. 'You look like a hooligan! A street ruffian!' Appa had screamed while slapping him again and again. 'Is this the animal we have raised in this house …'

Appa had said more and slapped some more, but this is all Arvind remembers, pieces of the noise. His father had not asked him any questions. The scene had not felt heavy when it was happening to him, and he can feel its tiny weight dissipating like wisps of smoke, easily blown with the lightest of exhalations.

With the gun, he has found not just an offensive weapon, but a shield—its presence itself driving all the bad things away. All the feelings of helplessness and despair that clung to him—they now hide from its light.

Amma was harder. The dinner and the fussing. The tears. The apologies and the where-were-yous. It is harder to lie in the face of her love. But he did it. He hid his pain and hid his joy, and then he went to bed, secrets flowering safe within his heart.

Now awake, he finds that all the slaps and recriminations have slid off of the surface of him. Everything since finding the Gun is a clean slate, and everything leading up to it seems too vivid to be real.

The mad dash into the crowds of the fair. The scramble as he avoided the seniors. How he grabbed the pole and pulled, causing the tent to collapse. Slithering on the ground in the heart of that kaleidoscope of chaos. The big man whose legs he had crawled through. The shelves giving way. Him on his hands and knees. The bag upturned just so, and how it shined in the dark and the dust—silver grace pouring out of the upturned bag … and how his hands moved on their own and grabbed it, the way it felt hot to his touch, and heavy, so much heavier than he had thought it would be … And then holding it tight against the flesh of his stomach, he crawled some more and it was then a thing of moments to shove it into his schoolbag before anyone noticed …

Sri tosses in her sleep, her back turned towards him. As he watches her fidget, a steady electricity builds inside Arvind, an urge to move charging up his limbs—he wants to throw off the sheets and climb up to the terrace and look his destiny in the face in the morning sun.

But he does not. He waits. Lying in place on his narrow bed, staring through the ceiling, eyes focused on the liquid shine of the Gun as it drips through the stone above his head.

•••

The house awakens and familiar routines take over, and as Arvind plays his role within them, he finds that the water sparkles as it falls out of the tap when he prepares to brush his teeth, the foam in his mouth is that of oceans meeting fantastic shores … Today there is joy in every movement, and with his deliverance in hand, he feels a peace that he has not felt before. A confidence with which he moves through the world as it parts before him, a world of absolute beauty, a thing truly belonging to youth.

It hits him, when the salty yellow Amul butter smeared on the breakfast idli tickles his palate, that yes, it is this way every weekend, but it never really tasted like this before.

Appa is quiet and does not acknowledge him beyond a grunt in response to his good morning. Amma is busy with the clothes and changing the bedsheets, and has Sri assisting her.

Bathed and ready, careful to not show any more happiness than is customary, Arvind leaves the house with feet that do not quite touch the ground.

•••

As he cycles to Sudipto's house, Arvind thinks about secrets and friends and comes to a decision.

•••

Sudipto is excited to see him. 'I am glad you are okay. When I turned around, you weren't in the tempo with me and then …'

'Yeah, but I was able to get away …'

They are sitting in Sudipto's room. The door is open but the family is busy entertaining guests in the lawns. There were a table and white chairs and a giant umbrella as he had walked in.

Inside, it is just his friend and him.

A deep breath.

'I have something to tell you,' they both say at the same time.

Arvind is taken aback, having believed himself to be the sole bearer of secrets—and as eager as he is to share, Arvind pauses. 'You go first,' he tells his friend, impatient to get any small distractions out of the way before his own big revelation.

Sudipto nods. 'I told my parents. I told them everything.'

'Huh?'

'We were in real trouble, all right … Jaggi is completely mad. We hurt his friend … Hurt him really badly, okay … And I was terrified they had caught you yesterday … I had to do something—'

'This was our problem—'

'It was too big okay. They are too big. But now it is all handled. My dad knows his dad … He is going to talk about it.'

'You do not get parents involved—'

'Trust me it'll be fine … He would have killed us. We cannot avoid him forever. You know this. Don't worry, my dad will handle everything.'

'Okay. I hope it works.' Something sputters to death within Arvind and he breathes out its dust. He does not share Sudipto's feelings about this solution to their problem. It feels hollow to him, a non-victory. It was not something he would have done before, even when he was powerless, and now …

'What is it that you wanted to tell me?'

'Oh, nothing much,' Arvind says, feeling the suddenly heavier weight of his weapon inside his backpack. 'There was a fight and everything. It was crazy …' He tells his friend about the chase in the market and the confrontation outside the temple but makes no mention of collapsing tents, toppling shelves and guns sliding out of shopping bags.

JAGGI

Jaggi hates hospitals in general but he has a specific hatred for this one. In his heart lies a deep distaste for everything about and within—the way the building stands ahead of him, dank and forbidding, the way the insides will smell of despair and disinfectant, and, worst of all, the way the tiny knots of people sitting on the patchy lawns outside all seem to have the shadow of death spinning about them.

He would rather be anywhere but here, but he also understands that being a man is about swallowing such distaste and so he bitterly spits on the hospital grounds, cursing it before it can curse him, and gets out of the jeep. Behind him, Swapnil swings out the back door, followed by Sonawane, the police constable assigned on guard duty today who will walk with Jaggi everywhere, his government-issue double-barrelled shotgun hung over his shoulder. Sonawane who is thin and dark and almost definitely a spy reporting to Jaggi's brother.

They all are, Jaggi thinks, these various cops and drivers on the security rotation, they all must talk to Om and if they talk to him then they are owned by him, such is his brother's power—his ability to completely dominate all who fall within his orbit. It would be impossible to lie or even shade the truth in front of Om. So yes, they all must talk to him, but this one, this Sonawane, with his deep yellow eyes that match his khaki uniform, this one likes the snitching.

The Rannwara General Hospital started life as the Army Field Hospital of Rannwara, a relic of an older time, before Independence, before even the mines, from when Rannwara was a long forgotten military outpost. They built a hospital here for British Indian soldiers who found themselves sick of TB or malaria or whatever killed people then, and Jaggi knows this because he was told this by the current dean, or maybe the ex-dean of this place, during some Lion's Club dinner, and the man had been insistent on him making a visit to see the architecture of the doctor's rooms. Jaggi wanted to tell him to fuck himself with a fork. Instead, he smiled and said, 'My mother died there,' and that was the end of that.

•••

The walls inside are puke green with patches of chalk white where the paint and part of the plaster have simply fallen away. The lighting is choked and claustrophobic, the anaemic tube lights doing little to remove the dimness. The windows are shuttered down with irregular rectangles of plywood, an attempt perhaps to keep the burning sun out; it helps only a little.

And then, of course, there is the smell. It is exactly what Jaggi remembered—the despair and disinfectant, and it is everywhere, pickling on the inside of his nose and feeling sweet inside his lungs. Even as he focuses to close his senses to it, a stray dog runs across them, down a corridor and out. A couple of old orderlies walking in faded grey uniforms do not even blink.

Behind him, Swapnil keeps talking about how he had spoken to Mahesh's mom, and it is pretty bad, the scooter is beyond repair and he is bad, the leg is broken badly, might have to drop a year. It is a story that Jaggi has heard a lot on his way here, and it is something they will see for themselves soon enough and he tells as much to

Swapnil who goes quiet and then says, 'By the way, I spoke to the printer in Aranagar,' and Jaggi has to angrily shush him because this is hardly the time to talk about this, and yes they can discuss it later, and he decides once again that Swapnil is a fucking idiot for even bringing this shit up in front of Sonawane.

'We are here to see Mahesh, so let us just do that …'

Mahesh, the supposed brains of the operation, isn't much better, and has landed himself in a fucking hospital after crashing a scooter while chasing juniors after school. A fucking embarrassment his boys have turned out to be, but they are all he has to work with.

They reach the patient wards, and in the corridor, on ancient wooden benches sit a middle-aged couple, who stand on seeing Swapnil, and these must be the chutiya Mahesh's parents.

Uncle looks drained and feeble with a thin face, his skin falling loose around his bones—a shapeless blob in a brown shirt and darker brown pants, and Aunty is just an aunty who gives a pained smile. They look worried and when their eyes meet his, Jaggi can see the flash of anger and hostility before they hide it behind fake smiles. Uncle even moves ever so slightly towards him, wanting to say something, but Aunty stops him with a hand on his arm. They blame him, he can tell, blame him for this and other crimes. His presence a black magnet in their son's life, but he is determined to not care.

There is small talk led by Swapnil who is asking details of Mahesh's condition. Multiple fractures including a particularly bad one in the right leg, and some torn muscles in the hip and well it is not looking good, but they hope to have him home in ten days. He is conscious and can talk, the boys can go see him.

All these answers are from Aunty. The whole time Uncle just stands there looking at him, eyes bubbling with hate and a smile on his face, and the whole thing is so fucking hideous, Jaggi wants to laugh.

Inside, Mahesh lies broken. Pulled apart. Every limb covered in plaster and hung from a rack in the ceiling. He looks like something from a cartoon, the aftermath of when Jerry tricks Tom into slipping down a flight of stairs and then drops a piano on him.

Swapnil lets out a low whistle. 'You are genuinely fucked in the a— …' and then, 'You look like that thing wrapped in sheets … What is it … yeah, a mummy …'

A pained smile is all he gets in response before Mahesh looks at Jaggi.

'Those kids really did a number on you,' Jaggi says this and it is supposed to be humorous but it does not quite land.

A shadow moves across Mahesh's face before he opens his mouth and a mound of words tumble out, that it was in fact the scooter that slipped and something was wrong with the tyre and he did not know, it was the speed, you see, that he rides at—after all he is a motorcycle guy at heart …

Swapnil from behind. 'We can see that from where we are, quite the fucking hero you are. We caught those bastards later near the temple … The fucking hawaldars showed up otherwise we would have closed that chapter.'

The hawaldars had indeed intervened, but the boy was gone by then, escaped in the confusion. He is a quick one, that fucker, Jaggi thinks, I almost respect him, he is hard to kill, like a cockroach.

Later, Jaggi had enjoyed watching the cops slap Swapnil around. He had taken his time before stepping in.

'I am getting out and will proper murder them,' Mahesh says to Jaggi again and he means it proper serious but it is difficult to take him seriously because of his condition.

'Everyone knows that the seniors went out looking, and the boys fucked them up, and sent you to the hospital. They say they beat you up in the fucking market.'

'I told you, I slipped, it was an accident,' and then, 'Don't kill them before I get out, okay, I want a piece of them.'

It is all gas and noise. Mahesh is humiliated, the big fat pig, and his situation is not a secret and already half the boys from school are talking. He should leave. There is no salvation with these idiots around.

Jaggi taps Mahesh's plastered arm. 'It's okay, you do that, buddy. You do that. Just get better.' He turns to Swapnil, 'Let's go.'

They stand to leave and Mahesh says, 'Oye, one thing—Mom was saying I won't be able to take the exams … Just talk to Menon Ma'am … I do not want to drop a year … I just really do not want that …'

AMAR

Amar Singh has spent the afternoon tracking the Gun and has built a narrative of pieces.

They do not fit perfectly, but a pattern still emerges.

No trace of the Gun was found in the rubble, and there were no inquiries by the police, which would have definitely followed its discovery. All the workers and the hawkers are back in their regular places playing their regular roles, even Raghu Kalyan Sharma, an import from Banaras, the owner of a particular sweet shop, which was where the fracas originated, stands there unblinking and bored, no flash of recognition as Amar appears before his eyes. Some discrete questions—no man present that day is absent, or suddenly richer. There are a hundred things that men do to betray themselves, and Amar has found nothing. No one is here who should not be. He focusses on those who were there but who are not now. The schoolboy comes to his mind, the angry one, the one with the scar, the one they say is the son of a minister.

He too, was at the centre of things, and had in fact grappled with him near the collapsing shelves.

It was a simple matter to find the school. A trip to a tailor with a query about uniform designs, a convenient lie or two, and now he knows that the boy is called Jagdish Ranade, an established badmaash, son of Jagdeo Ranade, politician and strongman, and goes to the Rannwara Sainik School, and it may not be the answer but it sure smells like it.

His Gun in the hand of that boy. It is something to think about.

•••

Amar used to believe—and still does—that there are no coincidences, not when it comes to his Gun.

Eight years ago, the Gun had left the side of the old Kamani brother. Why, Amar is not completely sure, but probably because there was no blood in it. It was not in its nature to be locked away at the side of a king. It demanded a warrior, and so it found its way to one—one to lead it into fire and death, where it could touch its own destiny, and Amar, or the younger version of him had been exactly that. But not anymore.

The boy, Jaggi, seems a good candidate. Young and full of violence, he will not shrink from using it. This change over, from Amar to the new boy, is not an accident. The idea makes his guts twist in his stomach. But he won't give in to despair. This is a test, that is all it is, and he will find and reclaim the Gun, prove himself worthy again.

His investigations take the whole morning, and the sun hangs high and angry in the sky when he heads into the old city. It is time for his appointment with Bilal.

Like old cities everywhere, Rannwara seems to sprout from under the shadows of a forgotten fort, the old walls now co-opted for new-ish buildings housing moneylenders and hardware stores. The town is crowded and dusty, and here in the old town it gets dustier and more crowded still. Rickety motorcycles nudge pedestrians, who in turn casually kick dogs who sit in their way. The dogs don't complain or bark, simply slump onto another patch of shade.

The address is not hard to find, and locals looking at him with their kohl-stained eyes direct him ahead, always ahead, deeper into the narrow lanes. All he thinks as he walks is that this is the kind of place that is hard to run from.

The lantern shop, for that seems to be the front of this business, is small and mouldy, despondence hanging in dull glass and thick dust. He checks his Timex watch; it is about to be 4 p.m. He waits till the second hand hits twelve and then walks in. Cradled in his hand is one of the packages, this one rolled up and resealed with some care.

The inside is dim, barely lit by lurid hues from a hundred little lamps everywhere—on the shelves, on the small table, hanging from the ceiling, forcing Amar Singh to hunch over as their pointed brass bottoms brush his hair. The air is thick with oil. On the other side of a low table sits an ancient man with fair skin, eyes cloudy with cataract, a delicate skullcap perched on his head. The man whispers in Urdu what seems to be a greeting or a question, the voice too soft to fully decipher.

'I have a package,' Amar says, his normal voice seeming like a hammer in this fragile cramped space. 'It needs to go to Muscat.' The code makes him think of old Dev Anand movies.

The old man nods sagely and presses a buzzer under his counter. Five seconds later, there is an answering buzz from behind a wall. With no change in expression, he points at a door concealed by hanging lamps from which emerges a little boy. He too is exceedingly fair and has fine features and is dressed in a light blue kurta. At a gesture, Amar follows the boy as he turns back in.

The boy leads him deep inside the dark-shaded walls of what seems to be a medieval workshop floor, a karkhana, perhaps once part of the original fortification itself. The corridor goes on and on with closed doors on either side—ancient doors, made of wood, pitted and holed, held together with bands of rusted metal and rings nailed into them with iron nails the thickness of his fingers. At random turns, some of the doors stand open, revealing low rooms with dark furnaces where darker men blow glass, their eyes shining like djinns.

The heat is a physical thing pushing into his lungs but the walls are cooler and look wet to the touch. The boy moves quick through these corridors, and Amar rushes after him, already losing his bearings. There is comfort in the cool metal of the naked Taurus revolver against his lower back. This is the baby hammer—a good choice for narrow corridors hiding ugly surprises.

The boy pushes through a door, no different from others before it, and Amar finds himself in light.

•••

Bilal sits in a wide-open room, his table piled with notebooks. He is an exceptionally thin man with a bearded face, dressed in white and wearing an intricately embroidered white skullcap. Two indoor coolers hum away, filling the room with hints of wet straw and soft gurgles of water.

He is reading entries in a ledger when they walk in, the boy and Amar, and he gently closes it and smiles at the new arrivals. The smile is pleasant and genuine but Amar does not trust it at all.

At a gesture from Bilal, the boy turns back to Amar with his gaze down, almost shy. He catches Amar's eyes for a moment, and then spreads his bird-like arms wide. It is a request. Amar mimics him. Very slowly the boy frisks him, going on tiptoes to touch his chest and shoulders with his thin fingers. He finds the Taurus stuffed into a modified holster at his lower back and then keeps going.

Done, the boy holds out a single finger to Bilal, and on an indication, leaves the room from a door behind the smiling man.

Bilal gestures Amar over to sit on the chair opposite him, bending his head in greeting, 'Amar bhai. It has been a long time, since Bambai …' and then, 'Don't mind the boy—he is a nephew of mine. Mirza. Doesn't speak but he sees everything.'

He did not fucking see the small knife strapped to the back of my calf, Amar Singh thinks, but that is perhaps a good thing.

'He is a sweet kid.' Taking a seat, he adds, 'It has been a long time, Bilal mian. You are doing well …'

It has been only few years since Amar saw Bilal, then a boy, hanging around Boss—a nephew of a nephew, like many such boys, dispatched to Bombay to learn the business. Amar had not liked him then either.

'Things are good, by God's grace. I run a trading business here, it keeps me busy.' The same smile again. 'It is good to see a brother from another life. How has time been keeping you?'

'Time does what it does, Bilal. Makes old men of all of us.'

'Ha, that it does, but it also does many other things. Okay, tell me—where are you staying? You must stay with me tonight, or however long you want to be here ... Let us host you. I can send my boys to get your things, you need not worry. We have rooms here, good rooms and good food. Stay as my guest, as my brother …'

'Thank you, but it's okay. I have made arrangements. Some other time, Bilal. This time I have work to do.'

'Still a loner, Amar bhai, time has truly not changed you. I find that this business of ours is very dull without friends.'

'I distrust friendship, Bilal. I find that respect among "traders" goes a lot further. How many princes, after all, die from the swords of enemies?'

Bilal laughs and it is the sound of coins clattering on marble.

'Let us do it your way then. Business with respect. I think it suits me just fine. Better in fact. You talk of princes'—he waves a hand casually taking the room, the building, the whole old town and all of its futile buried past—'princes lived without consequence and now they are very hard to find. Above the ground anyway. Under the ground, however—'

He is cut off as the door creaks open and Mirza returns with a tea carrier with two glass tumblers. The conversation dies while the boy sets the glasses full of steaming black tea in front of the men and walks out of the same door through which he came, shutting it behind him.

'Have some, it is excellent.' When Amar does not move, Bilal smiles again and continues, 'I was talking of princes, and this is a princely delicacy. We call it Shahi Kahwa here. Even when boiling hot, the presence of mint and wild honey makes it surprisingly cooling inside the body. Useful in this weather.

'It was the secret of Akbar's armies, you know, as they marched in here—how they conquered these hills of Rannwara. Kumail Gaffar was his general then, and he had campaigned with Turks who shared the recipe … and the secrets of its power. They say he had entire elephants loaded with these ingredients, and they walked into the desert in the height of summer. No one campaigned in the summer in those days—imagine it! Eight hundred kilometres to Delhi, the metal armour, the frothing horses, the unforgiving sun … It was hell, but they made it, thanks to this chai.

'One fine morning, the local ranas looked out of their palaces and found the great imperial army on their noses. The rest, as you must know, is history.'

Pleased with his story, Bilal stretches across the table, grabs Amar's glass and brings it to the centre. 'I assure you, it will do you a world of good.' Then he places his own next to it and sits back, waiting for Amar to choose.

Amar takes the same glass he was offered initially, holds it to his lips and then downs half the glass in a single sip. It is hot as it enters his throat and then cools instantly as it goes down. It is unfamiliar but entirely pleasant.

Bilal notes the appreciation and sips his own tea before opening one of the identical registers piled neatly to his side.

'On to business now. Is that the package?'

Amar keeps the package on the table and slides it across, and then watches Bilal slice it open without hesitation using a small penknife removed from a drawer. His work is quick and expert, and inside, gleaming black, is one of the guns—the Walther PPK.

He whistles. 'This is good. Very good. The one like James Bond …'

Amar nods. This is not the first time he has heard this. He has never seen the films himself, but he knows that the gun is a famous part of them. It is not his best gun, yet look how easily Bilal is impressed just because of a film.

'Chacha had told me that the product would be amazing, but not in my wildest dreams …' He holds the gun next to his chin and smiles. He looks like a child. 'I am happy, very happy,' and then, 'What are you carrying—show me …'

Amar is reluctant but does it anyway.

His reaches under the back of his shirt and carefully removes his current handgun—the black snub-nosed Taurus—pops open the cylinder and shakes the bullets into his hand. They are heavier than they look. Popping back the cylinder, he slides the gun to Bilal.

Bilal looks at it with a frown. It is clearly not what he was looking for.

'It is a good piece. Very rare. Very powerful bullet. Magnum bullets. Can shoot through a door or a wall, no problem.'

Bilal isn't really listening. 'Amar bhai, I didn't mean this. I thought you carried that special one everywhere …'

Fucking bastard. 'Sometimes yes. Sometimes no. Why?'

'It is such a piece of art. Nothing like that ever comes our way here … It is a gun of rare beauty. I saw it once in your hands, and it has been in my dreams since. I was hoping to get a closer look today. To hold it in my own hands—that would be a special thing. All those stories about you—and it …'

It all comes back so easily.

The thrill and the magic of it, the calm in the centre of the storm, where all the chaos of the world contracts to one blinding white point. The locations do not matter, and race past each other:

the beaches at night, inside the mad lanes of the Dongar, in hotel rooms and container ships, and they are all faceless as they shoot with eyes closed and mouths frozen wide in grins of manic bloodlust … And moments later, when their bullets do not work, do not hit, do not do anything but wound the sky in sparks, the same faceless men frown and sulk and cry and laugh and Amar Singh guns them down with perfect shots, sternums cave in and heads come apart in red mist and sometimes groins cause it is funny to see grown men hold their blasted apart crotches as they wail in blood. He had held the flood of emotion back for a whole twenty-four hours, but Bilal's words have pierced the dam. He must find it again. Claim it again. Whatever it takes.

Bilal has been talking, seemingly oblivious to the storm raging inside Amar. 'When the big Boss told me it would be you, in person, who would come with the package—my hopes did rise. I thought maybe after all these years you would part with it …'

'It is not for sale, Bilal. Not now, not ever.'

'That is a pity indeed. Are you a superstitious man, Amar mian?'

'I believe I have made my own luck.'

He has been Untouched, all these years. Not even a scratch. Odds that madden, that make no sense … that make a man believe.

'Hmmm yes. You are still here, after all. Anyway, it was good meeting you. Please tell Boss that everything is as agreed, yes, share my gratitude with him.'

Bilal closes his register as a signal that the meeting is over. Amar is already reloading the revolver.

'Alongside these—what do we have?'

'Another similar revolver. Big, strong, very good. Another pistol—Russian. Extremely good. Very expensive. Very rare. And a machine gun, but small.'

'How small?'

'Can fit in a briefcase or a shoulder bag. Even a women's bag, if it was big enough. It is a scary bastard.'

'Good. Good. I will need to see the others as well and then we can make the trade. Perhaps I will buy all of them though sometimes I wonder if I need any at all. The requirements are more … basic … here in Rannwara. Let me think for a day or two, after that we shall meet to complete this transaction. Maybe then I will see your real gun?'

'Maybe.'

'Is there anything else you need here, Amar bhai? I ask again—I can arrange rooms, here or elsewhere …' and then, 'Drinks? Afeem? Girls? Boys even … Do not hesitate. You are our guest here, yes?' Even as he says this he opens another register, fingers already turning the pages.

Amar shakes his head. 'I am fine. I have all I need. Thanks.'

'Give my love to my uncle and to the rest of them—Wendell bhai? Ramanna?'

Ramanna is fucking dead with a hole in his head. It happened two days ago.

Amar wonders if Bilal knows and is baiting him and if he'd be better off just shooting him, emptying the now loaded revolver into his smiling fucking face and being fucking done with it, but instead he just nods and stands up and carefully tucks the Taurus into the back of his pants.

'The tea was good, but I have to say one thing. I am no student of history but even I know the Mughals didn't win because of their tea … They won because of their guns.'

ARVIND

It is another day of sandwiches and video games at Sudipto's and while he is physically there and smiling, Arvind's mind races through realms of possibilities. He must decide his next steps. Planning, he has realized, is key, or the advantage the universe has handed him will be squandered.

First, he will not reconsider his decision to keep the Gun a secret from Sudipto. He had meant to share this joy, this sign of providence with his friend. The excitement inside his twelve-year-old heart had demanded it, demanded that he tell the story and unveil the magic weapon, that they hold it together and laugh into blue skies.

But he is now aware that such a thing shared will quickly lead to such a thing lost, especially if the news reaches a single grown-up. And it is obvious that Sudipto is not a person who can keep a secret and swallow it deep, waiting for the perfect time to use it. His friend lacks the resolve.

In this new adventure, Arvind decides, he is alone.

Second, and more importantly, he slowly builds a mental list of things he knows about the Gun.

The Gun, like all guns, has limited bullets. This is known. These could be anywhere from six to twenty. Six because that is how many there are in revolvers, he knows this from old movies, but he thinks this should have more. Because the hole in the barrel at the front of the weapon is thin, a lot narrower than he had thought it would be, about the width of a pencil. The bullets too then must be small. Not like the fat cartridges hanging from the belts of the security guards at the bank.

If the bullets are smaller then more of them should fit in the magazine. This he can tell visually by approximation. Also, in the movies that he has seen, the heroes often shoot more than six bullets. However, to be on the safe side, he is going to assume six bullets till he finds out more. And six bullets, he thinks, should be enough.

The Gun is heavy, dreadfully so. It is unlike the toy guns of his childhood past, or even the half metal half wood airguns used to shoot balloons in melas. No, this is far heavier. It weighs as much as a full-size cricket bat. He had tried lifting it earlier with one hand, again like the movies—he had succeeded but it had seemed an impossible task to aim it anywhere. Two hands seems to be the only way forward.

He knows what triggers are, and so he was extremely careful to not touch it, for the absolute fear of the thing going off. He knows it will be loud, at least as loud as a Diwali bomb, and will attract attention—something he will not be able to explain away easily. The testing of the trigger and the actual shooting of the Gun will have to wait for a different time and place.

The Gun is also a lot more complex than he had imagined it to be. Its body covered with little buttons and levers with no labels or instructions. He knows at least one of them releases the magazine, allowing him to determine the bullet capacity. But the rest could be anything at all …

As Sudipto dies, impaled by a flying wall of knives on the TV, Arvind takes the controller handed to him with a smile. He knows that he does not know much, and that the scope for experimentation is very limited, but he is confident that the answers will come.

JAGGI

Today there is no school, so the boys waste time on the chhoti terrace of Jaggi's father's house, sharing a cigarette and sipping on bottles of cold Maaza, condensation dripping down the glass sides and onto their fingers.

It is hot under the awning, hot in front of the large standing fans groaning with the effort of throwing only hot air, but Jaggi sits with grim resolve, defiant of nature and the world. This is their spot, and this is where they will sit, the weather be damned, because here they can smoke cigarettes unseen from the windows of his father's house.

Jaggi had once thought of this space as his mother's terrace, where she spent her mornings and her evenings surrounded by her thousand gamlas of flowering plants. With time he has become better at not thinking about her at all, and today he thinks instead about the two kids and how they escaped yesterday with guile and providence. I have surrounded myself with idiots, he concludes yet again as Swapnil runs through his stupid scheme for 'Stealing the Papers'.

The scam is an old one and he is not sure when exactly it started but it was already loosely established by the time his elder brother—Jai, not Om—took the lead on it and then set it into hard ritual. Jai and his gang of absolute legends—it's been four years since they left school and still their shadow stretches over the rest and pinches Jaggi, who looks at Swapnil next to him and then thinks of the mummified Mahesh hanging like a marionette from the roof of his hospital room. What do I have to work with, he wonders, as the sweating Swapnil proudly makes plans for doing what has been done so many times before.

The task is simple. Every year, the boys of the eleventh standard—and not just any boys but the badmaash boys—must get their hands on the question papers for the term exams. These are then copied and sold off to desperate juniors … It is not so much about the money—though there is some money in it—as it is about continuing a tradition. Being the ones to show their daring, and declaring to the school and the world outside that they are no less than the boys who came before—it sets reputations that endure for years.

And it is important that Jaggi does this. The train starts here, he can see it, and so can his friends. Get on with him now and in the years to come they will own petrol pumps and clear land disputes, maybe get a wholesale dealership or two. These are the established routes to prosperity in the district. This is the tangible value of being proximate to Jaggi, who himself sees this train as a fundamental function of his position in this town—because power, and Jaggi understands this very deeply, increases with its use. He must allow the others to push under his name—for his own reach grows larger alongside them at every step.

He encourages them, in this and in other ventures, he really does, but they make it really hard.

Swapnil tells him, once again, how Mahesh had already made a deal with the printers and it will cost about four hundred rupees to buy a copy of the question paper, copies of which they plan to sell for about six hundred rupees each to a few of the kids in the class …

'How many?'

'Huh?'

'How many kids do you plan to sell this to?'

'Eight to ten …'

'You plan to sell the paper to eight to ten kids in a class of eighty?' Jaggi keeps his tone level as he reaches out for the partly smoked cigarette in Swapnil's hand. It is wet at the end. Fucking idiots.

'Yeah, I think so …'

'They will talk. Increase the price and sell only to a few kids. Else you'll get caught.'

Swapnil nods, his eyes on the cigarette in Jaggi's hands.

I don't know why I even try, Jaggi thinks, and this is when the terrace door opens and he turns to find Mukesh-ji standing at the half open door. He looks both eager and agitated.

'Jagdish bhaiya,' he says, 'your brother is calling you …'

Mukesh-ji, who is now old, has been with the family since he himself was a boy—from when Jaggi's father was a young man. Jaggi likes him but doesn't like how the cigarette suddenly feels strange and alien under his gaze. He takes another drag with purpose, taking his time and replies, yeah, that's okay, I will go see Jai in a bit. The old man smiles again and says, no, it is not Jai bhaiya but Om bhaiya who demands his presence, which, Mukesh-ji does not need to add, is an entirely different fucking situation …

Jaggi stubs the cigarette on the roof tiles and follows Mukesh-ji into the corridors of his father's house without a word to Swapnil, without noticing Swapnil's eyes stuck on the half-smoked cigarette lying crushed on the floor. He does not head to Om directly—Om, the eldest, the unwavering, the perfect. Unforgiving, cunning, cold as ice Om, the planet that rotates closest to the sun that is their father.

Om's summons cannot be denied, and nothing good has ever come out of them.

No, in this, the first step is to find out what is going on and for this he has to meet Jai.

•••

Jaggi finds Jai, his elder brother, the second of three, slamming through push-ups on his bedroom carpet, long hair cascading down, music from the movie *Khalnayak* blasting on large Philips speakers.

Jai notices Jaggi as he enters, does not stop the push-ups, and then shouts over the music, 'Did you bunk school today?'

The question is a simple one, without any judgement. Jaggi says, no, I was at the hospital, and it is fucking Sunday don't you fucking know. Jai grunts and doesn't have any further questions. Nothing about the hospital—why did you go? Who was inside? What happened?

Jai has limited curiosity, and confidence that all relevant information will find its way to him in time. Jaggi likes this about his brother.

He also really likes the room.

A bedroom slowly transmogrifying into a gym, a temple to his brother's own ongoing and continuous transformation, his progress marked not just in thicker trapezoids and defined lats but in the ascending order of heavy iron lying along one wall—from smaller baby rattle-sized dumbbells to monsters that Jaggi would be hard-pressed to budge from their resting place, let alone lift. Painted green, their edges scratched and shining with flecks of rust, partnering the thick grooves etched into the mosaic floor below them.

Above this collection of metal, the wall is covered in posters of Arnold and Rocky and, of course, Sanjay Dutt. It is an aggressive room, smelling of wet straw and sweat and testosterone, and Jaggi loves it the way he loves everything about his brother.

'Come sit on my back,' Jai says on the apogee of the push-up movement, arms locked, all vines of tight muscle, shoulder blades retracted—sticking out through the thin cloth of the tight white vest. Jaggi does exactly that—moving smoothly to perch on his brother's back, distributing his weight across the shoulders as evenly as he can, marvelling at Jaivant Ranade's godlike strength, for there is no discernible give in his body. It stays flat like a bench of stone.

'Do you know anything?' Jaggi asks as the movement begins and he can feel the tension in the back and the immediate sweat break out on the neck of his brother. 'Om has been looking for me ...'

'Wait.'

His brother completes the repetition and does it again and then again, his breath a wheeze that Jaggi feels but does not hear under the music which too is repeating itself.

'Same song?'

'Always the same song,' he says with a burst of air and then up and then down, hard, and Jai collapses with Jaggi on top of him. He has done six reps with Jaggi's not inconsiderable weight on top of him.

'Okay, so tell me, why has he called me?' he moves off of his brother who lies flat with his face down, turning his neck this way and that.

'It is not just him. Baba wants to talk to you.'

Baba. Bhenchod. 'What? Why?'

Jaggi did not much like being under the terrifying eyes of their father, the Ranade patriarch, preferring to live his life and plan his exploits far from where it might attract attention. His was a life without rules, this he was aware of, and the only constraints he felt were that of Om and, rising above him like a demon-god, Baba himself.

'Something to do with your school,' Jai says as he turns his body to face the ceiling and looking at him, as he raises his knees and begins doing crunches in his jeans and blue suede Adidas shoes.

'What do you know?'

'There was some conversation about boarding again, but it was the usual shit. Om remains adamant, but fuck him.'

'I didn't even do anything.'

'I think it will be fine, just go talk to them,' and then, 'Go fast, best to catch them now,' and then, 'But wait, punch me first,' and Jaggi uses all his prodigious strength, really throws his back into it, and punches Jai at the final moment of the crunch, smack in the middle of the abdomen, and his brother, his hero, the light of his life, grunts and there is a grimace and then 'again' and then 'eight more' and Jaggi stays kneeling next to his brother's form, throwing punches every other second.

•••

His forearms are tender all the way up to his elbows when he walks to the 'office' wing where his father holds court and where his brother now stands waiting, a spectre in white and grey with the smile of a fucking butcher.

The office stretches over most of the east wing of the large Ranade residence complex, an entire section of rooms and corridors and meeting areas devoted to Baba's political career—his election office, his rooms for party functionaries where he stands as a member of the state general committee, the multiple charities, a few construction companies and even a smaller office dealing with the Ranade family's interests in agriculture.

It was a part of the house that Jaggi had liked a lot when he was younger, running through the wide marble corridors, dodging the secretaries and the managers and the many PAs, gawking at the giant pictures of historic election rallies, and, of course, all the images of his father—vintage Jagdeo Ranade, young and vigorous, trademark light blue kurta, a hand raised in the thumbs-up of victory, and surrounded by thousands.

In the intervening years, the place changed or he changed, and it was no longer welcoming, the floor felt strange under his feet, his father's eyes burning into Jaggi from his father's many faces.

He was rarely asked here and he rarely came. Jai and he both. This is a place for them, the politics-walas, Baba's empire, now ruled ever more by his brother Om.

Fair and effete, Om is the image of their mother, and is wearing a white shirt tucked into grey pants as he waits for him, his expression plastered into practised pleasantness, eyes following Jaggi even as he whispers instructions to an assistant who disappears down the corridor with a nod.

Om's oppressive neatness makes Jaggi feel extra scruffy, unwashed, still sweaty from the terrace heat—he fights the urge to touch his own face to ensure that it is not covered in mud. He stops a few feet away from his brother, but Om closes the distance with a frozen smile and casually grabs Jaggi by the upper arm, the grip like a vice, fingers hard as steel, pulling him closer.

Jaggi does not resist. As soft as Om may look, and as much as they may hate him, Jaggi and even Jai would never dare challenge his primacy in strength of all kinds.

'Where were you? I sent for you twenty minutes ago.'

'I came as soon as—'

'Ugh. Look at you. Did you even bathe today?' a whisper, dripping with acid, burning into his ears. Eyes fixed on the smile, stuck on the softly feminine face, unchanging, he is dragged through the corridor to Baba's office.

'Fix your hair,' and sharp fingers descend on Jaggi's scalp, probing his skull, pushing the hair into shape, giving up with a grunt, dissatisfied. Om reaches for a small flower vase sitting on a side table, tilts and collects water before slapping the wet hand on Jaggi's head and trying again.

One day, Jaggi thinks, pliant in his boundless rage, one day I will skin you alive.

Final instructions outside the door: Do not talk. Do not explain. Apologize, that is it.

There is no time for questions as the door swings open and they are in the chamber.

It is Baba's personal office—that Jaggi has not been inside in a decade and immediately he can sense its age push onto his shoulders, far heavier now than he remembered. The physical age of the room is not much. The room and this wing which arose with it are only a few years older than him, but the psychic age of the room is in the centuries—an age that is borrowed from the thick ornate wooden furniture, from the giant porcelain jars with Chinese inkwork, the giant jade lion staring with its mouth open and the red jail carpet which his mother had once told him was a hundred years old.

Two men sit in the ancient chairs with lion feet for legs—the fair one in a grey safari suit looks familiar in the way that all the government service types do to Jaggi, and the other, wearing a blue open-collared shirt and blue pants, is another thing entirely—expensive-looking glasses frame a wide-open face and there is an intricately combed spattering of hair on his head, though he does not seem very old. They are in conversation as the brothers enter and immediately fall silent with expectation.

Baba sits on the other end of a massive table, bigger now than in his memory, when he could slip under it without slouching, and with some trick of the light, find the shadowed space underneath greater in its extent than the entire room outside. Baba is much the same—Jagdeo Ranade, the champion of the people, the lion of Rannwara, large as a mountain, breathing into the small oxygen mask, not saying anything, yellow eyes embedded within black folds of overlapping skin and he does not smile or nod or greet the boys, but Om, always having a link to Baba, a connection almost telepathic, nods to the guests and begins.

'Here he is, gentlemen, my idiot brother—Jagdish. He is a good kid, just a bit naughty in his nature.' The smile remains stuck on his face, his voice now pleasant and dripping charm. 'Jagdish—this is

Kapoor sir, you have met him before, he is the Rannwara SP, and this,' he says, motioning to the bald man, 'is Mr Chatterjee, the GM of the steel plant. His son … Sudipto … goes to your school.'

Jaggi just nods and mumbles a polite 'hello uncle' to both of them. What is the police doing here? He stands there, fidgety, mind racing as he calculates the set-up of the play he has walked into.

Om continues, 'We were talking to Chatterjee sa'ab—and we got to know you and his son are having some … trouble … at school.'

Om waits and turns to him and he, Jaggi, mumbles a 'sorry uncle' while giving the most contrite look he can muster.

'He is a new boy, Jagdish. Take care of him, okay,' Om says. 'Be good—show him around. You are his senior … look after him.'

'Yes, we were just …' and then thinking better of it, he says, 'yes, I will. Don't worry, Uncle, you will not have any trouble from me.'

The Chatterjee fucker, looking more embarrassed than him, as if he was the one beating his own son, smiles now with an 'Okay, beta.' And then, 'These things happen … Yes I was a boy too once but fun has its place … Well … Om, I am sure the boys will get along now.'

The matter seems resolved here, until, with a grunt as initiation, his father speaks.

'Don't worry, Chatterjee sa'ab, Jagdish is a smart boy and he will understand. He doesn't have to be told twice.'

Baba's voice is thin, reedy, like water dripping somewhere out of sight. It is unnerving, the remnants of Baba's voice after the cancer, but what is left is enough.

His piece said, Baba breathes into the mask again, the plastic cup looking dainty in his short thick fingers, and the men smile and Om smiles and indicates to Jaggi that it is time to go.

In the hallway outside the closed door Jaggi wonders why that little fucker is so important and asks his brother, 'I don't understand this … that kid is a fucking insect—' He hears it before he feels it, the instant absolute clear pain of the slap follows the sound, and he is on his knees on the floor, face burning with pain and humiliation, looking up at his angel-faced brother.

'You do what you said you will do. You will say good morning to that boy every day. You will not let any of your friends fuck with him. If anyone fucks with him, I will assume it is your fault. He is not to be touched. Baba has spoken on this.'

There is a sharp stinging sensation on his cheek, a trickle of blood where a stone from one of Om's many rings caught his skin, and Jaggi fumes in terrible rage but does not say anything or scream or fight or cause any manner of scene right outside Baba's room. Om holds his gaze till he can sense the fire die down and it is a lot of pride to swallow but Jaggi does it and his brother nods and says, 'Good. Another word and I will break your face.'

•••

The rest of the day Jaggi stays locked in his room playing with his best knife, gifted to him by Jai, and it is a small one but sharp, and not a switchblade but a straight metal into the hilt—the switch makes it weak, his brother had told him and had also said that these are the ones they throw in the kung fu movies. Jaggi had paid attention, and now he throws it at a cupboard where it sticks and around it are a hundred other notches and he is burning burning burning even though there is a cooler running on high, and cold water bottles, and the rain outside, but within he burns. He walks to pick his knife from the cupboard and throws it again, edge straight and perfect and it is not a challenge to guess the target he has in mind.

ARVIND

It is evening and the sky is overcast. Arvind stands within the abandoned Imperial Steel Factory, built by the British, but now empty and forgotten—a place he had once visited with his father and some others, a kind of tour to show him the old factory floors and explain the complexities involved in the manufacturing of steel for war eighty years ago.

Five large work sheds rise out of the ground nearby, their walls are old stone and have eroded to a neutral brown. Some have holes in them. He had entered them that one time with his father, and they were empty of everything except malevolence. To his mind then, they stood like things haunted—and in all the times he has been here since, he has never actually stepped inside one again.

He used to come here to explore, to hide out. It is not far from the colony, simply further along the road and the tracks, the road he walks with Sudipto, the road where he fought with Mahesh. There is a new plant now, the plant where his father works—but that is much farther away, a full half hour drive beyond the school. The plant changed, but the colony stayed where it was, a colony where he had no friends at all, and so he would jump gates and explore instead.

Getting here is not the easiest thing, he has to leave the road behind and cycle through wild shrubland, over deceptive slopes, till he finds the perimeter of the complex. It does not take him long to find a boy-sized hole in the rusted metal fencing, and then he is in.

He stands alone, the ground uneven and rough, a once concrete floor now cracked, and a thin layer of dust that blows in lazy circles around his feet. Around him now is the sound of the still functioning scrap processing plants, a few hundred metres away, releasing some smoke and an almost constant din of clashing metal and machinery. The vibrations hurt his ears, and make it hard to think, a sheet of teeth grinding, palm clawing noise falls over him, but there are few locations better than this for his experiments with the Gun, for here in the day—with the scrap plants running—there are no men, no birds, no dogs even, they've all been chased away by the deluge of sound. Deluge enough to drown a gunshot.

Here, there are no witnesses. Here, then, is the place.

It is cloudy but not yet dark, and in this light Arvind, with eyes tuned in like microscopes, takes in the details of the weapon. He sees nothing that is not already etched unwavering on the surface of his mind. This, then, is the time.

He lifts the Gun, holding it in a bizarre double-handed grip in front of his narrow chest, arms extended, but not fully, and there is a quivering along his twelve-year-old muscles—excitement and anticipation mingled with the considerable strain of holding the Gun, weighing more than a kilo, away from his body in a stable way.

A shiver goes down his spine as he feels the cold steel of the trigger against the soft pad of his finger. He aims at a discoloured stone the size of a football located waist high in the wall of the first work shed. He tries to find the sights—line them down with his intended target, back and front, like he would with an airgun—but this Gun is heavy and it is hard to keep it still in his shaking hands, and so to hell with it, he pulls the trigger. Which does not move.

He pulls again, pushing in his thin left finger over the right one and both into the trigger but it still does not shoot. It is locked in.

Undeterred, he begins to examine the buttons and switches along the body of the Gun, all the while mindful of keeping his fingers away from the trigger and having the barrel point away from him. The precautions seem prudent and self-evident, and concentrating on the weapon he does not think about the origins of such thoughts and how they arose within him.

He finally pulls a lever to the right of the handle—it resists him at first and then there is a click and a sliding movement and the magazine pops out before he catches it. The magazine is a dull grey and he sees a single bullet peeking out the top, shiny and bronze—looking largely like he had imagined bullets would look, except the very tip of this one is flat, seemingly cut off.

He wonders if this is normal or if his own weapon is somehow defective, and that these bullets are not as lethal as the ones that are sharp and pointy, after all how were they to pierce skin and bone and organs otherwise? It is a troubling thought but he deletes it, for why would destiny hand him a half-answer? Moreover, now with the magazine in his hand, he understands that it can hold inside it a lot more than six bullets—maybe ten or even twelve, and the thought leaves him giddy with excitement. Ten is a lot more than six. Ten is a lot of revenge, a lot of protection and a lot of justice.

Pushing the magazine in, Arvind finds another switch where the handle meets the barrel and flicks it, and it moves and behind it is a red mark, which means danger. In this moment he does not need the mark to tell him that he has fixed the weapon. The energy he feels from within the Gun, which was already a steady hum of power, has now increased in frequency and volume and the weapon is like an infernal engine that has just awakened. It quivers in his hand and he is surprised to not see sparks emerge all around it.

Whatever this is, he believes it has now awoken, and with this burning inside him, he extends his arms, and with the Gun gripped tight, squeezes the trigger.

BOOM!

The kickback is tremendous and it throws him back a few steps, and he slips and falls. His ears are ringing, his hands are shaking and his eyes were shut and the target stone is intact, undisturbed, and he does not know where the bullet went and he does not care. The sound of it, the power of it … it rages in his blood, boiling, churning, pumping till he is sure he will burst from within.

This is love. This is life.

Arvind shoots two more bullets this evening. He is able to keep his eyes open for the third pull, and see that his aim was off by a significant distance. He is, however, not deterred in the least. He has enough bullets—even accounting for practice.

It begins to rain.

Arvind packs the Gun in layers of polythene bags before putting it inside his schoolbag. He remembers and then takes it out again to engage the safety, and he can almost feel the cold sigh from within it.

•••

It is dark when Arvind rides his bicycle back home, wet and breathless in a technicolour world, still pulled along by the thread of destiny that rises from the inside of his chest; all movement is effortless and the world around him filled with the excitement of a dawn at a time of the sun setting.

As he rides, he targets the whole world with his eyes, pointing small brown fingers at parked cars and unfortunate trees—lasers erupt from the tips of his fingers and they all burst apart into super-bright pixels.

Interlude

FELL OMEN

RAJ SHEKHAR

Bombay, five and a half days ago

Raj Shekhar sat in the back of his large German car contemplating the idea of lateness, and the many facets it contained within it. In that moment he was late, he knew that, and it was a situation that did not surprise or trouble him at all, for those he was going to meet would wait for him, and in this scenario his lateness, to him, was power. This continuing disregard of time was a recurring theme of his life, he knew this about himself and understood it to be not so much a hesitation, or some kind of lethargy, but instead a logical outcome of his ownership of time, both his own and that of others.

It is time that is man's only true resource—he had read this once as a boy, and it had stuck sharp, and it became instinctual for him to treasure time: protect all of his own, and push others to squander theirs. This, after all, was the game, if there ever was one. He had waited, and had hated waiting, once often and rarely of late. It is as sure a measure of his growing stature as the size of his car, now others waited for him, waited on him, establishing the primacy of his time over theirs. This was real influence, for their waiting was the only true human cost he could extract. Everything else was just business.

As Raj leaned back into the plush leather and closed his eyes, time compressed into a perfect moment. It was as close to nirvana as he could be, seeing himself as a central unmoving node at the heart of a whole world. He, his body, his car—all poised in time, even as the city rolled itself under the wheels.

It was helpful that Raj Shekhar—builder of buildings, constructor of highways, charmer of women and fucker of boys—had wisdom enough to recognize the transient nature of human supremacy, and managed to draw it out, for it came crashing apart in … three … two … one … Now.

There was a bang of metal against metal and before his senses processed the sound and the cause—an accident of sorts—he found his hand grasped tightly by Pratham, his bodyguard of three years, even as his driver cursed in Marathi and then screamed, the sound overlaid by the dull pop-pops of gunshots and then the car was in reverse. Pratham held him by the back of his neck, pushing down hard, such that he was now bent double, his head level with his knees, and then pushed lower still as the car moved fast, its 6000 cc engine roaring its Teutonic roar, and his face was inches from his shoelaces when there were more pops and then the pings of bullets hitting the body of the car, and a steady shower of glass fell next to his brown Italian shoes.

The shower of glass turned thick red and liquid. The grip on his neck slackened, replaced by a fleshy weight on his back. The car jerked and then rose with a sick long crunch, tossing him and a limp leaking Pratham into the roof and down and on impact Raj felt small muscles tear off of his spine.

The world was in shards and each shard was piercing agony, and he could not move or crawl, wedged as he was in the extra leg room of his executive saloon, bent double, pressed into the back of the front seat with his dying bodyguard on top of him. Raj pushed his hands against the floor, now covered in glass and pooling with blood, and achieved nothing.

The car had settled, even as the engine continued to rumble. There were still gunshots on the outside and he wondered what they could be for, and that was when the car door opened, not his but the one behind the driver, Dharmesh, his name was, and Pratham's massive body was pulled off of him and the agony faded to a mere blaring alarm.

There was a shot and he heard it before he felt it: it was like a dull punch in his shoulder and then two others followed, the sound exploding inside the car … The thought 'I have been shot' was still forming in his hormone-dumped brain when he was dragged out by strong hands. Something in his back tore with this action and the pain was still a distant flood hurtling towards him when a gun was pressed into his forehead, it's red-hot tip burning a circle into his skin. Raj Shekhar closed his eyes as time slowed further, a single second stretching out to a minute and then more and in the slightest change in the pressure of the hot barrel against his skin he could feel death coming for him. There was a click and then nothing.

•••

Glimpses of the attack flit through Raj Shekhar's fevered mind, mismatched pieces of a jigsaw that do not seem to fit together. It was less than a minute from the car ramming into his own to when he lost consciousness, his assailants escaping in a hail of gunfire, but he struggles to structure the chaos within any definitive chronology.

There is one memory, however, that is clear from the very first time his eyes open in the ICU of the Hinduja Hospital, an immaculate thought diamond embedded at the very heart of the whirling kaleidoscope of his mind.

He tells the doctors, the nurses, his wife, his mother and finally the police about the gun.

Every detail of it is stark and urgent, even when he can only form mere hints of words amidst shining acres of anaesthesia—a bright angel of death dressed in gold and chrome, eclipsing the universe as it was pressed red-hot into his forehead. He bears its mark, a gift, a red splotchy circle branded on his face, his new third eye.

He bears many other wounds but is alive, and the shining gun had gone *click* instead of going *boom* and the third eye was marked but not thrown open, and with it the rest of his skull. It is a miracle for Raj Shekhar, and a mystery for the investigators, for the police cannot understand why the hit, meticulous and brutal, was not seen through to its logical end.

SARDESAI

ACP Sardesai could barely breathe when he heard of the almost dead man, fighting for his life with three bullet wounds, a shattered back and shattered mind, who only spoke of a gun of shining gold and silver, like it was some weapon out of mythology. Sketch artist in tow, he rushed to the bedside of a now conscious Raj Shekhar.

•••

Later, outside Bombay Hospital, Sardesai looked at a piece of paper with an exacting sketch of a Beretta 9mm pistol on it, decorated with carvings and exotic enamel work, and recalled a party at a farmhouse in Alibaug years ago when he was still a young IPS, a master of his destiny but lost in the big city; an innocent time, when he still had much to learn and live. It was to celebrate the birthday of the Kamani brothers, twins, already ascendant in Bombay's own twin construction and mafia businesses. It was there, surrounded by people so shiny they looked like they were dressed in stars, that he drank his first sip of Johnnie Walker and ate his first Szechwan fish finger. But more than those things he remembered the gift—from one brother to another—a gift of shining perfection: a gun that shone like a sun.

Trilok Kamani, younger by eight minutes than Jaslok, laughed and shot at bottles of Vat 69—quickly arranged as targets and as each exploded into sparkling amber under the dark open skies there were cheers and claps and honeyed voices singing his glory.

Much was forgotten of the revelry that followed but Sardesai never forgot that gun.

•••

Sardesai knew it would be the gun when the news first reached him. Call it a policeman's instinct. And he was right. It stared back at him now from the page in his hand, rendered in detail, remade from the broken mind of a man who ought to have been dead, fixing the weapon as the intact lodestone of a psyche that fragmented around it.

The excitement of discovery, however, faded fast in the glare of the call he had to make.

THE MAN IN BLACK

Jaslok Kamani always wore black and it is because his father always wore white.

A black phone rang on a table topped with black granite and Jaslok answered. His fingers were thick and white and covered with rings.

Sardesai did not waste time getting to the point. 'Bhaiya,' he said, addressing him thus even though the men were not that far apart in age, 'I think I have a lead on Trilok bhaiya's gun.' Which, of course, meant that there was a lead on Trilok's killer and that meant the world to the man in black.

Jaslok Kamani had loved his brother, younger by a whole eight minutes, and like many twins they were linked deeper and more essentially than other siblings—a single soul split into two bodies—and his brother's violent death had destroyed half of Jaslok on the spot. Since then, it was with extreme care that he had grown and manicured his grief into delicate dreams of revenge.

His search for his brother's killers had never stopped. No one had taken responsibility and all his leads had gone cold. Over the years, intermittently, rumours had reached him—of some shooter or the other with an exceptionally decorated weapon. He had paid much money for them, the shooters and their guns, but there had never been a match, and the men responsible for the killing had vanished into goddamned shadows.

'You better not be fucking with me,' Jaslok said keeping his voice level even as a vein began to throb against his temple.

III

NOOSE

BILAL

It is almost dawn and Bilal is doing his accounts like always and he thinks of his business here and his uncle's much larger business in Bombay when there is a knock on the door and a fax is brought to him. It is a new thing, this machine of his, and useful. The fax is a simple one, but it stuns him in place.

It is a sketch of a gun, a unique unmistakable weapon, a weapon he has seen once before and remembers clearly—and this, of course, changes everything.

•••

Bilal, observer of man, student of history, has long understood that the secret to life is in the spending. It sits within the opportunity grabbed; the gamble taken, the waiting for a lifetime for that one chance, the divine conjunction of stars when all must be ventured. And it is this … the ability to recognize such a moment, and to wield in an instant the resources that have been accumulated over decades … this is the domain of kings. It is not just the movement of armies but extends to the spending of coin, to the calling in of collected favours. The perfect opportunistic betrayal of trust.

He does not contemplate this lightly, his mind afire with a hundred branching contingencies, but hours later, still in his office, fax in hand, he comes to a decision. He summons Jamshed, a nephew from his sister's side, an elder brother of Mirza, a boy who can handle himself. To Jamshed, he says, 'Call the boys, and get the guns ...'

'All the boys?' Jamshed asks him. 'All the guns?'

Yes, Bilal says, all the guns and all the boys and tell them to be ready by tonight because maybe that is when they are going to fucking do it.

Jamshed senses the mood and just nods and walks out.

Bilal reconsiders his decision and finds it sound. It is quick, it is decisive though not without risk.

The fax had landed on him like a hammer. A message from a gun-running intermediary working under Jaslok Kamani himself. Bilal does not know why Big Don Jaslok Kamani is desperately looking for a gun and its owner, but there is here a shining light of opportunity, a door sliding open. He can call his uncle sitting fat in faraway Bombay, an old man with his best days behind him, and warn him of whatever approaching hell this search surely augurs.

But he is not going to do that. He is going to get the Gun, and Amar Singh's fucking head, and then figure out the rest. His uncle is not going to like it. Maybe it traces back to him somehow, but what can you do? None of this is personal, and after all, in history, this is the only way princes become kings.

Much can happen, but he needs more information, and he must be careful not to get ahead of himself. Focus on the enemy in front of him, a cunning and dangerous bastard of an enemy.

Bilal knows the stories, knows that Amar Singh is no street goon. This is an experienced killer of men, and is currently armed to the fucking teeth with the most sophisticated weapons money can buy. He makes a few revisions to his plans.

He calls Jamshed again, and tells him to call Raju.

'Raju-*ji*?' Jamshed repeats.

'Yes,' Bilal says, 'find him and get him to that hotel. Fast. I don't want him out of my sight.'

ARVIND

It is Monday. In the morning, Arvind sees a spiderweb with a wasp stuck in it, and believing it a sign, he studies it for portent meaning. The wasp is twice the size of the spider, yet it struggles, and the spider does nothing, absolutely nothing, waiting patient. The wasp will tire and then the spider will go and eat him.

On the way to school he contemplates the concept of action. It has been two days since he got the Gun and while he is still upbeat, once again the real world encroaches. The day is real. The school is real. Within it, the classes and the teachers and the other kids—they are all real.

Jaggi. On this morning, made of sinew and rage, Jaggi is real.

He thinks of drawing the Gun and shooting Jaggi in the middle of the school corridor. It would be terrible and glorious. Picture-perfect, like the drawings in his head, like the stories he played out with his broken toys. Jaggi, the first name on his list of absolute justice, and he thinks hard about the other senior boys and if they deserve the list—ammunition being limited and all that—and he is unsure as he can see each name on the list birth branches from which emerges an endless list of names that grows and grows …

But the list is not important. Keeping the Gun is.

And so, tempting and obvious though it is, he knows he is not ready yet to use the weapon, for to use the weapon is to set up the conditions to lose it. His continued possession of it is reliant on its remaining a secret. He thinks of the man from whom he took the gun, and wonders if he is searching for it. That seems inevitable. It is too beautiful a weapon to not be treasured when owned, and pined for when lost. He understands little about guns but he knows that what he has is a true wonder of the world, and the man who had it will never sleep, and Arvind finds himself searching for him, with his long face and thin moustache, in the background of things, as though he might emerge from walls or rise like a ghost from the stone of the ground and steal it back.

•••

Later, in between the first and second periods, Arvind sits in class and listens to Sudipto tell the boys about the incident with Mahesh, and their eyes widening like saucers as with an arc of his hands Sudipto makes Mahesh fly ten feet then twenty feet and now he is somersaulting in the air, turning cartwheels, the scooter spinning wildly behind him … All from Arvind's actions and heroic throwing of the bag.

He thinks he should be enjoying this more, the way his classmates look at him like he is their saviour, a hero, someone who dared to fight a senior, not just any senior but one of *those* seniors, and win, and break him as they themselves have been broken. They have light coming out of them, exultant, the boys want it again with more questions, always more questions and Sudipto relishes the answers, builds them up more and more with every rendition, and together they stitch the legend of Arvind and the Bag and the Mangled Mahesh.

He thinks he should be enjoying it more, but he is not. Yes, it was necessary, and it was smart and well executed, and yes, it was deserved a hundred times over, for Mahesh's role in the daily humiliations Sudipto and he suffered. But it is already a thing of the past and could have happened six months ago or a year.

Sitting in the classroom, smiling through Sudipto's stories, Arvind comes to realize that it is indeed the Gun, and how the mere possession of it has thrown him far away from such small battles, and the fear that his classmates shake off for brief moments as they hear the story again has completely slipped off of his bones.

AMAR

Amar wakes late with the ugly taste of whisky drying on his tongue.

He finds himself slumped on the chair, facing the door of the room, a pistol—the Walther PPK—clutched tight and sticky in his right hand, his fingers calcified claws around the grip, unresponsive. He uses his left hand to pry the gun loose. It is some time before life returns to his hand and to him. On the table in front of him are five quarter bottles of whisky, Royal Crown, all drained. Two have been used for ash trays. The bottles explain the state of his head which is intent on tearing itself apart down the median line. He looks at the Walther like it has an answer he could use. It stares at him, silent, dumb.

Waking up in this fashion jars him into a watchful sobriety. As he shaves in the tiny mirror hung on the bathroom wall, his feet balanced on either side of the latrine, he thinks that this is not like him. He drank, yes, he always drank, but rarely to excess and never so carelessly. And while he may have had the presence of mind to face the door before succumbing to blackness, gun in hand no less—he knows he would not have twitched even if the door had been beaten down with hammers.

You are losing your touch, he tells his reflection, you are letting your guard down, you are forgetting the basic things. You have seen this before—when they forget the basics is when the motherfuckers die.

The face in the mirror just looks back at him hollowed out.

In his time as a shooter, Amar Singh has seen all the signs of the many sicknesses that breed inside the minds of men for it is a lot of life to be lived in a very short period of time. His is a stressful profession peopled by mavericks and die-hards, with men living on the very edge of human existence. It does things to you, he knows, impacts you and shaves away parts of you, and every time you go out on a job, you can never be entirely sure if all of you has come back.

There is Ramanna, who shoves powder up his nose and stays up for days following a job, releasing his pent-up nerves in a fog of cigarette smoke and a constant fury of broken bottles and broken heads for anyone who said something wrong or really anyone at all. It was dangerous to drink with him in those times, no one wanted to, but then the fucker would whine—Come baba, one drink baba, sit sit, he would say, and then half a bottle in, he would kick the poor bastard's face in for breathing too loud. And the girls, the endless stream of girls, in and out, like a fucking parade. Ramanna the man, so afraid to die that he hung tight to all ideas of life. Drinking and fucking. How he got the energy to actually shoot somebody, Amar never quite understood.

There is Wendell, who just sleeps and drinks Pepsi and eats mutton biryani by the kilo till it is time to go shoot. Blow up some heads. Come back. And it is the same again. Fat old fucker who can move real silent when he has to. Can sneak up on a fucking cat. They say he has a woman somewhere, but no one has seen her ever. Heh. They have bids out—betting that he likes fucking little boys. Amar laughs at the jokes, but does not believe it. After all Wendell taught him how to fucking shoot when he was a boy. Lived with him for months. Nursed him back to life after the Kamani job. Never tried to fuck him though. A big man, who grows bigger when the job is on and things are heated. Few better than Wendell.

Then there is Sudhir with his fucking AKs, a whole collection of them, all named after old heroines. It is always chaos with him because the bastard can't aim, cannot hit a parked bus at a signal. So he figured he might as well shoot out the whole street.

Maybe they will do a job again together, God willing they will.

Nothing with Ramanna now, though. He is dead.

It was bad luck, the police jeep coming when it did halfway through the job, and their having to run—him and Ramanna, there was nothing in it to stick around. It is very bad luck to shoot at cops, even if they are shooting you. It was a morning of bad luck, all around, bad luck that a bullet caught him in his shoulder, worse luck that it went through Ramanna's neck on its way to him. The fucker dropped instantly, his blood squirting like a watercannon on Holi. He had known then and kept running, known that Ramanna was dead, and that his own luck had finally turned.

Amar doesn't know if he ever really liked Ramanna, fucking unpredictable raging asshole. Boss did though, always screaming about the girls and the money—how he cost too fucking much just in overheads. Expensive fucker to maintain, he would say, more than a mistress, this bastard costs me, and not worth the fucking. It was not a good joke but everyone laughed cause they knew the old man meant it. Ramanna had been there from the start, him and Wendell alongside Boss as they crawled out of the gutters of Dongar, dark rats with blood in their eyes.

Boss loved the boy, forgave him a lot, but he too stayed away from him after a job till he calmed down. No chances, that is what Boss would always say, no chances, zero risk.

It is a shit life, but a lot better than others. Binary, like a coin toss. Heads, you are king of the world. Tails, you are dead with holes in you. Nothing in the middle. It was the simplicity that had appealed to Amar in the beginning, and it was the simplicity that had kept him in it. He knew that there was an existence out there, among civilians, an existence containing small wins and deep lingering losses—he had had his taste of it, seen the darkness that dwelled in defeated men, and he was done with it, and many years ago he had resolved that he would play to win, and he would lose only when he died, and it would be final and there would be no time left to be defeated.

The job is hard and it takes its toll on them all. He has been told that you start young and hot and you are invincible, and later, after some blood, you think you are alive because you are good at it, faster and stronger than the ones who are gone, and when enough time has passed, and better men than you have fallen, you finally believe in luck.

Amar believed in luck, and believed he carried it with him, his totem of luck, his taveez of bent circumstance—burning hot next to his body, melded to his skin. A hundred times the fell coin was tossed, and a hundred times it had landed right—a hundred deaths dodged and avoided, bullets and knives and swords and bricks, all falling where he was not.

The Gun had protected him, not just from defeat but from the fear of defeat, and it is this fear that has infused his blood these last nights, choking his breath, and which now lies shrunken in his belly, drowned in alcohol, but not dead.

He consciously does not think of the moment when he, Amar, had held the Gun to the forehead of that whoreson builder and pressed the trigger and ... *click*. It was the only time it had misfired in all the years he had had it since that first misfire in the hands of Kamani, the great moment, the choosing, the beginning of his second life.

He had become frantic then, and he had run. He got a bullet in him, in his shoulder, his first since that first day. He had known then that a time had ended, a boon had lifted—and he stood naked and unprotected in a field of spears. Then had begun a countdown, a desperate scrambling of the hourglass as he tried to understand what the fuck this meant and how it could be averted. Luck, so beloved, so revered, was leaving him, and from this root thought sprouted a thousand dark spirals ready to drown him …

Is this why he had left it unattended at the temple? To test its love? Its loyalty? If I walk away and come back and it is still here, does that mean it is still mine?

He got his answer all right. His Gun-God had left him, after it had told him that it would leave him. The way it had left Kamani all those years ago. His time was coming and he had not been ready to face it.

There is real fear in the eyes in the mirror.

He takes a deep breath. What has been lost must be found, regained. It will allow him. It must. His was the best arm and the best eyes. The Gun will see it. He alone deserves to wield its awesome power.

Now, a fresh focus. Time to get his luck back.

A shave. A bath. Redressing the wound—today not so angry. Fresh clothes, this time packing the CZ75 at the shoulder and the Taurus around the ankle. The added weight in his stride feels good.

He puts his weapons back carefully before stuffing the bag under the bed. When he leaves, he uses his own chain and padlock against the handles of the double door.

As Amar makes his way down the stairs, a mountain rises to meet him. An enormous man, more bull than human, is on his way up. Shoulders stretching out the kurta the size of a double bed. Ugly brick of a face with large liquid eyes. No smile. The giant takes up the entire width of the staircase as he moves, slowly, shifting his weight from one tree trunk leg to the other.

Amar stops and holds his breath as the man passes him, the hair on the back of his neck rising. The animal inside him screaming to run or to kill. Shoot this fucking man! The guns are close, burning against his skin. He thinks he is quick enough to get it before the giant crushes his skull with one hand. He holds it in somehow, nerves jolting with the urge to move.

The man passes without incident. Heart hammering, Amar continues down, not looking back.

•••

At the reception, the desk is empty and he pauses to look at the wooden board holding the room keys. Three empty spaces there, on his floor and the floor below—a cluster of occupied rooms forming all around him.

He thinks about the guns still in the bag inside his room. The giant he saw on the steps. He contemplates going back up this very moment, grabbing the weapons and getting out, counting on the fact that they would not want to engage now, not in daylight. But what if they do—the ones who wait for him to walk into the web? The dark crooked walls of the reception seem to be bearing down on him. It does not matter. He must keep his eyes on the prize.

He walks out of the guest house into streets he now knows well from all of his fruitless walking. He takes a meandering pattern and can spot no tails. The task is simple but Amar does it with care, sensing the pressure building around him, hostile eyes burning into his back. He is still playing out the scenario from the hotel and concludes that they will not make a move now unless he forces it. They will wait, confident in their numbers and for the night and for him to come back to his weapons.

His guns are hostage. Well, he will be back for them. But for now, he has a more pressing mission. This too, he feels is part of the test. A challenge by the gods to probe the single-mindedness of his quest.

•••

Near the railway station, he strolls into an alley and kneels among parked scooters and unscrews a pair of licence plates, front and back, with a flat metal card he removes from his wallet. Still unnoticed and holding the plates in his hand, facing into his body, he walks into an adjoining lane, past two red motorcycles before choosing a nondescript grey Yamaha. He swaps the plates. Then, with a quick look around to ensure he is still alone, he takes out his ankle knife and from here it is merely the cutting of wires and the joining of them and the engine is on.

And just like that Amar Singh has a motorcycle.

JAGGI

It is recess and they are in the secondary section boy's bathroom, Jaggi shadowing Swapnil as he lays out the plan to three skinny juniors who are nervous and doing their best to not act like it.

Swapnil does all the talking, telling the boys that the question papers are going to cost eight hundred rupees each, and the payment must be made now, and they can be collected from Nathu's where he will sit in the evening for the duration of the exams.

'You get them the day before, that is it'—this was an input from Jaggi, and then, of course, the warnings—'and no one finds out about it, no matter what. Do not take them anywhere with you. Do not bring the fucking papers with you to school, if I find you brought it here on the morning of the fucking exams ...'

They nod warily, shifting from foot to foot.

'Also, if I fucking find out that you've shared this with anyone, if I even hear a fucking rumour, even if a totally different set of fuckers managed to get a paper all by themselves—I am not going to care, I will find all of you and strip you and fuck you up the ass.'

Swapnil shouts the last part.

The performance is overdone. The boys are still paying attention but they are less afraid than before. There are things you learn about the idea of transmitting menace, and Swapnil has a way to go. He is not a natural at it. Always overcompensating.

There is now a silence that grows.

'So, give me the money, you idiots … What the fuck are you waiting for?'

The tallest amongst the boys, wiry with glasses, who looks familiar to Jaggi, asks Swapnil about the answer sheet.

'What answer sheet?' Swapnil is too stupid to not act surprised.

The tall one, having found his balls and some of his voice, 'The answer sheet for the paper?'

'Find the answers yourself, you little shit. I am giving you the paper, aren't I?' he barks, his swagger slipping.

'If we get the paper the night before, we need the answer sheet. Without the answers it is only three hundred rupees—'

'What?'

'Everyone knows this, Abhimanyu bhaiya told us, it is eight hundred for the paper with the answers … Who has the time to find the answers? I mean if we knew the answers we would not be buying this—'

'You motherfucker, shut up! Do you want it nor not?'

'That's the thing, right, you'd have bought these in your time. You always get the answer sheet with it … Abhimanyu bhaiya is my first cousin and he told us. It is three hundred just for the papers … everyone knows that …'

Fucking hell. Swapnil cannot touch the boy and he fucking knows it. Is he really Abhimanyu's cousin? This is a farce, and it is time to intervene.

'Wait,' Jaggi says and it is not loud but it does the job and the mood in the bathroom is once again nice and tense.

'You will get your fucking answers,' and then, 'Give him the money ...'

The boys nod and immediately comply Well, at least they're still scared of me, he thinks.

'The rest of you go. Glasses—you stay, I want to talk to you.'

Glasses, Abhimanyu's cousin, stays while his friends walk out without a second look.

Glasses tells Jaggi that his name is Piyush and he is indeed Abhimanyu bhaiya's first cousin and that the topper of the class is a boy called Nikunj Goyal, and no, he is okay, not a snitch and yes, he lets people copy during exams and yes, of course Glasses knows him and can point him out right now if Jaggi would like to come to their classroom.

It is on this walk that Glasses tells Jaggi the story of what actually happened to Mahesh and how the runts of his class—the Bengali and the Madrasi together—are bragging about how they sent a senior boy, and not just any senior boy but one of Jaggi's senior boys, to hospital.

Abhimanyu is a very close friend of his elder brother Jai, and even then Jaggi almost slams the fucker's head through a wall for saying all this with a fucking smile.

•••

Nikunj is easy to find and easier to deal with, understanding immediately what is expected of him.

He simply nods his triangular head and does not argue or ask for money. Smart fucker that he is, he has seen his angle in getting access to the exam papers far in advance, and knows that nothing is gained by being on Jaggi's bad side.

He takes the papers handed to him, says 'Yes bhaiya' to all the warnings and the threats, and promises that the answers will be ready in three days. Of course, he is not going to share them with anyone directly, not even Glasses.

The bell rings, recess is over. Nikunj and Glasses join the other kids in the corridors as they float back into class.

Jaggi stands outside, waiting, his eyes fixed on Arvind and Sudipto, sitting on the tables, surrounded by other kids.

The fat white one is talking and talking and talking. Their audience laughs and giggles. He knows they are laughing at him, or at Mahesh, which is not very far from them laughing at him. They would not have dared do this last week. Not a single one of them.

He must do something, but not now, not when recess is fucking over. But soon. That Bengali thinks he is untouchable? Just because his daddy had complained to Om? Well, first he would manage Om, and then these boys. Soon.

AMAR

Jagdeo Ranade's house is a fortress.

At least it was not hard to locate. It took only the most basic inquiries in the town for Amar to find himself cruising the tree-lined streets of Rannwara's Civil Lines district.

It seems to fall on him from a great height, a mountain of endless white stone with spikes on the walls. He takes it in and takes a turn, does not stop, and over a couple of hours, meticulously makes lazy circuits through all adjoining lanes to get a read on the contours of the gargantuan property.

There are no surprises, not in this. Every jungle has a big bad fucking king, and the boy's father just happens to be him, accumulating wealth and power for more than three decades, and his house shows every bit of it. It is big and ugly and white with a twenty-foot-high wall that stretches all around the compound, a constant beat of giant political hoardings peaking over it, showing a hard man with hard eyes. Amar Singh has no clue who this man is but he is familiar with the look. It is a look that makes a promise. It says that if you let him fuck you just a little, he will scare away all the other fuckers trying to fuck you.

A couple of police jeeps are parked in the shade, outside the closed main gate, like sleeping guard dogs. They look empty. They sit inside, Amar is sure, along with a complement of groundskeepers and civilian guards and an army of servants. An assault will take a lot of blood. With a little luck he can sneak in at night. There are a few trees along the road, close enough to the wall, that he is sure would make it convenient to get in, but there is no way to get advance intelligence about the inside layout. It will be a blind play—there will be blood in the coming out of it. A lot of blood. And that is if he is able to find the boy and the weapon before the shooting starts.

It is not impossible. It is always good to assess the fallback options, the plan Bs, even the uncomfortable ones. He rides away, convinced that catching the boy at school is still his best play.

ARVIND

The pain is a burning white electric current, running along Arvind's finger bones and up his forearms till it seems to sit deep inside his elbow, flexing and reflexing, tying itself into knots.

He stands with his arm extended, palm down as Mr Satchitananda Ray, the mathematics teacher, smacks the skin off of his knuckles with a wooden ruler. He is used to being hit but this … getting hit on the knuckles … this is new, a fresh hell unleashed by Ray Sir who has decided that the boys, now in seventh standard, are old enough and he no longer needs to mess about. It is time to get serious.

'You are never going to dare do this again,' Ray Sir says, almost out of breath from the effort, and then to the class, 'this is a lesson for all of you,' and then looking at Sudipto with 'especially you', which is a bloody joke because it is only Arvind who is getting hit. Something is said in Bengali to Sudipto that has him soberly nodding even as Ray brings the ruler up in the air, the edge touching the ceiling of the room, this weathered piece of wood, 30 cm long, too chipped and faded for it to be of any use other than as a weapon, and he waits, watching the terror build in Arvind's eyes, before bringing it down, and it makes a swoosh sound in the air and then *thwack*.

The sting melts his face off.

It had begun with Bakshi Ma'am, who at the end of her civics class—this one spent revising something about local government—admonished Arvind and Sudipto for their public exit from her class the week before, which was fine except Ray, evil, sadistic, monstrous Ray, was early for his own class and overheard the story.

Now Ray Sir, being Bengali, is extra fond of Sudipto, who is his shining light, his Made-in-America boy wonder—a circumstance already disadvantageous for Arvind, who only looks worse in comparison. But this specific instance caused Ray Sir to explode in fury, all of which was targeted at the tiny snivelling creature who had led his darling Sudipto astray.

Arvind had had him the year before as well, and Ray was terrible even then, quick and merciless with the ruler, a monster of anger and violence, but not like this … not with the upturned knuckles, which is an entirely new universe of trauma …

Five of these on his right hand, pink inner skin peeking through where more of the dark outer skin peels away after each hit—all this in front of the whole class, and all this with Sudipto, his partner in crime, staying quiet and looking down fixedly on the ground, pointedly not looking up while Arvind's bones are cracked hot and cold.

He cannot bear to see my pain, Arvind thinks, and in this we are alike.

•••

Arvind takes the punishment, not that he has another option, telling himself that the power does not lie with Ray, nor with the ruler that is tearing his hand up. The power, true power, actually lies with him, inside his schoolbag, and it is only due to his temperance, his hesitation, his forbearance in unleashing this power that the world is balanced.

When it is over, Ray Sir smiles a wide smile of stained teeth. Arvind and Sudipto return to their seat, Sudipto avoiding his eyes the whole way, with Ray Sir telling him to stop sitting with this useless idiot donkey of a boy, and then mumbling something about how south Indian boys are supposed to be smart, and how Arvind remains a pale shadow of his sister, before returning to the equations on the blackboard.

Arvind's eyes have an edgeful of tears but he does not stop them like he usually does, for he now sees it simply as his body's reaction to the attack, an autonomous thing, a response to a pain that does not mean anything, that remains skin deep and does not contain a spiritual component.

A pain that is borne by choice and choice alone. With the Gun in his possession he stands above the world, watching the games of action and consequence play out below him. He can consider all possibilities before he needs to pick his path. He knows he can shoot Ray now, kill him maybe, and he knows he will be valid in doing so but then whatever happens later he cannot use this weapon on Jaggi or to right other wrongs in the future.

It is far better to have the option of grand absolute vengeance available to him while he plans other less ambitious solutions to all his problems. Ray Sir can wait. He is a vicious little man in a world of vicious little men, and will still be here ... like he is now, standing at the board next to a long set of equations, scratching his balls through shiny polyester pants and leaving giant chalk stains on his crotch.

And so, with this piece of enlightenment shining inside his heart, Arvind finally allows himself to begin to think about Jaggi.

Arvind had seen him. He was outside the classroom, standing with Piyush, and had definitely noticed the boys. Arvind is certain that the only reason he is not getting thrashed behind the school grounds or in the bathroom at this moment is because the class bell had rung and saved him. Sudipto is living in a dream world where he believes that the conversation his father had is enough to protect them. Arvind does not think it is—not for Sudipto, and definitely not for him.

Not since the story of what happened to Mahesh has raced through the school. Already boys from the other sections knew. He had been stupid, he should have anticipated this and told Sudipto not to make a big thing out of it. It has made them bigger targets. And not just for Jaggi and his gang. All the seniors will want a piece of them now. It is a question of pride after all.

Arvind feels that maybe Jaggi's boys will aim to do some terrible permanent damage. The school rumour mill claimed that he had once stabbed a boy and cut his arm off ... He does not want to lose a hand or a leg or anything else.

He is going to have to find an answer.

When Jaggi was outside with Piyush, Nikunj Goyal was also with them for a bit. There had been a conversation. Nikunj and Piyush were not friends. In fact, Nikunj was a complete loner, and had no friends. Moreover, Jaggi does not think of boys like Nikunj as anything more than insects—to beat and berate. Yet, today a conversation took place and no one got punched.

As Ray Sir continues explaining simultaneous equations, Arvind stares at Nikunj, who sits in the row ahead, his giant triangular head moving in time to the teacher's words.

AMAR

It is a simple thing to grab a hold of his tail. All it takes is a parked bike and a quick walk into the scrub bushes next to the highway, a walk with intent. The man is too smart to follow Amar immediately down the dirt path, choosing instead to continue riding along the road and stop a hundred metres ahead. His job after all is simply to track the stranger, not confront him.

Amar is counting on him doing exactly that. The first inkling the man has of Amar's presence is the back of a pistol smashing into the back of his skull.

Amar became aware of the man at a tea shop where he was waiting for the school day to end. The tail was dressed casually, thin, barely more than a boy, sitting on his parked scooter as he read a newspaper. Nondescript, unremarkable. But to Amar's trained eyes he was a professional: it was the way he sat, not making waves, waiting for something to happen.

They had staked out the hotel, he was sure of it; it was a simple thing to post lookouts in the lanes leading out. He should have made the tail at the very first instant. A week ago he would have. Not having the Gun was making him careless.

In that moment, Amar Singh threw his cigarette and moved out on the bike, turning down the highway, away from the city and the school, the tail following him, unaware that the game had turned.

In this moment, the tail tumbles without sound, and then it is a quick thing to drag him off and smash his face in to make him talk.

Close work.

Amar is not a big fan of it, much preferring the art and angles of a good gunfight. Life is made of unpleasant tasks and it is a far worse day for the tail, who is unarmed, calls himself Saurab, is a robber and bike thief by trade and confirms that he is working for Bilal, and has worked for Bilal now and then—often serving as a lookout.

Amar had been pointed out to him outside the hotel, though they had lost him soon after.

'Please do not kill me,' is all he says, his face a piece of toothless, bloody meat, and Amar does not.

BILAL

What is the price Jaslok Kamani would be willing to pay for the head of his brother's killer? It is a delectable question to contemplate—one Bilal is sucking dry with all his mental capacity. The answers come, and he has to bite down upon them before they get too big, dwarfing even his sweetest dreams.

It will have other consequences too, he is sure. Jaslok will not likely stop at one head, and will pull the thread of the dead shooter till the whole conspiracy unravels. War will follow—and will surely drown Uncle and all his people, his whole operation. Maybe the old bastard will talk his way out of it, make a compromise, but Bilal doubts it. By killing Amar, he will be pumping bullets into his old uncle's chest. It is an absolute betrayal.

But the prize? The prize could be anything at all. Uncle's whole business. His own growing as well. Avenues of power, and pipelines of money he has not even imagined. The size limited only by the gratitude of the Kamani organization. He wonders how he would fit within it. Could he run his own independent shop? Maybe Bombay.

But no … first the task at hand. He re-evaluates his plan. He will have to do it all himself, he concludes as he sips hot kahwa. His instinct on this is right. Mere information will not get him past the line. He needs the Gun, and Amar's head. His dead body rotting in some quarry.

It has to be quick, a simple whisper of the gun's presence, a gun once owned by Jaslok Kamani's dead twin, and there would be a mini fucking army disembarking at the station in minutes, and with it his leverage would vanish …

No, it would have to be done fast, tonight, and ideally somewhere else. With no one the wiser about his role in this … Not till he got the head and the Gun to Jaslok Bhai himself…

This is when Jamshed runs in to say that Amar has left the hotel and vanished. There is no news from the boys sent to track him.

It takes immense self-control to not throw the hot tea in Jamshed's face, and in the end it is the thought of his sister screaming that stays his hand.

Amar has run and this has all been for nothing, the fucker could be halfway to Bombay, and he, Bilal, should start thinking about his lies to his uncle already, about how Amar Singh's paranoia was so extreme that no deal was possible or that maybe … wait …

'Did he take his guns with him?'

'What guns?'

'He has a bag of guns, which is stashed in his hotel room. Did he take it?'

Jamshed looks confused and Bilal is rethinking the tea, family or not, when Mirza, who has also entered, silent as always, shakes his head with confidence. Ten boys like him and I would fucking take all of India, is what Bilal thinks and then says, 'He will come back for them.'

He knows Amar, knows that he is dangerous and has innate tactical knowledge and is reckless and unpredictable. But there is also a sense of his having been touched by God. Riven by superstition, Amar is a man who sees himself as living outside the rules of nature, his mania fed by his impossible victories, and his stupid obsession with his guns, a man who will return to take back his beloved guns and prove his invincibility. He will not simply leave them for Bilal to take.

So the ambush will still work, though he will lose some boys now. Nothing has really changed.

'Wait there, and keep an eye out. Quiet. Don't drink. Don't touch his room. When he comes back, shoot him on sight.'

ARVIND

An hour later, at the end of the school day, Arvind collects all the pieces of his resolve and makes his way to confront Jaggi directly. There is no Sudipto with him to complicate matters. Arvind had slipped away from his friend at the final bell with rushed goodbyes. Sudipto nodded, and then, 'Let me come, they won't touch you if I am with you,' and Arvind had just laughed, saying, 'I am faster without you,' and walked off before his friend could follow.

Jaggi is sitting, as he often does, on his jeep with his senior boys outside the school gate on the main road that turns in from the highway. It is a bit of a walk for Arvind, as he moves past the parked school buses and the other children, clumped together, voices shrill with excitement.

He has a plan, a manner of thinking, the setting up of a negotiation—which is beginning to seem less substantial with every step. He can see the senior boys now in the distance, through the gaps in the school wall as they laugh about something, and it makes his insides flutter.

He is strong now, stronger than before, but walking towards his still much stronger nemesis is hard. The fear that he was sure he had left behind now comes back tenfold, and his confidence withers under its onslaught, but he wills himself to continue.

There is a plan and he has to believe that it will hold. If it does not, the seniors would not even have to chase him today, he would be right there, an offering to be devoured. It would be bad, but nothing he has not survived before. The beating, if it were to come, should not be too bad, not now, not with all the kids around, and the teachers still milling around the buses, not here, just ten metres outside the school gate.

And if it was too bad, if they broke his nose and his legs, well then, he would just have to heal up and then come back and shoot them.

•••

They look at him, Jaggi with Swapnil beside him, and the others whose names he doesn't know, familiar faces with vicious smiles turning towards him with intent. Jaggi relaxes them with a word. He sits on the bonnet of the jeep, his feet hanging a foot off the ground, the pose is relaxed but the eyes contain considerable menace.

Arvind stops about six feet away. Jaggi is still looking at him … curiously. Curiosity that might buy him some time, minutes perhaps, enough to say what he has to say, to talk about what sits inside his bag even now. He takes a few more steps forward, and with these he is now too close to make a run for it. The die has been cast, the gambit opened, the head placed inside the lion's jaws.

'It is good that I did not have to run after you,' Jaggi says, and then motions for the other boys to go away. 'I have some business with this little one here. I will catch you later.' They are keen to see what transpires, but it is Jaggi, and he does not look like he is fooling around, so they nod and walk off. Only Swapnil remains standing by Jaggi's side.

Jaggi turns to Arvind now, with his full attention. 'I heard what you are saying about Mahesh … Everything reaches me. It looks like I am talking to a fucking hero. So, tell me, little hero, what are you going to do today? Are you here to say sorry, you little fucker?'

There is a pressure here, in his presence, a force that makes it difficult to talk, but he pushes the words out somehow, 'I have your paper,' he says, the words dying as they leave his lips, too light and too weak they are blown away by the breeze before they reach.

'Speak in Hindi, you chutiya,' and then to Swapnil, 'I think I am going to drag him behind my car like a little dog, maybe it will teach him something.'

The boys laugh.

'I have your paper.'

Swapnil shuts up. Jaggi's smile freezes into something nightmarish.

'I stole the paper from Nikunj,' he says, 'and I don't have it with me. It's gone. I gave it away for safekeeping.'

Jaggi glances at the police bodyguard who is standing a few feet away near the back of the car before turning to him.

'I am going to kill you,' is all he says as he walks towards Arvind.

'Don't. If something happens to me, or if you hit me, the paper will reach the principal.'

Swapnil grabs hold of Jaggi, but he does not stop. Arvind sees now there is a Band-Aid stuck on the left side of Jaggi's jaw. 'Just wait,' Swapnil says.

The Gun is a red-hot coal inside the bag against his spine, and with that strength he says it again, 'I am just keeping it, I will not share it or give it to anyone.'

His Hindi is breaking, even in parts where it used to be intact, the words he knows, the words he practised in class are getting mixed up, pieces of English papering the cracks. He knows better than to speak too much English here, it is the kind of thing that will make the situation explode, but he has few options.

'Give it to me now, or I will bury you right here.'

'Listen to me, if anything happens to me the paper goes to the principal. It is just one paper, for one subject, for one exam. I know you have to sell all of the others. For other exams. If this comes out—they will change the printer. And the question papers for the exam.'

His words are fast, with no borders, slipping into each other in his rush to get them out. At this distance he can feel the heat radiate from Jaggi's body, his intent to kill boring a hole inside his half-sized child sternum.

'You fucker. I am going to fuck your mother.'

The words are harsh and shake him but it is too far gone now.

'This way you do whatever you are doing, I will not tell anyone, and you do not touch me … till the exam anyway.'

Time is slow for Arvind. He can feel his heart pounding. He watches the microscopic changes in Jaggi's expression, even as Swapnil whispers in his ear, his hands grabbing Jaggi by the shoulder, trying to calm him down. Behind the jeep, the bodyguard smells some action and moves closer.

'I don't get anything by sharing this, any of this. You boys do what you have to do. Just leave me alone.' And with this he turns and walks away, his bones shaking inside his thin body, bracing for a blow that does not come.

JAGGI

This is the fucking end of the world. It should not be, but it is, and it is not the time for fucking words. It is the fucking time to break heads.

Threatening him? Blackmailing him? That little fucking shit, who does he think he is? Does he not understand what the fuck is going to happen now?

The whole time just talking talking talking in his shitty little accent, that no one can fucking understand, he is lucky his head did not get bashed in with a brick, that little fucking fucker. Swapnil is talking to him about money. Money? Like he, fucking Jaggi Ranade, gives a fuck about money. Fucking Swapnil going on and on about money and fucking plans and schemes and exams and punishments and principals ... Jaggi does not fucking care. Why should he? He is going to set the whole fucking place on fire. Start from the bottom and keep going till there is fucking nothing left. Who can touch him? Who? No one, no one can fucking touch him. If that bitch principal even tries anything he'll hang her upside down with her own fucking saree. If Swapnil does not keep his fucking hands off of him, he is going to pound his fucking body into the ground too. Let them fucking watch, both him and that bastard Mahesh, useless little cunts, let them sit in the fucking hospital together, staring at each other's eyes as they finger their fat pussies. This boy, this fucking Madrasi boy won't be there, no no no he won't, he won't because he will be fucking dead, his head bashed in at this fucking moment.

He is still talking, the little shit. Broken fucking words coming out in this reedy, twangy, fucking voice. And Jaggi knows, oh he knows, that the temperature is building and once it has fucking built it will be the fucking end no matter the fucking circumstances, do they not fucking understand … Blackmailing him! Fucking this no-name Madrasi yam-yam-yam-yam shit fucker telling him what to do, and fucking Swapnil clinging to him, and he is going to get fucked if he does not let go, the fucking chutiya. 'Stop it, Sonawane is here …' Swapnil says, barely keeping the fear out of his voice and then Jaggi turns around and sees the guard in his constable uniform staring at him, and this is when he starts punching the bonnet of the fucking jeep, each blow leaving a dent in the metal.

It takes what seems like hours for the rage to cool and then it settles like sputtering sparks of white electrical heat deep inside him as the situation becomes clear. There are multiple subjects for the term papers across the different classes, and the deal the boys have made with the printer's boy is for eight of them … It is a bulk investment, which has already been paid out. Each of them has been promised forward—to be delivered in four weeks' time to the students who have paid in advance. The thing is already in fucking motion.

In case the copy of the paper reaches the principal, there will definitely be action. Maybe more screaming, possible expulsion, definitely suspension. Swapnil will get proper fucked at home, and while he, Jaggi, will be able to protect himself and probably get off with just a warning, Swapnil is going to be made an example of.

Even if the principal cannot prove that the boys are behind this, not only will the question papers be changed, but also the printer will change. All the money paid so far will go up in smoke. And just like a few years ago they will once again start getting the papers copied out the morning of the exam ... And then this scheme, this most sacred tradition of the senior boys, past and future, will be gone.

Jaggi understands the situation but also does not care. Fuck the money, fuck the school, fuck the expulsion—that remains his philosophy at this moment, pride and white hot rage allowing no surrender on these aspects. Pride above everything—today these brats are bragging about fucking up Mahesh, tomorrow they'll talk about how they made a total chutiya of Jaggi Ranade and then where will he be? Fucking nowhere. Jai, Abhimanyu, and all his seniors, what the fuck will they think when they hear this? He will have no place to even hide his face.

The Sonawane problem is a valid one though. It was clear from Om's tone yesterday that he did not want any chaos in the school, no violence, nothing linked to Jaggi at all. This kid, he is close to the Bengali boy, and that boy's father has business with Baba. And when it comes to his business, Baba is fucking ruthless and Om his weapon of choice.

No, the school and the principal and the money—all that is bullshit. In this moment Jaggi is quiet because he cannot have anything go back to his home. This is the chain around him, one that Om has tied around his neck, and he is contemplating the links and designs of it when Swapnil, looking to him with scared eyes, says, 'There is another problem.'

It's a simple thing, Swapnil explains, and it could happen to anyone you see, these are unforeseen circumstances. The paper that this boy has stolen, well … it was the only copy of this paper. They will need to find another copy to give to the boy, the one who was going to prepare the answers, so that he can actually write them out.

'You had one copy?'

'No … I mean … yes.'

'That is the copy we gave, which has now been fucking stolen?'

Swapnil is too smart to answer, but even then Jaggi reevaluates the idea of using the brick but this time with Swapnil's head as the target. It is too thick though; the fucking brick will break. He takes another deep breath—the fury inside him is starting to bubble again. And from this come the beginnings of a plan.

'Take the car,' he tells him, 'right now, and go get another fucking copy.'

'Oh, but you?'

'What about me? One of these fuckers will drop me home,' he says, not even bothering to point to the fuckers in question. 'Go and fucking sort it out.'

Sonawane looks at him, confused. 'Take him to Aranagar, he has some work,' is all Jaggi tells him, and when Sonawane protests, 'How can I go without you …' and 'Om Bhaiya had told me …' and finally, 'Please come with us,' he snaps again and says, I am not a fucking child and it is important work and just take him with you and I will see you at home.

They both want to object, but seeing his mood they leave, Swapnil telling him, 'Just relax, we will solve this,' and he nods already thinking ahead and then watches the jeep turn into the highway, rushing out towards the city.

He then walks over to the other boys and takes Dheeraj's scooter and then asks, 'Does anyone know where that girl Srilekha lives?' One of the boys says it is the Steel Colony. He rides on to the highway, convinced that he will catch up with the little bastard, feeling the vibrations of the engine under him and the wind in his hair, allowing slowly the temperature of his anger to rise again, his skin incandescent in anticipation.

Such is his focus in this moment that he does not notice the rider driving down the highway on the other side, but who sees him and makes a sudden U-turn.

ARVIND

A different Arvind walks alone along the tracks on the way to the back entrance of the colony. He crosses the spot where the old Arvind won his great victory against Mahesh three days ago, but it might have been years. It feels like an opening skirmish.

The war is on now, and the different Arvind moves ahead, wondering if his ruse worked and if it has then how much time he has actually bought himself. The exams are not far, which is a positive—asking Jaggi to put aside violent retribution forever is an impossible ask, and this delay might be short enough for him to digest, yet long enough for Arvind to find the next solution.

Three days ago, the old Arvind had bought himself three days, allowing for the birth of this new one. There is much that he can do in the few weeks that lie ahead of him.

The day cools fast as he makes his way, and fat grey clouds begin to build. Arvind can smell a storm coming. The route ahead is largely deserted. In the distance, three bone-thin men watch the skies as they usher along a herd of goats with sticks and whistles.

He smiles. Today too was a victory, another small one, but they all count. Snatching the paper from Nikunj's bag was the hard part. Once he realized what he had in his hands, putting together the rest of the scheme was not.

Suddenly a roaring sound and before Arvind can understand what is happening a powerful impact pushes him off his feet and he is flying through the air with two arms locked around his waist like steel cables and as he lands the wind is knocked out of him and he finds himself prone on the ground with Jaggi sitting on top of his chest.

He begins to struggle and there is a punch straight to his face and it does not hurt but his vision becomes blurry and then Jaggi gets up to kick him between the legs, just the one time, and it is as if every bulb in his body flares up for a single moment of pure agony and then the world falls apart in pieces around him.

Arvind is dazed as he is pulled upright by the larger boy, and dragged off the road, stumbling over the broken paths, legs like complete jelly, his bag still stuck on his back ... and there are broken young trees and through them he goes, the branches scratching his face and arms till a moment of respite as Jaggi lets go and then it is a hard shove and he is propelled forward with serious momentum, and he crumples on the hard, chalky ground.

Rough hands pull the bag from his shoulder and he fights this, he really fights this, with nails, and with teeth, clawing and biting, but it does not help, and one of the straps of the schoolbag rips and he curls in a foetal position on the ground, hooking his elbows around the one intact strap and gripping it with both hands even as Jaggi kicks him in his stomach and his legs to get him to release it, and he endures the blows but does not move and does not let go, and finally Jaggi changes tactics and begins to stamp the hands that are holding the strap, and the pain is too much and the strength shows and it is snatched from him, torn away from bruised hurting fingers.

Jaggi throws the bag to the side, and stands shaking with fury.

His entire body is rocked by pain but Arvind fights through this and raises himself up on his elbows. The kicking he had received on the ground was brutal, and he can feel the bloom of bruises all over his body, but it has allowed him to recover his breath and take stock of his surroundings.

They are at the edge of a large clearing, one of the old limestone quarries, now refilled. Nothing grows here, not even a tuft of grass. Beneath his fingers he can feel the jagged edges of stone flakes and small sharp pebbles. Jaggi towers over him, all lean muscle and murderous rage. Staring him down.

'I told you I don't have it,' Arvind says, not even sure if it will work.

'I don't think I really care anymore … It was fun and games with you, boy, it really was fucking entertaining but I am fucking done playing'—he takes out an oblong object from his back pocket—'you are never going to fuck me again—'

'Wait, I will give it to you, I have it, it is in my bag …' The words tumble out, his mind whirring so fast he cannot think, as Jaggi removes the cover to reveal the steel blade of a knife.

'I don't give a fuck about the paper. Keep it. Report me to the fucking principal, you fucker. But how will you talk? You will have no tongue left after this afternoon.'

Panic rises within Arvind as he realizes he has overplayed his hand—he overlooked the simple fact that Jaggi does not respond to fear or threats. He is a creature of blinding pride and ego, pushing back against him does not work as it might with lesser bullies. A monstrous ego, now bruised, will swallow him whole. An ego that must be fed.

'No not the paper … the game, the game, I have the video game … I will give it to you,' Arvind says, and seeing the senior boy pause, he continues, 'I will tell Sudipto I gave it to you, ensure he doesn't tell anyone, or talk to his parents … What a chutiya, huh? Who does that … getting parents involved … a total chutiya,' he says and it is the first time he is saying it, and the word 'chutiya', so common in Hindi, sounds alien in his mouth.

Jaggi is smiling now, standing in place, 'You have the game … How did you get it …?'

'I borrowed it from him. I didn't ask … he is a rich fucker, a fat rich fucker who does not deserve it … Wait, let me get it for you,' and he starts to crawl towards the bag.

He does it slowly, dragging his lower body behind him, keeping an eye on the blazing steel of the knife even as he moves … It is for effect, this worm-like motion of his. He could stand but he chooses not to, even though this hurts, the rough stone of the ground scraping the soft skin of his chest and stomach.

'It has so many games,' he says, staying low, 'let me …' sticking to Hindi, letting the words mumble out, talk, talk, only moments more, and then he is at the bag, 'so many games … that fucker,' and yes, there it is, the Gun, and his hand closes around the grip and remembering, his thumb goes to the safety, flipping it, even as his fingers shake, as his whole body shivers, and maybe it is something in his body, or maybe he has not quite entirely shielded the gleam of the weapon in the sun—but Jaggi moves towards him, knife extended.

'What the fuck—'

And then—*boom*.

IV

DELIVERANCE

ARVIND

It is a hard shot at a bad angle. The sun was behind Jaggi who was quickly moving towards Arvind who, bruised and weak himself, was prone on the ground and had no time to actually aim the Gun, no way to spot the sights or level the barrel or anything, with his upper body twisted into position such that the recoil threw his elbows back hard into the ground.

It is, however, a perfect shot. The bullet, a 9mm dumdum, hits Jaggi at the base of the throat, near the clavicle, shatters it—and then immediately mushrooms into a piece of hot sizzling shrapnel about the size of a large piece of popcorn. This piece, already slower than the 381 m/s it left the Gun at, still carries enough kinetic energy to rip through the insides of Jaggi's throat, shred the soft muscle tissue and about three major blood vessels before exiting from the back of his neck and destroying some of the nerves at the very top of the spinal cord. As all motor control leaves his body, Jaggi falls to the ground, turning with his own momentum, and lands on his side with his face up, eyes open seeing clouded skies. His hand, still clutching the knife, twitches slightly.

The blood from the wound is now flooding his lungs and there is a wheezing sound as his body tries to breathe, throwing up tiny bubbles from the entry wound in his throat.

•••

Arvind, deafened by the sound of the weapon in his hand, his small frame shaking with shock and emotion, on his knees beside the body of his great nemesis, lets out a long wail, a scream, a primal call to murder, as old as cave drawings and bone clubs—he screams as tears roll down his dusty cheeks, mixing with blood from his own face.

In his heart, in all three languages he understands, he praises the gods that allowed the Gun to fall into his hands, he thanks them all, and this, this right here, is the greatest moment of his life.

This moment.

Jaggi lies fallen on the ground before him, blood leaking weakly out of the wound in his throat.

Arvind watches. Exultant.

On his knees, exhausted, empty, beyond conscious thought and animal instinct, he watches, sheared of all memories, outside of time. He watches with purest joy singing softly in the absolute stark present moment. Fulfilled, he watches.

The raindrops fall fat and there is the Diwali cracker smell of burning gunpowder and his skin is scratched and he is bruised and beaten and his throat is hoarse from the scream, and he breathes deeply—a breath of acid and rain, of bitter smoke, but this breath feels like his first real breath in a lifetime.

The Gun is weightless in his hands, a thing made of skin and bone, a part of his own hand. There are no lines between them now, between the sculptor and the hammer, and his art is the broken flesh that used to be Jaggi—he too is a part of this union, now and forever, sanctified by blood.

And there is no surprise or emotion left in him. He sits empty and content and one with the universe, when once again, twice in the same day, arms reach out and grab him from behind.

V

STILL LIFE

BILAL

Bilal is asleep when he is woken by Jamshed, his face covered in blood and with more holes in him than the fucking moon—screaming horrible nonsense about demons and death, his words interrupted by gushes of thick dark blood that pours out of his mouth.

•••

Hotel Jaipur is a slaughterhouse. All his boys are dead, the wounds from the bullets inside their bodies still smoking, a hundred empty shells sizzling in the pools of blood that flow down the stairs, seeping through the ceilings …

What in the name of all hells happened here?

Rafique, dead, his face torn apart by a knife, dead while crawling for life. Charu, only fifteen years old, found splattered flat in the back alley, his entire torso missing. Bhola, his best, dead, bullets through the eyes and throat—his pistol still in his hand, unfired. And like them the others, all of the others, all of his boys.

How could one man, any man, do this?

Bilal, no stranger to violence, cannot comprehend the scale of this carnage, as if it is too ghastly a scene to be truly absorbed by his brain, a circumstance that his cognition rejects—and it is here, with his mind racing down a thousand routes, that Bilal wonders: Where the fuck is the police? They should be swarming all over this like flies on cow shit. This was not a quiet, small shooting among two or three men; here lies enough spent ammo for a fucking border war. This is really bad, Bilal thinks, really bad indeed, cursing Jamshed for having baited him here, and his own stupidity for having walked in, to have been seen here.

Fear is a natural ally of man, keeps him alive if he is smart enough to listen. The men that ignore these calls out of hand in the name of courage are idiots, their deaths already written in their stubbornness.

There is no victory here.

Turning to those of his boys who have come with him, now standing in stunned stupefaction, 'Burn it,' he says, 'burn it all. Get some petrol. Burn this whole fucking building to the ground.'

•••

It is only later, once he is back home, locked in, and secured and guarded, and still wondering how the damned fucking whorehouse of a place was not crawling with cops, that he hears that Jagdeo Ranade's youngest son was shot dead the same evening.

And this is when he knows he is truly fucked.

SUDIPTO

He is dead and the world is better for it.

•••

The news came to Papa in the evening. A blaring phone call on the official line just as he was sitting with his tea, and he sounded serious on the phone and sombre and worried. After the call, he put his coat back on without even waiting to finish his tea.

His parents had a quick chat—he could not hear, strain his ears as he might—that left his mother looking frantic. 'Do not leave the house, lock the gates,' was all Papa said before taking the personal car and driving off. Their driver had already gone home for the day.

Sudipto knew it was very serious then, for Papa rarely drove.

It was not a normal night. Ma and he stayed up watching *The Wizard of Oz* on the VCR. He is rarely allowed to watch movies late after dinner, especially on a school night, but it was something he did not question too much then, understanding that for whatever reason Ma needed his presence close to her—her grip around him almost uncomfortable in its tightness.

Papa, when back, too seemed particularly tender—not saying much, just stroking his hair and watching the film as Sudipto dozed off on the sofa between them.

He woke a little later to the hushed sounds of them talking and feigned sleep. The TV was off and the lights were dim and Papa was sitting with his whisky, talking in whispers to Ma and he heard him say, 'That boy is dead, Rina, that boy is dead. I saw him just a few days ago.' As things slowly started clicking in Sudipto's head, an emotion swelled inside of him like a great tide, so much so he could not breathe, and when he heard the word 'Ranade', he was swept by a giant rush of cool perfect joy.

He wanted to jump up and ask if it was true but he knew that would get him sent away. It was better to just stay quiet and listen to the words and preserve them like butterflies made out of the clearest glass in his own chest.

It was morning when Papa sat him down for the 'chat' and broke the news of the death to Sudipto and it was like liquid gold flowing through all of him. He could not keep the smile away from his face and Papa, concerned, had to explain to his son in his sweetest voice, 'I know that boy gave you trouble, but it is still a terrible thing to happen to someone who was so young.' And he hoped Sudipto was mature enough to show just his sadness at a time like this. He was a boy, maybe an older boy, but a boy and 'If you don't have anything good to say, son, don't say anything at all. This is not the time to talk about what happened between you or your feelings at this moment, at least not to anyone outside of this house,' and Sudipto understood the importance of this, and he killed the smile on his face, forcing a neutrality onto his features, and it was this neutrality that he maintained for the whole day, making his heart a vault and stuffing all the elation inside till he was sure he was going to burst.

•••

The world pauses. They close the school. They close the plant. There is a curfew in the city and you can hear the sirens of the police cars as they chase each other all day, even through the lanes of the colony, where they do not otherwise come.

He died not far from here, they say, along the backroad near the quarries, near where they walk back home from school.

The details come in slowly, and Sudipto collects them bit by bit from the shreds of gossip from servants. The news is everywhere, like wildfire. He was killed. He was stabbed. They found him beheaded, and have called a doctor from Delhi to stitch it back for the funeral … There is talk too of causes—rumours of mafias and politics, and how the dark times are here, the deepest Kalyug written about in the scriptures, and how there are riots in the city, giant mobs flooding in from the surrounding villages and it will get worse tomorrow as the news spreads and some shops are burning and all of the police is patrolling the roads and it is all a complete breakdown of law and order in the city in the state and so much else and all Sudipto hears is that he is dead he is dead he is dead, like the words of the world's happiest song.

JAI

On the first night of Jaggi's death Jai punches walls and punches servants and then goes and pushes all his security away to get to his car and drives down to the hospital, demanding to see his brother. He speeds the whole way there but they don't let him enter the premises under orders from his fucking father. He hits a hospital worker and then bangs his car into the gates of the hospital and the fucking metal bends over and they finally relent and he is allowed to go in and see the body. On the cold metal lies the broken shell that once housed his baby brother and then it is all red for a while and when he comes back there is more police and they are dragging him out of the hospital and then somehow he is at the place where it happened and there is a crowd collecting there where they found him next to the back road near the tracks where Jaggi was shot like a dog. He cannot take it anymore and attacks every single onlooker, screaming at them to go back fucking home and not make a fucking mockery of the death of his brother till the police have to grab him and take him away. He punches them too and he would have kept punching through the city and the whole state and somehow punch his way through the sky to the heavens and everything else to possibly bring his baby brother back …

Things are a blur. Now there is no more police. Instead there are about twenty party workers who are crying and also focused on violence and there is shooting in the air. Some others from the party come and get him, telling him it is his father and how it is urgent and there is some other shooting somewhere else in the city and he is needed home and this is how he returns home under heavy security, dragged in like a criminal on the night his brother has been killed.

Inside he meets Om, the brother who lives, who is on the phone, surrounded by more police as he barks order after order but there are no tears and no broken pieces of furniture and this he does not understand at all.

What the fuck is going on in this house and this is when his friends come, Lucky and Abhimanyu with beer and cigarettes, and it doesn't help … none of it works … nothing nothing nothing

SRILEKHA

The tears come when she least expects them.

They come at home when she is struggling to concentrate on chemistry prep, the organic links of carbon that she is trying to decipher turn misty and then thick drops fall on the thin paper, smudging ink.

They come at the dinner table where she bites her lips and swallows hard and nods along to whatever Appa is saying before making excuses to run back to her room—'It is a problem I just solved,' she says as she leaves with a smile that should fool no one.

They come in the shower like a sudden stream, and this is good and easy, and this time she lets them out, but careful, with no sound, for she does not want to explain anything.

They come at night in the bathroom as she masturbates thinking about his thick muscled forearms. She does not stop.

•••

She misses him, her twisted love, her villainous dead boy dream of absolute lust.

•••

It was the first day of a new school in a new world when she saw him and it felt like a thunderbolt through the centre of her chest, that one memory rendered in high-resolution technicolour, shining amidst the grey vagueness that was the process of her perpetual adjustment, a process drained of all novelty, this being the fifth school she remembers attending in her short sixteen years of life.

Appa was a power supply engineer, and was sent across the country on deputation—and Rannwara had seemed like yet another hot dusty industrial town, just smaller and dustier than most, with people speaking a different language and eating different food—but same in all the other ways, in all the ways that counted.

This was a good posting for them, and it was something Amma had explained to her and it was something Srilekha understood though she had wondered who comprised the 'them' that it was good for. At the end of the conversation, Amma had asked her, 'Are you okay with this?' and Srilekha looked her mother in the eye and said yes, yes she was and she thinks her mother had not believed her but appreciated that her daughter had the good sense to lie. The truth in that moment would not have mattered—the decision was already made by the higher power—and it fell to her mother to enact it and pack up a whole life into thick steel trunks and move it to a place where she, not knowing a speck of Hindi, would not be able to speak to anyone.

Amma, Srilekha knew, had found a place for herself in Trichy and the move weighed on her as well but she would do all she could to smoothen it for her children. Srilekha and her mother never spoke of such things, their relationship was one that occurred in silences—two women matching eyes at all times, forever allies if not friends.

Perpetual adjustment. New school, new uniforms, new faces that you struggle to turn into friends as the new girl. She could never express this unmooring that she felt, after all she was staring at a board year as a child of a salary-class family. Friends were a luxury she had learnt to do without, like so much else—the exams looming so high on the horizon that they blocked out the stars.

So it was that an uprooted Srilekha, untethered and strange, large and with hairy legs, her body struggling with the awkwardness of a badly understood puberty, walked into a school which for all its alienness, might have been on Mars.

Some snide looks aside, the kids mostly left her alone, but even her broken understanding of Hindi was enough to put together words like 'black buffalo', and it hurt but she did not let it show either in class or at home, then or later. She remained untouched and unaffected by everything said and unsaid—with one glorious exception.

He had sauntered in that first day before the third period, hair ruffled, shirt half out of his pants, and as he walked past her desk on his way to the back seats, momentarily brushing the top of her desk with his fingers, everything stilled. She saw his bruised knuckles, scabbed and split with a pink redness peeking through, a redness that looked anything but soft, singing to her of the harshness of life, and these hands, like cords of old rope, were different from all the hands of men she had ever seen before, absolutely unlike her father's with their long sloping fingers, no, these fingers with their connection to the real world, leading to wide wrists and into giant forearms, and a flush began in the pit of her stomach and then headed lower in a hurry, a flush she never felt before.

Later that night was the first time in her life that she touched herself. It was something that just happened as she lay awake at night, thinking of his hands pressing against her skin, and she did what she did without thought and without intent and with the release came the shame and the secrecy and all of that but it was the dream of him that kept it going night after night.

•••

She wanted him in a way that she should not have wanted anyone, least of all him—and school and class became about him, and she no longer missed Trichy or friends or any other fragment of her old life, as long as she could watch him move, as long as every so often he would touch a thing close to her—his hands resting on a table ten feet away, unconscious but beautiful, an act of possession—a benediction as he acknowledged an object and thus allowed its existence, his touch extending solidity to all things, making them real where before, it becomes clear, they were made of smoke.

How she wished, then and again, that he would touch her too, make her one of his things, turning her from an idea of a girl into the real thing.

•••

Because no one spoke to her at the new school, she rationalized later, and so much of her being was engrossed in the daily survival of wrong language and classwork and the unique pressures of a board year, the wanton violence Jaggi liked to inflict remained a secret to her, a secret she never put together from all of the clues that were apparent, that she should have seen. The bruised knuckles, the swagger-y walk, the other boys following him like hyenas—all minor symptoms of the violence that bred inside his body, and how it exploded in all directions, at all times.

She understood too that Arvind had emerged as collateral damage of this violence, and though she hated herself for it, it did not stop her from wanting Jaggi, for her want was not a rational thing—to be measured and split and turned off when found to be inconvenient. So, she continued to want him, even as she watched her brother suffer, even as she noticed him being dragged out of the school bus, even as she caught him at home with bruises and scratches, even as she saw in his eyes the constant furtive desperation and how he had aged so fast in so many ways.

The new school and the new town weighed on both siblings. It was a difficult transition for her, at her age, in her class; for him, as a boy at his age, it should have been easier, but it was not and that was entirely because of Jaggi and his fists and his hands—the same hands that wandered the curves of her brain every waking moment.

So, she tried her best and supported Arvind in all ways that she could, and encouraged him and was—in action—the very best elder sister she could be, dealing with him with infinite patience, covering his absences and all of his faults, and interjecting for him with the family, building him up as best she could, trying to pull him back from the damage that was beginning to show even in the quiet times.

And after all that, with the excuse of a book, she would stay in the bathroom at night—touching herself, thinking of the boy who was destroying her brother.

KAPOOR

Superintendent of Police Virendar 'Barry' Kapoor can still smell Hotel Jaipur.

It has been two days since he stood with the city fire marshal, looking at the most disgusting sight he has seen in his life. Bodies—five, eight, ten—who even knew how many—piled in the corridor, half burnt. A single leaking ball of meat, flesh and skin and clothes melted and coagulated together.

The marshal, an ancient man, dark and curved, much like a piece of wood pulled out from the ashes, his words coming out in a whistle from under a giant shining white moustache, said, 'They were in a hurry. If they really wanted to do this, they should have flamed the foundation beams. It is old stone, it was an army building once you know … the British cut no corners in construction …' The old bastard had gone on about the history of the place while Kapoor watched a constable pick up empty bullet casings from the floor with his bare hands, like a child collecting stones from a riverbed.

He had had no sleep for thirty-six hours, not since the Ranade boy was found dead and the news spread and then the riots and the curfew and the press and the fucking stress of dealing with that fucking Family. And with everything going on, no one, not one of these fuckers had bothered to even tell him about the scale of this … this pyre of bodies … This fucking …

'They used petrol,' the old man had told him. 'But they used too much. You can see where the fire burned too hot,' he said as he poked at the sizzled flesh with a stick. The thing—the arm, the leg, the whatever—was charred but felt wet.

Kapoor swallowed bitter vomit. He had a hanky drenched in grain alcohol wrapped around his face. It did not help, the fumes turned everything lurid and sideways, and the stench came through undeterred. The old man seemed to need no protection, his face alone was uncovered as he talked while poking the body pile with his stick.

'The fire ate itself,' he said. 'There was not enough air.' Poke. 'They could have opened these windows. What were they thinking?' Poke poke. Something spilled yellow juice. 'Amateurs.'

Kapoor had left before he fainted …

•••

The world has gone crazy, reality no longer fits any pre-existing pattern. Now with seventy-two hours of no sleep, he is in a jeep, rushing to the main market where the mobs have set fire to a movie theatre. They protest violence with violence and will be put down with violence. It is the language of the state, the language of its people. A language he has been screaming in at the top of his voice.

This is all temporary, the real investigation continues elsewhere. The dead boys in the hotel belonged to the Bilal Ansari gang, and while he does not know everything, he can see the beginnings of a pattern emerge, a story told in shell casings and bullet holes. The fire was set by the gang—in this the old man was right; it smelled of panic and amateurishness. It had all the signs of an ambush, and one that didn't go so well for Bilal.

The question is: Who were they hunting? And what did it have to do with the dead Ranade boy?

He knows he will not sleep for a week, for a month even, but electricity is coursing through his body as he drives over the empty streets, siren blaring. The Ranade kid dying is the best turn destiny has shown Kapoor in half a decade: for he knows that finally, this week, he is at the very centre of the universe.

SUDIPTO

The prayer service in the school for dead Jaggi is held in the hall and the students and parents are here class-wise, to pay their respects. The entrance is marked by a giant garlanded picture of Jaggi's face—pulled from some fictitious past where he looked sweet and smiled warmly and had no scars, and in some ways it looks like a different person entirely. The teachers stand at the entrance with heavy eyes and Sudipto looks at them really carefully, trying to see if, like him, their solemn expressions hide secret joy, but cannot be sure.

All the families present are walking in a trance, small steps with their hands clasped on the shoulders of their children, each unit walking separate, closed within itself—a forcefield extending outwards from it, pushing away the evil miasma of unfathomable tragedy that drenches the room.

Other fathers just nod to Papa, the realness of this great parental tragedy is stuck to their faces—their own fingers tight over the arms and shoulders of their own kids, the bones thin and slight in their hands, like those of birds.

His eyes scan for Arvind from the minute they walk in, peeking through all the gaps between taller parents, trying in vain to spot some hint of his friend. Eventually he catches sight of Srilekha and then what must be Arvind's parents, though he has never met them, and then he sees Arvind following them, his face angry and rigid, a hardness on it he has not seen before. He goes up to his friend, quickly dragging his parents with him through the half-full hall with some determination and when questioned simply says, 'My friend is there,' and the parents look at each other and walk behind him as he leads them to the Srinivasans.

He calls out, 'Arvind,' which rings through the hushed energy of the room, and they all stop, all of the people around him and even the Srinivasans look troubled to be there, and Srilekha especially for she is the only one from her class here and should be attending the service alongside the senior secondary group of students which is planned a couple of hours from now, but she is here and she is standing, looking strange and awkward in a black salwar kameez with golden borders.

Uncle looks stern, a thin dark man with little hair and a prominent white tika going sideways along his forehead and now Sudipto notices that Arvind is wearing one of those as well. Uncle straightens perceptibly on seeing Baba and nods a greeting and Sudipto has already reached Arvind and dragged him away even as the sets of parents begin a polite strained conversation behind them.

The boys have not truly spoken since the killing four days ago, have shared no words of triumph and no screams of freedom, just a quick conversation on the phone the day after, when the news was still fresh and burning hot—a conversation that was terse and intense and stuffed with hidden things, where both were in sight of the parents, unable to share any response that rang true.

Words were limited to a 'Did you hear?' and 'Yes' and 'I will see you when school opens' for schools are shut and the town is shut and no child is allowed outside by anxious parents, and though they live mere lanes away, they might as well be separated by an ocean.

Here, alone in this crowd, with no parent in hearing distance, they share a quick hug and Sudipto says to Arvind, 'I am glad he is gone,' and Arvind smiles and to Sudipto it feels like it is a strained shadow of a smile, not the real thing. 'Yes. Yes, he is gone, and it is good,' and it is enough now and Sudipto finally relaxes. This is the moment he has been waiting for. From the very first night when he felt the shivering pangs of hope—he had hungered to share this victory with his friend, and only now is it real.

JAI

Jai thinks it is total sisterfucking bullshit that his brother has been dead for five whole days and the entire world is not yet on fire.

The days after the funeral are pure agony and he can still smell the smell of his brother's body burning where he had stood, taking breath after deep breath for the smoke is all he has left of Jaggi. He has had no sleep and no rest and no food, and cannot go through a single second without thinking of his brother's last minute of life spent drowning in his own blood.

Jai prowls the halls and at every turn he finds Om. Om who is always on the phone and making calls and making plans. Om who does not scream and wields no rage on his face at all. Their brother is dead, and this is surely a time for war, and not a time to sit and have meetings in that goddamned office. This is the time to round up the boys and round up the men and hit the streets and break heads and join the mobs outside these walls, join them as they burn the town, giving voice to the fury that blazes inside of him … But he cannot do that, is not allowed to do that, is physically stopped from doing that.

And so Jai drinks. All day and all night but it does nothing to drown the fire, and no oblivion touches him, no void rises to hold him and give respite from his pain.

This is how Om finds him, smoking on what Jai now thinks of as Jaggi's terrace—Om who looks extra fair and extra shiny, with sweat beads forming along the stubble growing on his shaved head. Om simply asks him to have a bath and wear a shirt because there is an important meeting with the police, and Jai should be there, and no, he does not know what they have found, but it is something. 'After that,' Om adds, 'we will have a family meeting.'

•••

In the meeting, Jai is quiet for he knows it is sometimes good to just listen and understand what is happening. The policeman Kapoor walks in with the DM—Bajpai or whatever his name is—and they both look like shit, and even Baba looks tired now that Jai thinks about it; his breathing is heavier and fills the entire room, a soundtrack he does not want to focus on too much.

Kapoor's white skin is even whiter, because his eyes are ringed with dark shadows as he waits to begin to talk. Om starts the proceedings and says, 'Go ahead, Kapoor sa'ab,' and then Kapoor dips his hand into his pocket and pulls out a clear plastic packet with something shiny inside and he holds it out and Jai being closest reaches out instinctively and it sits dense in his palm like a curse.

It is a shrivelled thing like a small rotten fruit or a piece of stone and it is what took Jaggi away from him. He is still staring at it when Kapoor starts talking and says it is the bullet and then falters because there is no need to fucking complete that sentence.

'It is not a local make,' Kapoor resumes, 'we have asked for time from the advanced forensic lab in Bombay and they will have a look at it and tell us more, but what we do know is that this weapon is imported ... it seems to be something from an imported gun and it's an expensive thing, not seen around here too much. Also'—he looks at Om, not Baba, he has not dared look at Baba at all through this—'see the size of the thing. They call it a dumdum bullet ...'

'I know what they are,' Om says and then he tells Baba, 'they are special, they kill badly.'

Baba's face is a wall of concrete—dark and unknowable.

Kapoor continues, and his voice is hoarse, like he is having to push each word out, and he tells them it was a professional hit, not random, very much a mafia hit and at this Om looks at Baba like he always does and Jai knows that look, it says see-I-told-you-I-was-right-once-again and it is the look he always gives Baba and it always works and Baba like always nods in acceptance.

The DM finally finds his balls in time to squeak out some words and it is the usual shit about locking down the district and setting up checkpoints and police checks and how even a bird cannot leave the town before his words wither to nothing as Om stares him down and he is left wringing his hands anxiously and Jai smiles at his fucking discomfort and it is the first time he has smiled in days.

'There is another thing,' Kapoor says, 'there was a shootout the same night,' and then tells them about how the same night someone killed a dozen members of Bilal Ansari's gang and set them on fire.

•••

Later, when Kapoor and the DM are gone, it is only the Ranade men in council, and Jai realizes this is the first time he has been included in this and does not speak though he wants to say much.

It is Baba who talks to his remaining sons and he says, 'They have hurt us but we do not know their faces. They have hit us where we are weakest. They have hit us where it shall mean blood … blood forever … rivers of it.'

He has to pause for breath and it goes in, an extended splutter of air in thick fluid through the oxygen mask and then he says again, 'This is not a sortie or a small battle to realign some map, this is a war.' His yellow eyes deepen in concentration.

'They came with machine guns and an army and they shed the blood of this family. They must know that a truce after this is an impossible thing.' Baba stops again, the brothers wait, unified in silence.

'They want to kill us all. They are not stupid, so this means they are not weak. We must move carefully. They may not have run. They might still be lying in wait, waiting for a crack in our shield. One rash step and they will strike again.'

'Jai,' he says, pausing for another long lingering second, 'this is for you. Om will manage the situation. You were close to Jaggi. He was my son, and while he troubled me sometimes, he was my son. So trust me. Trust Om. We will manage this, and for some time now I need you to listen to Om and do what your elder brother says. Things now are truly dangerous. I am counting on you.'

•••

Om finds him on Jaggi's terrace, sitting at the spot where Jaggi used to and he is drinking and Om comes close but does not sit and does not drink. He just says, 'I know you are angry and you must know that I am angry and there will be revenge for this but I need you and Baba needs you to just stay quiet and stay safe and that means staying inside the house.' A house that has been barricaded into a fucking fort with all the cops and other security types floating around.

'Here no one can hurt us, here we are safe. Here we sit and wait till we know more. Our eyes are everywhere. The motherfuckers cannot hide forever. Just stay here and don't go out and don't do anything stupid.'

In this moment, Jai realizes that while both their heads are shaven it is Jai and Jai alone who truly mourns Jaggi. He is disappointed in Om and even in his father—they have become rats in their fear. They are hiding like rats and making plans like rats but he, Jai, is no rat, he is a fucking tiger and knowing these two things he also knows that he is no longer scared of them.

SUDIPTO

Today is the first day of school after the monster died a week ago. Today Sudipto did not have to sneak an extra pair of uniform shorts into his schoolbag. He feels his smile will tear apart his face.

He gets out of the car and waves goodbye to his mother, who remains in the backseat. She nods, her eyes still red after her night of tears. She has never dropped him to school before. This, the car and her riding with him, is the only way she will even let him out of the house.

As he climbs the steps into the main building, he sees the picture of Jaggi, the one from the school funeral the week before. It rests on a giant wooden frame—garlanded by pink and white flowers, and in front of it on the reception floor stands a giant brass lamp. The tip of the lamp is at level with Sudipto's eyes and four perfect drops of flame stand at attention, equidistant along its top edge. The flames don't move, as if they are made of glass, like they too are a picture, cold, never-real, like the boy framed behind them.

As he turns right towards the stairs that lead to the junior secondary section, he glances back—the car, with his mother inside, is still there.

•••

Sudipto knows Ma is scared. He understands that because he too has been afraid. He wishes he could sit her down and tell her that he gets it, that he understands the contours of fear, the paralysing, energy-sucking nature of it, but he lacks the words to explain. He wants to tell her that now is a time of victory, of celebration and of freedom.

Instead he had settled for, 'There is nothing to be afraid of, not now. He is dead.'

This was last night, when she was sobbing quiet tears holding his schoolbag in his room, while Papa had his drink at the dining table. He had meant them as words of comfort but she got angry, her wet eyes turned sharp, and she pinched him on his upper arm, hard, 'Don't ever repeat these words again …'

Later, in bed, the pinch still smarting, he could hear his parents fight. They were not loud, but angry voices had a way of carrying across dark empty corridors. They had fought every night this week. About him, about school, about continuing their life in Rannwara.

'This was the same boy who was bullying Dimpoo. Huh, Debo … the same boy! And he is dead now and they're saying it is a "mafia" thing? Are you fucking kidding me! I have to leave, Debo, I have to absolutely leave this place with my son. Children are being shot in the fucking fields—'

'The children are safe, Rina. It was a political thing … and we will have the cars dropping him and picking him up …'

And then, 'They use the same route, you know. The same fucking route to come back sometimes, him and that friend of his. The same route where they killed him, Debo. Please … why can't you see?'

Sudipto was not used to seeing them like this, disagreeing, angry, irritable, like opposing poles of a magnet being forced together. Before this week, his parents had been a unified whole. This, their recent separateness from each other, felt like a precursor to their eventual separateness from him.

•••

Arvind comes late so they do not get to talk much before class begins. Ray Sir again, this time with science. The science teacher Chandra Ma'am is off, and Ray is the substitute. She is the class teacher as well, so Ray takes the attendance and then sits on his chair in silence looking for words.

'What happened was very sad, but we have exams coming up in a few weeks. So, let us get started,' is all he says on the matter, and it is a bit of a relief.

Later, between classes, they finally talk. 'We should be happy, I know I am,' and Arvind nods and says yes, yes he is happy, but he looks distracted, like he is thinking of things that are elsewhere.

'My maid told me they cut off his head,' he says undeterred.

'Oh …' and then, 'Why would they do that?'

'I don't know. They found the head on the other side of the highway.'

'Oh.'

'Yes, I mean my father went to the funeral and I asked him if the head was attached and he told me he could see the stitches.' Sudipto lies, 'You see, they cannot burn you without a head. So, they must have had to put it back …'

'Your dad went to the funeral?'

'Yeah. They reattached my friend's finger after he cut it off in an accident, they put it on ice and then they stitched it back.'

'I do not think we should talk about it.'

'What?'

'Jaggi. And him dying.' Arvind looks at him. 'I don't think we should talk about him. Someone might hear us … It is not good to hate dead people.'

Sudipto's heart breaks. 'Have you forgotten what he did to us?'

'No. And I never will. He was here and now he is gone. Just remember—it is not good to hate dead people.' He pauses and then says, 'Whatever happens, do not ever tell anyone anything about all that happened between us, the bullying or the fights or anything …'

Sudipto wants to say that the 'all' that is to be un-mentioned makes up most of the 'all' that he has ever shared with his best friend, but does not.

•••

At the end of school they exit the classroom together, but Arvind vanishes before Sudipto can say goodbye.

Outside the main building, inside the school grounds, his father's car waits with his mother inside.

He knows she has been here the whole time.

ARVIND

Arvind leaves the school without saying goodbye to Sudipto. He can almost feel his friend call out to him, but he does not stop. He walks with gritted teeth and resolute steps and does not turn around. He is terrified of questions.

It is once again the back wall and the tree, the same escape route they would use, often, when running away from the enemy. Now the enemy is dead. And he uses this route to run away from his only friend.

It is a long walk to the city, but he makes it at a steady pace.

He walks to an alcohol shop. It is called Janta Wine and Beer. It is empty when he walks over to the counter, with carefully counted cash in hand. The man has light eyes and is eating greasy samosas wrapped in newspaper.

He asks for two quarters of whisky, Royal Crown.

'You are here again,' the man says.

He shrugs and lies, 'It is for my father.'

'Tell your father to come here himself.'

'He is drinking at home,' he responds. 'If I don't get this, he will beat me.' He calmly raises his uniform shirt to show the still purpled bruises along the front of his body.

The man nods. His face is expressionless. He hands him the alcohol in a paper bag. 'Don't drink it yourself.' He shakes his head and the man believes him.

As he is walking away, the man calls him back and gives him a samosa.

•••

Next, Arvind heads to a medical shop.

There he buys gauze and fresh cotton and antiseptic fluid. He also buys four strips of strong painkillers. There is no prescription from a doctor, just names scrawled on a torn piece of paper.

He says the medicines are for his mother. She has a lung infection and cannot breathe. The old compounder nods. If he sees the alcohol bottles in the black bag in his hands, he does not mention it.

Arvind takes the medication and heads out again. Carefully he packs the liquor and the medicines into his schoolbag after checking that he is not under surveillance. Then, like every day this week, he once again makes his way across the tracks.

•••

He reaches the fence and the hole is there, waiting for him.

He is back in the old Imperial Factory compound. It looks deserted but he still keeps an eye out for men and errant dogs and does not find anything. It is just rubble under his feet and the discomforting, jagged wall of sound that hits from the smelting plants next door.

He heads straight towards the old sheds, giant structures of stone and rust, the metal vibrating softly as he gets closer. They have been abandoned, stripped away, left to wither.

As he walks, he picks up two stones. He throws one onto the rotted corrugated roof of one of the larger sheds. It is a good throw—the stone hitting metal and making a sound clearly audible over the din. He counts to five and throws the next one against the same roof.

This is the signal.

And now, having given warning, Arvind turns and ensures there are no pursuers and no witnesses before entering shed number three of five.

It is a giant shop floor—a metre-thick slab of concrete under his feet, stretching for a vast open expanse—pockmarked with sun where the roof has given way. All of it now covered with soft dust and rotting cable, screws and orphaned gears. Giant brackets of red-brown metal rise twenty feet from the floor, securing nothing. Embedded in the concrete, they are too hard and too heavy to be scavenged, stabbing out around him like the rib bones of ancient monsters.

Leaning against one of these giant brackets, wounded and broken, with patches of dried blood on the dirty shirt draped around his shoulder, eyes bright with all the light in the world and smiling a toothy smile is his teacher, his mentor, his hero—the divine provider of the Gun, Amar Singh himself.

Interlude
HARVEST

AMAR

The Gun spoke clear, the Gun spoke loud.

The dead boy fell in pieces, legs going limp, landing on his knees even as his spine folded into itself. It was a good shot. Lucky. A one-shot kill shot. He had seen enough dead men to know that it was done—bodies did not fall like that unless the entire nervous system had short-circuited.

Amar was frozen in place, stunned by the tableau that was playing out.

He had followed the now-dead boy from the school, recognizing him as he rode out like a man on a mission. He had let the boy take a long lead, then tailed the scooter easily past the bypass and across the tracks and had felt his patience paying off as they entered more deserted surroundings … This would be the moment to strike.

He could feel the pull of the Gun like a chain nailed into his heart.

Then things got more complicated. His target vanished into the trees. He followed quickly on foot and found the scooter but no boy. The skies grew darker, the heavens mirroring his spirit. Amar dove in further, hearing something, and then he could see the boy again, but he was no longer alone.

He kept his distance, watching as the boys crashed through the foliage, his breath catching, unsure of what evil he may be forced to witness. Grappling with the moral responsibility of intervention, and the weight of inaction.

He should save the young one—he knew this but he did not move. It was as if his body knew that this was not the final act of the play, there were lines yet to come.

That was when the kicking began, and he had seen such kicking before and it never ended well, and he got ready to act, peeling out his handkerchief and wrapping it around his face, but still he waited for some unnamed line to be crossed, the taveez of God burning hot against his skin as if to say no, no, not yet, even as his own muscles cramped with each blow that the small one swallowed, feeling it all in his ribs that held long memories.

The fighting stopped, and the two boys exchanged words. He was too far to make them out and he began to move closer, a ghost, feet finding spots with no sticks and no stones. The big ugly one, the one with the scar, the target, took out a knife from his back pocket even as the young one crawled on the ground and reached the bag and there was a perfect glint of perfect metal and the world stopped.

BOOM.

The fucking sky exploded and the dead boy fell.

The small boy on his knees wailed into the gaping sky, and it was a mid-pitched keening sound, throaty and scraped—a scream that rent Amar's insides.

Eventually, the wails faded but the boy stayed there, unmoving.

Amar moved on instinct, fast and sure, limbs cutting through the now falling rain, grabbed the boy, lifting him clean off the ground, and vanished into the trees.

•••

The eyes stared back with a depth of void that shook him. The Gun stayed in the boy's hand, and now four days after losing it, after combing the entire city in his search, after yearning and drinking and yearning, Amar could not reach out to touch it.

'Take it back,' the boy said, 'and don't kill me.'

The Hindi was tilting and heavily accented, comic even. 'I know it is yours. I am sorry I stole it. I needed it for something, and now it is done. You can take it back now.'

The boy had no fight left in him, he extended his hand, and the Gun, held in loose fingers, began to slip out. Amar's hands grabbed his, overlapping his child fingers, feeling the vital heat of the weapon within his grip.

Amar didn't take it. He held the boy even as he screamed at him, his voice loud and high, calling him names, fool, sisterfucker, motherfucker, idiot.

Amar told him it was not a toy.

'I know it is not a toy,' the boy said, 'it is God.'

•••

There is no will and there is only fate and men dance on strings they cannot see. It takes a wise man to sense the direction of this pull and not resist it; a stupid man fights.

He had been a stupid man, blind in his interpretation of destiny and he had pulled and pushed and fought against his thread with everything in him, but no more.

Amar asked the boy to hide. The Gun was still in his hand. Amar did not take it back. He knew that it was no longer his to take. It no longer belonged to him.

The shot was loud, there was a chance a passerby had heard it.

He went back and searched and searched and found and picked up the expended shell from the quarry floor. It was the work of many moments. He scanned for tracks that had survived in the mud and removed them, fouling every footprint leading in and going out, taking care to not leave his own as he worked, patiently, taking minutes, his ears tensing for the merest sound carrying over the thick deluge of water as he erased all the perceived signs of what had happened here.

Finally, he took the knife from the dead boy's hands. It was perfectly sized and sharp. Today, Amar had lost a weapon, and destiny had given him another one.

The boy was where he had left him, drenched and tiny, hunched over the Gun cradled against his belly, protecting it from the water that fell incessantly. Amar led him out of the trees, watching with approval as he wrapped the Gun in clear plastic to protect it before putting it back in his bag.

Moments later, on Amar's stolen motorcycle, they rode out in the pouring rain with the boy stuck to Amar's back, his tiny hands clutching the sides of his shirt in desperate fists. That was the only way he knew to ride.

Outside his colony they said goodbye.

Amar told him that he has been chosen.

That the Gun is his now and he must take care of it.

That he must be careful and not be afraid.

That he must never say anything, even if he is questioned directly.

That he will need instruction and training in the use of the Gun.

That he, Amar, will meet the boy in two days and they will begin.

•••

Amar watched the boy limp away into the darkness and thought about his options.

A kilometre behind him was a by-pass that would put him on the Ahmedabad highway. He had a motorcycle, he could ride till dawn and that would be that.

But here, here an inferno was building. In this town, this killing would be like a bomb going off among pigeons. The dead boy would be found. And from there would begin a hunt with the bloodlust of mad dogs, a wave that would crush everyone caught in the way.

He knew the dead boy's family, he had got a measure of the father, seen the house and the cop cars, and it had been enough to give him pause. He had decided to not act in haste. To wait and watch. To do it without spilling blood if he could.

It was too late for that now.

There would be a fallout from the actions of this night—big, hard consequences like giant flagstones falling from the sky. They would fall on this boy. A child, weak and untrained, but chosen, already anointed in the blood of his enemy. Like him. Just like him when he was chosen, himself a boy only a little older than this one.

He had been living in a fog since the day Ramanna died, when the Gun-God first forsook him with a misfiring *click*. He lived in dreaded anticipation of the fate already written, a fate he knew was coming for him. Then the Gun had left him, and he had chased it, his luck and life … Now it had been found again, but it was no longer his, and just like that all doubt flaked away and his purpose was revealed, crystal clear.

The child was weak and untrained, soft. Unworthy of Grace. Unless Amar Singh did something about it.

AMAR

Killing a man was easy. Killing a man without his friends finding out—that was damned hard, and to do this again and again in quick succession was nearly impossible.

He would take his time.

He was back at Hotel Jaipur, and inside, waiting for him, were Bilal's men. He knew this because he could see the dim light through the cracks in the closed shutters of the rooms on the same floor where his own room was pitch dark. There were probably many of them, distributed across the floors, coiled to strike. In his mind, he saw the hanging board at the reception, with all the keys that were missing. The rooms stood highlighted on the map in his mind—clustered around his own.

There was excitement. He could smell their confidence from here as he sat unseen, a creature of murder in the darkness. They thought they were waiting for some shooter from a big city. They thought their numbers and their positioning and their dubious element of surprise would be enough.

They had no fucking clue.

The skies had opened their guts—and it rained and rained.

Guns.

Always guns.

On him, he had only the Taurus and the CZ75. Simple, sturdy, nineteen bullets between the two of them. Which was both a lot of bullets and not enough bullets. It depended on how hot things went, when they got hot, and how many were left at that moment in time.

He thought of the bag of weapons in his room. He would need them, need them all now that the Gun rode elsewhere. They may have taken them, moved them. But he didn't think of this now. Simple plans. Simple targets.

There were three possible entrances to the hotel. The reception and the back service gate would both be watched. So he decided to enter direct from the first floor. It meant climbing a wall with an old iron railing on the top in the dark. In heartbeats he was on the other side, shimmying up a drain pipe, hanging from the ledge of a first-floor window. He listened for sounds inside the room on the off chance that it was occupied. His shoulder simmered in silent agony but he willed away the pain in less than a breath.

He pushed the locked shutters in, it took strength and he had to do it one-handed. It was loud but the noise was lost in the rain. Outside, the storm continued to build. Inside, there was silence as he climbed through.

He walked across the room like a ghost. It was empty, and the wooden bed did not even have a mattress. The now open windows rattled behind him.

The double door of the room, such as it was, was a weak thing of bad wood. Thin. He could kick it down easily, but it was better to be quiet. He knew this floor was occupied, somewhere in the rooms around him they were waiting.

He went to work on the hinges instead. It was slow patient work in the dark, he worked with the feel of his fingers as they traced the image of the door from his room above. From his wallet he extracted the metal card and the steel wire and tackled the hinges on the left panel. The screws came off first, thick metal, rusted red from another age—he loosened them with the card and then it was not hard to loop the wire around the exposed plate of the hinge and yank them off the soft rotting wood. He swung open the double doors as if they were a single panel behind him. He was in. The hunting ground lay ahead, spread out in a grid …

Sounds in the corridor to his left, towards the main stairs. He went right first, confirming that each room was empty, each door barred and padlocked from the outside. Back near the stairs there were two rooms with lights on. One quiet, the other with sounds—loud conversation, music on a radio. They were having a party in there, the fuckers. He locked the door from the outside, the latch sliding into place with the slightest groan. The revellers had no clue. There was no chain or padlock, but it would slow them down. Buy him a few precious seconds. Then he pushed the door of the second room and it swung open.

Inside, a man was sleeping fitfully, tossing and turning. The room smelled of cigarettes. On the coffee table were some beer bottles, two iron rods and what looked to be a machete. The man had a country pistol hidden under the rolled-up sheets he was using as a pillow—the edge of the cheap metal grip was visible.

Amar slid his new knife out, the one he had taken from the dead boy, and slit the sleeper's throat, one hand clamped over his mouth. He did not wake. A thick river of blood flowed out and his limbs thrashed weakly as if they were underwater. Then he was still.

Amar exited the room, turned off the light and left the door unlocked. The dead boy's knife in his hand still dripped blood over his fingers. As he passed by the other room he slid one of the iron rods through the door handles. Sealing the fuckers in.

Upstairs would be harder.

He climbed the steps on silent feet, body hunched, knife in hand, feeling the pressure of the Taurus at his waist. It was still time for the knife, the time for the gun would come. There would be chaos soon enough. He did not think too much about what he would find and what he would do about it. Trusting his instincts; no elaborate plans, not when the dance had started—this was his secret. Plans blinded, and he needed to be flexible.

Halfway up the staircase, he crouched and peered into the shadows. Two men smoking in the corridor. Right outside his room. They conversed in whispers. The corridor was barely lit, a single light bulb working on the far side. That was good.

Cigarettes destroy dark vision. The fuckers should have known that. It took a little time for the eyes to adjust, but it was enough for him to run full tilt into the back of the first guard and sink his knife into his kidneys. Together they fell on the second guard and he collapsed under the impact …

The knife was pulled free fast—it was sharp and double-edged. Amar thanked the dead boy as he pushed the men down and then stab stab stab stab … quick motions at what he thought was head height, and the second guy at the bottom, crushed below his dying friend, screamed as the knife slipped into his eye.

It had become loud now and doors swung open behind him, but Amar had already turned and was facing them on one knee, the Taurus in hand. Four shots clustered at chest height. At the door that opened first. The gun kicked like a cannon in his hand—giant .45 ACP bullets tore into the first movers. He knew it was important to kill the first ones, show the others the cost of bravery. All movement ceased. He followed up with two shots at the bulb, and it was the second bullet that took it out. Now the corridor was pitch-black.

The men by his feet moved but not convincingly. The knife was still buried inside one of them, it did not matter which one. It was dark and there was the bitter smell of cordite but his blood was singing, and singing loud. He dropped the empty revolver at his feet and drew the CZ75 with the other hand as he moved to the door of his room. Less than twenty seconds had passed since the first barrage of gunfire. There had been no returning shots.

The men in the other rooms were scared: it was dark in the corridor and they could not see anything and there was gunfire and their friends were dead. They were scared and so they were slow.

His room was still locked—just as he had left it. He kicked the door—the gun held one-handed and pointed down the corridor. He kicked again. It started to give way.

Someone fired from down the corridor, once, twice, three times. The bullets bounced off the walls around him. He shot back. Another cluster of four bullets. Double-handed this time, tight. Into the gaps and then through the doors. The CZ75 was loaded with 9mm FMJ bullets designed for high penetration—they pierced wood like butter. There were shouts and grunts. Some of the bullets had found a home.

He turned and kicked the doors again.

The men now stuck their hands out and peppered the corridor, shooting blind. Fireworks in a tin can. Just as ricochets filled the confined space, the door finally broke apart and Amar tumbled in. He picked himself off the floor and began to count. One. Two. Three … And as he counted, he thought.

In a firefight, once bullets began to fly, the only thing he could do was play the odds. Shoot where he thought they were. And not be where they shot. The rest was the play of God. As a lone shooter it was in his interest to always increase the chaos. To keep them unsettled. He had eleven bullets left in the magazine. Crouched at the edge of the door, he listened for sounds of movement over the moans and death cries as they tried to organize and build their courage to charge him. On the floor below this, they were finally awake—and struggling with the sealed door, trying to kick it down. So far the rod was holding. Kicks and more shouting. Someone down the corridor screamed for a torch.

The count hit ten. Lying sideways on the floor, bracing his shoulders against the door frame, he popped out. There were three of them in the corridor now, outlined in the light spilling from their bright rooms, blind as bats, guns in hand. Amateurs. He fired. Three bursts, three bullets each, head and neck height. Their response hit the ceiling as they fell, dead before they hit the ground.

He rolled back in.

The guns were where he had left them, in the bag, untouched. They were confident and it was this confidence that made them weak. He dropped the CZ75, picked up the big Taurus and fit it into the waistband of his trousers, and pulled out the Mac-10 with its double clip extended magazine. He smiled as his blood sang louder and he knew the gods were singing with him. It was a quick motion to fold open the stock and switch off the safety.

A crash below—it was the doors. They were quiet, no shouts and no screaming of instructions. They were circumspect. He had killed at least six of them, maybe eight. They too were learning as this went on. They finally turned off the lights in their rooms—darkness, they had realized, was their friend too.

They shuffled outside.

Deep inside the room, stock braced against the uninjured shoulder, gun trained at the open door, he waited, counting once again. He hit ten and threw the switch. The bulb lit up just as they burst through, eyes mad, charging with rods and hockey sticks. He shot them in the face with focused semi-auto fire from the Mac-10. And they went down and ones behind them went down and it was just a cloud of blood as he pounded bullets, three at a time at the doorway, counting a single count between trigger presses. At this point he could not hear very well at all—the Mac-10 was a short weapon that sang loudly. It was when he felt a sudden pulling sensation in his arm that he realized he had been shot but it did not matter for the fight was here and the hot metal was screaming through the air, crashing into walls and floors and pieces of furniture all around him …

This was madness and this was life and things slowed down and thoughts slowed down and it was all fucking habit and he trusted it and fell into it.

He ducked behind the narrow bed. There was no way to aim anymore so he switched to full-auto and sent a blind spray towards the door till the gun was empty and then it was a quick flip of the switch as he released the extended magazine, flipped it, and pushed it in—*click*, loud and perfect, telling him everything would be all right.

There was no movement and no more shots. Just some groans but no footfalls and no steps. Everything near the door was dead or playing dead.

He stood up, gun sight stuck to the empty doorway. Blood and sweat. Sweat and blood. A bright naked bulb in a room shot to shreds. There were no colours and no shapes, only targets. His ears rang and the only sound he heard was his fucking heartbeat. Going off like a drum. His arms felt weak—the Mac-10 was thick and heavy, a brick of metal in his hands.

Abruptly, he felt a blow to the back of his head and again on the side. He spun around and saw him, a boy with eyes like black diamonds hanging from the now open window behind him, shooting a revolver in one hand.

It was the one-handed shooting that saved him. The boy was young. The gun was not his, obviously a weapon scavenged from the dead, probably minutes ago. He must have found a route around the killzone, sneaked out of the rooms and hopped parapets to get the drop on him. But his nerves made him shoot too soon, and the single-hand grip on the fat revolver made the recoil unmanageable—ensuring that all but the first bullet missed. The boy was still shooting at the ceiling somewhere above Amar Singh who opened up with the full-auto Mac-10 and emptied all thirty bullets of the magazine into the little bastard before he disappeared in a shower of blood and wood and torn flesh.

The barrel of the Mac-10 was molten red. He tossed it on the bed, drawing the Taurus, cocking the hammer. It was habit.

There was nothing from the corridor, but he stood with it in his hand and started a count in his head.

One. Two. Two. Fuck it. They were all dead.

The song had begun to fade. Adrenaline pounds through his body even as his vision wavers. Spots around the edges of things. He had been shot. Fuck. His teeth hurt. There was a trickle of blood in his left eye.

Swear to Hanuman, none of these sisterfuckers can come close to you.

Amar Singh felt the monkey god's hand at his own back.

You're fucking lightning. Nothing can touch you. Nothing.

He moved.

The empty Mac-10 and the CZ75 went into the bag. It had the weight of worlds, but he lifted it. He wanted to swing the strap over his shoulder but with the blood still pumping hard in his head, his brain could not seem to figure out the motion.

He clasped the revolver in a single-handed grip, right arm extended, and walked in a tight shuffle—always keeping the right leg ahead to balance the shooting of the gun. He scanned the world through the sight. This was not something he consciously thought about at all.

The corridor was an abattoir. Blood pouring out of sacks of flesh that were once men. Stark shadows in hell light. There were at least ten bodies here. Most at the door itself. So considerate of them to line themselves up.

Some had tried to crawl away and had died on the staircase—leaving trails behind like snails out of the rain. Some still moved a little. He did not bother finishing them.

He was at the top of the stairs when the giant hit him.

It was like being hit by a truck. He flew through the air, and the impact with the stone of the landing destroyed every soft tissue inside him. The gun was lost instantly, vanishing from fingers like it was never there.

The bastard landed on his back and his weight was immense and as his massive fists pummelled into the back of Amar's head, he remembered crossing paths with the giant on that same stairway. He knew he should have fucking shot him then, the fucker. He knew it and he did not and now he was going to die.

Amar turtled and the giant punched his sides and his arms—crushing bone. Amar could not kick out. Or turn himself under the onslaught. Kicks landing like blows from cricket bats. Things were breaking inside. He would die here. He was sure. He tried to scramble away. A kick lifted Amar off the ground. And then hands the size of frying pans grabbed him and threw him, and he was flying through the air again, now to the floor below. He should have died, but a body broke his fall. Soft, squelchy and wet. And somehow, with the last shred of his life, Amar crawled.

It was pure instinct. Down, all he knew was that escape was down. He could feel the vibrations of the fucking giant descending the stairs. Amar tried to move faster but his body was no longer listening … limbs entangled with the dead man under him.

The giant grabbed his ankle and pulled.

Instinctively, Amar clutched at the dead man. Fingers clawed through his wet shirt, slipped over his arms, and then somehow Amar caught hold of the knife buried in his face. It slid out, smooth and sharp—it was the dead boy's knife. Stab slash stab even as he got punched in his face, in his shoulder … there was no blocking the giant, he could only attack, and he stabbed again, and it was in the ankle and a giant weight fell on him and Amar kept stabbing and stabbing and the blows kept on coming, relentless …

VI

HEIR APPARENT

SRILEKHA

When the police come home, Srilekha is in her room grappling with thermodynamics.

It has been forty-five minutes since she opened the workbook, and in this time all she has been able to do is scribble figures along the margins of pages and they, the figures, swim in and out of her head, and she knows that last week, just last week, this used to be easy.

The bell rings, her attention drifts as Appa opens the door. It is the police.

Distracted already, and hearing strange voices, she peeks out of her room to see two officers, both in uniform, skins shining dark brown, with thick black moustaches. The younger of them is wiry thin, and the other is thick, built like a cabinet. To her they look like movie villains. Appa talks to them in broken Hindi and they smile and come in and sit down in the living room. He waves her away as he sits, calling to Amma to serve tea.

Srilekha goes back to her desk but her curiosity is murdering her and she tries to listen in but it does not matter because soon it is Appa, his skin paling, at the entrance to her room. 'They want to talk to you.'

The senior cop, the bulky one, whose name she forgets immediately on hearing it, tells her not to worry, that 'this is just routine questioning'.

Dull terror begins to throb in her stomach as he starts speaking and his words in Hindi hit her ears and then get jumbled up like building blocks in her head. It takes her a while to decipher them, and the whole time she is slow she worries about the meanings he will derive from her slowness.

All his queries are about Jaggi, he tells her, and that hateful last day. 'We are talking to all the classmates,' he says, addressing Appa, 'it is such a high-profile case, after all.'

She tells them what she remembers of her day, the school and the classes. Yes, Jaggi was in her class. No, they did not interact. No, she does not know if he was present in the last period. Yes, he sometimes left early. No, she does not know when that was.

The last entire part is an absolute lie as Srilekha can even now see how his shirt stuck to the straightness of his back as he slipped out of class following the history teacher. It was the last time she saw him. But she lies as she is scared her words will betray her feelings.

She thinks they believe her.

He leans in with difficulty, his thick stomach seems like a stone slab, not bending under his chest, 'Did you speak to him that day? Or to any of his friends?'

'No. I never spoke to him or to any of his friends.'

'Not even for homework or for an exam?'

'No, never. For nothing at all.'

He nods and then he tells her and her father, and her mother who is listening from the kitchen door, that last time he was seen alive, he, Jaggi, was looking for her and asking for her house address before he drove off from school.

She is stunned. Panicked. How did he know she existed?

It is Appa who speaks. 'I do not understand this—what do you mean he was asking for her? She just said that she didn't know him, never spoke to him … How can you say these things sitting in my house!' He is agitated and has slipped into English for the last part before controlling himself.

'That is the report from the other kids. Classmates. He asked where she stayed, and then he borrowed a scooter to come here.'

'What are you trying to say?'

'Please sir, do not make me raise my voice in your house. Let your daughter answer.'

Appa is red. Amma is a statue at the kitchen door, too scared to even breathe. The big cop looks suddenly bigger in the cane chair.

'Do you know where he was found? Huh? He was found on the backroad of your colony. The scooter was also found there. He was coming here when he was caught and killed.'

'I don't know anything about this … I don't know …'

'Do you know the boys—Saaransh and Swapnil?' The thin one smiles and his voice is soft.

'No, I don't know Saaransh, he is not in our section. Swapnil, yes, I know him. He and I are in the same group for physics practicals … But we are not friends. We don't really talk …'

'Where were you that afternoon?'

She tells them that she was home, having taken the bus at the end of the day. But as she says it, she realizes how thin it sounds, like the thing a murderer would say.

'And after that …'

'I was home studying.'

'Anyone with you?'

'No, not really, Amma, my mother, she was out shopping and she came back by 4 p.m.'

He nods like he understands, smiles at his partner and then, 'It is clear that Jagdish Ranade was coming to see you. Was on his way here when he was killed … Why would that be?'

She thinks it had something to do with Arvind. He had come home later than usual that day—a full hour after her, she remembers now, and he was hurt, scratched and bruised, uniform torn from some fight he had been caught in. She had not paid any attention, as it happened sometimes …

The shock of Jaggi's death seems to have burned this out of her, for she never made a connection, that maybe Arvind had seen Jaggi or had a run-in with him the day he was killed, and maybe Arvind had fled and Jaggi decided to chase him down to beat him again, and it is a chilling thought—but in this moment as the policemen stare at her, she is determined to remain silent.

'I cannot say, I have not spoken to him at all … You can ask anyone in class …'

'Beta,' the evil one says, smiling with little teeth, 'beta, it is better if you tell us everything now. Don't worry—nothing will be a problem. If you tell us now this matter will end here. Otherwise, we might have to call you to the station—'

'What?'

'It's okay. It says here you have a brother …'

'Yes, Arvind. He is not home right now.'

'Where is he?'

'He is at Mr Chatterjee's house. He is friends with their boy, they spend a lot of—'

'Ah yes, Sudipto. We know of this. The boys had some trouble, na? Between them … some scraps some fights … Do you know of this?'

'Arvind never told me anything.' It is a dead whisper. 'I know he was having some trouble with the senior boys, but that is just—'

'Boys will be boys, huh?'

'Yeah, I guess—'

'So yes, back to you, did you give him a note in class? How did you tell him you wanted to see him? Did you tell him that your mother was going to be away and the house would be empty?'

'What? No! No!'

'How dare you speak to my daughter like this … She is a good girl from a good family!'

'Mr Srinivasan, be quiet!' He is louder than her father and it takes no effort from him to be louder than a man in his own house. 'You are a decent man, so we are behaving decently. This is a serious case, a very serious case, a murder. And you know who he was? Huh? Do you have any idea? It will take us minutes to throw all of you behind bars and no one, but no one, not in this city or this state, will be able to help you … Do you understand? Please, I beg you, do not fucking interrupt again.'

Appa is silent. His face is red, the blood vessels in his temple are throbbing.

'Not another word from you. I am talking to this idiot daughter of yours.' The officer turns to her once again, 'Did you call him here?'

'No, no, I did not … No, I …'

'Did someone pay you? Huh, did someone ask you to talk to him?'

She is crying now and Amma is crying and Appa sits with his head in his hands, and as the tears flow all she can say is No No No No No No No …

•••

The policemen leave.

Appa hits her, the first time in years, perhaps ever. He slaps her again and again, the whole time shaking like a leaf. Unable to say anything coherent afterwards, he locks himself in his room.

SUDIPTO

It is the evening of the next day when the police come to meet Papa. A large fair man, who looks senior, and a stout dark man with a policeman moustache. Papa was tense in the hour before they came in, fussing over the tissues and the coldness of the mosambi juice and checking if the good coconut biscuits are the ones being served. Sudipto has never seen him do this before.

He is not there for the conversation but the past week has made him an expert in listening in from his room—and it is polite and light-hearted, and they laugh and they talk and Papa tells them about his visit to Jaggi's family, constantly underlining the fact that while yes, there had been some fisticuffs and bullying between the boys, it never got to a genuinely vengeful point.

'It is a new city, sir ji,' Papa says in unaccented Hindi, 'it takes time for kids to settle down.'

They laugh and chat about the district and the plant and the plans for a new hospital. They eat the coconut cookies—very nice, why yes, they are imported—and they sip the juice … They talk a little about the investigation—'this is most definitely a mafia hit, sir, you know, some political thing out of Bombay …', after all nothing this dire could have been birthed in Rannwara.

'My wife was worried about the law-and-order situation here ... There was that big gang shooting inside the city also …'

'Yes sir, it was possibly related, we are investigating. But be assured, we have combed the place, it is all secure. This was a big tragedy, but Rannwara is safer than ever. We have the responsibility to the public after all.'

They laugh some more.

Later Sudipto is called from his room to meet them.

Kapoor Uncle, the fat fair one who talks to him, whom he instantly likes, says he can come by the police station at any time if he wants to see walkie talkies or take a ride in a cop car. 'Anytime, beta, anytime you want … we will go get ice cream.'

The men shake hands. 'Sorry to trouble, sir,' he says in English and Papa smiles and then says, 'No problem,' and then 'Come over anytime,' and then 'Keep me updated,' and the policemen nod and leave.

KAPOOR

A large plastic bag sits on the table in the middle of the special investigation office.

The office has been hastily put together in an old guest room, one of the thirty-plus bedrooms in the imaginatively named Police House, the colonial-era mansion that is Kapoor's official residence as the superintendent of police. Rannwara was more important once than it is now—its chief of police meriting a house like this, a monstrosity of excess that needed twenty servants just to maintain the damn thing.

Those days are clearly past, for both Rannwara and its police chief.

The inexorable decline of the town, and this whole region of the state, is written clear on the walls. Kapoor stares at decades of chipped paint fighting for space with mysterious brownish-green splotches that seem to have emerged from the stone wall itself. They have been cleaned, they told him, the walls washed and rewashed with soap water—but all efforts have only revealed more rot lying in wait. It doesn't stink, or at least he cannot smell it under the thick antiseptic scent of phenyl.

What even was this room? Too large for a bedroom and no bathrooms nearby. Yet it is on the same floor as the giant still-sealed formal drawing room, and the in-use-but-barely sitting room which itself could seat forty on its mildewed sofas. It was a zoo, he thinks, a fucking zoo. They probably tied their horses here and their dogs … maybe even the servants. That is a fucking thought …

It has been four years here, an age and a half. The Virendar Kapoor then had been younger, sharper, working at the state HQ, had still been called Barry, and could still fit into his college jeans when he was called in and told that a stint at a district job would be a good idea. An inquiry was being conducted into one of his old cases and Rannwara had seemed like a prudent retreat. Away from the capital and its department politicking, and people from opposing camps waiting to scalp him. This, he had thought then, will be a safe space.

Rannwara, though, turned out to be this, the entire town—a decaying monument with holes in its walls and no police work, no fucking police work at all, because the whole thing was run by one family, and the Ranades had it pretty well tied up. Kapoor, of course, reading the situation then, did what he was expected to, which was find a place within the flesh of the district set-up, and burrow deep like a worm, content to feed and wait.

It has been four years since he arrived in this fucking hellhole, because of course a government changed and things were shuffled around at the HQ, and everyone back there found it convenient to forget about Barry Kapoor. Stuck here, orphaned, with no friends upstairs and no transfer in sight, Kapoor was certain he would rot here for eternity, and with every breath in Rannwara the ore dust would settle deeper into his lungs—and he could cough and hack and spit till he was raw and it would still be there, sticking to his insides.

This was the deadest of dead ends, with zero hope of deliverance.

Until a boy was shot to death.

The perfect case to rebuild a career, to give the first desperate spark to a phoenix.

Which of course brings him back to the here and now, and to this decrepit room which is the functional HQ for the Ranade murder investigation. Considering the high-profile nature of the case, and his own 24/7 involvement, Kapoor had thought it best to move the investigation in-house, literally. He could have done it at his offices, another ancient sprawling wing within the district infrastructure, but no, this was better. It ensures that the chutiya DM does not keep barging in for status updates at all times, and it allows Kapoor to be the star of the investigation.

The room has a giant ornate table, one he has never seen before, and a mishmash of chairs—all corralled from different parts of the police house, and on the extremely heavy table, in the centre, sits the bag, exerting its very own gravity. Kapoor stares at it. He has been staring at it for fifteen minutes and it has not vanished.

Show me, he says finally, and one of his constables calmly upends the bag, showering its contents on the table. Brass casings fall on old wood, clinking like stolen treasure, they pour out in a steady stream, piling up and rolling off each other everywhere, spinning along the surface of the table and falling over the edges.

They make a perfect *ting* as they hit the stone floor.

The stupid fucking sisterfucking constable is grinning with the empty bag before he catches Kapoor's eye and then he falls to his knees on the floor, scrambling to collect them ... Stupid, stupid fucking sisterfucker ...

Looking to Qureshi, the sub-inspector who was on location, he asks, 'How many?'

'Sir, eighty-five—from different guns. Fifty are of one type only. This.' He holds up a cartridge—a short fat bullet, brass colouring, fatter than the .32s he puts in his revolver. 'They were all in one place, these, all in one room.'

Kapoor does not recognize the spent shell. Qureshi holds it, moves it in his fingers, convincing himself it is real.

'Fifty?'

'More, sir, we feel it was two magazines of thirty each. And others besides …'

Qureshi drones on, takes him through the bullet sizes, calibres and numbers. Unfamiliar bullets, the lot of them, strange, imported. Steel-tipped and hollow-pointed. Like the one dug out from the Ranade boy's throat, now being tested in Bombay.

Kapoor has heard enough and stops him. 'What do you think?' he asks.

Qureshi looks shaken. 'Twenty years, I have never seen anything like it.'

The investigation has a clear agenda, a path it is following.

In this moment, everything Bilal Ansari has ever touched is being torn apart in their search for him. Every member of Bilal's family, every boy who has ever worked for him, every member of their families, they are all on Kapoor's shit list. They have raided every business that has ever done business with him, jailed all known associates and have sealed the town tighter than a priest's bumhole. They have a list of the dead boys, identified through shirts and belt buckles. They know of the boys who are still alive—their brothers and fathers are inside, now, getting their faces slapped off. Kapoor is making no secret of it.

If this pressure does not work, Kapoor will arrest the mothers next. The boys will emerge from the underground, they will come crawling on their knees. These are old methods, vintage police work. Crude and effective. Bilal too will be found eventually.

The constable has now picked up all the bullets from the floor and stuffed them back into the bag. Kapoor feels the weight of the bullets and the stench of the melted bodies comes back to him and he has to swallow again the bitter liquid building in his throat. It haunts him, that smell, and he thinks it always will.

Kapoor stares at the weapons hanging from the shoulders of his men—Royal Enfield .303 rifles, magazine-fed, single-bolt action.

Tough, good accuracy at a great range. Cutting edge of warfare in his grandfather's day. The department also had two shotguns of similar ancestry—double-barrelled, hand-fed. They had lathis and eight rifles. And four service revolvers—one each with his two SIs, one in his leather holster, sitting inside his bedside drawer in a room barely a hundred metres from where he is now, and another, no longer working, in the armoury.

This is all that he has against a trained manslayer armed with machine guns.

There is just one killer, he is sure of it. All this is the work of one man.

They had found a witness, a boy caught in the next district, in Dagarjunu. A history-sheeter, a known associate of Bilal Ansari. He was in lock-up when Kapoor found him, his face a shattered dinner plate.

'Not our doing, sa'ab,' the constable had told him, 'we found him like this.' The boy—Saurab—in his mid-twenties, is blind in one eye. Someone has done a good job on him. He has orbital fractures, and as he weeps, along with his tears, there is an incessant seeping of thin blood out of his very broken nose.

He is eager to talk. Scared shitless. Kapoor barely asks the question and the story tumbles out.

A single shooter, a stranger who had come to make a deal on guns, imported guns, with Bilal. This was the man whom he had tailed as he moved towards the Sainik School, the man who had beaten his face in with a handgun. The same man who had killed Jagdish Ranade.

A man who, if Kapoor is right, slaughtered a dozen more men who were waiting to ambush him. Cut them to ribbons using an advanced arsenal, of a kind Kapoor could not even dream of.

'Isn't this a lot for Bilal to be involved in?' Qureshi asks, and Kapoor recognizes it as a rhetorical question. They both know that there is absolutely no way that Bilal even had the remotest fucking clue about what was going to happen.

'He was always ambitious …' is what Kapoor says, deciding that there is no way Bilal planned this, the killing of the Ranade boy. Even his idiot mind would know that it would surely be traced back to him. And there is no discernible angle, no possible prize worth making blood feud with the Ranades.

'And sometimes you get caught in the wrong side of things.'

'Just so.'

Bilal has dealings with this killer and then learns of his plans. Terrified, he tries to kill the man and erase all links between them—but only succeeds in poking this rabid lion, a rakshasa that promptly slaughters most of his gang in a single gunfight.

A rakshasa that, Kapoor is sure, vanished that very night, and took his reasons with him.

He is glad for it.

If this killer is found, the trail will lead out of Rannwara—go statewide or, worse, all the way to Bombay. Those fuckers over there in the cities, Kapoor knows, do not share the glory.

It is a lot better that this stays local.

It will be easy to get confessions from the boys he has grabbed, now weeping in cells, that the meetings between the killers and Bilal were long and entrenched. This Saurab boy will say anything. Other boys, when captured, can be made to see the same logic. If a later Bombay involvement comes out, so be it. But the local side of the plan should be seen as significant, even primary.

'I don't think we will find the shooter. We should focus on Bilal.'

Qureshi nods in agreement. He has no qualms in this. He has been a cop for some time. He knows better than to let truth get in the way of evidence.

AMAR

Amar wakes in sweat.

He scrabbles about next to him, finding the cool hilt of the CZ75. It takes him a few breaths but there is no one trying to kill him. His heart is hammering inside him, he can feel it over and under the dull drone of fever that still ravages him, unbroken from the night before.

Nightmares. Nightmares after nightmares of burning desert sands and fires, with talking demon heads, with all shades of terror and despair—specifics already turning to vapour, leaving dark hostile spaces inside his mind, not empty, no, these spaces are filled with seeds to birth the next lot of them, venomous and writhing, intent on eating him alive in his madness.

He knows he should be dead, but he is not, and so he will fight. His muscles scream as he tries to turn and finds that he can only move his body in degrees. It takes concentrated effort to let go of the gun he has grabbed in panicked instinct—he has to send separate instructions to each of his fingers, one by one, to get them to relax in turn, and once the gun is on the floor, he fumbles about for the plastic water bottle. It sits outside the periphery of his vision and he has to feel for it blindly, careful to not knock it down out of reach. There. He pulls it in and it sits fat in his hand, red and cream, a schoolboy's water bottle, like a thermos. Next to it, in a small stationery box, are the medicines. This he can see. He opens the box with one hand and grabs for the pills—a mix of antibiotics and painkillers he remembered from a different life. Then too he was shot, and should have died. They worked then, and he hopes they will do the trick now.

It is hard to swallow the pills. Unable to lever himself up to his elbows, he has to settle for turning his neck to the side and swallowing the pills one by one with tiny sips of water. The water inside the canteen is still cold and feels good in his mouth and throat. He has to drink sparingly. It will be a while before the boy returns.

The light streaming in from the high windows on the walls tells him it is well past nine. He would know for sure, but his watch is broken. Much like the rest of him.

He is not dead and is unlikely to die now. There have been moments in the last few days when he has wished for it, but they were fleeting—it is not in him to surrender.

He should have died in the damn hotel.

It would have been easy—he could see death waiting for him like a dark heavy blanket. He could have closed his eyes and exhaled and it would have enveloped him and snuffed him out. But he had crawled instead—crawled out from under the body of that fucking giant, crawled down the floors, knees sliding smooth over stone wet in his own blood, like some kind of snail from hell. Reaching the lobby, he had pulled himself to his feet and stumbled into the gaping night.

Then the bike and then the boy. Somehow, he found the boy, or the boy found him. And now he is here.

Here is a mattress of old sheets, spread out on an abandoned factory floor.

He thinks he is safe here—the boy, Arvind, told him there is a curfew and that the police have gone crazy. Hunting everywhere, racing back and forth in their jeeps, checking everyone who walks in and out.

'They think it is you who killed him.'

Amar had nodded. 'It is better that way.'

'No one comes here, it has been abandoned for years ...' The boy had added with some confidence, 'There is a security guard who walks through sometimes, but he never enters these buildings.' And then, 'No one will find you.'

Yes, Amar thinks, but they will never really stop looking.

•••

First among his problems is his body.

It has two flesh wounds from the bullets—one that passed clean through his left bicep, and another that took part of his ear off and grazed his face. The hole through his bicep hurts, but no longer bleeds as much. He has somehow managed to retain control of the hand, though the strength is greatly reduced. The bullet that took most of his left ear is the one he did not notice.

There is a third bullet that sits deep inside his back, and he can feel it digging into the muscle under his right shoulder blade, tearing against everything. Every time he moves he can feel it, grating inside him, melting all movement into viscous agony. But at least he can breathe, so it is not inside a lung. He thinks this is the one that is making him sick, that is infected and full of fever.

He worries it has gone bad. That it will get worse. It is a terrible way to die. But there is nothing he can do about it, no doctor will take him, not now. He can only swallow the pills and hope.

He continues to audit his inventory of pain, and now, past the headline items of the bullets, he gets to the rest of it.

His leg is broken—close to the ankle; one shoulder—the one with the bullet from a week ago—was dislocated in the fight, and he had popped it back in before he got on his bike that night, and it is still a little loose; and he is carrying a bunch of cracked and bruised ribs from his encounter with the big fucker, the giant. His own face, from what he can touch and feel, is a mass of hurt and swelling.

He has vision in both eyes now, though for the first three days he could not see out of the right one. Even now the world that he does see when he closes the left is hazy and off-kilter, like something has fucked with the wiring in his brain, and all the connections are loose.

In short: there is a bullet in his back that could kill him, he cannot walk, let alone run—till he gets his leg looked at—and both arms are compromised. He can still hold a gun and point it, but he is not sure if he will be able to shoot.

Amar Singh's legendary luck seems to have run out. This is the second time this month he has been shot. Untouched, since the first job, for years and years and now this. He thinks about this a lot, and thinks about the Gun.

The Gun and the boy and the boy and the Gun. It has led him to this, his Gun-God laid a thread of destiny that he has followed without blinking, without consideration. There has been chaos and revelation, and now within that lattice is a single flame of clarity—the boy, Arvind. He must protect him, for that is his mission. It is the only reason he still lives. He is sure of it. He is not blind to the miracle of his life. The bullet inside him could have taken a lung. The bullet through his ear could so easily have been through his brain. He could have lost himself to nightmares and fever but no, his work is not done. The Gun has chosen the boy, and it falls to him, Amar, to train him, break him and build him, put strength in his stride and stuff guile in his heart.

Do to the boy what was once done to him.

Wendell. That fat bastard who had found him after the first job, after the doctors and the cutting and the stitching, before he could walk. Wendell was in front of him, smiling, calling him a cunt.

'You are a cunt,' he had said. 'A two-paisa cutthroat who got lucky. And it is my bad karma that I have to make a real shooter out of you now.'

One-armed, one-legged, even then he had answered, 'I have killed five men'—the words dripping with pride. For was he not the lone survivor? The hero? The boy who killed Trilok Kamani? Gunned down his best boys with him …

'It was a fluke. You shot a little faster and a little straighter this time. But that is not how you kill a man.'

Wendell was right, Amar had been extremely fortunate. He can see it now. And as much as he had hated him then, Wendell was right about many things regarding the killing of men. 'You have to eat his mind, fucker, you have to eat his mind. Once you have eaten his mind, you will 100 per cent be eating his liver.'

Wendell. Ramanna. Boss. He is not going to see them. Not for a long time. Maybe not ever. Bilal. That snake fucker. He has fucked it all up. Boss, he needs to talk to Boss. Warn him …

He fades, Amar Singh, into trembling sleep in the day, into a sweating fever. These fevers are cold and these fevers are hot and his body shakes uncontrollably and at some point the dogs come back and they are howling outside the shed, and he joins them in his shredded voice, screaming into nothing till they leave, and then he falls into dreams of endless deserts that surround him and in those wastes, under the full moon, marches an army, with their horses and their camels and their heavy armours of fat brass, and they have trekked a long time and the animals fall and turn into sand and these men fall to their knees in prayer with their weapons held straight up overhead, even as their legs sink into the dunes, and then the rest of their bodies, and it is just the eyes left staring from beneath a soft layer of sand, and the guns—ancient muskets of wood and stone held in skeletal hands—presented to the unforgiving skies … And it is here, hiding in a giant hut, wearing a black robe and a helmet with peacock feathers, that Bilal sits, and he is sipping tea and tells him, 'The secret is in the guns …'

WENDELL

Wendell arrives in Rannwara in the same train Amar Singh took ten days ago. He knows this and the irony does not make him feel better.

In his hand, he brings a small suitcase with some clothes. His guns are with the boys who have arrived ahead of him. This precaution was useless as the station is clear. There are no police brigades to welcome him. Whatever security there is seems to be focused on the people getting out, not coming in.

Kamal, the older of the two boys, meets him at a cigarette stall outside the station. He hands Wendell a gun, a well-used 9mm that goes into his waistband. Kamal has a scooter with him, and they head directly to the old city.

•••

The safe house, such as it is, is on the top floor of a decrepit mansion, its best days slipping into ancient memory. Kamal leads him up the side stairs into a large hall filled with discarded furniture. The smell of dust is thick. A young boy meets them there, and indicating to Kamal to wait, ushers Wendell through a door.

It is a small room, probably once a pantry or the like, though now it looks like a mausoleum. It is afternoon and yet almost completely dark. There are no windows here, nor electric light. Bilal stands in a white kurta, his face ringed in darkness. They face each other in flickering lamplight.

Bilal is unhappy to see him.

The feeling is mutual.

'They sent you,' Bilal says. His face is neutral, but he is wringing his hands.

'They did.'

'Will you be able to do it?'

'Yes.' And then, 'You said he was hurt in the fight against your men?'

'He was wounded. He has been shot, and Raju …' Bilal's voice quivers with agitation, 'my man Raju said that he almost had him …' And then with disbelief, 'He should be dead.' The last bit is a screech.

'Do you have any idea where he could be?'

'No. I cannot look for him. I have enough problems of my own. Can you not fucking see that?' he says, waving his hand around him, gesturing to the room—and, outside, the whole city hunting him down.

'You brought this on yourself.'

'No no no, do not do this, do not put this on me. This … what we have here … is not on me. Did you know'—Bilal pauses, having caught the look on Wendell's face, softens his tone—'did you know about this … this hit on the Ranade boy?'

'First, no. There was no hit on the boy. Second, you get no answers from me, and you don't get to question me. That is not how this relationship works.'

'But—'

'I could shoot you right here and no one would care. But that is not my decision, and lucky for you, matters have moved past you. I am here to clean it up. Your best chance of surviving this is to do exactly what I say. We finish here quickly, and then we get you out—'

'But, Jaslok—'

'Jaslok bhai and Boss have spoken. Their arrangement does not concern you. All you need to know is that under the current terms of this arrangement you get to live. Do not give anyone any reason to reconsider. Do we understand each other?'

Bilal's eyes close for a moment as he mourns all possible futures. Wendell enjoys how difficult this is for him.

'Yes,' he says finally, 'we understand each other.'

'How many of your boys survive … from that night?'

'Four. They are all here with me. Two will not last the night … The police have grabbed my doctor.'

'I will need to talk to them.'

Bilal has shrunk during the conversation. The tiny embers of defiance have faded. Wendell is looking at an old man.

'I had heard the stories, but …' and then, 'He killed twelve men in fifteen minutes. Is he even human?'

•••

Raju the giant sits with no shirt on. A mountain of flesh folded over itself, each fold thick and unmoving. Waves of menace emanate from his pores. Wendell thinks about the 9mm in his waistband, and of Kamal outside, similarly armed. But these little pistols won't stop this man. If he begins to move, it will take nothing less than the full clip of a Sten gun. And even that may not be enough.

Wendell can see that Raju has been shot and stabbed multiple times. The left side of his torso is one giant wound—the skin mottled and angry red where it peaks through overlapping layers of bandages. Raju has few words—his jaw is wired shut. Amar Singh had ripped half his jaw out.

Raju says that they fought, and Amar stabbed him and managed to get away.

'I broke him,' he says. 'Next time I will rip his head off.' He stares at Wendell with a single wet gleaming eye.

Wendell tries to imagine the battle between them. It is difficult—the scale of the fight almost too big to fit in his brain. A contest unconstrained by human dimensions. It is something legendary, from an ancient time when men fought demons with the heads of beasts. Amar stands tall, a hero from the epics, grappling with this mad bull of a man at stabbing distance. It is insane. How did Amar survive?

Well, he is alive—he has to be, he is too hard to kill—and he is hurt. Wendell does not think he has run. Even if he could get out of this sealed city, there is no way he has left Rannwara without taking Bilal's head.

Wendell knows Amar Singh, has known him for years, from the day he was reborn, baptized in blood. He has tasted Amar's thoughts over many hours over countless weeks. Amar Singh is a creature of habit, and Wendell is confident that he will find him.

Of course, that leaves the question of what to do when he finally faces him.

•••

Things had moved quickly in Bombay with news of the Ranade boy's murder by mafia hitmen blazing through the streets.

It could have been a coincidence … it should have been a coincidence, but even so, Wendell felt his guts twist inside him on hearing the news. Amar and Bilal were both out of reach and when further accounts of the hotel shootout filtered in, there was much tension and many cigarettes were smoked.

And then the first raid began.

The cops were relentless, swarming over them like flies, hitting every office, every bar and every house till it felt like the Boss did not have room to put a foot in.

The pressure was palpable, thick threads of panic, because they did not know their enemy. They had vacated the main office in Marine Lines and were sweating it out at the farmhouse in far-flung Nerul. Invisible walls seemed to be closing in on them from all sides, and that was when Boss had summoned him. He had just received a call from the police, it was Sardesai. Wendell did not have to be told that this meant Jaslok Kamani, and it meant that ghosts dead and buried a decade ago had risen up again to haunt them.

'How did they know?' is all Wendell could think to ask, and Boss waved that question away in favour of immediate concerns.

'I lied to Sardesai,' Boss said. 'I told him Amar did not work for us then, and I don't know who he worked for before us, and we took him in later, maybe a year after.'

The twist in his gut tightened as if folding into itself.

'I told them I didn't know, and I didn't care in those days. Never asked him who he was running with before he came in,' Boss continued while staring at Wendell, the lines sat thick on his white face as he peered through his gold spectacles. 'I have given him up. I had no choice in this, Wendell, we cannot afford this war.'

'Boss, this is wrong, the blood is on all of us … on me.'

'We never thought the boy would succeed. We could not foresee who he would become.'

'You cannot do this. It was years ago. He was a kid, he didn't even know who he was hitting.'

'I understand. But the price must be paid. And it will be a big one. Maybe I can limit this.'

'There has to be another way … He is family—'

'Then we will mourn him like family. You think this is easy for me? He is my fucking kid too, just like you. But he has been unpredictable, Wendell. Emotional. He has been half crazy for fucking years, don't think I don't know, don't think I don't see you lot cover for his shit. He let Raj Shekhar live. He had his gun to the man's forehead—that bhenchod builder is walking around with a muzzle burn mark between his eyes … 'cause fucking Amar Singh's fucking Gun told him not to fucking kill him! Huh, Ramanna died for that? I barely understood that … And now, now the bastard has gone and killed a child.'

'That might not be him—'

'It is him. It is him, dammit. They matched the bullet to the Shekhar shooting, and others. Sardesai knows it too. There is no hiding this. I have spent four hours swearing on all generations of my family, living and dead, that we had nothing to do with it. I don't think they believe me.' Boss closed his eyes.

He looked tired. 'He is dangerous, Wendell. His direct actions have almost killed us all. We can manage Jaslok, somehow. Times were different then, and I am an old man. But this Ranade thing? It has left us no room to manoeuvre. We will not be able to ride this out. None of us, none of our families. You cannot imagine the forces that are pressing against us here. It is a matter of survival.'

'Boss … we can do something, anything …'

'Wendell, I am not asking.' For just that moment he sounded like Boss again, young, full of an old fire. 'Can you do it?'

He could. He was perhaps the only one who could. He would hate it, but he could.

'Yes.'

'His head. They want his head, and they want the Gun. Go fast, before the cops or anyone else gets him. This has to be us.'

ARVIND

Dead Jaggi is everywhere.

Not all the time, but enough that a part of Arvind is always on the lookout. Expecting him to walk in through a wall or to be simply present when Arvind turns his head—sitting on a desk in class, or on Arvind's bed at home when he walks into the bedroom after another forty minutes of a family dinner where no one talks to each other.

Jaggi in death is much like Jaggi in life, he seems to sit with swagger, his legs spread wide apart and some of the old aggression in his shoulders. His face is arranged in an expression of calm hostility, a threat of violence behind a curious look—a look that sees through Arvind—fixed at something very far away. Of course, not all is the same, there is the gaping hole in his throat which leaks thin streaks of blood that vanish underneath the open collar of his school shirt.

Arvind has seen films where the avenging spirits of the victims trouble and torture their murderers. This ghost, however, if that is indeed what he is, doesn't say anything to him or chase him or scream or accuse him or anything—he just is, existing in a fixed place in Arvind's world, and when Arvind looks away and looks back he is not there anymore.

He wonders if he should ask Amar this question when he meets him next, this question about ghosts, but he worries that Amar will look at him like he is a child for believing in such things. Maybe he will think that Arvind is fearful—and that too is not true.

Or maybe it is a secret known to all killers of men, and shared only between them.

•••

'Ghosts?' Amar says the word slowly, as if tasting it in his mouth.

Arvind wonders again if he should have asked, but it had fallen out of him. And now he worries—what if Amar thinks he is a fool or, worse, weak? He wants Amar to see him as brave—a proto-hero, a warrior–prince. 'I am not scared of him,' he adds quickly.

A smile, as if Amar can read his thoughts, and then, 'Sometimes when people die, they leave behind their shadows. And these shadows stick around in our world for a while—that is all. They are powerless here now. They can do nothing but scare you, or worry you. They have no words for you, they cannot touch you or hurt you in any way. So to answer your question: yes, they are real, but they may as well not be.'

'Do you see them?'

'No. But I know people who did, and still do. It happens to some people. You cannot let these shadows decide anything for you. You have to not care or give them any attention. They leave on their own … most of the time.'

'If not?'

'Well, you can always try eating them,' and then he giggles at his private joke but Arvind does not respond because Jaggi's ghost is no laughing matter and Arvind is sure the apparition is here to stay though he does not contradict the older man.

Amar is sitting on his makeshift bed—a pile of sheets and discarded clothes—with his back against a wall, eating an idli out of Arvind's tiffin. And so they sit together—man and boy, the two chosen of the Gun, past and future, killers both.

•••

'I will teach you,' Amar had promised at the end of that maddening afternoon when the heavens raged with electric fury, and Jaggi was just dead, and Amar had taken a trembling, bleeding Arvind back home.

'The Gun is yours now, and I will show you how to use it,' he said at the colony gates, standing tall, a mountain, untouched by the storm bursting around him.

Arvind had then told Amar about the abandoned factory and made a promise to come there, to learn, to get better, to walk the road the fates had drawn for him … And driven by that commitment, as the greater part of Rannwara burned in chaos, Arvind sneaked out of his bedroom window, down the pipes and down empty streets and over the locked gate no. 4, and made it here to find Amar more than half dead …

And he had come every day since, from home, from school, through curfewed streets and brought with him medicines, cigarettes, food and water …

The first days were bad and then quickly turned worse. Three days in, Amar didn't wake up at all, not with sound and not for whisky. He just lay there, contorting in fever, lost in delirium and Arvind sat next to him in silence as Amar writhed and burned, calling out garbled names in waves of screaming hot breath. Arvind waited after sunset, into dinnertime, knowing it would get him into trouble at home. When he could wait no more, he threw the medicines into bottles of whisky, thinking Amar would wake up and need both.

The fourth day his feet were heavy as he walked to their hideout, certain he would enter and find a corpse or something worse somehow—but Amar was still there, still alive, asleep, his thin chest rising and falling in gentle waves, and the whisky bottles were empty.

The worst had passed and on the fifth day Amar was sitting up and hungry and Arvind finally asked the questions he had been waiting to ask. 'Who were they? They said you killed men at a hotel. Twelve of them. Did they try to kill you?'

Amar nodded and didn't say anything else.

'They should not have done that,' Arvind said. It seemed obvious to him, no question or doubt in his mind. It was not a thought that rose from morality, it seemed like a natural rule of the world. They had hunted Amar, attacked him, and were now dead, defeated by a predator far more dangerous than them. They had brought it upon themselves.

'Did you get all of them?'

'No. Not all of them,' he said. 'But I will.'

It was Arvind's turn to nod, and with a heart full of anxiety he asked, 'Can you teach me how to do that?'

And that was the first time Arvind saw Amar laugh, and it did not begin as a laugh, but a smile that widened into a grimace and past it, wider still, till the teeth parted and the sound escaped him with a sharp intake of air. It exploded out of him, and it was a good laugh, not a big one or an extra loud one and it ended in coughs and obvious pain but the mirth once born didn't leave his eyes. The transformation was instant, and when complete it was like the wounded Amar had been discarded like old clothes, and a new one, face shining, sat in his place and began to tell his story.

About the Gun, how he got it years ago when he was little more than a boy, only a little older than Arvind, and how he was a man who used the Gun to make a living. And how the Gun itself had dragged him to Rannwara … and straight to Arvind.

•••

Today, as Arvind packs the tiffin away Amar turns to him. 'Do you have the Gun with you?'

The air becomes still. Arvind nods and reaches into his schoolbag and takes out the weapon wrapped in the layers of thick plastic. He begins to unwrap it.

'You keep it well,' Amar says. 'Keep the barrel pointed away from us—always. Point it only at things that you want to kill. If you don't want to kill something, point it at the ground. Always.'

Arvind nods and does that.

'Hand off the trigger … Give it to me.'

'Do you want it back? You can have it back if you have changed your mind,' but the boy's heart shrinks as the words leave him.

'No, it is yours now. But I want to show you how to hold it properly, how to maintain it. This Gun,' he says, 'this is your life. Tell me—what would have happened if it had not worked when you needed it to? Now let me have a look at it.'

He takes the Gun in his hands and feels it. His hands move smoothly over the surface. A look of great sadness touches his face and then is gone.

'Well,' Amar says, handing it back, 'it is time I start teaching you … but you have to promise me to not talk so damn fast …'

•••

They begin that very day.

On this first afternoon of training, Arvind walks circuits of the factory floor with bricks in his hand. He holds four of them cradled in his hands in front of him and he walks, they are heavy and with each step the rough exterior of the brick peels off more of the skin of his palm but he does not stop and does not even think to question.

Later, nursing burning hands, he watches as Amar sits, lit cigarette in mouth, with the Gun placed in front of him.

'You fired it last when, ten days ago?'

Arvind nods.

Amar disassembles the gun and puts it back together again, his hands moving slowly. If his wounds bother him, there is no outward sign, except the slightest tremor in his fingers. There are no words. No change in breath. Heart hammering, eyes dilated, Arvind watches as the very concept of murder is reduced to a tool, and then a collection of metal pipes and springs, and he takes in every angle of every brushstroke as Amar starts to clean and oil the components till each piece shines like a mirror.

Amar's fingers begin to tremble with the strain, sweat beading his forehead, and sitting close on full attention Arvind can feel the subtle changes in gravity, how the very world seems to bend around them as piece by relentless piece the Gun is reborn.

SRILEKHA

On Monday, the school looms over Srilekha as if the entire building changed dimensions while she was sleeping. This morning she feels shrunken and strangely threatened as she goes through the now suddenly lengthier corridors, corridors that take a lot longer to cross, corridors that are now bursting with other children who stop and stare at her as she walks past, their eyes are daggers wielded openly, and the scrutiny sucks the air out of her lungs.

In the lunch break, some girls approach her, girls she only knows from the roll calls in the morning—Avni B, Avni G and Garima S—who collect their will between them and ask her about Jaggi.

'Were you having an affair?' they ask, and it is in a stage whisper and the world is still and you could hear a pin drop.

'No,' is all she manages.

They nod as one, and they say, 'Yes, we thought so, but something was definitely going on.' They look at her and she has no answer, for what is she to say? No, there was no affair but I wish there was, I love him, I want him and with every one of my breaths, I can feel his rough palms push into my skin? She does not have the words so she just stays there silent and in shock till the girls start laughing and turn and walk away and then it is not just them … it is like a trigger has been pressed and everyone around her is laughing and they are all laughing at her.

In this entire time at school, Srilekha had no friends, and no one to talk to. She had made her peace with that idea. She was unknown, a nobody, just the weird south Indian girl with the unusual name who mispronounced everything and sat in the middle of the class and did her homework on time. It was not a good space, but a comfortable one for her to occupy. She had few expectations of it, the world was agnostic to her existence—and while not benevolent it did not go out of the way to fuck with her. That delicate truce, she now understands, is gone forever.

Later, at home, she finds that she cannot study, cannot concentrate on any of her work and her thoughts of Jaggi have only increased in their intensity, as if fed by the shame of the day gone by.

Fed too by his death, for now all guilt is gone. For dead Jaggi is kinder, dead Jaggi does not hurt her brother, dead Jaggi acknowledges her existence, dead Jaggi actually touches her …

All the truth of him has been stolen by death. All futures for him made equally possible. Who can say that he would not have come to want her? Not be consumed by her in time …

Thoughts of him burn her and chase her around the house, threatening to choke her, so she writes when she should study and all she writes is about him. She writes in half sentences, her pen carving into the paper the heated sagas of her desire, the want and the filth, words after words. She can picture him as he stands inches away from her, always inches away from her, the heat of him letting her melt, the words sketching the contours of his hands and the spaces where they would have met her body … She writes love letters to a dead boy, and it is the only way she can breathe.

She writes when she should be taking prep tests, with the setting sun of the endless summer falling across her back from the tiny bedroom window. She writes into the night, a storm without end, in

English and Tamil and then words of her own invention when known words fail. She has to stretch her fingers into darkness to find words that will do the trick, her mind forming sentences without meaning trapped in mobius loops without end …

ARVIND

It is maths class again and there is chaos, and it is once again Ray Sir but this time it is not about him, and for this Arvind is glad.

The class is receiving their answer sheets for a unit test held before Jaggi's death, and Sudipto Chatterjee, who is roll number 8, has gone to collect his sheet, quickly followed by Akash Chaubey, who is roll number 9, and they are nothing alike. Sudipto—fat, white, like a puff of a cloud. Akash—scrawny and so black that his skin shines like freshly laid coal tar in the blazing sun. So much so, that Akash, though generally liked for his exemplary fast bowling, is still called 'Dambar' with love, which Arvind eventually found out means 'coal tar' in Hindi.

As they collect the sheets, Akash tries to look at Sudipto's marks over his shoulder, but Sudipto shields the paper, and Akash must be suicidal, considering Ray's special connection with Sudipto, but as the boys walk back, he snatches at the paper and Sudipto pushes him and there is the beginning of a genuine scuffle. Ray Sir begins to shout, but the two do not listen and so he throws a piece of chalk that hits Dambar in the face and he immediately goes down, acting like he has been hit in the eye, and all the boys start heckling the teacher, saying things like, you killed him, he is blind, and he is now going to be stuck with one eye, a 'kaana', and chants of 'Kaana Dambar, Dambar kaana' spontaneously take over the class.

Maybe it is the strain of the moment, or the fear of actually having injured a child, but the otherwise sadistic Ray rushes to check on Dambar and then not seeing blood tells him to shut up and sit down, which is all great except he says, 'Dambar, stop your fake crying and sit down.' Oooooooo … the class begins to hoot and Dambar, with a face of perfect innocence, says, 'Sir, why are you calling me Dambar, my name is Akash,' and then Ray Sir gets stuck mid-sentence, looking like he is having a seizure, and the whole class is laughing with half of them still singing 'Dambar kaana, kaana Dambar' as they begin to bang their desks and then someone from the back begins an old Bollywood song about how if you are dark skinned you can still have a heart …

It is a perfect moment and Arvind is laughing at his desk and Sudipto is laughing as he stands next to Dambar who is still acting like he is deeply offended, and their laughter merges with that of the other kids. For the first time Arvind feels that his laugh is included and Sudipto's laugh is included with all the others around them, and Jignesh and Vatsal and Mukund, boys who always looked past them are not looking past them now, and maybe never again.

Through the mirth, Arvind alone can see that in the place of Ankit Pujari, who usually sits in the next row and who has not come to school, sits Jaggi, looking none the worse for wear, making strange faces at the teacher as if trying to remember how to laugh. No sound comes out because he cannot breathe because there is a hole in his neck and the blood falls drip drip drip onto the desk in front of him, and collects in tiny pools around his shoes on the floor.

•••

During recess Sudipto and he trade parts of their lunch. He gets a cheese sandwich in return for two idlis. They are both happy with the exchange, though Arvind does not eat and simply keeps the food away. Later, they walk the grounds and Sudipto asks him where he goes after school, and says he should travel with him in the car to the colony.

'I don't know if you are still scared of the seniors, but they cannot trouble us in the car.'

The seniors have not bothered them in the two weeks since Jaggi's death and Arvind knows that the car should make perfect sense and is trying to think of an excuse when he sees Swapnil on the other side of the playground. The senior boy looks strange without Jaggi and Mahesh with him, like a monkey without limbs. Swapnil keeps staring at the boys as they walk and Arvind tells Sudipto that he will think about it and then, to prevent the conversation from pooling around this discomfort, begins to tell him about the movie he watched some days ago on cable, where the hero can turn invisible, and it turns out that Sudipto had also seen it and that is what they talk about.

•••

Today again there are rounds along the outside of the sheds, except now he is running with a brick in each hand, held by the very tips of his fingers. It is hard. The bricks keep slipping out of his grip, scraping his skin as they go. His fingers have not recovered from the strain of days past, and each individual muscle in his arms is throbbing past exhaustion. But he does not stop. Inside the shed, Amar is eating Sudipto's sandwich. He cannot see him, but Arvind does not cheat, and keeps moving, blinking the sweat away from his eyes, round after round, hour after hour.

It is late afternoon when Amar calls out to him. Once again the Gun, his Gun, sits in front of Amar.

'Do you remember what you saw yesterday?'

'Yes.'

'Show me …'

Arvind dismantles the weapon in front of his teacher's eyes, straining to pull the levers with bruised fingertips. Once done, he puts it back together, mirroring Amar's movements from a day ago. He has made no mistakes.

They do it three times, Arvind growing in confidence.

KAPOOR

On the fateful day of Jagdish Ranade's death, Police Naik Prakash Sonawane had ridden around the market with the boy, Swapnil, on some stupid errands—and then dropped off the car at the Ranade house before heading home. He did not check on the whereabouts of his young charge, and in his limited defence, not one of the guards at the house had said anything to him about Jaggi not coming home.

When the news of Jaggi's death reached him, Sonawane, among the last people to see him alive, the man who was supposed to literally guard his fucking body with his own, realized he was properly fucked. And in the smartest move he ever made he wrote out a signed statement detailing his actions and whereabouts, including alibis, and promptly left town, claiming a dying father. His intention was simple: explain himself while avoiding the first burst of volcanic rage from the Ranade family.

Of course, turns out he was not so smart after all, because the police retrieved him from his father's house, exactly where he had said he would be.

'It would have been better if you had run,' Kapoor tells a panicking Sonawane as they make the drive to the Ranade compound. 'Actually fucking run. We would have found you a month later when things were cooler—we could have transferred you or dealt with you in some other way. Kept you out of their notice somehow.'

He breaks his tirade to finish his cigarette, which he then throws out of the vehicle. 'You have given me a new fucking headache. Have you any thoughts on how I am supposed to keep you alive?'

Sonawane is silent, his head hangs like that of a man trampled by destiny. In this Kapoor does not grudge him, for it is true. But his sympathy is strained, a weak sentiment choked out by endless late nights and casual violence—all because this fucker could not do his job.

'Fall on your face,' he tells Sonawane as they enter the large gates. 'Fall on your face and just don't get up. Cry, weep, wail all you want, but say no words. Give no excuses, tell no stories, say nothing. Absolutely nothing. If they hit you, you let them hit you. If I hit you … When I hit you, let me hit you because I will hit you a lot less than they will.'

Sonawane nods, incapable of speech. His hands are white.

'I will save you, don't worry,' Kapoor tells him with a confidence he does not feel.

•••

Later he slaps Sonawane. Kicks him. Lifts him clean off the ground by his ear, almost tearing it off. The policeman cries and weeps like his life depends on it, which it does. The service belt comes off—held aloft in Kapoor's right hand, a whip of justice, the weapon of truth. It is a melodramatic gesture, but these are melodramatic times.

They are in the Ranade family office, with the big table and the big throne and on it the big man himself, breathing through his giant tanks, but otherwise saying nothing, his eyes are small stones in his granite face, expressionless at the scene playing out in front of them.

In the room also are the sons. Om, the older one, says little with word or gesture. As unreadable as the father—and Kapoor keeps trying to spot a reaction, any response at all, even as he brings the belt down across the constable on the floor, the thick leather biting into his back. As the room reverberates with the sound of impact and Sonawane's high squeals, Kapoor catches a twitch in Om's mouth, in disdain for this obvious charade.

The younger one—once the middle brother, now again the youngest—the hoodlum with bloodthirsty eyes, he wants to join in, his muscles tense at each smack as Kapoor continues his assault. Kapoor can tell, having spent a decade around men of violence, that this one—though maybe the least dangerous of the three Ranade men in the room—burns with bottled rage that will soon explode.

'We asked him a hundred times,' Kapoor says finally, catching his breath, lashes uncounted, splotches of sweat building under his uniform shirt, 'and he sticks to the story. The same story we got from our other witness—that boy, Swapnil Chaube. He took the boy to the main market ...'

'Jaggi sir had told me, he only ordered, sir, you have to believe me ... I would never ...' the words come from the carpet, a high-pitched wail ...

'Shut up, you little cunt.' A kick, sharp, hard into the midsection. Sonawane needs to shut up. Needs to understand that the only chance he has to survive is to keep this as official as possible. An investigation that is complete. A waterproof organizing of the past that has moved beyond the realm of emotion and into the nation of fact. It is important to keep the conversation away from ideas of duty and loyalty and most of all forgiveness. All these just point to their common black shadow of betrayal.

'Well,' Kapoor says with marked viciousness, 'I could hardly doubt him. He is a stupid man, a very stupid man. You were on VIP security and you left your fucking post.' He raises his hand again, the fat brown belt hanging below his elbow.

'Stop it now,' Om says, and if there was a communication between father and son, Kapoor did not spot it. 'Is he telling the truth?' Om is looking straight at him and Kapoor feels fresh sweat break out along his back.

'Yes. Yes, he is. He is too stupid to be a traitor. It was just that … bad luck that he was not there when the attack took place.'

'And if he was present, what do you think would have happened? Do you think Jaggi would be alive?'

'It is impossible to say.' Kapoor realizes he may have overplayed his hand with his performance.

The moment builds. On the floor Sonawane stops breathing.

'No,' Kapoor continues, 'it was planned—the killers, they were professionals. They had guns, automatic guns. He'—Kapoor points to the bloodied constable—'he would not have helped. Not meaningfully.'

'Hmmm. So it was good luck. Wouldn't you say that? That it was in fact really good luck that he is alive now … Kapoor sa'ab, you are a man of the world, what do you think are the reasons for such good luck?'

Kapoor can sense it moving away from him.

'I don't know. But today, this … this was his idea. He is here, and he is filled with shame, and I know he is not praising his luck now.'

'What will you do with him?'

'He will be with us. He is not going anywhere. We will hold him in remand …'

'Okay. Get him out of here … Then come back. We have things to discuss.'

•••

Sonawane cannot stand without help, and crumples to the marble floor outside the office—in pain and relief. Streaks of blood are prominent against his white shirt where the belt cut through fabric and skin. Two other uniformed constables are waiting outside and at a glance they rush to grab him.

'Take him to the station, and radio a car for me.'

They nod and head out, no words, Sonawane held between them. They know they must be fast because moods can turn.

Kapoor closes his eyes to savour victory. He takes a breath, checks the belt for blood and puts it on. Another breath and then it is back into the lion's den where the mood is tenser. There has been an argument while he was out. The boys have changed positions. Om now leans on the father's desk while the younger one, the thug, paces along a wall.

'I thought cops didn't do third degree on other cops …' Jai speaks before the others. It is the first time Kapoor has heard him, and he sounds just how Kapoor thought he would.

'We don't. Not usually. Not good for morale. But this guy …'

'He got off easy. I would have—'

Om interrupts him, 'We know what you would have done. There is nothing to it.' He is firm and then looking at Kapoor, he continues, 'What is the status now? Where is Bilal Ansari? How long do we have to wait for this?'

'He is still in the district, sir, we are sure of it. We are on his trail. He is moving from safe house to safe house and he is running out of options. We will get our hands on him, there is no doubt about it. We caught two of his boys, and they have confirmed that Bilal had some men following Jaggi.'

'Following him? Who was following him?'

'Our investigations show the shooters were from Bombay, and they had meetings with Bilal. They were following Jaggi sir, we know this. Written confessions. Then there was a problem between them—the shooters and Bilal's gang. The shootout at the hotel …'

'Are the shooters still here? In Rannwara?'

'We think so. The town is airtight, sir. Nothing has come in, and nothing has gone out. We have upped your security here, sir, as was requested—and we will keep searching. Our best bet is the Bilal gang. They are breaking. We have arrested the families, even the mothers. The boys will crack, sir. They have nowhere to go … It is just a matter of time.'

'What about the girl?' the young one again.

Kapoor has to swing to face him. 'Huh?'

'You interviewed the kids from the school. Jaggi was going to meet some girl. Who is she?'

'We spoke to her. There is no link—'

'Arre! What do you mean there is no link? Did you question her? Why was he going to see her? He left his car and borrowed a friend's scooter to meet her … You don't think this is a problem? Are you an idiot? Get her into the station and give her two fucking slaps and see what story she has then.'

Kapoor wants to give him two slaps. The things he has to do as a part of his job.

'Have you seen her, sir?'

'What?'

'Have you seen her … this girl? Looked at her?'

'No.'

'If you had, you would not ask me this. She is fat. She is black. She can't even speak properly. Even if your brother *was* chasing girls—I very much doubt he would have anything to do with her.' And, 'We spoke to the whole class. We asked them, each and every student. The girl and he, they didn't talk … they didn't have a relationship at all.'

SRILEKHA

On Tuesday, Srilekha enters her classroom to find the word 'RANDI' scratched out in Hindi on her wooden desk. In that moment it feels like her whole body has shut down. She spends the entire day with her notebooks spread out over the desk so no one finds out.

During history, Neelam Ma'am walks up and down the aisles as she talks.

A voice from the back. It is one of the boys. 'Ma'am, please check Srilekha's desk.' Half the class giggles.

Neelam Ma'am looks down at the utter terror in her eyes, and goes on teaching.

•••

On Wednesday, Avni G comes to her in between classes and says, 'He is dead, it is not right to start rumours about the two of you. Have some shame.' This time Srilekha breaks down and cries fat hot tears in class.

Later she would agree with Avni G, her accusation held logic. After all, who else in their right mind would even imagine anything romantic between Jaggi and her, let alone start a rumour about them …

Her days at school pass in a complete daze, interspersed with moments of sharp derision; time exists like an endless ocean with no cardinal points—it is just time, thick and shapeless, coagulating around her ankles as she walks, choking her vocal chords so she doesn't remember her own voice.

•••

Home is not the refuge it was.

The police seem to have forgotten her completely. There have been no visits and no summons and no calls at all, and it is like the investigators simply threw a stone into her life and walked away, leaving her alone to deal with the ripples that are still upheaving her whole life.

Appa does not talk to her anymore. He does not smile at her, does not ask her questions about her day, quiz her with maths problems, or show her crosswords that he has found difficult to crack.

He looks straight through her the half dozen times their paths intersect in the house. Dinners are the worst of them all—dead affairs of oppressive silence, with no sounds except those of chewing and Amma asking quietly about second helpings.

He does not talk to her and she understands that home for her was never a place but a single relationship. A relationship whose immediate and complete sundering has left her emotionally marooned. Appa's coldness invalidates her existence.

•••

She lives within a window of time, a sliver of hours when she can breathe—after she comes back from school and before he returns from work. Then she rests and eats and showers. Amma tries, in her way. She cooks for her too now, her mother, more so than before when her affection was directed more clearly towards her son. Now Srilekha finds more of the fried rice crackers she enjoys and more korambhs, and avials, and homemade coconut barfis waiting on the dining table when she is back from school.

Srilekha never spoke to her mother, their bond held affection but little understanding, their relationship running along expected courses as they played roles to one another: caring mother to demure dutiful daughter. They have always been like this, in her memory, but surely, Srilekha thinks, surely, we had something more complete when I was a baby. Between then and now there has been a chilling between them—and for Srilekha there is a simple answer.

Her mother resented her relationship, her old relationship, with Appa, who saw in Srilekha a piece of himself, a flower to be nurtured, an intellectual equal. Something he would never see in Amma, and Amma knew it, and it ate at her insides. What could she do then but resent her child—the first born sacrificed to the love of her husband …

It is not very noble of her, Srilekha knows, to think this way, for whatever may be the feelings within her, Amma does everything for her, and more besides. This she can see on the lunch table. They don't talk but Amma cooks her love. Beans poriyal and tamarind rice. Small helpings, single portions enough for just her, meant for just her—a secret dialogue between mother and daughter, an acknowledgement, a gesture of support in the language Amma knows best.

Arvind does not eat lunch at home anymore. He is away all afternoon after school, and during the weekends. He walks in every evening, a precise half hour before Appa returns from office, and is bathed and at his study desk in time for the doorbell …

Arvind goes home with Sudipto now, the GM sends a car for his son to school—he has told them, Amma and her. He spends the afternoon there as the boys study together before he meets other colony boys for cricket or football. She has her doubts about it, and at another time Amma and probably Appa would have got more involved and cracked him open like a walnut but they don't seem to worry about him now, he is no longer the problem child in the family.

Well, someone in this house should be happy. And happy he is—in fact, Arvind is transformed. This is the happiest she has ever seen her little brother. His posture, his voice, his actions seem to have dropped the sulkiness they had within him. He bounces as he walks, each step taking him further across the shiny flooring than it should. The shadows no longer stick to him.

She does not recognize him. Who is this boy? Even before Rannwara and his problems at the school, back in Trichy, surrounded by friends, she does not remember seeing him quite this animated. There was always a lovable sadness about her brother, a deepness with which he would see the world.

Something has changed.

•••

On Wednesday, fifteen days after Jaggi's death, at about six in the evening, she sits by the window, looking out for Arvind.

She is not sure why she does this, but feels she needs to see him when he feels himself unseen, as if in this moment of voyeurism she can discern the locus which now guides him. In time, she sees him walk down the street towards her and there is something about his movement that strikes her as wrong.

She moves out of sight as he comes closer and as she hides she realizes that her brother is approaching their home from the opposite direction of the Senior Officer's Enclave where Sudipto lives.

She puzzles over why he would be lying about his whereabouts—what can he be doing, and how is that activity related to the new Arvind that she is seeing around the house—when it occurs to her that she has not heard the doorbell yet. It is only three flights of stairs up, and even a tired Arvind should have made it up already, and a cloud of suspicion descends on her as she waits and watches the clock on her desk, the one she uses to time her tests, and it has been ten minutes and still there is no Arvind at the front door. Crouched at the tiny bedroom window, she is sure she hears the faintest scraping sounds from the terrace above, and multiple questions are writhing in her mind when a further ten minutes later the doorbell finally rings.

•••

On Saturday after school, with Arvind gone who-knows-where, Srilekha goes to the terrace. She knows he spends time here, this is his oasis. This space belongs to him and now she is trespassing.

It does not take long to find his hiding place behind the water tank, and she feels dirty as she pulls out the old, tattered blue Spiderman bag. It is small in her hands, she could not fit even one of her chemistry books inside it. He used to love this bag when he was younger, she remembers, often sleeping with it.

Inside, stuffed in the front section of the bag, she finds his toys, neatly wrapped in plastic, folded and closed tight. It does not look like it has been opened in some time. The back section of the schoolbag is empty except for two plastic bags—one is empty. The other contains a seventh-grade question paper for the term exam, scheduled ten days away …

AMAR

The boy helps dress the wound on Amar's back. He does not flinch, his fingers remain constant and stable as a piece of fresh cotton, dipped in disinfectant, is pushed against the tear in his flesh that the bullet has left. The bullet that still sits within him. He tries not to think of it too much.

'It is better today. It is filling.' A pause as the boy collects his words. Hindi does not come naturally to him, and the accent is strong. 'It is small. I had thought it would be bigger.'

'It does not need to be. It tears through everything inside. I was lucky with this one. It could have killed me easily.' The wound burns, the disinfectant setting his nerves on fire.

The boy begins to secure the dressing with medical tape. Once he is done, his fingers touch another point on his side. Another hole, now just a scar, from another time. 'This one? Did you get this on that first day? The day you got the Gun?'

Amar nods as he turns over. Reaches out for his shirt and slips it over his shoulders like a shawl. He knows what the boy is thinking, the conclusion he will reach. 'The Gun protected me for a long time.' He doesn't add that he had once thought it would protect him forever.

'Why do you think it chose me?'

It is a natural question, but one Amar does not think about for even a moment, not in the long hours he has spent staring at the cement walls as he heals. He has never thought about it because he knows the answer—knew it instinctually when he saw Arvind for the very first time, on the ground and crawling. When he saw him fight off the much larger Ranade boy with everything he had—hands and teeth and unyielding heart. When he saw him stare with blood-drenched face at a knife. And through it all, Amar, desperate to intervene had not been able to move.

The boy was beaten. Defeated completely. In that clearing in the rain, there were long moments where no hope could be imagined, and yet, the boy had scrambled with his body and with his mind. He had lied and playacted for a single extra moment of survival. A single moment, when a tiny slice of opportunity would reveal itself.

That is the essence of a shooter. To manoeuvre with everything you have … all to survive one more moment.

But it would not do for the boy to know this, not yet, so all he says is, 'I am not sure.'

The boy nods and goes to put away the medical supplies. The bandages and tape join the pills on the side of his 'bed'. Amar takes a swig of the whisky, finishing the bottle, and then asks, 'Why do you still want it? It did the job for you. Saved you. You don't need it anymore.'

'Like you, I don't know. But I know I want to be better, to deserve it. If I am good enough, maybe it will stay with me, like it stayed with you.' A pause, and then, 'I have nothing else.'

'It is not an easy thing to keep. It will keep testing you.'

'I know. That is why it brought you to teach me.'

•••

Amar Singh has never thought about the future, or what his legacy might be.

He has never married, nor ever wanted children. His own nature, and the life he leads makes such dreams impossible, he understands that. But as he watches the boy pack the Gun in plastic and keep it in his bag, he feels a shade of happiness that he has never felt before.

Arvind is intelligent, frighteningly so. An intelligence that is only matched by his curiosity—a curiosity that swallows everything, questions everything. He has to see something just once to be able to replicate it perfectly thereafter.

Night has fallen. The far factories have ceased their noise. He sips on his second quarter of whisky. Back when the Gun was his, back in Bombay, he never wondered about the end point of his story. Like all others in his profession, he was invincible till that one moment he would not be. It was enough then to live every day like it was one of an everlasting list of todays. There had never been a hint of a different tomorrow.

He lights a cigarette. The last of the night. He is still unsure of what part the Gun wants him to play, to what ends it guides his destiny. But he is glad. Teaching the boy, being witness to his transformation—it is a gift. Something he can leave behind, something that will outlast him. He is sure that he does now a more noble thing than he has ever done before.

JAI

Jai is smoking on Jaggi's terrace when Om shows up, looking the same as he always does—determined, focused on a pattern that only he can see, a frieze that remains hidden to the likes of Jai. It makes him feel stupid and so he blows the cigarette smoke towards his brother's face by way of greeting.

The expression does not change, only the eyes narrow and then Om stretches out his hand and a surprised Jai hands him the cigarette and watches as his brother takes three neat puffs of equal length before inhaling the smoke. Om hands the cigarette back and then exhales through his mouth, to the side pointedly away from Jai, who cannot help but smile. 'You still do not like it.'

'No, I still do not like it.'

The brothers stand in silence.

'Your friends are not here today.'

'No, they are not. I am afraid I will not be good company. I hate to see my brother's killers walk away freely from our house.'

'Ah the constable … What did you want to do? Kill him in Baba's office? With Kapoor standing there?'

Jai wants to scream at his brother. Punch him, make him see sense—but that is what Om does, turns him into an animal who can only rant and froth at the mouth. No, Jai will not let his brother instigate him. Not tonight.

'Better than letting him go …'

'He is not important, Jai. He is not important in the least. They would have killed him too. These men … they are professionals. Did you see the report on the hotel? Did you see how many of them died? And those killers are still out there—'

'Good.' And he is happy as his response has paused Om's words. 'It means I can fucking smash their heads myself.'

'You really don't understand, do you?'

'Oh, I understand all too well. I understand that our brother was killed. *Our* brother—he was your brother too. Remember that. And it should be us out there, in the hunt, looking for these bastards—'

'Do you know animals can smell blood?' Om's voice goes quiet. His face has become grim stone, implacable, dangerous—their father's face suddenly stares out from their mother's bone structure. 'Animals can smell blood, Jai, even from wounds that they did not inflict. And once they smell it, they start planning how to hunt down and kill this wounded prey, a prey that is in pain, a prey that is not thinking straight. You are too young and too angry and, honestly, at this moment, too stupid, to see this, but there are a lot of people who would do us harm. And they are all circling like hyenas.'

'So, that is your plan? Go into a cave and hide?'

'No. We don't react in predicable ways. We don't run through the streets, making targets out of ourselves. We protect ourselves and we make plans that will destroy them. Utterly. You are right, Jaggi was my brother too. And every attack against this family will be returned a hundred times over.'

'It should be us.'

'It will be. Don't worry about that. But in the meantime, it is still very dangerous to go out. And you have to promise me that you will stay inside, with the security. You cannot slip out like you did last night.'

Jai thinks of the vast web of informers, all the servants and the drivers and the PAs, that Om has spun around himself. All the whispers that reach him. 'That is your problem brother. You stick so tight you don't let anyone breathe.'

'Where had you gone?'

'We had just gone to Lucky's Gym, all right? No one was there. It was empty, just me and the boys. I needed to get out—'

'Your boys … Abhimanyu and that lot? You have a gym at home. You boys can exercise here. Baba doesn't know about last night. I know he will be a lot happier with you here, with us.'

Om grabs his shoulder, and it would have been the moment for a hug but it passes, his brother is already walking away.

'I hear you. I just want one thing.'

'What?'

'The driver. I want him here. In the house, where I can see him. Give him to me as security.'

'Why?'

'I am listening to you. I swear I won't touch a hair on his head. But I want to watch the bastard sweat a little.'

'Okay. I will speak to Kapoor.'

Jai lights another cigarette as he watches Om vanish into the shadows of the old section of his father's house. It does not look like it, but it was a small victory.

•••

The night before, at Lucky's gym, Abhimanyu had mentioned something that still rings in Jai's head. He had told him how his younger cousin, Piyush, was going to buy term papers from Jaggi and his friends, and how they had discussed this on the day of his death.

Abhimanyu had not meant much with the information—it was just a chat in between sets, his way of simply remarking on how Jaggi and his friends had been following paths laid down so many years ago … See how like us our brothers are, he means to say. See what could have been …

But there is something within that story. The cops don't know about the stolen exam papers, or if they do, Kapoor has left it out of all his reports to the family. He can understand that—it is not something that any of the kids interviewed would voluntarily share. It could be a small thing, but it is not nothing, and since it is the only thread that Jai has in his hand, he intends to begin yanking it and see what comes out.

He thinks he should start with talking to Sonawane, and hear what he has to say that he hasn't said to the other police, and later meet Jaggi's school friends, the fucking donkeys that Jaggi kept around him, and have a conversation about what exactly was happening that day.

KAPOOR

There is a call for him, and it is from Bombay and his heart sinks as he answers the phone, afraid that this most wonderful case is somehow going to be snatched away from him.

It is ACP Sardesai.

'This is not official,' Sardesai tells him, 'but pay attention. The bullet we received from your office is a custom made 9mm dumdum. It is the exact make and manufacture as one used in a case we are currently investigating. Even the barrel etchings seem to match.'

Fuck! There it goes. Kapoor can feel his whole career slipping through his fingers.

'The shooter is a person of interest in an ongoing investigation. It is my personal request that you do not engage with this man. He is dangerous. If you get anything on him, any information on his whereabouts—you let me know personally. Find him if you can, but I do not want you going in on this—'

'Sir, this is a very sensitive case, as you must know. Pardon my language but my balls are in the fire, sir.'

'I know. And I appreciate your situation. Break the case in all other ways. I hear there is some involvement of a local gang. I think that is a good lead. Follow up on that.'

'If this man were to find himself in my custody somehow … Let us say he walks in and surrenders, what do I do then?'

'That is unlikely to happen. He is a seasoned killer. You will have to kill him before you can arrest him.'

'Okay.'

'Good. You are handling it well, Kapoor. Political cases are tough. This is a good case to end your stint in Rannwara. I don't think you will have to wait very long before you find yourself somewhere more … prominent.'

And with that bare shadow of a promise, Sardesai cuts the call and that is the fucking end of that.

AMAR

Arvind's movements are fast and precise as he brings the Gun up to shoulder level in a smooth motion using both his hands. At this stable position, the boy locks in his shoulders, skinny elbows bent to better compensate for the recoil. Even in this—with the weight of the weapon pushing straight down—his wrists stay firm. A count of five.

Then down and then up again.

Strong hands. It is the first rule of the Gun. It comes before the aim and the intent. You cannot aim what you cannot hold.

Today is the boy's fifth day handling the Gun—it sits heavy on the end of his arms and there is discernible effort in his movements, even so it feels like a part of him, as if the Gun has accepted the boy. It helps him—Amar can see it in the sweeps, as the Gun seems to pull and correct at the very apogee of the movement, as if to say till here and no more: here, we are level with the eyes … here, we hit our mark.

He watches the growing synchronicity, the timing of the dance, and waits to feel the sharp stab of jealousy but there is none, just a critical eye that would make the right foot move inwards just a bit at the raise, and demand stronger wrists—always stronger wrists. The boy still seems just a tad off-balance to make the second shot, but these are just nudges towards a higher perfection. Mostly what he feels on this day, with a cigarette in his hand and the sun on his face, is pride.

He had not been wrong in his assessment. The boy, of course, is a natural. He couldn't not be—after all the Gun doesn't make mistakes. It has an unerring eye for potential. The boy has been the perfect student. He learns fast, and with startling intensity. He walks with bricks in his hand, his arms extended, thin muscles pushing against tight skin. He stores and maintains the Gun with a focus and patience that rivals Amar's own. His concentration does not falter, not even in the hundredth iteration of a task. He strips the weapon countless times. Aims and swings and aims and swings. He truly is everything.

It is as if the boy heard his thoughts. He turns to Amar, a toothy grin on his face. He knows he is doing well. He tries lifting the gun with a single hand, but it is way too heavy for him—the swing jerky and out of control. He gets it up, somehow, with no aim but his arm is too weak—he cannot hold it there. The right arm slips down, till the left comes in to help it out. He is out of balance, and he knows it.

The smile now is an embarrassed one.

You are too weak, Amar tells him, too weak to shoot with one hand. Fortunately, God has given you two.

•••

Amar knows the value of patience.

It has been almost three weeks of hell. He sleeps. He eats. He crawls to shit. He drinks. He sleeps again. He pisses in a bottle. He drinks some more. He hurts. He stuffs his ears with torn rags to survive the wall of blaring sound during the day. He has even made friends with the dogs that come visiting at night.

Today is the first day he can walk.

Or hobble, if he is being truthful … The broken leg refuses to mend further, or has mended badly, he cannot tell, but outside of that the rest of him is better. The shoulders move. The back turns. The bullet is still in there, a dull ache under his muscles, but it troubles him less every day. There is no fever now, and even breathing is easier—good enough to actually enjoy the deeper drags of a cigarette.

He has shaved, passing the blade carefully over the misshapen contours of his face, and even changed into a shirt found rolled up in his gun bag, a new shirt, unworn, bought the day he lost the Gun, in another lifetime.

It felt right to wear it. It felt like victory.

•••

He leans on the boy as they walk to the motorcycle, the one he had stolen that fateful day, that now lies stashed outside the fence lining the factory compound.

It is a walk made longer by the bad leg, and he thinks he may never walk properly again. These things have to be fixed right the very first time. He had an uncle back in the village, a cousin of his father. Got drunk and fought a bull. Broke his arm. There were no doctors then and they just splinted it with a set of sticks. It withered like a dead root, and in a year it got so bad he could not even wash his ass with it. Amar pushes the thought away, It doesn't matter, He would have to be stupidly optimistic to expect to live past the month, let alone a whole year.

The boy has to assist him through the fence. His knee does not let him kneel or bend enough, so he crawls out on his back, feebly propelling his body forward with his elbows even as the boy pulls his shoulders through the gap. He has taken the shirt off for this part, not wanting it destroyed in the dust. On the other side, the boy has to help him up.

The bike lies flat, in a clump of thigh-high thorn shrubs, hidden from prying eyes. Apart from a thick layer of desert dust, it looks unmolested, tyres intact, petrol un-stolen.

It represents options.

'Now that you are better, what will you do?'

The question takes him by surprise and he answers without thinking, still studying the pipes and checking for leaks.

'I am still healing, then I have some business to finish.'

The boy nods in understanding, the value of vengeance is clear to him. 'After that?'

'Go north. Maybe. Go far away from here.' He does not even consider the probabilities of survival.

The boy is silent as he looks at the bike, then, 'Will you take me with you when you go?'

'Sure,' he lies, 'if you want me to.'

VII

A BETTER TOMORROW

WENDELL

Wendell thinks about killing Bilal.

It will not take much. He can be back at Bilal's safe house—the traitor remains ferreted in that old mansion—in the next half hour, demand a meeting and shoot him in the face.

But Bilal will get off easy if he does that. Wendell is not sure about the sequence of events here in Rannwara, but he is sure Bilal is to blame for all of it. Betrayal—there is no other word for it, and for it, by all laws of earth and heaven, he should die. Maybe he should shoot out his knees first and watch Bilal crawl around for a while. Sadism is not his style; he is too professional to play with his 'food', but he'll be happy to make an exception this time.

It will be easy. And it will feel so damn good.

Instead, Wendell masturbates. It is a quick wank—he thinks of nothing in particular as he stands at the bathroom sink. Just goes through the motions as he searches for release. He comes and it is nothing special. It just feels like a long exhale.

Then he sits and he eats. Rannwara is known for its meat and his boy, Kamal, has found a dhaba that makes mutton that melts off the bones. He eats it with fat rotis dripping in butter. The food, now cold, is still delicious. One day, after this is done, he will go and eat it fresh and hot. The thought makes him happy.

After lunch there is nothing to do but wait and a few hours later he once again thinks about killing Bilal.

•••

Kamal has rented a house for them in Rannwara. A small one in a neighbourhood of government clerks and schoolteachers. It has no kitchen and only two plastic chairs in the living room. The bedroom has a single bed with a thin mattress. It is hot, hotter inside than outside, a kind of bone dry, knife stab heat that Wendell would not have believed possible. The fan in the bedroom doesn't work and Wendell keeps the shutters of the sole window closed. Old habits from Bombay. Outsiders can always see in, more than you can see out.

Four guns lie on the bed. All pistols. All 9mm. Different manufacturers. Replaceable. Nothing remarkable about a single one of them.

Boss had wanted him to take an AK. Sudhir had almost insisted on it, even pulling a couple of his own out from underneath the seats of his car. 'It is *him*,' he had said as he held the guns aloft by their necks, like they were chickens.

It was a good offer, better for the spirit in which it was made. But it is simply not how he, Wendell, works.

He had never put much faith in the weapons themselves. Bigger did not mean better. The 9mm is more than good enough for him. Standard calibre, abundant ammunition. Reliable construction. He leaves these obsessions to the others. Sudhir would walk in the streets with a fucking machine gun if he could. And Amar? He had his fucking love-mother-religious bullshit with that gun of his.

He should have thrown it into the fucking sea all those years ago. That would have been better for everyone.

It had seemed harmless then. Harmless and funny, and they had all laughed behind his back in the early days. The boy with his 'chamatkaari ghoda', they would say, when he would not be in the room. Amar was sensitive in those days. Sensitive and ferocious—a mad dog, ready to bark, readier to bite.

But good, so very good. Unflinching, brave and with an unteachable awareness of the fight as if he is seeing things moments before they happen. Amar Singh is the finest pure shooter in Bombay, one of the best ever, Wendell thinks, a born killer. It will be a challenging hunt. Even now, wounded, Amar is a worthy target. This is by no means a done thing. There will be risks. He has guns enough and even Wendell cannot know what kind of madness rules him now.

Killing a child.

He liked Amar. Maybe even loved him. But Boss is right—their business is a wretched one, which does not ask much, but they cannot be unpredictable. Bilal played his stupid games, but Amar, he cannot go around shooting kids. What provocation did the boy give you, Amar, Wendell wonders in the darkness of the room, that you had to shoot him dead. A bloody sixteen-year-old. As young as you were, when you first came to me.

So young you are still. What life have you tasted at all.

It is hot. Wendell cracks open the window. Outside, the houses are asleep. Narrow lanes empty in peak afternoons. Bilal's days are numbered. Wendell has decided as he wipes moist eyes. He will kill Amar. And then he will fucking avenge him.

JAI

Swapnil looks worried, he bites his lips and blinks his small ugly eyes and Jai decides that it is a good thing, that a scared Swapnil is an honest Swapnil. He keeps touching his cheek, red and swelling where Jai has just slapped him. Stupid bastard, one would think he has never been slapped before.

They sit in Mahesh's house, in Mahesh's room where Mahesh lies on his bed, trussed up like a cartoon animal. He too looks scared, though Jai has not touched him, not yet—he has thought about it, but he cannot figure out where to hit the super-injured motherfucker without outright killing him.

'Tell me again,' Jai says, 'what you were thinking.'

Mahesh stays quiet, his eyes look big and watery, dancing around like fried eggs on his black saucepan of a face.

It is Swapnil who takes a big breath and starts again, 'It was the papers you see, we wanted to—'

Slap.

It was a light one, lighter than before, a slap of warning, of encouragement … of clarity.

'I know about the papers. You've already told me about that.'

'We didn't want to get into trouble. Not with the school and the cops … We didn't tell them about the papers—'

Mahesh intervenes, 'I didn't know, bhaiya, I didn't know anything about this papers wala plan—'

'You fucker. He was part of it—'

Slap. Again. This one has some bite in it. Swapnil's thick head lurches to the side. His ear touches his shoulder before it bobs back up. There is a soft sound. *Crack.*

'I didn't say anything about the papers, bhaiya … I didn't understand what this was about … You've got to believe me.'

'So, you lied to the police. You lied to the police who are investigating the murder of my brother. You lied because your little cunt was all fluttering and upset about what would happen if someone found out about the exam papers.

'THEY KILLED MY BROTHER, YOU FUCKER! THEY KILLED MY BROTHER.'

All control is lost as Jai falls into a frenzy of punching and kicking. Swapnil is on the floor, turtling up, but Jai cannot stop, not now, never now. His fists bounce off of Swapnil's head and his shoulders and it's not enough, not nearly enough. He looks around the fucking room, Mahesh's small shitty room, and standing in the corner, against the cupboard, is a cricket bat. Two steps and the fucking bat is in his hands. Swapnil is exactly where he was before and Jai swings, he puts his shoulders and back into it, and it is a big swing—too big and it hits the wall as it comes down, and misses mostly, but still sinks into Swapnil's body. Jai lifts it again and brings it down but someone grabs it out of his hands.

It is that bastard cop Sonawane—he must have been waiting at the entrance—who snatches the bat away. Jai pushes Sonawane who falls against a wall, still hugging the bat, and then turns back to the miserable fat loser cunt Swapnil who is on the floor. He knows what he has to do. He has to beat this fucking cockroach to death. That is the only way forward now. He is finally feeling a little better, so he kicks again and again, now with improved rhythm, his black boot connecting satisfyingly with Swapnil's body. Sonawane, at his feet, grabs him, 'Sir, stop, please stop.'

There are shouts outside. Mahesh's mother bangs against the door. Sonawane shouts again. 'Everything is okay, madam, you go sit.'

Jai pushes the bastard off and grabs hold of a crystal tray next to Mahesh's bed. He lifts it and brings it down on Swapnil's head and the tray shatters in his hands, thick pieces of glass going everywhere. With that the spell is broken and he takes a deep breath.

Swapnil is lying on the floor in a foetal position, hands wrapped around his head. Sonawane has stood up. The bitch Aunty has stopped hitting the door, but is calling out to her son, 'Mahesh beta, are you okay?' Mahesh the stupid fucking buffalo has not moved and is just lying in his bed because that is all he can do.

Swapnil's sniffles make Jai want to hurt him again.

'Motherfucker. You and the fucking papers. Fuck your fucking papers. I want to know what you were thinking when you left him. Taking his car, and his guard'—Sonawane stands by the door, not meeting his eyes—'and leaving him. You think it is a fucking joke?'

'Sorry … we are so sorry, bhaiya, please …'

Jai crouches on the floor. 'Fucking shit. Okay, so tell me again now, and slowly.'

Swapnil sits up, shaking, and tells the whole story again, and it is the same as the last three times. The stories have not changed at all since the slapping began.

'And this boy, Arvind, the one who stole the papers, is the same one who did this to you?'

Mahesh nods. 'Yes, bhaiya. He is a cunning bastard, that boy …'

'He is the brother of that girl … Srilekha … in your class?'

'Yes … he is but—'

'Ssshhh. Quiet. A fucking junior has broken you in half and … fuck. I should kill you. I really should fucking kill you. But I am not going to. You two will stay here, in this city—and when I call for you, you fuckers will come. You will come that minute and you will come on your fucking knees.'

The boys nod. Snot drips out of Swapnil's nose.

'Good. Okay. You will show me this boy. And this fucking sister of his.' And with this he gets up.

Everything looks better now. There is a clear path leading to a clear enemy.

This boy was recruited by the men who killed his brother. He is smart. He ensured that Jaggi would be alone and without support. No guards, nothing. Alone, defenceless. Maybe he promised to give the papers back. Maybe it was something else. Something to do with that fucking sister of his …

Jai doesn't know where this boy is, but he will fucking find him and finger him, make him spill his damn guts till he tells the fucking truth. He smiles, and when he leaves, he takes the fucking bat with him.

SRILEKHA

It is not a plan consciously made or consciously acted upon. Srilekha cannot claim to have deliberated over this, or even articulate all of the knots of logic that have led her to this. To her, her actions this evening are beyond instinct, they are inevitable.

It is Monday again and once school was over, she looked for Arvind in the chaos of exiting children and school buses, and to her complete lack of surprise, he was nowhere to be found. She mistrusts him entirely, he is no longer her little brother—and so she gets off the bus two stops early, and walks to Sudipto's house. She has never been there before, but it is easy to locate. Everyone knows the GM's house.

She does not even bother with excuses to tell Arvind, for she is sure he will not be there.

The gate to the bungalow is intimidating but she rings the bell and a maid comes out. Srilekha asks for Sudipto. The maid nods, slightly confused. Right behind her, though, walking down the driveway, is Sudipto's mother. She looks like a bird—fair, dressed in a yellow sleeveless kurta with her dupatta draped neatly over her shoulders.

Srilekha asks for Arvind, and Sudipto's mother smiles and says, no he is not here, but she can ask Sudipto if he is going to come over and, 'Won't you come in … have some cold coffee?'

Inside, Srilekha sits on a large brown sofa with the cooler on. Meanwhile the maid brings her water in a glass made of glass. The surroundings envelop her. The large windows, bright curtains and the cabinets with shelves full of delicate porcelain figurines. She realizes this is the first time she has been inside a rich person's house.

Sudipto enters, freshly changed out of his school uniform. He too, just like Arvind, looks better than he used to, fuller somehow, more complete. He says hello, and it is all very polite. They chat about schoolwork for a bit. She asks about his test scores and exam prep. She tells him that Arvind has been playing cricket with some new colony kids. He looks surprised, hurt even. He nods yes, yes, he knows, he too goes with them sometimes, but she knows he is lying. She can tell that he resents being caught out like this, so naked in his pain. He does not want to be embarrassed in front of his mother …

He is fidgeting and wants to escape.

The mother picks on the vibe quickly. 'Sudipto, you should go do your homework now—then in the evening you can play your Nintendo till dinnertime.'

It is now just her and Sudipto's mother, and before Srilekha can make her excuses, Aunty speaks, 'Do you think the school is safe?'

Srilekha is ambushed by the question and is unsure of where it might lead. She just nods and the older woman continues, 'It is not just the murder. Did you know about the violence in the school? The things that terrible boy used to do?'

She knows which terrible boy Aunty is talking about.

'The teachers did nothing. The place is not safe, not safe at all … How …' and the first tear rolls down her face.

'Sudipto has been talking, did you know he was being beaten up every day by those boys? Even the maids knew about it, but they told me only now. The things they said! Every day they would beat them … This Jaggi and the other seniors … All the children would talk about it … I feel as if everyone knew except me … Did you know? Did you know any of this?'

Srilekha shakes her head, saying nothing.

'It is not safe. How can a school run like this? Violent hoodlums in the classes … Do you think there is still any danger there? Huh, it sounds like a prison … The stories I have heard. A few years ago—my cook told me this just yesterday—a few years ago this Jaggi actually stabbed a boy … What is even happening? Can you believe that these boys were bringing weapons to the school …'

•••

At night after dinner, when Arvind is in the bathroom, Srilekha checks his schoolbag.

All his books are stuffed in the front section. The larger section in the back is empty but for layers of plastic bags. Containing nothing. But the emptiness inside has a weight to it—like it was made out of ghost stuff.

She passes her fingers along the edges and touches something cold and metallic. She pulls it out and in her hand is a bullet.

WENDELL

'Boss, we have found something.'

It is Tony—eyes glowing yellow in the white tube light. Tony whose real name is Tarun, and who lived somewhere in this area before boredom or tragedy pushed him to Bombay.

He looks excited. Behind him, Kamal can't stop smiling either.

'What do you have?'

For more than a week, the boys have been scouring the city while Wendell waits and eats. Kamal playing lookout as Tony walks around and asks a lot of questions—he knows the dialect, knows the villages around, knows the people. They talk to him. Tell him things they wouldn't tell outsiders, or cops.

'We found a shop that sells Royal Crown, that whisky you told us about.'

'Okay.'

'Not too many shops carry it around here, so that helped—and this guy has been selling two quarters of it every day to this boy who shows up at the store.'

'A boy?'

'Yes. A boy.'

'Same boy? Every day?'

'Every day. But only in the last twenty days. He comes in and picks it up. He says it is for his father. He pays cash each time.'

'There could be other boys that buy liquor for their fathers…'

'There could, but this same boy stops by a medical shop near there and buys medicines for his mother. Some painkillers, some bandages and the like. Not every day, but a few times a week.'

'So the father gets drunk and beats the mother,' Wendell says, keeping the excitement out of his voice. 'Do you have the prescription?'

'There was no bill … but the chemist's boy remembered some of them. Here are the names … We wrote them down in case we forget.'

The names of the medicines seal it for him. Excitement turns to dead certainty. These are the same drugs Amar used eight years ago. Opioids. Antibiotics. Something for blood infections. He doesn't know the details, but he has not forgotten the names. Wendell himself used to buy the refills for him all those years ago. I got you, you son of a bitch. You should have paid more attention to me. You should not have remembered these pills.

All men are creatures of habit. If you eat a man's mind, you will 100 per cent be eating his liver.

'It is him.'

Tony smiles with more teeth than before. Kamal slaps him on the back. They have done well and they know it. They are excited about what comes next.

'What do we know about the boy?'

'He shows up in the afternoon, after school—he is still wearing his uniform—and makes these purchases … He talks in a funny accent, like a Madrasi …'

'You got close to him?'

'No. The chemist's boy told us.'

'Okay, good. I think you should follow this boy. Be very careful, make sure you're not seen following him. See where the boy goes, but keep your distance. The man we are hunting is not a joke. The slightest change in the air and he'll know he is being hunted. He is a ghost … no, he is worse, he is a living nightmare. He will come out of thin air and slit your fucking throat. Do not let him see you. Do not come within hundred metres of him. Pay attention, both of you, concentrate. I will not tolerate any screw up. And yes, do it in turns.'

They nod. Their smiles fade …

'Shouldn't we just …' Kamal mimics a gun going off in his hand.

'No. You don't touch him. You don't get close to him. He will see you coming. He will kill you. And worse, he will hide further underground. Just follow the boy. Make your plans now—how you will do it. Tell me in the morning.'

They nod again.

'Do this right and I will take you with me on the job. We will do it together.'

That makes it better. Now they will listen to him, this promise of glory will keep them in check, stop them doing anything foolish. Shooting a shooter, it is not a thing you do every day. They should be okay. They know their jobs. Tony used to be a lookout for another mob and has some experience following paranoid men. Kamal was a chain-snatcher before he became a dabbawalla, boys trusted to carry guns and other deliveries between gangs. He too can vanish into crowds …

It should be enough, Wendell thinks, rubbing his palms, it should be enough.

AMAR

Dawn is a dagger drawn along the edge of the sky, and Amar Singh is awake to see it, having walked on his own to the outside. He is not fully healed but he is better and now, being better, he has decided to begin preparations for what is to come. Of the six guns with which he arrived in Rannwara, only three remain, which he feels is apt considering he has been halved as well, straddled as he is with a broken leg and an arm that still struggles to lift a water bottle.

The CZ75 and the Walther both use 9mm ammunition, which is good, for he has a total of fifty rounds left of those. The Mac-10 uses .45s—he has about forty of these, also good but not enough to fill its extended magazine to capacity. He has two knives, his own smaller one, and the one he got from the dead boy, the one that is still crusted with the blood from the fight at the guest house. They are sharp deadly things, he can definitely do some damage if his targets stand absolutely still and let him fall onto them.

The boy has brought him pieces of chalk from his school, which Amar has used to draw an image of Lord Hanuman on the low wall of his factory, telling himself as he moves untrained fingers that an imperfect likeness does not imply imperfect worship. The monkey god is flying through the air carrying a mountain in his hand, bringing the Sanjivani, the elixir of healing, to heal the god-princes so that they may enter battle again. The symbolism hits him halfway through the sketch and he laughs to himself. He would do much for such an intervention, but all he has are the strips of medicines the boy brings him. Medicines he needs more and more of, their efficacy fading with time even as he heals. This morning he took four and the pain is still there.

He uses his own knife to cut one of his bedsheets into long, wide strips of cloth, and fashions a sling for the Mac-10, adjusting the height so that it sits comfortably at his waist. He no longer has the strength in his arms to hold it up. He now switches to the knife of the dead boy, marvelling at the quality of the steel. He looks at the trees outside, trying to spot branches that he can fashion into a crutch, or some kind of brace for his leg, allowing him to get around. Make him more mobile.

All the empty whisky bottles are still there, stacked neatly next to his bedroll. He thinks of his plans for them. There is little time ahead. Sanjivani or not, Amar knows he must go to war again. In the larger world, three weeks have passed and the hunt for Jaggi Ranade's killer continues, and he knows it will not stop till he is dead.

SRILEKHA

It is Monday night and the family is at the dinner table as Arvind tells a story. It is about some boy in class who has a funny name and how he had a fight with Sudipto and the maths teacher threw a piece of chalk at him which hit him or something. Srilekha does not follow the particulars of the story because she is watching Arvind, for he doesn't tell the story as much as perform it and does the voices and by the end of it Amma is laughing, unable to eat, and even Appa cracks a smile.

She sits in silence, their laughter grating against her skin, her breath stuck in her throat. She no longer knows who Arvind is, what monstrous evil sits inside his skin, growing fat, threatening to burst, drowning them all here. She used to be able to talk to him, her brother, but what can she even begin to say? How can she even confront a crime so large that her brain refuses to outline its contours. She has not slept a wink since she found that bullet, which she had immediately put back, terrified that he will know that she knows …

She cannot bear to look at him. He doesn't notice her either, so enraptured is he with his own story, so seemingly full of light. Her mother is who she is, and Srilekha has limited expectations of her, but Appa? Surely Appa can see past it—past this paper-thin veneer of goodness to the darkness inside.

She loves him, her baby brother, she really does, and she keeps telling herself this even as the acid pools in her stomach and her heart grows spikes that are poking out from between her ribs.

He worked with them, whoever they were and they paid him back with the exam papers, or money or something else. It is clear to her; the pieces have fallen together with a hellish exactness. He worked with them and now her Jaggi is dead. He worked with them and now the police are threatening her. He worked with them and now Appa cannot stand the sight of her, her life is in tatters, absolute tatters. He worked with them and now she cannot study, and her scores are shit and she won't get through to medical and Appa will never love her again.

•••

She watches him at night, his thin body close enough to touch, his face calm like a Buddha. He did this, whatever this is and it is not fair that he be happy while her world falls apart. No, no, she will not allow it … She wants to wake him up and shake him and attack him and beat him and make him cry and—

'Sri?'

Panic. He is awake. She tells herself that whatever he may have become, he cannot read her mind.

'Why can't you sleep? Was it a bad test?'

She wants to laugh loud at his fake concern, as if the only thing that can touch her life is an academic setback. But it seems convenient to lie so she says, 'It is nothing, just exams, and it will be all right,' and he turns in his bed and tells her to pray, because prayers make all wishes come true and it was something he did not believe once but believes now. 'Good things happen to good people,' is how he ends it without even noticing his hypocrisy.

•••

In the morning she wakes early to supposedly study, and while he sleeps she stares at his bag with the bullet. It sits heavy in her vision, bending reality as her eyes pass over his study table. She thinks of revelations, and concludes that the cost of the complete truth will be too high. The bullet will remain hidden, for now. That particular storm will be unstoppable. She knows, and for now it is enough. Eventually, there will be a reckoning.

So instead, she steps outside, makes coffee for Appa who is awake and who gives her no acknowledgement at all, and then she goes up the stairs to the terrace and removes the question paper from Arvind's secret little treasure bag.

She does not want to destroy her brother—she loves him, truly. She wants the best for him, like she always has, wants him to be free of his corrupt criminal joy. If she didn't, she wouldn't hand Amma the paper just before they leave for school.

ARVIND

The bottle explodes into a cloud of stardust, gleaming with wet sun. The moment goes on forever, he can feel every twitch in the small ligaments of his wrist as they stretch out and pull in to keep the barrel level with the line of his eyes, the muscles along his spine making micro-adjustments to spring his torso back to the neutral position, just so much and not much more. His feet have not moved, staying along the chalk marks drawn into the ground by Amar.

This time he managed to keep his eyes open.

Amar lights a cigarette. 'Better.'

It is one word and it slips into his ears through the cotton balls stuffed inside, and within that word is everything. Arvind wants to laugh, to scream and jump ecstatically but he does not because it is not something that Amar would do.

'Do it again. Slower this time.'

He brings the gun down in a steady arc. He engages the safety and brings the gun to his side. There are tremors within him and his forehead is beaded with sweat. With both hands interlocked around the weapon, he tries to blink the drops away.

He is firing with Amar's Russian pistol and not with his own Gun. It is of similar weight, and uses similar ammunition. 'It will be close enough, though no two guns are the same.' The Gun-God, Amar doesn't have to tell him, is not for practice.

He shoots twice more. One hit and one miss, making a total of two out of five. He wants to shoot more but Amar has explained to him that ammunition is scarce. 'We will train more,' he promises, 'but this is it for now.'

The moment is enough and it stays with him, the cadence of the shooting flowing through his mind like an elaborate song, each note falling just so, the transition in the stances, the shifting of weight between the lead and rear legs, the exhalation that goes on and on till that final moment when you are squeezed empty and all movement ceases and you pull the trigger.

•••

Arvind bunked the last two classes of school to be early.

This, the training with Amar, this is where his heart lies, and any time not spent here is spent counting the minutes and the hours to when he can be here again. Willing the sun and the stars to run faster across the sky.

All of him hurts. His wrists, his shoulders, his back even. The skin of his fingers is scraped raw, seeping blood because it has no time to heal at all. He oils his fingertips with coconut oil before he goes to sleep, and has learnt to not wince as he eats Amma's spicy rasam-chadam every night. There is pain in his training but it seems to become less important with each passing session.

Today Amar is walking all by himself. There is a length of wood tied to his leg, from ankle to mid-thigh. He hobbles as he moves around, and Arvind can tell it hurts even though he tries to not show it. Right now he stands ten paces away, with a bunch of stones held in a giant left palm. Small sharp shards of incentive.

'Did you understand?'

'Yes.' Arvind nods. This is a new thing today, a new piece of training. Counting, Amar calls it, making it seem so simple. All he has to do, Arvind, is run to a tree forty metres away and touch it. As he runs, he must also count the seconds inside his mind. While he does that, Amar Singh is going to throw stones at him. Hard and fast.

The first run, Arvind simply makes a mad dash to the tree. Falling into crouches, and dodging left and right as he runs and—*bang!*—a stone hits his back, and before the sting can settle in, another catches his shoulder. 'You are dead. Do it again.'

The next run. Arvind has learnt that with no cover between him and the tree, he must move slower, keeping Amar in sight at all times. He should know when to dodge. This time he runs to the side and turns, keeping Amar in his view, making a circuitous route to his mark. A stone still catches him on his forearm when he is barely five metres away.

Again. And then a few times more. It is on the sixth turn that Arvind makes it. He has dodged every one of Amar's attacks. He turns to the older man and smiles.

'What is the count? How many seconds has it been?'

He has no idea.

More rounds of this. He dodges better, and later. He reads the shift in weight as Amar begins to flick the stone. Only a few more stones clipping the edges of his skin, only half dodged. This one time he keeps the count.

It is not a complete victory but Amar nods. Lights a cigarette. It is the signal that the exercise is over. That he is satisfied. Arvind thinks he has begun to read him just a little, this mysterious mentor of his.

'Why do we count?'

'Fights have a rhythm. Like a song, and in time you will hear it. It allows you to predict what will happen.'

'You can tell what your enemies will do?'

'Not perfectly. But most times. More importantly, it allows you to not be where they think you are. The counting allows you to focus, to hear it better.'

'Where did you learn this?'

'I picked up some things from people around me. If you keep your eyes open, you can learn a lot.'

'Your friends?'

'You could say that. But they don't matter now. They are all far away.'

'In Bombay, right? What was it like?'

•••

It is with light steps and a light heart that Arvind heads home, his mind aflame with the idea of Amar's Bombay. A city with towers that block the sun, and where people choke the streets at midnight. It feels like a magical place to him, something out of a fable. Filled with guns and adventure …

A door has opened now, between him and Amar Singh, and today he asked many questions and each answer he got birthed still more questions … No, gunpowder from crackers cannot refill bullets, and yes, bullets are expensive and very hard to buy, and no, they cannot blow up cars like they show in the movies, and on and on it went till finally Amar had to point out the growing shadows around them and tell him to go home.

A month ago, Arvind Srinivasan was finished, daydreaming impossible scenarios, an escape, any escape from the hell that was his life. He was weak, truly weak and struggling to survive, and he had no real hope—he can see that now. Now, he holds the hope in a double-handed pistol grip. But even he knows, of the two gifts that destiny has handed him—his new Guru is the greater part.

Such is the electricity flowing in his veins that he does not even think up an excuse for his lateness till he is at the door. It takes three rings before Amma opens it, her face pale and her eyes red.

Inside is chaos. From the threshold he can hear Srilekha sob, and above her cries Appa roars.

SRILEKHA

Srilekha returned home from school to Appa frothing at the mouth, calling her a slut and a whore and other words whose meaning she could only guess as he threw sheets of paper at her face.

She did not have to pick them up to know that these were her letters to a dead Jaggi, the ones in which she had poured her heart out, which indicted her in the absolute crime of not being an absolute daughter. These papers that were hidden away and now had been found, for Appa had gone searching the room, and not content to simply search Arvind's desk, had of course searched hers as well. As the sheets of paper fell on the ground, she knew nothing would ever be the same again.

It should not have been this way. It should have been Arvind as the accused, not her. She knew she should have got rid of those pages, burnt those sheets of shame but she could not for they were the only parts of her that were solid, tangible in any way, the only proof that her feelings existed and were valid, lending them continuity so she would not wake up in the mornings convinced she was going crazy. And so she had kept these pages, scurried behind completed test-books, hidden in physics notes, stuffed within the piles of scrap working paper.

Now, these pages with the secret history of her heart and her body and her aching terrible shameful desire were thrown at her face by Appa, who stood shaking in the drawing room, all bones in his thin vest and veshti, eyes popping out of his dark delicate skull, and the papers—her own willing confession of her depravity—had not yet hit the floor when he struck her.

She did not say anything. He had no questions. His rage was a deluge of monstrous accusation and heartbreak. He hit her again but she did not register it. His words, having pierced her, were powerless against the truth she knew about herself, screaming, ravaging her insides. Amma tried to intervene with her own fury but Appa shoved her and sent her spinning across the room. He took a breath and began again. Traitor, ungrateful child, pervert, deviant, criminal, slut … Her ears burnt as he raged against her very existence and through it all was a loud keening sound and it took a few minutes before she realized it was coming from her and she was indeed crying as she collapsed on the floor.

•••

She stays on the floor and cries like she has never cried before, even as Appa kicks her with his slippered feet and she crumples further into herself and there seems to be no end to the space inside her that she can shrink into, her bones and cartilage are now water—all of it pumping out of her eyes ... Another sound and she thinks she has been hit again but it is not so, and she looks up to see Arvind standing above her. Her brother, in his uniform, his bag still at his back, is pushing against their father even as Appa brings his fists down on Arvind's thin shoulders, and in the scuffle Appa loses his balance. He falls backwards on the drawing room diwan, and in the fumble, his veshti, one end of which is trapped under Arvind's foot, comes off.

He lies there stunned, exposed in front of his children, his dark skinny legs sticking out of faded brown underwear. All Arvind does is hold his own arms up—palms together in prayer and obeisance—saying in Tamil, 'I don't know what you think, but she is the good one, she is the good one, do not ever forget that she is the good one.'

Whether it is due to Arvind's pushing him or the veshti that came undone and Appa's nakedness, Arvind knows that something has broken between them, a chasm now extends between father and son, a point of no return.

Maybe it was the perfect redirection of the hate Appa feels for his daughter, or perhaps this crash between father and son was fated, or both, but such is his fury that he leaps at Arvind, tackling him and hitting him and kicking him and throwing him into the furniture as the rage melts off of him in layers.

Still in his dusty school uniform, Arvind rises with a grim look in his face. His posture has changed, he holds his palm up firm against his father and says, 'You should know the difference between right and wrong—you always said it. In this moment you are wrong, Appa, if you don't trust her, you are wrong,' and it is the other hand which holds a gun.

ARVIND

The Gun is out.

It should not have been, never ever, not in the house, not in this way, so maybe it was a reaction from the drills he has done all day, but he knows that is not true.

He was scared, scared of his father, scared for his sister. Yes, that is perhaps true.

But true-er is the fact that he does not want to continue this sham anymore.

This play of power that exists between them, he does not want to fuel it any longer. He is done with it. Is done with getting pushed around by a man who does not stand up for what is right. Someone who, within the four walls of the house, behaves like a god, terrorizing the family, but holds no moral value whatsoever within himself …

There was an Arvind who was helpless, who was afraid and who fought back with his teeth and his nails, but he is gone now, burnt in a flash of gunpowder—and in his place stands another Arvind, who holds destiny by its throat and is willing to shake it to get his way.

And so, without conscious thought, the Gun is out. It is pointed low—there is no aim here, no call of death, and there is no intention to threaten. His hand had moved before he could stop it and then the Gun was in it, out, pointing at the floor, undeniably real—and they can see it.

Appa pauses, eyes riveted to the weapon in his hand—like a whirlpool it seems to be collecting all the energy in the world. 'Appa, please, it is not her fault.' His stare remains hooked on the weapon, even as he picks up his veshti and wraps it around his waist.

Arvind can sense his mother move a moment before she does—as if her intent has flown across the room to him—and he shouts, 'No. No. It is not a toy.' And she looks at him and walks forward … and slaps him. He takes it across the face and when she tries to grab his arms, he pushes her hands away and slips out of her grasp … It is easy, like there is no strength in her.

'Please,' he says, 'please.' He doesn't know what he is pleading for, does not know what it is he intends to do.

'This thing in your hand … Where did you—'

'I found it, Appa, it is mine now.'

'Tell me where you—'

'You did it, you killed him! I know you killed him …' Srilekha screams.

Appa's face turns to ash as the significance of everything—the Gun, the murder, the police—begins to dawn on him.

'No, not you … not … I don't believe it.' This was Amma.

Sri is crying again but the nature of her tears has changed, thicker now they flow as a deeper growl emanates from her throat.

His mother on his right, and though he steps away from her slowly she seems to walk alongside him the whole time.

'Amma please … Stay back …'

He steps away slowly, but she follows, without conscious thought, closing the distance. Her eyes boring into his.

'Did you do it?'

'Yes. Yes I did it,' he blurts out between choked tears, 'and I would do it again.'

'It's okay, Appu,' she says, 'just put it down.'

But he knows he cannot. He knows they want the Gun. If they get the Gun he is done for, finished. His life is over. They will beat him and keep him. His father is probably stupid enough to go to the police with it, and then everyone here will be dead.

She stretches a trembling arm out, her thin gold bangles shivering against her dark skin. 'Just give it to me …'

His willpower shrivels under her gaze, and the Gun seems to hold within it the weight of mountains, and this is when Appa decides to move and from now everything that follows feels inevitable. The branching probabilities birthed in this moment collapse into something terrible. Appa is moving and Arvind has the Gun in his hand and it would be the easiest thing to just point it at his father and hope that the safety is on. But he knows now, from Amar, the truth of these things: you only aim at what you intend to kill.

And so, he puts the Gun against his own head.

•••

It is only moments, but it feels like forever, his entire family arranged around him in this infernal tableau, a mockery of everything.

Srilekha, tears streaming pouring, stands like a statue, her hair undone. Appa standing before him, face knotted in anger and confusion, one end of the veshti clutched in his hand, the rest trailing across the floor … And Amma, somewhere behind him stands Amma, no longer moving … Amma, whom he cannot face, whom he may never be able to face again … And there is this enormous pressure building inside his chest, pressing against his ribs and it needs to come out and the Gun at his head offers a dark promise, but it is his legs that respond, and he runs, pushing past his father and out the door.

Arvind runs out of the apartment and out of the building and he runs through the colony streets, his feet bouncing off the hard concrete, and he runs past the playgrounds and the senior kids playing cricket, cursing in Hindi, their voices sharp and carrying, and he runs without stopping even as the breath seems to explode inside his chest and he runs to the closest colony gate, which is gate no. 4, which is always closed. He glances left and then right to confirm that there is no one there who might see him and this is when he realizes he still has the Gun in his hand.

He understands that for now and forever more it is just him and the Gun and he slips it through the bars of the gate, gently keeping it on the ground on the other side and then scrambles up—the gate is high, many times his own height and the top of it is guarded by metal spikes but they are not enough to deter him and his small feet and thin legs easily fit in the spaces between them and then he is up and over, careful to not let his bag snag on the spikes. He lands with significant impact right next to the Gun, which he picks up in his sweaty hands even before he gets to his feet and then there is nothing but the dark unlit road ahead of him …

•••

He moves on pure instinct. He slows but never stops. He is invisible, a black shadow in the black night, both hands tight and sticky on the pistol grip, and his head scrambled with different strains of the same thought playing on repeat, loud and out of sync, a screaming cacophony of guilt and sustained panic.

It is over, it tells him.

They know about the Gun and now he can never go home again.

SRILEKHA

She saw *it*, and everything instantly made sense.

She saw *it*—the source of his happiness. His power. His joy. The central node of his many secrets. Her suspicions turned far truer than she had dared imagine.

She can see *it* even with eyes closed, its brilliant light, its awful gravity that sucked out the colour of the world. This then was *it*, the instrument of his petty vengeance, his toy of damnation.

This was *it*.

The spring in his step, the smile in his eyes, the death of her dreams, the dust of her life.

•••

It is just Amma and her in the house. Appa is out, having chased after Arvind, and Srilekha is unsure if it is to bring him back or kill him or worse, to go straight to the police to confess the crimes of his son—her brother, a killer. A boy who would shoot his own father.

He killed Jaggi because of course he did. He tricked him into the quarries and shot him dead. It is so obvious in hindsight—her brother and his bloody secrets, the absences, the exam paper, the damn bullet. The darkness that she alone glimpsed inside his soul … It was all there and her every instinct had picked up on it. She knows it and she knows now that she always knew it. He killed Jaggi. He killed her whole …

'Sri!' The voice is loud and it pierces through. It is Amma who is sitting on a dining chair. 'I need water,' she says, her hands gripping the table, failing to calm the shivers that wrack her body.

After the water she asks, 'Amma, are you okay?' and her mother asks staring at the floor, 'Do you think he is okay?' and then 'Do we need to go?'

Srilekha knows which him she is talking about—her only son, her little man, her star who is now out there, her star who drew a gun in the middle of the house. Srilekha worries about the other him, the one chasing after a mad son who has a weapon. She prays for Appa, even now, prays that he will not catch up with Arvind.

'I am going out,' she tells Amma, 'I am going to find them.'

'Okay, yes, you do that, wait, I will come with you.' She says this but she does not move, her hands still shaking in her lap.

'No. Ma, you are in shock. You stay home. If someone returns while I am away, you should be here.'

'Okay,' and then, 'Wait,' she says, 'is this the boy who hurt him?' Taking Srilekha's silence as an answer she nods again. 'Then so it is. We will get through this, and may God protect my son.'

ARVIND

An hour or maybe two or maybe half the night has passed while he was lost in the bushes, getting turned around with no landmarks and no light except for the thinnest sliver of the moon, or maybe it has been entire weeks but he is here finally, back at the fence demarcating the Imperial Factory. He walks in a half crouch on legs that are rubber, unsteady along the treacherous path, his heart exploding on the inside of his ears, his schoolbag pulling down against narrow hunched shoulders, one hand feeling the fence next to him, searching for his opening …

He has walked through here every day for the past few weeks, but a deep night has fallen and fundamentally altered the topography of the land into something more sinister. The rocks have sharper edges and the ground underneath is playing a game of illusions. Arvind slips often, cuts himself often, and each time he recovers quickly and moves again, as if every minute is somehow eating him and relief lies only inside.

Tonight, he thinks, Amar and I shall leave tonight and never come back.

There it is, finally, the gap in the fence, and Arvind feels around it and crawls through and with this he re-enters the real world from the nightmare he had inhabited for the last hours. Instantly more confident on the familiar ground, he quietly and efficiently makes his way to the main building, the third out of the five, Amar's home, and as he bends to pick up stones to signal his arrival, he perceives the slightest movement out of the corner of his eye, and freezes in place.

One second. Two. A whole ten seconds of no breathing, willing his heart to beat silent. It is nothing. An interplay of his imagination and the gloom. He is convinced but he waits, stationary like a rock, the half crouch burning his thighs, eyes ripped wide, scanning for the barest hint of movement.

He sees it then.

Black against black, the silhouette of a man against the stars. It is gone before his brain can comprehend, but he is sure. Arvind knows this location, this ground, he has walked and marched and sweated over every inch of it. This intruder, he may be careful but …

Another sound. The faint crunch of gravel under a shoe, this time from his far left, and he knows the spot where the once-tarred base of the service road has eroded into grit the size of rice.

They have come. He is sure of it. The unknown, unnamed them from Amar's past have risen and arrived in the moonless night like ghosts to slay him, his wounded, unwalking friend, his mentor … Who even now sleeps his restless sleep, oblivious of the threat that rises around him. Arvind must do something, but he does not know what, for any movement may be detected by the assailants and they might grab him and beat him, kill him even.

He can shout, or scramble away or try to sneak past these men, their numbers unquantified, and wake Amar but even as they rise in his mind he knows these solutions are not guaranteed to succeed. There is little time, and they are getting closer while he thinks … and then he knows the answer. It sits, as ever, in his hand, gravid with ominous impulse. With all doubt gone, Arvind lifts the Gun, aims into the black nothing where he believes the silhouetted man to be and pulls the trigger.

VIII

UNDER THIS DARK MOON

WENDELL

Wendell is not superstitious. He does not believe in magic guns, and divine interventions in the lives of killers. God has a plan, he agrees, but it is not the work of man to unravel it.

His apprehension at this moment, he concludes, then lies simply in the identity of his target.

•••

The boys are in position.

Wendell waits some distance away. Telling himself that all is according to plan and the plan is good enough, simple in its execution, tailored according to the resources available with him, with layers of redundancy. It should be enough.

There are seven of them in the field ahead, dressed in black, armed with pistols, spread out to avoid any bunching that Amar can take advantage of with that fucking machine gun of his.

Five of the boys are final leftovers of Bilal's gang, its last gasp—two of them are survivors of the hotel massacre, only lightly wounded, alive now because they hid then, played dead, amidst the corpses of their friends. They were scared on the way here, these boys, terrified. They won't admit it, but Wendell can see the shame and guilt clouding their faces, the shame of cowards, the guilt of the silent—they walk like men craving absolution.

The other three are not much better, worse even, naked in their terror. These were the ones who had done the clean-up, poured the petrol, burnt the bodies. The ashes of their dead companions stick to their skin, even as they joke and talk of vengeance. Big brittle words about killing the killer, an unholy spectre now grown past all reality in their dreams. Their fear melts out of their pores like wax.

His own boys, Kamal and Tony, are different, better, walking the thin line, eager but not excited. They have done well, these boys of his, and for digging out the scent of the target it is right that they get to be part of the hunt. 'Stay on the outside,' he had told them, 'keep your eyes open.' They had nodded; they know that it is easier to shoot a man shooting at someone else.

The giant, Raju, is there too, stalking the edges. 'Don't worry about me,' he had said, his voice thin and wet as it slipped out of a still wired jaw. 'I will find where I have to be.' He had a gun with him, an ancient double-barrelled shotgun, comically small in his massive hands, a child's plaything. It was impossible to picture him shooting someone, he seemed more liable to club someone to death with it. Of all the men moving in the dark, he is the most dangerous. It is easy to underestimate big men as stupid and slow, a bias that has served Wendell in his own career, but Raju, Wendell is sure, is neither.

Wendell thinks about him and what it will take to kill him if he has to, which is likely once this night is over—he is sure it will not be easy—and that is when he hears the shot, splitting the night into two. It is too early, they cannot have reached the buildings yet. There are shouts of men and the barking of dogs and the plan is done for and cursing the heavens, he begins to move.

AMAR

The note strikes with perfect clarity and in an instant Amar is awake. He knows the texture of this sound in all its intricacy and there is no doubt in his mind, the Gun is here, and that means the boy is here too, and it has spoken again and this time it is indubitably a call to war.

He scrambles to his knees, instantly reaching for his bag of weapons, kept ready at his side. Right on top sits the Mac-10 with its makeshift sling which goes across the left shoulder, the gun hanging at perfect height just above his right hip. The bag with its extra magazines and extra pistols, oiled, ready, safeties off, goes over the right shoulder. Also inside are some of the surprises he has been working on …

It is an effort to stand, his leg buckling under the weight. The pain is sharp, but he moves anyway. He does not know how much they know so he must assume that they know where he is. Hiding away is not an option and in any event the boy … the boy is outside.

He keeps his trusted CZ75 in his right hand as he walks along the wall—he had slept with it, a thin strip of cloth looped along the trigger guard and tied to his wrist—as silent as he can be towards the exit which is a hole, twenty feet wide, filled with a lighter darkness. Suddenly torches illuminate the outside—cones of white light stabbing the night before they are hurriedly turned off in response to angry shouts. But it is enough to tell him that they are many and they are moving to surround him …

There are voices now, one, three, half a dozen, rising and falling alongside the howls of the dogs. Then another shot and another. He can see no muzzle flashes, and the stone structure around him makes it difficult to trace the source by sound. Amar does not know who is being shot at but it is not him. The sound of rushed movement is now a lot closer so he sticks to the wall just inside the big exit.

'There is no place to hide, you motherfucker.' The words are spoken right outside.

It is time.

Amar goes into his bag and grabs his own homemade brand of fiery death—two whisky bottles filled with a deadly mix of petrol and motor oil. He closes his eyes and sparking their fuel drenched wicks with a lighter, flings them out flat and hard. The Molotov cocktails hit the ground ten feet away, shattering into liquid radiance—the flames licking the feet of two figures, who were about to rush in, guns drawn, but now hop and jump in shock as the cloying fire rides up their legs. Ringed as they are by light, it is an easy thing to switch to the looped CZ75 and shoot them in the torso, twice each. As they drop, he sparks another bottle and throws it underhand, high and looping into the sky, a fiery beacon of danger, and without checking to see where it hits the ground, he slips out the side exit.

The distraction is a momentary thing, but it works well enough, and he is out of the killzone precious seconds before more shots ring out, tearing through the walls a few feet behind him …

ARVIND

Bullets have missed him by inches. Arvind knows this because he can still feel the unmistakable woosh of air brushing the skin of his cheek as he dropped to the hard ground after he shot the Gun into the darkness.

They shot where they thought he was but he was no longer there, barely, and then he was up and moving once more. He shot again to his right, a blind shot into the darkness where he thought he heard movement, but there was no time to take a proper stance and his grip was all wrong, so of course he did not hit anyone. This was a bad idea as they saw the muzzle flash and then there were more shots from directions he could not discern and it was a total miracle that he was not hit.

He trips and falls flat behind a short wall, and he is happy because he now knows where he is. There is a semblance of cover—a short boundary wall to an access road, barely the height of his knees, but when prone, as he is now, it is enough to cover his thin body. Gripping the Gun till his knuckles hurt, he reminds himself that the magazine has fifteen bullets and he has shot twice, which means he has thirteen bullets still. He forces himself to breathe the way Amar had taught him, focusing his entire being into the sensation of the ground under his body, pouring his entire panic into the ground, but it is really difficult to do when his heart is about to burst.

Surely they are coming for him at this very moment, for he was not quiet, and he is debating the risk of looking over the wall when there is more shooting and sudden bursts of light and screams. Something explodes not far from him and he smiles because his gambit has worked and Amar, now awake, has joined the party.

AMAR

The man chases him while shooting, his bouncing stride throwing off his aim and it is the work of a moment to pause, aim the sight and pump four bullets from the CZ75 into his face at a distance of thirty metres.

The man falls and Amar lets the now empty pistol drop to the ground, resisting the urge to crumple himself as he stumbles, his broken leg giving way—and something having twisted inside his knee when he burst out of the exit.

It is hot, really hot, but he should be used to it—this is when his spirit should be singing, his senses inflamed by the sound and the scent of burning cordite. But tonight it is not so … tonight, his leg is faltering, and his lungs too are betraying him, he is already fighting exhaustion and it is clear to him that his body is not prepared for the battle, not in the least, but the battle is here. He has made it to the back of the factory buildings and ahead of him now lie open fields that extend to the horizon dotted with other smaller factories and scrap plants, but he knows he cannot run, not with his leg, and not with the boy still out there …

Three are down already, at least, and the rest are in disarray and all around him is fire and chaos and somewhere in that chaos is

Arvind. Still alive? He has to be. His student, his only friend, his heir apparent … There is no way to be sure, but they, master and student, are both inside the storm now. He has to trust the boy and his fate, for he has the Gun, and Amar must believe that the Gun will protect him. It is an artifact fuelled by belief, and he will not allow his belief to waver.

The path is clear. The only thing left to do now is to kill as many of these sisterfuckers as possible. Now that all strategic options have been whittled down to this single piercing edge, he feels more in control.

With his nerves pumping electricity, he pushes his body forward, readying the Mac-10 and stuffing the Walther in the back of his pants. It is time to get serious. They are disorganized, their plan blown to bits. But they will take a breath, regroup. They will think him likely to run, and get ready to chase him—even now they see themselves as hunters. The last thing they will expect is for him to fall on them like the fucking hammer of God.

TONY

Tony has just figured out that there are two shooters. He was shot at from behind and now, a separate shootout is taking place ahead of him near the factory buildings. This one sounds really fucking dangerous, and so he decides that he will leave it to the others, while he turns to confront the threat at the back.

'Let's go. What are you waiting for?' The words are a gargled whisper, and Tony is suddenly aware of a giant mass next to him. It is Raju, Bilal's monster, and he has sneaked to Tony's side without him realizing at all. How can this fat fucking fucker be so silent?

A hand against his shoulder pushing forward, gentle but inexorable. 'There is someone behind us …' he says, the giant's voice is a single dried leaf. 'But they do not matter. He is ahead … Come on. Let's go.'

There are others too, two more of Bilal's boys, locals, and together they move forward, guns out, into the gentle circles of firelight in the clearing. Tony follows them, slower, hesitant to leave the protection of the shadows. Ahead there is no cover, and Tony is feeling naked and exposed, but he walks, one step in front of the other, an impossible pressure building at his back as Raju pushes him forward … It is not the smartest move, he knows, but here, far from Wendell, he is terrified of the giant. He cannot make words, or reason, or even turn around … So, he holds his gun up in front of him as he turns his torso in slow wide angles, staring into the darkness that seems to press from all directions. Now that he is closer, he can see the two bodies lying at the entrance, still smoking, and Tony wonders where the rest are—are they all dead, where is fucking Kamal …

Suddenly, there is a spark in the distance. Tony frantically reels off a couple of shots and then a giant ball of fucking fire explodes in his face.

AMAR

Those were all the bottles he had: eight of them, strung together and thrown. The explosion did not disappoint, engulfing one target completely in a flash and outlining two others. He steps out of cover and makes a sweep with the Mac-10, the compact machine gun held in both hands at hip height, and then another salvo into flickering silhouettes and two are down and maybe the third before he swings back past the edge of the wall, only to find that he has been shot again, this one is in his side, a gut shot, through the stomach or the liver or the spleen or something essential, and it is a fucking death sentence.

Well so it goes. Chaos cuts both ways.

There is a shuffle of movement on the ground next to him and he raises the Mac-10 and shoots at the still moving body. It is a short burst, probably three bullets or maybe four. The magazine is empty. It is quiet except for the fucker who ran back, maybe he has decided to run all the way back, and maybe he will have to chase the fucker. It is quiet. He may have won. One more guy and then he can call out to the boy, and see him. The boy is alive, he knows it. He has to be. He has the Gun.

The fire ahead is growing, stray embers carried in the wind land on dry grass and all is silent but for the sound of the flames.

The men on the ground in front of him are dead or pretending to be. He begins to reload the Mac-10, pressing the release button but the magazine slips out of his weakened fingers and falls at his feet. He takes a breath, braces the bad leg, tensing the muscles as much as he dares, and bends at his waist to pick it up.

The effort to stand straight is almost the end of him. The bullet has torn him up. All the muscles in his mid-section are cramping and loosening of their own volition, far outside his conscious control. He closes his eyes and wills them to act, forcing them to ignore the damage and knit together. Somehow he is upright, but it is slow, too slow, and he knows it is not for long, but just a bit longer and he can see the boy and the Gun once again. He takes a step, gritting his teeth and then there is movement, and the fucking giant from the hotel is there, barely ten metres away, not dead, inhuman jaw grinning in the fire, shotgun pointed right at him, and he cannot even raise an arm before the shotgun roars, a cannon at this distance …

ARVIND

He has been moving carefully, testing each step for sound before committing to it, ensuring there is no noise, nothing to give his position away. He tightens the straps of his schoolbag, till they dig into his shoulders. He considers discarding it, but rejects the idea—it is too dangerous. He may not be able to retrieve it later, and it will lead whoever finds it straight back to his family …

His thoughts are interrupted by a bright flash followed by two bursts of machine gun fire and he knows without being told that it is Amar with that fat Mac-10, laying out death, and that will draw all their attention so he can afford to move a little faster.

The courtyard is well lit, what with half a dozen small fires burning here and there, and he is running quickly between them when he senses something huge moving ahead of him and it is a man, unlike any Arvind has ever seen before: he is the size of a truck and he has a gun with him and he is aiming, but not at him, so he must be aiming it at Amar.

By pure instinct, he raises the Gun in his hand, smooth and up, like he drilled just hours ago on this very ground, and he pulls the trigger and the night explodes, and with his eyes still open, he pulls it again.

The shotgun is some distance away from him, maybe twenty metres but it roars and it is the loudest sound Arvind has ever heard. The giant pivots, as if only slightly troubled by the two bullets Arvind is certain he has put in him, and the shotgun is pointing at him and—BOOM!—it explodes again. Arvind is frozen, unable to move, he does not know who the giant was expecting but it was not a boy, barely four feet tall, and maybe that is what saves him for none of the pellets touch him where he stands, the hot metal flying above his head. The giant, confused, throws the gun at him like a dart, and it comes flying through the night at enormous speed and crashes into Arvind's chest.

AMAR

The shotgun does not miss, not fully, and his left side takes the brunt of it. It feels like half his face has been scraped off with hot razor blades.

Blinded by viscera, ready to die, he waits for the second shot, and when it comes but does not hit him, he wipes blood and tattered skin off his right eye and sees that the giant has turned his back on him, and has shot elsewhere, and then flung his gun forward. He spots Arvind, a tiny figure collapsing into the shadows, and he should be shooting but the Mac-10 in his right hand is empty, waiting, and his entire left side is just a collection of trauma, but somehow he has managed to keep a hold of the magazine in his left hand, an involuntary death grip he cannot feel, the fingers warped around the metal, the nerves within short-circuited.

Amar drops the gun to let it swing from its strap and screams at the giant with all the air he has in his burning lungs. His challenge has no words, but no words are needed, not between them. The big man turns away from the boy to stare at Amar, and the next instant is in a full sprint, running right at him. Nothing this big should be moving this fast, and a surprised Amar fumbles for the Walther in his pants with his one working hand, but his fingers fail to find traction on the bloody pistol grip, and he tries again and again, to somehow anchor the index finger in the trigger guard, but it is too late.

The tackle lifts him off his feet and he is flying through the air, only to be driven into a wall, the impact erupting through his body and switching the lights off.

When he comes to he does not know how long he was out, but it cannot have been too long for he is still on the floor, with the giant fucker on his chest, his fingers like steel cables wrapped around his throat, choking him. There is no removing those fingers, he knows this from experience, but he fights anyway, clawing at them with his nails and then there is a shot, and two more, and something thick and warm falls onto his face and then another one, a final Boom! The fingers around his throat relax and the enormous weight is lifted as the giant topples to his side …

ARVIND

It takes him no time at all to find the Gun at his feet, the steel flickering with a blaze all its own, light emanating from the metal itself. A count of three to stand and locate the giant, now sitting on Amar Singh. A single count to raise the gun in a double-handed grip, and ignoring every lesson he has been taught, Arvind shoots as he walks, one trigger press with each step in the dark, adrenaline bursting through exhausted muscles. Bullets number five and six disappear into the massive back and when he gets a little closer, and more careful, bullets number seven and eight in his gun, go through the head of the monster, and that is the end of that.

Time slows further, moving in fractions of inches. There is a shot from ahead of him and then another and the Gun is up again, and he fires three successive shots, nine, ten, eleven ... He does not know if he has hit anyone, shooting as he is into absolute darkness, but there is no return fire.

A battered and bloodstained Amar crawls out from below the giant above him, and Arvind rushes to him and helps him up and all he says is 'move', and so they do, limping together, the weight of the older man on him, following the edge of the wall and around the corner, safe for the moment. Amar grabs his arm. 'Wait ...' Arvind is surprised at the strength of the grip that pulls him in, his guru's dark eyes shining like stars in the darkness, burning into his head. 'Good work, boy,' Amar says and the words sink into his heart and remove all the fear and make him soar on the inside. 'Now listen to me, you need to run, we cannot let these fuckers get their hands on the Gun …'

'You are hurt—'

'This blood is not mine,' he says, and then, 'We should not be standing together like this, making one big fat target … Now go! Remember where we first met? I will meet you there.'

'I am not leaving you …'

Amar carefully draws the Walther from his pants. A gunshot rings out, probing, aimed at nothing. A reminder that the survivors are out there, still hunting.

'The Gun is what is important. And I cannot move very fast with this anyway …' Amar says patting his leg. 'There aren't many of them left. One, maybe two. I can handle them. It will be easy. Do not sit here looking at my face. Go! You must keep the Gun safe.'

As if on cue another shot is fired. This one hits the wall near them, it is closer, so much so that he can hear the distinctive metallic ping of the bullet striking stone.

Amar pushes him away and scrambles into the shadows.

•••

Arvind runs.

He runs not because of Amar's words, but because he is not fooled by them. He runs not to escape, but to be a target, a prominent target, leading the surviving attackers away, out of the factory complex, deeper into the fields … He runs to give Amar a chance to regroup, to live …

He shoots the sky as he runs, screaming loud in the night, zigzagging past the still sputtering fires. He hears another shot, and then another. Puffs of dust at his feet as the bullets miss and then he is past the courtyard, and into the deep shadows, and this is when he turns and shoots in the air, bullet number twelve, and then runs again. There are answering shots but he does not care as long as they are aimed at him and not at Amar. He can hear the steps now as a single pursuer breaks into a run somewhere to his right …

Arvind leads his pursuer through the fields towards the boundary fence, just as he had planned, then turns and shoots bullet number thirteen, blind. He knows that he has not hit anything, but he focusses on running, pumping his legs as hard as he can, flying across the broken ground, not caring for where his feet fall in the darkness. He knows the fence is coming up, it must be, it has to be here, and he sprints faster, calves burning. There it is, the fence, and outside is the whole world to run to but the gap … it is not there, he cannot see it with his fast frantic eyes, so he forces himself to breathe and remembers the two bullets that are still in the magazine. He spins around and crouches and begins to scoot backwards to the fence, feeling for the gap even as he stares back out towards the factory, peering into the darkness, hoping to catch sight of his pursuer—and there it is, a flicker of a shadow, but he is not sure if he is imagining it. Boom! A bullet hits the fence behind him and all he has seen is the spark but he shoots once and he knows he has missed and then he shoots again, and this is the last bullet, and a scream cuts the air.

He finds the gap in the fence and he is through and out.

AMAR

The boy is fucking crazy. Shooting like that at the bastards to make them follow him into the darkness. Ha! Stupid little bastard. It hurts to smile, but he does.

He can hear the fucker chase after the boy, a quick scramble of running feet over the dirt, but cannot make out his shape in the darkness. His vision is not what it was a few minutes ago. If he could just rest his one working eye for a moment …

No. He must go after the boy, protect him. Kill the fuckers … the fuckers will not let him go so easily.

So what if you've been shot? It isn't the first time, he tells himself. It's just fucking pain. He can move, he must move. Today there is something worthwhile to be won. There is, he tells himself, only one of them out there … maybe two. He will just have to seek that last fucker out and shoot. That won't be hard, he can still move, can't he?

One more kill and then the boy will be safe and all this will be over. Rest then, maybe die even, but later … He can do it. It is just a step. The leg can move, come on, just move it. It is a question of will—

A bullet hits him.

It feels almost familiar now, the punch and pull, an old friend. It does not hurt, it simply feels like something giving away. Another. This one feels like a push, like a game with friends when he was a child, and he is flying now, for a time, a long time, enough time to fill his lungs with cold air a cubic inch at a time, and now he is on the ground, his face in the dust. He does not remember falling. Did he trip? Slip maybe … He cannot turn his neck to look. His eyes see nothing in the darkness but he is sure they are open. His mouth is open and pressed against the ground. He tastes blood, his own, and there is grit on the insides of his lips. How did it get there? He does not know it is the shattered pieces of his own teeth.

He feels rather than hears the footsteps that come close. It is hard to concentrate over the soft, ever rising, whooshing sound in his head. Fuck, all he wanted was one more—

WENDELL

Wendell shoots Amar Singh in the back of the head.

And then again for good measure. There is no twitch in the body.

Wendell turns him over with his foot. His friend looks frail in death. Using a camera he has been carrying in his pocket, he takes a picture.

Amar Singh is holding a Walther in his hands. Wendell searches him, but finds no sign of the gun. An additional annoyance in a night when nothing has gone to plan. He will need to be quick. The shootout has gone on too long. Amar was a hard fucking bastard to kill. Wendell looks again at the body, and all the damage it took to take him down. Amar should have been dead thrice over. But then again, he was the most stubborn bastard Wendell knew.

He glances at his watch. It has been twenty-two minutes since the first bullet was fired. It is an eternity in these things. The police could be breaking down the gates at this very minute. He has little time and the job is only half done.

•••

Wendell searches Amar's body for the gun for five dangerous minutes, even braving a lit electrical torch. He finds an imported knife but nothing else. He expands the circle of his search, thinking the gun may have fallen somewhere, anywhere, but it is a hopeless task. The light reveals a hellscape of discarded shells and blackened skin, but no gun. He finds the giant Raju, with his head blown off and what looks like at least three bullet holes in his massive back, and Tony, or what is left of him, his black polyester shirt still smouldering. He finds no other survivors.

At a sound behind him, Wendell aims his torch and gun together to see Kamal, out of breath, shuffling along, clutching his thigh. The torchlight reveals a large, growing circle of blood on his jeans.

'Where the fuck were you?'

'I … there was another shooter … I just …'

'Another shooter?'

'It was the kid. The one we followed, Tony and me. Fucker shot me, got me good. It is in my leg. Is it over … We got him, didn't we?' Then, 'Is Tony okay?'

Wendell shoots him in the head. It is a pity, he liked the boy, he had potential. But this is no time for him to chaperone the wounded.

IX

NEXT OF KIN

KAPOOR

Kapoor gets a call in the middle of the night on the home phone. It is ACP Sardesai from Bombay.

'It is done,' he tells him, 'an hour ago. Go and close your case.'

At the scene, the carnage is fresh. Again, bodies that are shot up, bodies that are half burnt. Again, there is no one left alive.

Inured from the clean-up at the guest house, Kapoor and his men do not react.

Away from the others lies a single body with half his face blown off. A loaded pistol in his hands, a single knife on the ground next to him, alongside a pack of Capstan cigarettes. There is a small machine gun looped around the left shoulder in a cloth sling.

It is him, Kapoor knows. His manslayer. He looks at the dead man at his feet and realizes that he is standing at the centre of a circle of carnage. The violence seems to radiate out from him, in every direction he can see it, other bodies forming spokes on a wheel.

A grim harvest. One man, Kapoor thinks, just one man. If they gave me ten like this, what couldn't I do?

Round them up, he tells his men, round them up and keep them ready. The constables are not too happy to touch the fresh corpses, but he glares at them and they get to work. Qureshi, his SI, says, 'These are all Bilal's boys. I recognize them. This is Raju … I have heard stories … I didn't think he was real. Sixteen murders. They say he ate their hearts.'

Fucking hell.

'Seal it. I do not want anyone coming in. Tell the boys to get their guns ready. We need to stage this properly. You will handle it?'

'Yes. But … All the other bullets?'

'We will figure that out. Don't worry about it. This will be the biggest ever … There will be promotions everywhere on this one.'

'What about him?'

'No. Not him. This one is special delivery.'

Some minutes later Kapoor smokes one of the dead man's cigarettes as gunshots ring out behind him. Qureshi is out there setting the scene. He was a veteran of the mining violence in Rannwara, the bad days of the eighties. Quite a thing this town was, quite a thing it can be again.

•••

Dawn. The ambulances come in to collect the bodies, now all lined up neatly. More police, as they wake, are dispatched. Someone gets him tea and biscuits. A settlement nearby, he is told, by way of explanation. About twenty houses. 'They didn't hear anything?' he asks.

'Don't worry, sir, I spoke to them. They heard nothing at all.'

A crowd has gathered in the distance, beyond the old steel fencing. Mute, dark faces look at him. Locals all, labourers and goatherders, starting their day.

Qureshi tells him it is all done. Hands him a knife. 'What is this?'

'Found it next to our hero. Look carefully,' he says, 'there are initials carved in the hilt.'

The letters *J* and *R* stare at him. Kapoor feels like he has won the lottery. 'Good job over here. It will work?'

'Too many wounds via 9mm,' is all he says, before saluting. Kapoor makes a note of it. Another call to make this afternoon. Right now though, it is time to call the Ranades.

He drives out of the location, following the ambulance carrying his manslayer, the ticket to all his dreams. The crowd parts for the cars to pass, and among the men he sees a brown boy in a dirty uniform. It is too early to be dressed for school, he thinks, and it is not till much later that it strikes him that he knows the uniform.

ARVIND

Arvind waited for hours in the same clearing where Jaggi had died. The ghost was there with him. Sitting on the same spot where his body once lay, expressionless and unchanged the whole time. Arvind spent the night crying softly, clutching the Gun, now empty yet larger and heavier than ever. His fingers cramped from holding it but he could not let go, the metal, ice cold, was his only grip on reality, and if he let it slip it would all have been for nothing, and so he sat there in the darkness with his eyes wide open even as waves of fever wracked him, straining to hear the steps of men. The night grew very cold as he sat, crying in bursts, no longer understanding what was happening to him. He checked his body for wounds, for secret bullet holes, for Amar had told him stories of such things happening, but he found none, just unbroken skin which shivered and trembled with ever greater frequency.

He slipped away, but it was not like going to sleep, more like blowing a fuse, a light bulb unable to handle the voltage burning out, hitting darkness in an instant …

In his nightmares the earth below him opened up, angry and full of fire, and a fire leaked out of the crust, like juice from a smashed orange, and the hot molten lava flowed everywhere, absolute rivers of it around him. As he walked to one such orange river, it cooled to a duller red, showering sparks like the raw iron hammered by wandering lohars working on the edges of the road, and it was now level and smooth and he found himself on the edge of a ridge that extended for miles, arching around him in a gentle curve, and he realized he was looking at a trigger, and the entire planet was merely an egg for the weapon growing inside it.

•••

He woke up and it was dawn. There was a sharp pain in his stomach and he saw that the hard edge of the Gun was digging into his stomach as he slept with it tucked into his shorts, the school uniform shorts he had been wearing since the day before. The events of the night flooded his mind and he realized with a sinking feeling that it was dawn and Amar was not there with him.

He was weak but the fever was gone, broken into sweat with the morning sun. He pulled his schoolbag from where he had tossed it, and he packed the Gun again, carefully, in overlapping layers of plastic. It took him an hour—his fingers weren't moving as they should have.

He began walking, noting that the ghost of Jaggi was walking next to him.

•••

Amar Singh is dead.

Arvind knows this the instant he returns to the factory, and then he thinks he has known this the whole walk back. He looks through the fence, and there is activity inside, men in police uniforms patrol the area even as others, reporters maybe, take photographs in silence.

He considers sneaking in, past the fence, past the police, and seeing him, Amar, lying dead like some of the bodies he had seen last night, like how Jaggi had lain, wounds large and gaping, radiating some black-edged menace and he cannot, he cannot, and the thought of his friend's body breaks him and he pukes and pukes but his stomach is empty for he has not eaten in a day and nothing comes out, not even bile, only dry air squeezed out of his bones.

He walks along the fence till he finds himself at the old factory gate. Ambulances. More police. Here he stands with a group of people, bystanders buzzing with quiet awe as a covered body is loaded into an ambulance, overseen by a senior cop, his skin shining like white marble in the morning sun. Arvind watches and knows that the thing over there is just some dead meat, not his friend, and as the ambulance drives out, siren wailing, he knows this is goodbye.

•••

His walk to the town is a strange one and while it is still morning, within him is this great heat which rises and rises and makes things look a little faint. As he walks, he realizes he has nowhere to walk to, his only island has been ripped away. He feels weak for he has not eaten in the last day or had any water or rest and thinking is hard and all he can do is walk.

Maybe it is muscle memory but he realizes he is on the way home. That is not where he wants to go and so he walks some more but it is getting hard to do it and he is thirsty … ever so thirsty … and there is a handpump around here, there has to be, he remembers it, his and Sudipto's handpump. It is here somewhere yet he cannot find it but maybe he just needs to walk a little bit more …

•••

He wakes up at the colony gate with someone pressing a bottle of water to his lips, saying, it is okay, it is all right, and his eyes open to see the moustache and dark eyes of the watchman of gate no. 3 as he swallows. At first there is fear and panic and then just thirst, and he finds standing next to him a familiar man, the owner of the alcohol shop where he stopped every day, and the man tells the guard, look he is okay, just please get his parents, I will wait with him.

Arvind sits up to complain but he cannot speak, the words seem to get lost between his brain and his vocal chords and then realizes he does not have his schoolbag with him—it has the Gun, and it is in the watchman's hands as he walks towards his father's house. Each step taking it further away.

A rough hand with callouses on the palm caresses his cheek gently and he looks at the man who is standing there, the man from the shop, and he has tears in his eyes as he says, I am sorry if your father is an alcoholic and I'm sorry for everything you have to go through, but running away is not the answer, and I am sorry I brought you back here but I didn't know what else to do, I panicked when I found you, you were unconscious and wouldn't wake up and I found your address written on your bag and so I just brought you here.

He then says that his father beat him too, a lot, when he was young and that is just how fathers are. Some are good and some are bad and you cannot do anything about it, not when you are young, and sometimes not even when you are older.

•••

Arvind is picked up by Appa and Srilekha who looks like she has been crying the whole night. Appa gives the man from the shop a fifty-rupee note, and the man says no, says it was his duty. He tells Appa that he needs to do better for his son than he is doing right now. 'There are many ways to be a father, and I am not here to tell a big officer like you how to do things … You have a good boy here and you can still fix this. My father was like you, and now he is dead in the village, and I didn't light his pyre.'

SRILEKHA

The twelve hours of the night were absolute hell, with no one sleeping, with Appa taking one trip after another on his scooter, hoping to spot Arvind, somewhere, anywhere, and no one talking for what words could explain what had happened, except for Amma, who sat on the same dining chair, chanting, 'He will come back, he will come back in the morning,' as though this mantra was the only thing protecting her from absolute madness.

And maybe it is her words that worked, for he is here now, standing in the living room at the very same spot. Of course, now all is changed. She sees him looking like a thing half dead, a wet rat pulled out from a gutter, and anger wars with pity for a while until anger wins. It is a silent anger though, building on the inside because there is no space to express it, not with Appa losing it at him. There is much shouting and screaming and accusations, and her brother just stands there taking it. Then are beatings, horrific beatings, with hands and belts and sandals even and he stands there and takes it, offering no excuses and no explanations, till he cannot stand anymore. And then he breaks, and it is like a dam bursting. He cries and cries and cries … howling like a baby, his thin shoulders shaking and Amma falls upon him, tearing him away from Appa, who tries to pull her away but does not succeed.

•••

They decide to lock him in the bathroom. They initially plan to lock him in his bedroom, but she tells them that will not work, not with his habit of sneaking out through windows. He does not react at all at her words, content to simply weep.

They leave him biscuits and water, and he is thrown into the bathroom and that is where he spends the day, while Amma and Appa are inside their bedroom, arguing a thousand arguments, and Srilekha is outside, staring at the door, wondering how it came to this, how their little imperfect life broke down so completely in a matter of weeks.

•••

It is after an argument with Amma that Appa stomps to the bathroom, opens the door and slaps a still weeping Arvind, saying that he is no longer a son of his, and that he is dead to him and then he leaves—shouting to Srilekha to close the door behind him.

As she does so, her little brother looks her in the face and says, 'Last night, all I did was only to save you,' and she thinks that there are no limits to the lies that we are willing to believe about ourselves.

ARVIND

He could have fought harder, he could have been braver, he spent too much time hiding, he didn't shoot straight enough, and if the first bullet itself had killed the pursuer he could have turned back and saved Amar, he could have if he had trained harder, run faster, shot better …

He should have known that Amar was lying, that he was not just behind him, that there were more like the others, but he was scared of the big one who did not die and so he listened and he ran and he should have been braver instead of hiding in the darkness for half the gunfight and maybe he could have done more, after all, how many bullets did he waste? He fired fifteen bullets and only killed one man, and maybe wounded another and had he used them properly and killed the others then maybe Amar would still be alive.

JAI

They have brought the killer's corpse home for Baba to see.

The body lies in a glass coffin, a refrigerated box with steel edges and a glass top and sides, rolled in on a stretcher. Rolling next to it on a wheel barrow is the diesel generator that powers the cooling mechanism.

The ambulance that carried the body had a simple police escort, no sirens, and the cars slipped in along the service gate. There was barely any staff, just a driver and one attendant from the morgue, and of course a couple of cops and the fucker Kapoor shining in the morning sun.

The stretcher was heavy, with the weight of the coffin and the mechanism, and it took fifteen minutes to figure out how to bring it out of the ambulance, and finally it was Baba's attendants, the ones who carried him up and down the stairs, who had to help.

The coffin carrying the dead killer was brought into the garden—so as to not have his blood pollute the house—and set on the grass so that even Baba, on his wheelchair, could look down on the man who killed his son.

Baba sits and stares at the body, as if he can scare it into talking, spilling all its secrets. All the reasons his son had to die. They ask if he wants to be wheeled away, back inside, but he seems determined to stay.

Other members of the household—the guards, the servants—are allowed their time, and they come and curse the body and the soul of the dead man. The party workers were told to stay away, but a few who apparently live in the house, stand along the edges of the garden. One of them begins to chant, 'Long live Jagdish Bhaiya,' but it is shut down immediately.

Jai studies the killer. This is it. The man who killed Jaggi. Now dead, he looks like nothing at all. Shirtless, it is a thin body, with ribs sticking out. One eye open, staring at nothing, a half smile on a young half face, the rest is missing—a mangled lump where the bullets have done their job. All over the body, shining pale and white in evening sun, is a whole other story of scars—leftovers from a life of violence. Some of the wounds are fresh, half healed and angry, helpfully outlined in black marker pen, fat circles drawn around bullet wounds in the shoulder and chest that played a part in this killing. It was not an easy death.

The killer looks worse than Jaggi had and that is something of a relief. Some manner of justice has been served but it is not enough.

With his enemy dead before him, Jai feels empty. Jaggi's murderer is forever away from him now, safe from his vengeance. He thinks of breaking the glass of the coffin, of pulling this body out to fight it, to punch it. To drag it through drains, to piss in its face. To somehow make an accounting for the pain he still feels, but they are all useless gestures. And those watching will stand and nod. No one will interrupt, not the guards, the police, not even Kapoor—he can do whatever he wants … and maybe this is what stops him.

Look at him, they will think, for they would never dare to say it, Jaivant Ranade can only punch dead men.

•••

He walks in on Om and Kapoor talking in the house, this time not in the office, Kapoor drinking tea, Om drinking nothing.

'We got a tip off about some of Bilal's people heading out to the old Imperial Factory buildings … So we moved in. We were a little late though, they had started the party without us. We had to … well … clean it up.' It was these killers from Bombay and the Bilal Ansari gang, Kapoor explained, a continuation of their earlier fight. 'He is the guy from the hotel. We have recovered the machine gun and other sophisticated weapons and ammunition from his possession. We believe they will match the bullets found there. There were two others with him, both out-of-towners based on how they were dressed, boys we did not recognize. We think the three of them were working together.'

And on his body, he says, we found this, and he takes out Jaggi's knife. Jai recognizes it instantly—he does not even need to rush forward and take it, see it up close, check the carved inscription … The dead man outside is truly the man who killed Jaggi, and the cops got him, and all the ends are tied up, and Jai could not avenge his baby brother or do anything to harm even a single hair on the men responsible for killing Jaggi, and that of course is the end of that.

'Are we sure this is the last of them? No one else hiding in the shadows?' Om asks.

'Absolutely,' says Kapoor. 'The case is closed.'

•••

It is well into the night when Baba finally allows someone to wheel him back into the house.

SRILEKHA

In the evening, things settle into some kind of exhausted calm, and Amma lights all the lamps, including the ones that are lit only on festivals, and offers prayers, longer and louder than usual. Appa sits in silence in the living room with the TV on, acting like he cannot hear her. Both of them ignore her so she sits in her bedroom looking at Arvind's empty bed and his empty desk, stewing in the collected insanity that surrounds her, and she tries to shield herself from it, push it away, but it is everywhere, dripping like dark treacle from the edges where the walls meet.

During dinner, on the TV, there is news about a big shootout in Rannwara this morning and the police are confident that they have eliminated the gangs associated with the violence seen over the last few weeks.

•••

After dinner Arvind is brought into the living room and standing before them, he tells the story of how he found the Gun outside a temple during a festival and kept it, believing it to be a gift from God, and how he was attacked by Jaggi Ranade and had to shoot him in self-defence. He tells them about Amar Singh, the hitman whom the Gun belonged to and how the man found him and took him under his wing, and how they would train with the Gun after school, and it was just that, nothing more—he didn't steal anything or hurt anyone. He tells them that he knows Amar is dead, and that no one alive suspects his involvement in anything.

It is a short story and has a lot of holes but her parents do not seem to be asking any of the questions that she wants to ask, and they stay stuck inside her, the questions, like how was he sure that Jaggi was going to hurt him, and why did he steal a Gun in the first place …

He tells them that no one can know anything because the men who killed Amar are still out there, and other people who are hunting for Jaggi's killer and this information cannot go out, no matter what. You do not know who they are, he warns, and if they find out the truth, they will not care about any excuses, they will kill me and everyone in this family with no thought at all.

'I know you think they will not, but they will. You do not understand these people. You cannot turn me in,' he tells his father, 'you cannot because they will come after you and Srilekha and Amma as well. They will destroy your lives. I did not want to put you in this situation, but this is how it is. Whatever happens to me, whatever you choose to do to me, we have to keep this secret as a family.'

The Gun, he says, must be kept carefully—at home. 'I will tell you how to fix the safety. Do not try to get rid of it, because it must not be found or somehow traced to you otherwise things will get very bad. No matter what, you cannot give it to the police.'

Appa is silent, his rage abated by a full day of violence. 'I will not have a murderer in my house, I will not, I will not,' he says and then, looking at Amma, 'I don't care what you have to say about this,' and that he will send Arvind to boarding school in the south and pay for his schooling and that is it, and that Arvind is dead to him and he wishes he would change his name and remove the stain from his entire family.

'You are no son of mine.'

Arvind nods and says that it is okay, it is better this way, and there is nothing to worry about because only one other person knew the whole truth and he is now dead.

WENDELL

Right after the events at the factory, Wendell rode his scooter to Bilal's safe house, only to find it abandoned. He walked through dusty corridors, and kicked down ramshackle doors but discovered no trace of Bilal or of that little nephew of his, nor any indication of where they might have gone.

It was not unexpected. Bilal would have headed out at night knowing full well that whatever the outcome of the hunt, his own life was worthless now. He would have realized it the moment Wendell arrived in Rannwara as Jaslok Kamani's representative. Bilal was no fool, one look at Wendell and he would have begun planning alternatives. Fucking bastard knew how to survive.

Maybe if things had turned out differently last night, it would have been him, Wendell, lying next to Amar with a hole in his head. If Amar Singh had not single-handedly taken out the whole fucking lot of them. A final favour from his friend. Wendell could feel tears rise within him but he squashed them. His work was not done yet, and there would be time enough for nostalgia.

Later in the day, Wendell mailed the camera roll hidden inside old newspapers to Boss—proof of Amar's demise at his hands. It would reach in a few days. He would have liked to speak to the old bastard, but he had been told not to make direct contact for a while.

Maybe it was better this way, Wendell was not sure he would be able to control what he said.

He had spoken instead to a man in Pune, and though no names or details were exchanged, Wendell was certain he was a cop. Something about the voice you just cannot fake.

Done for the day, Wendell headed to the second safe house. It was in the same locality as the first one, the one he had shared with his deceased assistants, but in a different lane. He was the only person who knew about this house, having sent a different boy to Rannwara for exactly one job. He was wary of repeating patterns. On the way, he checked for tails, but didn't spot any.

The house, like the last one, was bare but for the most basic furniture. No bed. Just a table and some metal chairs with tattered cushions. He turned on the fan and slumped down on the floor to take a nap.

•••

The gun remains the only unfulfilled part of his mission. He was shocked to not find it in Amar's dying grasp. But he is confident it is out there, somewhere in the fields … Maybe the police will find it, and then it will become somebody else's problem.

At night he rides out on the scooter and picks up multiple portions of mutton curry from the dhaba Kamal had discovered. Wild meat, marinated in curds and chillies, and cooked over coals. Back at the safe house, behind a locked door, he stares at the mountain of rice in front of him, covered in meat and spicy gravy. He allows himself to reminisce. There is great sadness mixed with some joy as he digs into the food, as he thinks of Amar Singh and all the times past, as he chews every spoken word and swallows every bit of laughter down with the food, bite by bite, making them a true part of him, imbibing Amar's spirit, leaving nothing unresolved so that his ghost does not haunt him.

SUDIPTO

There is another curfew in the city after the most recent shootout, but the mood is different, jubilant, a fever raging through Rannwara. While there is a curfew in name, and the shops are closed and there is no school, there are celebrations in the street as mobs once again descend from surrounding villages—a thousand mouths loudly cheering the lifting of darkness, the defeat of shadow, a true festival of the old feudal spirit. They came in and killed our son, our collective son, they scream, they killed our noble prince, and now it is their bodies that lie in the dust.

There are rallies and agitations, trucks set on fire in explosions of happiness, highways blocked in displays of joy. The plant is shut and production is stalled in a commemoration of the justice that has prevailed in the land. The district administration is in on it, encouraging it, Papa says, shaking his head, revelling in this bloody nonsense, because it has just saved their careers.

Every day, there are pictures of the dead gangsters in the news, their names and ages and speculated motives. Sudipto spends hours peering at their faces, which dissolve unclear and patchy in the cheap ink, for all he gets to see are the local Hindi papers, obtained secretly from the cook. There are pictures in the English paper too, surely much clearer, but those pages are removed by Ma at the breakfast table before he gets his hands on them.

He cuts out a copy of the picture of the killer of Jaggi. There is a lot written about the dreaded shooter Amar Singh who is linked to some fifty shootings in Bombay, gunned down by Rannwara's brave policemen in a daring shootout, during which the heroic Rannwara Police ambushed not one but two gangs, one of them from distant Bombay, and shot dead all the criminals. It is the victory of good over evil, the papers scream, a celebration of Diwali in June in which the killers of the young boy, our young boy, have been brought to justice.

How little they know. Sudipto whispers a prayer of thanks to the photo of the dead killer. His private hero, his secret deliverer. He whispers thanks to the gods who brought him here, to Rannwara, to save him. He does this with complete sincerity before hiding the picture amongst his books. And with this he feels a chapter is closed.

It is over now. This experiment, India, Rannwara, all of it.

He wants out, he wants to go back to his old life in America and his American school where there are no guns and his American friends who were all white and smelled strange but some of them, at least, were nice enough to him. His thread here, with the sputtering out of his friendship with Arvind, is quite run out.

•••

School reopens on a Thursday after the curfew is over, and a slower, more considered Sudipto says goodbye to his mother in the car and walks up the stairs to the classroom, heart heavy and mind on fire. There is a conversation to be had with Arvind, his best friend—even if it is now a one-way relationship—and it is a difficult conversation, tinged with sadness, and Sudipto cannot help but feel that he is betraying something larger than him, that with his choice some great potential is unravelling.

Maybe they were friends only because Jaggi had stalked them together, and with his death, Arvind believes there is no longer a cause that binds them, and is okay to let the relationship go …

He wonders if he can ask this question, and whether he wants an honest answer, but this is all to no avail as Arvind is not in class. After the assembly it is Srilekha who talks to the class teacher with a letter saying that Arvind is severely unwell and will not be coming in this week. They are hoping he will recover by the end of the week, enough to come in and take the term exams.

Later, during the recess, he finds her waiting for him, large and swaying her weight from leg to leg, and she asks him if she can borrow his class notes for different subjects so as to copy them out for Arvind.

'What happened to him? Is he okay?'

'It is fever,' she says. 'Also a stomach ache. Bad stomach ache. Something you boys ate together maybe …' She looks at him a certain way, like she is trying to reach into his soul for an answer, but to what question, he cannot guess.

ARVIND

What is the source of this agony that drowns every thought and every action? Was it all for nothing? Just a waste of time and effort? All the medicines and all of the care and the sleepless nights wondering if he would die in his fevers and the relief in the afternoons when he had not?

The Gun is gone. It has been locked up or thrown away or melted into nothing. He asked once, and this time Srilekha hit him. Stood over him and punched his arms as he cowered behind them. It didn't hurt, not much, he is used to much worse, and also he understands that in this period all answers were beatings and without the weapon with him he feels weak, helpless like a baby. Each strike pains him and takes something essential away from him, leaving him with less of himself. This amputation is its own wound. All the stories Amar told him, the stories he himself believed, about being chosen by God to wield a divine weapon—those too seem like lies in this harsh afternoon. All the training and all the work, everything he has learnt, everything he had become, has been for naught.

What can he do? He lacks the language to articulate the completeness of this loss. He wants to mourn for it, but there is no way he can even comprehend it.

Arvind cries and cries and cries. In the bedroom, in the dark, as he eats, as he showers. He cries, trying his best to ignore the giant's ghost looking at him, half his face blown off, sitting next to dead Jaggi. He cries, terrified that soon Amar will join them.

He cries for the loss of possibility. He cries for a future truncated. He cries for the death of goodness. He cries because he misses his friend.

JAI

Jai is drunk and is at home though he does not remember driving back from Lucky's. The evening had started with a workout and then Abhimanyu had brought some beer and then time became muddy. Now he is in his father's house, stumbling in the corridors, when he finds Om poring over a pile of papers in the living room, still dressed in his official white kurta.

'Where were you? Did you have your security …?'

'I had my fucking security with me,' Jai says as he slumps on the sofa opposite. 'Don't worry, brother, it is the security that I want to discuss with you.' It takes effort to keep his words clear, to iron the slurring out of them. 'I want him,' he continues. 'The cop. You know he was in on it. He had to be.'

'Not now,' Om says, the papers still in his hand. 'The cops are fucking untouchable, Kapoor is untouchable now. They are calling him for a commendation to the capital. There have been'—he counts—'twenty-two dead men in two incidents spread over two weeks. The fucker is flying. He is a hero. We have lost control of him.'

'I don't care about Kapoor, I just want Sonawane.'

'You will get him. Be patient. Let Kapoor get his new posting. He is being called to Bombay, Crime Branch. It is how these things work.' Om looks him in the eye. 'Relax Jai. It is done. We got them … just as I told you we will. Things are looking better for us everywhere. The tide is turning.'

'Do we know who was behind this? No, we do not. You told me you wanted their head—'

The look Om gives him sobers him right up, reminds him why his elder brother is the most vicious of them, the one not to be crossed, the one who, on the inside, is most like their father.

'Come, sit by me,' Om says as he keeps his papers aside. It is not really a request, so Jai gets up and changes seats to be next to his brother, becoming the sole focus of Om's considerable attention. 'We have some ideas. Someone in Bombay has reached out to us … to broker peace. The man, this man, the one who shot Jaggi was associated with them. But this hit on us … it was unsanctioned.'

'You believe them?'

'They have been very convincing. They had no reason to attack us. Nor any reason to apologize and come clean. In fact, it was they who cleaned up this entire mess themselves. They gave us his head.'

'So wait … Kapoor and the cops?'

'They reached in time to click the pictures and take the credit. The matter was already resolved. It seems the killers were contracted by Bilal Ansari. There may be someone standing behind him, some other old enemy paying the bill. We will find out in time—'

'And that is enough for you?'

'It is enough for now. The important thing is that Jaggi is avenged. His killers are dead. Everyone who worked with his killers is dead. We have flexed our muscles. No one in the whole state, or even the whole country, is going to come up against us now. Twenty-two men, Jai, twenty-two.'

A righteous anger sparks within him, evaporating the liquor. 'Not one of them was taken out by us. We have done fucking nothing!'

'We will get Bilal. He cannot run forever, and we will get him to talk. Get more leads. As I said, we will get some more heads … soon. For now, the public has seen us take this revenge. It is a victory for law and order.'

Jai has no words as Om talks, just towering rage. He wants to hit his brother, consequences be damned. Jaggi's death has been washed into nothing, the blood spilt and drained away has been mopped up and sanitized into a game of chess that Om is playing against enemies he cannot see.

Om continues undaunted, 'There is going to be a rally next week. The home minister is going to attend. Kapoor is getting a medal.'

SUDIPTO

It is the day of the first exam and Sudipto is surprised to see Arvind enter the classroom. He was unsure of Srilekha's story about his sickness but seeing his friend now, he can believe it. Arvind looks pale and shrunken, like his frame has contracted within his skin, his head looking extra big and extra round, a football with dark skin stretched over, eyes heavy with exhaustion, and it is a disheartening sight, and in this moment he realizes he has never seen Arvind sick. Srilekha accompanies him till the door of the class, walking with him like he is in danger of fainting.

They nod a hello but it is a thing of formalities. The teacher is here and there is no time to talk. After the exam, which was maths and really easy, Sudipto waits in the class for a full half hour after completing the paper just so they can meet as they are collecting their schoolbags from under the blackboard. He asks his friend if he is okay and if he is feeling better. Yes, Arvind says, and then tells him he is most likely changing schools but he is not sure when. Before Sudipto can ask anything more, Srilekha is at the door to collect him. Arvind nods and after an 'I will talk to you tomorrow', he is gone.

•••

The second paper is English and this time they manage to talk for a bit as the invigilator is their class teacher, Mrs Chandra, who is a little more relaxed about such things. He is able to go to Arvind and say that he too is planning to leave this school and perhaps go back to America, and while it may be true, he knows he is saying it only to show his once friend that he will not be unilaterally abandoned.

Arvind is not surprised or otherwise emotional and simply says that maybe it is a good thing, and Sudipto will be happier there and get to eat all the good chocolates, and play in the snow and go on roller coasters.

It is towards the end of this exam that a policeman, a constable in uniform, comes to the classroom and whispers something to Mrs Chandra who is surprised and who then calls out to Arvind. The policeman looks serious and stands extra straight in uniform and just says that his boss has a couple of questions for Arvind and takes him by the arm and walks out with him. Arvind looks confused as he is led away, but is not arguing, and there is something defeated about him and Sudipto realizes this is really a different person, not his friend at all.

Sudipto is done with the exam and has already revised his answers once, so he feels comfortable submitting his answer sheet. Determined to help Arvind, Sudipto moves as fast as he can towards the exit, hoping to catch the policeman and maybe meet his boss, the officer … maybe it is the nice one he met before, the fat fair one, who was so friendly when he had come home for tea.

ARVIND

Arvind follows the cop to the police car, his mind racing a mile a minute, trying to understand what it is that the police know, and how they have found out. He is not sure if his father broke under the strain and went to the police to turn in the Gun and confess the crimes of his son, or if they have somehow linked him and the Gun to the shootout at the factory or even Jaggi's murder, or simply figured out that he was helping Amar or any of those things …

He thinks he will meet the senior cop, the one he has seen in all the newspapers, the one claiming to have killed Amar, even though Arvind knows it is not true.

They are outside the school building now, the area is empty, the school buses are yet to arrive. Arvind wants to stop and ask questions but is not sure what to ask. This is when he realizes he has seen this cop before. He was the guard, Jaggi's driver from the afternoon of the shooting. His feet freeze. He struggles to free himself, but Jaggi's cop simply lifts him into the air and carries him to the waiting car. When he opens his mouth to cry for help, the policeman simply clamps a thick hand against his face, squeezing the scream in and bundles him into the white ambassador where a much older boy with shoulder-length hair pulls him in. This one has a grip like hard stone and

Arvind has not felt anything like it. He twists his arm and the pain is blinding. 'Stay still or I will break it,' he says. Arvind recognizes the intent and the obvious capability, and stops moving entirely.

Suddenly he hears a shout. It is Sudipto, coming into view, running ragged, hands waving and cheeks red, and who is calling to them to wait and who says that he knows Kapoor Sir and he would like to come along …

•••

The floor smells of sweat and phenyl.

It is a sweet smell and it sticks to the back of his throat. He cannot help but breathe it in with his face pressed against the tiles. He has tried to move but it is difficult with his arms tied behind his back, tight, his elbows pinched together … Next to him, he can hear Sudipto sobbing quietly through his rough cloth gag, presumably tied in similar manner. Arvind is not crying. It is effort enough to breathe through the cloth with his weight resting on his chest. They have been here for some time, maybe fifteen minutes, maybe an hour, Arvind is not sure, but it has been long enough for the worst of Sudipto's cries to have quietened. Time enough for Arvind to panic and calm down, to empty his thoughts, to count his breaths, in and out, and wrestle his fear into submission.

They are in a gym with benches and the heavy-looking exercise equipment all around them—metal racks and steel rods with big green weight discs at the ends, rusting at the edges where the paint has chipped.

He does not know where in Rannwara they are. He had struggled the whole way here, their captor laughing as he held both of them—Sudipto and Arvind—down with remarkable ease while the policeman drove. Such was his terror then, his nerves withered away after this traumatic week, that he did not pay attention to where he was being taken.

'There is no defeat until you are dead,' Amar had said, and Arvind is still alive. He begins to move his fingers, trying to feel for loose ends of the rope wrapped tight around his aching wrists.

The sound of a door opening, and then footsteps on the stone. A pair of sports shoes come into view. It is the enemy, alone, the cop no longer with him, which removes the thin layer of comfort that was insulating Arvind from the worst possible outcome.

The older boy takes the gags out and sits them up, one after the other, motioning them to be silent with a thick brown finger against his own lips. Sudipto begins to mumble and scream and is instantly slapped. The sound is like a whip crack, breaking the still air. The blow catches him flush in the face and Sudipto falls to his side with the momentum. Stunned into silence. The enemy pulls him back up. One half of the boy's face is cherry red, and there is a thin streak of blood from a torn lip.

'This is going to teach you girls how to fucking keep quiet. Do you know who I am?'

Arvind shakes his head, though by now he is getting some ideas.

'My name is Jai Ranade. I heard that you were good friends with my younger brother.'

It is obvious now that it has been said. Jai is Jaggi made large, as if he has been stretched and expanded, filled up with a cycle pump. Jaggi, when alive, was larger than them, and this Jai stands larger still.

'I know you had some problems. That you stole a question paper, and made some sort of arrangement with him the day he was killed … So you,' Jai says, sitting on his haunches, 'need to tell me everything.'

'I had the paper. I have the paper. But there was no arrangement … I didn't call him anywhere—'

The hit takes him by surprise. He saw Jai move, just barely, when he struck Sudipto, but this time it is even faster. There is no time to brace for impact, the punch sinks into his body, just under the ribs and the world goes black. Arvind topples. It hurts so much, he cannot scream, he cannot breathe, just take in gasps of air that get stuck in his throat, he is not able to push them any further down.

Jai grabs his shirt and lifts him up. 'Who told you to call him there? Huh? Tell me …' Reaching behind Arvind, he grabs a finger, the hands still tied at the wrists, and with one hand, like an afterthought, snaps it.

Arvind screams. There is no breathing exercise now. There is no hope and no control and no calm centre and no focus, just pain … oh it hurts so much so damn much like pure black pain burning through the scorched nerves of his hand and he is howling and on the floor and flapping about and the pain is so bloody intense it goes up all the way to his neck and into his eyes …

'That,' Jai says, 'is only one. There are nine more. So just tell me everything.'

Sudipto is screaming too and there is another slap. 'You will be quiet if you know what is right for you.' But Sudipto is still blubbering and then another struggle and he is gagged and there is no other sound.

'You little bastards, I can see it in your fucking eyes. You know something. Well, don't worry, we have a long time ahead of us.'

He reaches out again. Arvind twists back and forth, trying to protect his hands and his vulnerable fingers but he is helpless. A hand like an iron vice grabs his body and Jai, looking him in the eye, breaks another finger. Somehow this hurts even more. Even as the agony drives a spike into his brain, he realizes it is the index finger of his right hand … his trigger finger …

•••

More time. More slaps. The same questions repeated in different forms with no answers. Another finger. He cannot tell which one though, both hands are a cacophonous jangle of pulsating trauma. Arvind is sure the pain has increased in magnitude, but he has exhausted the ability to compute it. His mind has switched off. It hovers on electric waves that have neither shape nor purpose, but on the edge of perception he can still make out the dead ghost of Jaggi, back after a week, now lying on the floor next to him, staring into his eyes.

Answers won't change anything, Arvind knows, he is dead either way. So he decides as he watches the blood spurt out of the dead boy's throat that he will never talk. This monstrous brother of yours, he may kill me, he tells dead Jaggi, but he will never ever know what happened to you.

'You won't get away with this,' he hears the voice. It takes many slow seconds as he swims to the idea that it is Sudipto, his friend Sudipto, who is talking, who has somehow managed to chew through enough of the gag to make words. 'My father knows your father,' Sudipto says, 'my father knows your father,' and he chants it, the words floating in the air, like some mantra of protection …

'We know nothing,' Sudipto says. 'We know nothing at all, please let us go.'

Arvind can see Jai moving towards his friend with sudden menace. 'I don't fucking care,' he screams and grabs Sudipto by his uniform shirt. In one powerful move, he lifts him off of the ground, feet dangling three feet off the floor, and as if on cue Sudipto's bladder gives out.

SONAWANE

What are the outer limits of loyalty? What are the contours of fear?

Sonawane feels he is physically pushing against the very edges of these concepts, loyalty and fear, terrible twin ideas that have driven him into a hell he cannot seem to free himself from.

It had seemed simple enough when it started. A request, Jai Ranade told him. 'You remember the boy from that day, that junior?' He had nodded and said yes he did, and then Jai had said, 'Come with me, let us go talk to him.'

The boy was in school and had to be brought out. Simple, right? And he, Sonawane, went and got him. It was such a little thing. Who even questions a policeman in uniform …

And he was happy too, as he did it, for the opportunity. It was just the display of unflinching loyalty that might still save him. Grab a boy from school. Thrash him maybe. Threaten him a little. A bit of a beating, he had thought, and if it goes out of hand, like the time with that Swapnil boy, he could intervene again surely … But not this, not this.

With this, he is dead and he is damned.

Two boys are in there, trapped with the monster. There is no going back from here. Whatever happens from this moment, they will hang him for this. It was he, after all, who marched into school in broad daylight and grabbed the boy. His face, they will remember his face, they will curse him and spit on him and hunt him down …

He is fucked—has been from the moment he abandoned his post and that youngest Ranade bastard got shot. All his time since has been borrowed and that has never been clearer to him. He can feel the noose tightening around his throat in this moment.

Once at the gym, he was told to leave. 'Go home,' Jai had said as he got out of the car, the boys tied up in the backseat, 'I will see you tomorrow at home. Not a word about this.' Sonawane had stepped out of the car, handed the keys to Jai and walked away knowing then that he was doomed. It was a low, flat building, surrounded by empty plots. There was no one around, no witnesses and no one to stop Jai from killing these boys.

And now he stands shaking, staring at the locked door of the gym thirty metres away, unable to take another step, half hearing the screams coming from behind its walls. Maybe he should just make a call to Kapoor Sir, who can come and probably save the boys. He is dead either way, but at least he will not die with the blood of children on his hands … unless it is already too late … and this is when the door of the building bursts open and a furious Jai stomps out.

JAI

The fucking kid pissed on him. What the fuck! It is disgusting and horrible and it is all over his jeans and his fucking suede Adidas shoes and he hopes there is fucking water in the car so that he can wash this shit off and he reaches the car and looks around him. The whole area is empty and that fucking Sonawane is nowhere to be seen which is good. He yanks open the door and inside the car he finds a water bottle near the driver's seat which he pours out on his shoes and the front of his jeans. It does not clean anything and to make matters worse it now looks like he has pissed himself …

He is going to kill the fucking Bengali kid and he does not care who his fucking father is … Just kicking the shit out of him is not going to be enough … The stupid kid will talk to his father who will talk to Om and then Om is going to ride his fucking ass again. Fuck him fuck his stupid Bengali father fuck Om. He will just have to kill both of them—the fucking Bengali and the Madrasi bastard with the dead eyes who just looks at him as he cries and even when he's fucking screaming with his broken fingers the fucker's eyes never show fear … He wants them to be shit scared and terrified and in pain the way his brother was.

They are not talking yet, but he is sure that they had something to do with it. He finds his packet of cigarettes on the dashboard and takes one out and now he can feel a wetness in his toes as the piss polluted water seeps into his shoes and wets his socks. He crushes the cigarette in his fingers and flings it away and then takes out another and in his anger he has a moment of clarity and he knows that the motherfucking Madrasi is for sure hiding something behind his fucking eyes. He was involved, he is sure of it and his brother is dead and they are the reason for it … Them and that fucker Sonawane … and no matter what it takes, he's going to make them talk somehow.

The water bottle is empty and there is a cigarette in his mouth and he is looking for a fucking lighter in the glove compartment and on the seat and he finds it and lights his cigarette and thinks of what he can do … He needs them scared, more scared than they are now and he sees the damn cricket bat in the back seat.

SUDIPTO

'I am sorry for this. Sorry for all of this.'

It is Arvind who is talking. Sudipto turns his head to look at him, really take it in. His own body hurts from the kicks he got, but the damage seems insignificant compared to whatever Jai has done to his friend.

'Arvind, what do we do?'

It is difficult to speak as there are still shreds of thick cloth inside his mouth, catching on his tongue. He is scared. What if this guy does not let them out … Surely someone had seen them being grabbed outside school, surely …

'I am not a good friend.'

Tears are falling fat and fast down his friend's face but there is determination there.

'I did it. I killed him you know, Jaggi, I killed him for us. I killed him for me.'

Sudipto hears the words but they don't mean anything, they're just a sequence of sounds with no specific arrangement. He is sinking in a soup of language without meaning.

'Tell him. Tell him I did it, and tell him to let you go. I don't think he will, but it is worth a shot. Tell him you will keep this a secret.'

'You killed him?'

'Yes. With a gun. I should have told you but … Well, you know now.'

The door opens and all thoughts fade away but the footsteps are different, lighter, faster, and Sudipto is confused and then he can see legs come at him and this time they are boots and not sports shoes and it is the policeman, the same one who had dragged them out from the school and he motions to them to be silent and begins to untie their hands.

'You boys have to run. You have to run, just stay with me, and you have to run,' he is saying and then Sudipto's arms are free and the man moves to Arvind who grunts in pain as the man struggles with the knots tying his broken-fingered hands.

Sudipto is able to sit up and starts pushing against the knots around his ankles which are looser and roughly tied and it is not long before they are off. He scrambles towards Arvind to help free him and once that is done the cop helps them to their feet and tells them, his voice creaking under the pressure, that Jai is outside and they will have to run fast and stay behind him. This cop, armed with just a lathi, holds it in front of him as he leads them to the only exit of the building. Sudipto walks unsteadily, his battered joints making it difficult, and next to him stumbles Arvind, who is just staring at his own hands which have swollen to three times their size, two fingers on his left and one on his right twisted all the way round like fat bulbous roots, purple and gross-looking …

They are almost at the door when it creaks open.

It happens in slow motion. Each moment standing clean and individual, separate, inside a longer tapestry, frozen and inevitable.

The policeman raises the lathi to avert the blow, but it is as if his hands are moving through water even as a cricket bat descends on his head with a sickening thud. He lands on his butt, his legs splayed out in front of him. He turns to look at the boys, blinks, and smiles just as the bat comes down and connects with the side of his face, wrenching his neck around, and he slumps onto the floor.

Sudipto looks up, frozen.

Jai Ranade stands over the twitching body of the cop, eyes red, nostrils flaring, the bloodstained cricket bat in his hand.

ARVIND

Arvind doesn't care anymore.

He has to go in. This is no time for plans. He must go straight in, no matter what. There are no tricks left. This is the moment you stand and fight with everything you have. This, he thinks, would have been a lot easier with the Gun.

Jai closes the door behind him and latches it.

Go that way, is what Arvind tells Sudipto, pointing to the right with a broken hand, and rushes to the left himself. As expected, Jai comes after him.

The gym is a large room, slightly larger than a classroom but it does not have empty space to run, not for long anyway. All you have to do, he thinks, is keep him on you and maybe Sudipto can get out.

Arvind moves fast, but Jai is faster, covering the distance with giant strides. Arvind dodges between the benches and the machines even as the taller boy, more agile, follows, cutting out routes as he moves around the equipment, swinging the bat in one hand like it weighs nothing, herding Arvind into a corner.

He senses the bat coming towards him before he sees it and leaps forward, and it misses him by a sliver, crashing into the cushioned back of a bench instead, and now there is nothing but wall in front of him and he is stuck and when he turns, Jai is looming over him, limbs outstretched, closing angles, and he, Arvind, rushes him, feinting to the left before darting to the right, hoping to move between Jai and the bench and to somehow pass under the bat. He ducks low and the bat sails over him in a wide arc and he is past Jai and free but then Jai swings the bat again, just as fast, and catches him in the middle of his back.

It feels like getting slammed by a bat. The impact sends him flying, his muscles spasming in mid-air. He hits the floor, completely winded, and when he pushes himself upright with throbbing hands, he sees Jai stepping over the bench, the bloody bat clutched in two hands.

This is when Sudipto crashes into Jai's leg.

SUDIPTO

Sudipto could have run but he did not. He would have if he had taken a moment to think but he did not.

•••

Jai struggles to shake him off but he is determined to not let go. Jai has just killed a man in front of them and this monster will most probably kill him and he will kill his friend and so Sudipto does not let go even though he shudders with each blow that rains down on his face and head but Sudipto does not let go and then an iron grip yanks at Sudipto's hair with enormous strength and it feels like his scalp is getting ripped off his skull, like a band aid, but Sudipto does not let go and he can see Jai's hand swing above him, now with tufts of his hair trapped in his fist but Sudipto does not let go …

ARVIND

Jai swings the bat one-handed but it is an awkward angle. He gets Sudipto in the upper back, once, twice, but does not get enough momentum to dislodge him, so he jams the bottom edge of the bat against the boy's face and neck and begins to push so as to peel him away from his left leg …

With Jai occupied, Arvind looks around frantically for a weapon of any kind and his eyes fall on a weight plate on the ground next to him. Crawling on his knees, he grabs hold of it using only the bottom two fingers of his hands. It is an impossible thing he does, the damn thing weighs half as much as him, and it is only his endless hours training with the bricks with Amar that allow him to move it, just a little, and fuelled by animal desperation the boy with broken fingers lifts it high with all of his strength, nerves screaming, knuckles cracking, then stretches his arms out and falls with it, edge first, on Jai's right foot.

There is a pulpy crunch as the plate flattens his toes and Jai screams, the bat slipping from his hand. Unable to balance, with Sudipto still grabbing onto his left leg, he drops to his knees and even so stretches out and grabs Arvind's head in his right hand and pulls him forward.

There is nothing Arvind can do to resist. His face is level with Jai's, which is just a mask of murder. His vision explodes into sparks and his mouth fills with a river of blood as Jai's fist crashes into his cheek and then *wham!* The second punch is worse, he can feel his nose crumple and his teeth cut through his tongue … He is still exactly where he was, his entire body limp and hanging from Jai's implacable right hand as he prepares to pummel Arvind yet again. He can see a third punch coming towards him through eyes that no longer truly see, and is entirely helpless, when Sudipto climbs onto Jai's back, eyes feral and blood tinged and bites his ear …

The hand falls and Arvind falls with it. He begins to crawl away on blind instinct. There is a scream as Jai finally grabs hold of Sudipto and flings him away … His friend goes flying, crashing into a thick metal rack, before sliding to the floor, a piece of Jai's ear still caught between his teeth …

Free of the boys, Jai stands, gingerly, his face stained with blood, a long flap of flesh hanging along the side of his cheek. He is confused and in pain, unsure of which prey to target. He picks up the bat waiting for him. Arvind, on the floor, his nose and mouth spouting blood, drives his elbows into the mat to somehow push himself away from this …

Jai takes a step towards Arvind, the bat held up like an executioner's sword. Another step and his bleeding foot slips on the thick puddle of Arvind's blood, and he falls, the back of his head crashing, with a sick crunch, against the metal edge of the bench behind him.

SUDIPTO

It is some time before he walks to his friend and helps him up, careful to not slip in the blood under their feet. Arvind sways as he stands, his face unrecognizable, a mask of red, a pulped piece of fruit. His nose is at an angle to the rest of him. He spits out teeth which fall on Sudipto's shoes.

'Sorry,' he says. More blood. It means nothing now. Sudipto can feel it in his own mouth, with a dim realization that not all of it is his. He can taste it, the ear, the thick fleshy texture of it and he wants to puke or scream or break down and sob. Instead, he holds his friend's shoulder and says, 'It's okay. Come on. We have to go.'

His own body feels like it was dismantled and put together the wrong way. Jarring stabs all along his neck and shoulders. Any movement brings with it nausea, and worse. He cannot see, he does not have his glasses with him and there is a burning around his eyes.

Arvind is looking at Jai, where he remains fallen, mouth open, milky foam oozing out, body still but for the shallow movements of his giant chest. His eyes flutter like he is caught in a dream.

'We need to finish this,' Arvind says, 'no half measures.' He says this and takes half a step towards the fallen body, unable to take another one.

Sudipto considers his friend. He killed Jaggi? Shot him with a gun? What does that even mean? But he knows enough to not mistrust Arvind. Nothing he does, Sudipto concludes, will ever surprise him again.

'He can't even breathe, Arvind,' he says, 'leave him. We need to go.'

Arvind resists but then his shoulders slump and he looks like he is going to collapse again but Sudipto is there, holding him up, pulling his arm over and around his neck and gently leading him out, his feet dragging.

They pass a giant mirror on their way out and in that he sees himself, not much better than Arvind, torn and bloodied shirt, piss-stained uniform, pale skin with bright purple bruises and of course the thick inches of bare white scalp shining in a strip from his hairline to the middle of his head, burning always, with thousands of dull pin pricks oozing thin pink plasma.

They step over the cop's body, so cruel and so brave, pointedly not looking at his face and stumble out of the gym into the blinding sun outside.

Sudipto does not know where they are, and now, with the weight of his half-conscious best friend bearing down on him, is not the time to figure it out, but to just walk and keep on walking as long as he can. He thinks of calling his father or the policeman who was friendly but these are hollow thoughts and they crumple as he mulls over them at any length. It is hard to concentrate.

The weight shifts and Arvind straightens up, just a little bit, and then he says, 'Why did you come for me? Back at the school ...'

Sudipto does not answer him because it is really goddamned obvious.

•••

They walk under a baking sun for a while before a tempo stops for them, perhaps looking at their bloodstained uniforms, and Sudipto explains in broken Hindi that it was a school fight, and no they do not need an ambulance, but could he please just take them home?

•••

The tempowala brings them to the colony directly, having agreed to take no other passengers, and has not asked many questions, assuming that boys will be boys.

Along the way, he is kind enough to give the boys some water which they use to wash off the blood that has dried on their faces. Sudipto, completely unsure of what answers he can afford to give to others, has pulled some of his hair across his ripped apart scalp. He waves at the guard at the colony gate who recognizes him and lets them through. Arvind sits deeper in the shadows of the tempo, his more extreme wounds hidden from view. Sudipto leads his friend up the stairs, helping him at every step till they reach the third floor of his apartment building and rings the bell. A few moments pass before the door opens and it is Srilekha and she looks troubled and is silent and says nothing despite seeing the boys' appearance.

Then a voice, heavy, with a strange accent, says in English, 'Let him in.'

She turns in silence and the boys enter and in the living room Arvind's mother is sobbing on the sofa even as Arvind's father comforts her with his arms around her. Sitting opposite them is a fat dark man whom Sudipto has never seen before, who sits casually with a gun in his hand.

WENDELL

The boy is short, brown, with long lanky arms that reach most of the way to his knees. His hands are broken, fingers fat like sausages, having suffered tremendous punishment. His face is large for his body, as boys' often are, feeling unbalanced on a thin neck sitting on thin shoulders. This face, too, is smashed, broken nose trickling blood. The eyes, one almost too bruised to open at all, look through to the inside of him, showing no surprise and no fear, and Wendell knows that this boy is the boy.

He saw a boy like this once before, also bloodied, with undaunted eyes, but where those showcased a soul burning bright in denial of the splintered shell that housed it, these reveal nothing.

Wendell came here looking for Amar's Beretta. Driven by the need to complete the mission, he had waited in this godforsaken town for days, hoping for news that the local police had successfully retrieved the weapon from the scene, but to no avail. In time, the improbable became inevitable, and Wendell pulled the only other thread he had. Kamal's delirious ramblings about a second shooter left only the boy—this boy now standing in front of him.

The Gun sits on the coffee table in front of him, all beautiful glinting chrome, taken from the shaking hands of the boy's father, and he, Wendell, sits on a chair with his own gun pointed at the terrified parents of the boy who, now weak, wounded, unarmed, stares back at him without flinching.

'You are Amar's boy.'

Arvind nods, and then, 'You are the one who killed him. I can tell. Have you come to kill us?'

'No. I wanted to see you before I left. I already have what I came for.' Wendell motions to the Gun on the table. The boy does not look at it, keeping his gaze fixed on him.

'You cannot take it. It was his to give, and he gave it to me.'

'He would never do that. Do not lie to me.' An edge in his voice, harsh, brittle.

'He said I was chosen. By the Gun.'

The boy does not lie. Fuck! Amar, you careless bastard, what have you done here.

He is so fucking small, comes barely to his waist, and looks like he has emerged from a car crash, uniform torn and bloodied, every inch of him marked by violence. Flanked by his sister and a very injured friend. Doubt sparks within Wendell, fragments of an idea begin to coalesce in his head.

His mouth is dry, his next words hoarse. 'Tell me, did he kill the Ranade boy for you?'

'No. That was me. With that Gun.'

No.

The fragments click into place with infernal clarity. No. No. No. This is not happening. How could he not have known? How could he not have fucking known?

The room grows cold around him and anguish builds up at the base of his belly and it swells and swells rising through his oesophagus and into his lungs and then up his throat, from where it spreads down his shoulders and arms and he somehow manages to keep his gun level and it threatens to burst from his lips but he grabs hold of it and squashes it with enormous physical effort, and pushes only the words out …

'You killed that boy? Why?'

'I had no choice,' the boy says, showcasing his purple bleeding hands by way of explanation. 'He would have killed me.'

The pressure breaks through, and a tear spills out and then another, and Wendell cannot stop them because it is taking everything inside him to not roar and rant and shoot himself in the head.

Amar did not kill the boy. Amar did not kill the boy. The idea, once formed, solidifies to absolute truth even as it burrows through the entirety of his being, looping through every vein and every nerve and he is shaking from the enormity of it. His hostages stare at him, a family of freshly terrified eyes, unable to move in the gaze of his gun, even as he weeps where he sits, cursing himself with every ragged breath.

There is nothing to be done here. Nothing at all. No salvation to be found. He was looking for answers and the answers have damned him to hell. He killed his friend. He could have spoken to him. Could have reasoned with him. Had a dialogue but he was too scared and too angry and so he killed him, shot him in the back, killed him like a bloody dog.

Inside his pocket is Amar's taveez, now burning through the cloth and into his skin and he snatches it out. 'This was his. He would have wanted you to have it,' he says, placing it on the table. Next to Amar's gun.

He says to the boy. 'My name is Wendell D'Costa. I was once a friend of Amar, a friendship I now realize I could not live up to. I loved him, yet I did what I did because I saw no choice. You do not have to believe me. If in the coming years you feel you cannot let go of this, and if your heart calls for vengeance, come find me.'

He walks to the door. 'They don't know about this, no one knows about this.'

KAPOOR

Barry Kapoor tells them that the gym was on fire when they got there.

He tells them that the assassination was perpetrated by the few survivors of the Bilal Ansari gang, a final strike against their enemies, payback for their own almost complete annihilation in the war against the Ranades. He tells them that they found some bullet casings, probably matching those recovered from recent crime scenes. He tells them that performing autopsies on the victims has been difficult, both bodies having sustained tremendous damage in the fire, and were only identifiable through personal effects.

He tells them that Police Nayak Prakash Sonawane should be commended for his bravery, for having given his life in the line of duty, sacrificing himself, truly guarding his charge's body with his own. He recommends a posthumous promotion to ASI and a police medal of gallantry.

He tells them that he is officially turning down all awards and commendations he is due to receive for his own actions in the preceding weeks.

'It is obvious now that the work was left unfinished, and the investigation incomplete. There is work to be done to win back the public trust,' he says.

He does not tell them about the story he found on the gym floor—Sonawane's obvious wounds, or the foreign-made child's glasses, or the tiny teeth lying in a pool of blood next to a then still alive Jai Ranade.

He does not tell them what happens to cop killers, no matter who they may be.

SRILEKHA

Appa and she are on the scooter, riding out of town and on to the highway, and it is not the longest of rides, just till they hit the bridge over the Dhej river. It is a narrow channel of water, a tributary to a greater river, surviving still in the peak of summer. It is not far, about fifteen kilometres outside of Rannwara, but it will do. This is the first time in her memory that Appa is riding in the day and she can feel the relentless sun erode her skin through her full-sleeved kurta, and through the whole ride she keeps her eyes shut tight against the glare.

The bridge is deserted and the road is empty and she keeps a lookout as he throws the Gun, wrapped in black cloth, into the water below. It falls forever and makes a small splash.

ARVIND

He dreams wet and sickly dreams, dreams in which he crawls in darkness through mud and soft filth, dreams that leave a layer of malaise inside him when he wakes, his mouth tasting of salt and chemicals.

The pain is still there, at a distance, like waves of an ocean he cannot see, formless and constant, slipping in and out of his young body.

It is evening, he is alone in their room, his and his sister's, as the sun sets in line with the window and shadows encroach across the thin sheet lying over his body. From the open door he can hear the sounds of Amma in the kitchen, the clang of utensils, steam escaping from a pressure cooker—there is a comfort here, and he allows himself to feel it as he dozes off again, and even in his half sleep he holds the taveez tight, the black thread wrapped around the unbroken fingers of his right hand. For a while, he was scared that they would try to take it away from him, but no one did.

•••

Amma helps him with everything, she is his companion, his caregiver. Her love showing in glasses of chhaas, coconut pachdi, endless bowls of vegetable stew. He suffers through it all in silence. She sits next to him in the long afternoons, reading aloud from magazines. He talks to her, through the pain, carefully forming words that are softer than the soft food, sliding off the surface of his true experience, an experience he cannot fully outline to himself.

The doctor has said he can perhaps start eating rice in a week. His jaw is intact, though he has lost two of his lower incisors, his cutting teeth. These were the permanent ones, they had shown up only a year ago. He can feel their absence like a cold patch with the tip of his tongue.

His fingers are altogether more complicated, flattened out and stuck tight to wooden splints. Two of them, those on his left hand, are clean-ish breaks, they should come back the whole way. The one on his right hand, his trigger finger, is a different story. It is the angle of the break, the doctor said, we have nerve damage there, and we will keep hoping for sensation to return, otherwise he will never be able to use the finger. This is the injury that crushes him, and he spends hours willing the nerves to repair and the flesh to heal.

When despair threatens him, he tells himself it is okay, he will do what can be done, he will not be defeated, not till he is dead. And if all else fails, he will just have to learn how to shoot with his left hand.

He wonders about the Gun and its eventual fate. His father took it after Wendell left, and Arvind was unable to protect it or protest at all. A dead-faced Sudipto sat in shock, waiting for his parents to come and take him away.

He has never spoken about it, Appa, not about the Gun or anything else that happened, not since that day. He has probably gotten rid of the Gun by now, acting with misguided speed in the aftermath of the invasion, defeated by the world of the Gun leaking into his house. Appa sees it as a curse, a poison, a harbinger of darkness. He does not have the true sight to understand that the poison is outside, everywhere, giant choking clouds of it, and always has been.

He wonders how they feel, his parents, now that they have been on the wrong side of malicious power. Has it altered their thinking? Has this experience given them the right kind of eyes, to see the truth of the Gun, the truth of the world. They don't speak to him of such things, he doubts they speak to each other.

He is confident, though, that those moments will take root in their hearts, growing deeper shadows, and in time, weeks and months and years, they will grow to understand him.

•••

On Day 4 or Day 5 Sudipto visits him. He comes with his parents, and it is a formal thing. The adults talk in the living room about parent things, in quiet whispers, two families keeping secrets together.

Sudipto, wearing a bright red cap to cover his now fully shorn head, sits on Srilekha's bed, next to Srilekha, talking to him. It is the first time his friend has really come home. He tells him he is leaving for Calcutta in a week, and this is goodbye. Maybe he will go to America after that, he is not sure. His father is going to continue in Rannwara for some time. Things are confusing.

In Srilekha's withering presence they cannot discuss anything that actually happened. So they talk of some of the brighter spots in the half year of their friendship and talk about things they might do in the future. Visit me, he says, in America, we will go to Disneyland.

When they leave, Sudipto gives him a package. It is his way of saying thank you for everything. In the package is a grey Game Boy with purple buttons—and newspaper cutouts. They are in Hindi and it takes Arvind some time to decipher them, to figure out that they detail how Jai Ranade died in a mafia hit at a gym.

Later that week, he learns that Appa has resigned from the plant, and they will be relocating to Bangalore. Mr Chatterjee himself has arranged a job for him.

•••

'Are you up?'

It is a question in the middle of the night and it takes him a minute to realize that it was real and spoken aloud, and it is his sister.

'Are you up?' she asks again, louder. 'I know you are awake.'

'Yes.' He sits up carefully, pushing only with the heels of his hands.

'The cop who came to get you at the school,' she asks, 'was it the same one who died? The one they found with Jaggi's brother?'

'Yes.'

'He is the one who saved you?'

'Yes.'

'What happened then … did you or your other friend do that …'

'My friend is dead. Was dead by then, I told you. And I have no gun. I don't know what happened after we ran. Anything could have.' In his mind, he can see the cops shooting dead bodies at dawn. And then, 'Don't tell Appa about this.'

'Are we still in danger?'

'I don't think so. No one else knows about us.'

She does not reply and they lapse, once again, into a choked quiet.

'Sri, I am sorry I killed him. I didn't know he meant something to you.' It is a lie, and it hurts him as he speaks it, but it is all he can think of as a concession.

She does not answer him, the silence stays. Unbroken. He waits for her reply, but there is nothing, and he thinks about all the different things he would like to hear from her, but there is nothing. He stays wide awake now, staring at the stars burning far past the dark ceiling, wondering if she has gone to sleep with her anger and her rage. Wondering if this is how it will be from this moment, from this moment to forever …

The killing of Jaggi seems like it was years ago, even his ghost does not follow him anymore, not since the day at the gym. He does not think it is forgiveness, for there is no true crime to forgive, he thinks it is because his brother died and joined him. Jaggi no longer needs the company.

He wonders if Amar too is a ghost now, haunting Wendell. They were friends once, the fat man had said, and Arvind believes him.

The Gun itself, he chooses to not mourn. He is now able to see himself as a waystation in its journey, like Amar. He had heard all of Amar's stories, and they sit within him, warmed by belief. The Gun will find itself in willing hands, in hands that need it … hands that could perhaps use it with more immediacy.

He has a long life ahead of him and the Gun will find its way back to him if it has to. He hopes it will, for the undone tasks that await him in his future. But if it does not, that too is okay.

He goes to sleep knowing that there are other guns out there, in the world, and they all belong to him.

Epilogue

The food is too spicy. Bilal can feel the insides of his mouth burn up. He would think that living in Rannwara his whole life would have trained him to handle this, but the local food really goes too far. Fucking Indore.

The boy does not complain anymore either, not after he had whacked him three nights ago. Mirza shuts up and eats, not complaining about the food or the heat or the bugs or any of it. He has stopped asking about his brother, Jamshed—Bilal is sure he is dead by now. Jamshed had little chance outside a hospital even without the police getting to him.

Fucking Jamshed, that inauspicious rat fucker. Nothing good ever fell out of his mouth, just like his mother, Bilal's sister, but that is nothing now. It is over, it is all fucking over. He had bet and he had lost. Lost big. He is still alive, though, no matter that all parts of his actual life are destroyed. No help, no gang, and no fucking money for chicken. Just roti and this fucking dal which is burning his mouth. Too afraid to move to the city proper, to even step out and get a decent fucking meal. Just holed up in this room with the boy.

At least the bastard Amar Singh is dead. He had not lingered in Rannwara that night, having seen the look in Wendell's eyes before they left. Raju was supposed to kill Wendell once they got Amar. A stray bullet or three. It could have worked, Bilal thinks, I could have got away with it. Jaslok bhai would have helped, another beginning somewhere far away, Indonesia maybe. But no. Now Raju is dead, along with the others, Jaslok Kamani is not taking his calls, and that cop, Sardesai, has told him to run and keep on running.

The Ranades are still looking for him, whatever is left of them. The old man is going to die soon, he has heard. Another attack, from the anger and grief of losing two sons. Fucker. The eldest son is the only one left, and he is half crazy with paranoia. Falling apart, yes, they are falling apart and after the father dies, there will be nothing—a vacuum in Rannwara. Maybe he will make a triumphant return then as the mafia boss with the balls to kill two of the Lion's sons in his fucking den. They talk about him differently now, he knows it, has heard the change himself. He could capitalize on this, walk in and shoot the third bastard himself. He will be a fucking legend then, the entire town will be his to take. He will be untouchable, yes, let fucking Uncle try something then.

Life is hope and times can change. His enemies are dying, one by one but he, Bilal, is still alive. Maybe there is a bright side to it after all.

As Bilal makes plans and Mirza stares at a wall with dead eyes, outside the hotel, a fat dark man steps out of a car and extracts an AK47 from under his seat.

•••

The truck is here, and the sad lives of her entire family are packed inside steel and cardboard. Srilekha stands with her father, watching the men load the truck, her eyes glued to her own suitcase, where hidden deep amongst her underclothes is the Gun, now dry, wiped clean, all remnants of the river removed. A miracle weapon that caught no rust and no damage, all she had to do was leave it in the summer sun on a terrace that her brother no longer went to. It will work, she is sure of it, the way she is about gravity, but she cannot trace the source of her burgeoning confidence.

There are changes ahead in her life, big ones, but now, with it in hand, she is no longer afraid.

The Gun had no bullets when she found it, but that is okay. She already has one.

Acknowledgements

A novel is a ship launched by a thousand hands—and it is difficult to list them all in a page or two. So with this impossible task at hand, let's get to it.

First of all, I would like to remember the real-world Amar Singh, my friend and companion through my teenage years, whose smile and spirit fill every page of this work. Wherever you are, I hope you are happy.

A big hug to my super-agent Kanishka Gupta, who has never wavered in his support and encouragement. Emailing him fifteen years ago remains the smartest thing I have ever done. A special thanks to Harsimran Gill, whose advice was so instrumental in shaping *Gunboy* to be what it could be.

And of course, the team at HarperCollins: Trisha, my editor, for her help in bringing this novel to light, and Shatarupa for her amazing work with my words. I am grateful to have found such a warm home with you.

Writing is an emotional and tumultuous venture, but it becomes a thousand times easier with the right people at your side.

I am a person fuelled by the awesome power of friendship and have been extremely lucky to get a lot of it from many of you, far too many to list here. You know who you are.

And finally, Mom and Dad, you are the absolute greatest and a thousand pages are not enough to capture what you mean to me.

Author Bio

Shreyas Rajagopal majored in Economics at St. Xavier's, Mumbai, and then got an MBA from IIM Calcutta at the age of twenty. He worked as an investment banker before writing his first novel, *Saltwater*. He spends his time between Mumbai and Jaipur. *Gunboy* is his second book.

HarperCollins *Publishers* India

At HarperCollins India, we believe in telling the best stories and finding the widest readership for our books in every format possible. We started publishing in 1992; a great deal has changed since then, but what has remained constant is the passion with which our authors write their books, the love with which readers receive them, and the sheer joy and excitement that we as publishers feel in being a part of the publishing process.

Over the years, we've had the pleasure of publishing some of the finest writing from the subcontinent and around the world, including several award-winning titles and some of the biggest bestsellers in India's publishing history. But nothing has meant more to us than the fact that millions of people have read the books we published, and that somewhere, a book of ours might have made a difference.

As we look to the future, we go back to that one word—a word which has been a driving force for us all these years.

Read.

Harper Collins · 4th · HARPER FICTION · HARPER NON-FICTION · HARPER BUSINESS · HCCB HARPERCOLLINS CHILDREN'S BOOKS

HARPER DESIGN · Harper Sport · HARPER PERENNIAL · HARPER VANTAGE · हार्पर हिन्दी · BOOKTOPUS